HERO IN THE HIGHLANDS

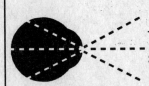

This Large Print Book carries the Seal of Approval of N.A.V.H.

A NO ORDINARY HERO NOVEL

HERO IN THE HIGHLANDS

SUZANNE ENOCH

THORNDIKE PRESS
A part of Gale, Cengage Learning

WITHDRAWN

GALE
CENGAGE Learning·

Farmington Hills, Mich • San Francisco • New York • Waterville, Maine
Meriden, Conn • Mason, Ohio • Chicago

GALE
CENGAGE Learning®

Copyright © 2016 by Suzanne Enoch.
A No Ordinary Hero Novel.
Thorndike Press, a part of Gale, Cengage Learning.

Thorndike Press® Large Print Basic.
The text of this Large Print edition is unabridged.
Other aspects of the book may vary from the original edition.
Set in 16 pt. Plantin.

LIBRARY OF CONGRESS CATALOGING-IN-PUBLICATION DATA

Names: Enoch, Suzanne, author.
Title: Hero in the Highlands / by Suzanne Enoch.
Description: Large print edition. | Waterville, Maine : Thorndike Press, 2017. |
    Series: A no ordinary hero novel | Series: Thorndike Press large print basic
Identifiers: LCCN 2016059139| ISBN 9781410499158 (hardcover) | ISBN 1410499154
    (hardcover)
Subjects: LCSH: Inheritance and succession—Fiction. | Large type books. | GSAFD:
    Love stories.
Classification: LCC PS3555.N655 H47 2017 | DDC 813/.54—dc23
LC record available at https://lccn.loc.gov/2016059139

Published in 2017 by arrangement with St. Martin's Press, LLC

Printed in the United States of America
1 2 3 4 5 6 7 21 20 19 18 17

For Monique Patterson,
who gave me some very good advice:
Sometimes bigger IS better.

PROLOGUE

Battle. Hot, bloody, dirty battle. Major Gabriel Forrester loved it. Strategy, bluffs, feints, maneuvers — fancy words, but it all came down to who hit harder, and who flinched first. And he'd never flinched.

Kicking Union Jack in the ribs, he sent the bay careening down the slope. Like everywhere else he'd been in Spain, the land around Salamanca offered little but shrubbery and dust and crumbling, steep-walled gullies. Except for the area directly in front of him, that was. Wellington and Marmont had found the one pleasant valley for ten miles around in which to slaughter each other.

A cannonball whistled over his head, and Gabriel ducked as sparking gunpowder rained down on his face. The allied forces had set their troops into a vast semicircle around the valley, with the intention of enclosing and crushing the French in the middle. A fine sight it would be, no doubt. He was supposed to be up on the hill himself this morning, watching with Wellington and his commanders. The word he'd said to General Wellington in response to that order would likely get him court-martialed later. It didn't matter; if they meant to take him away from battle because someone had pinned the word "Major" in front of his name, they might as well lock him up or shoot him, anyway.

"Humphreys!" he bellowed, calling for his second in command as he neared the position where the Sixty-eighth Foot was supposed to have been holding. They'd charged too early, damn it all, a ragged mob halfway across the valley floor and directly in the path of the French cavalry.

Angling Jack so sharply the horse skidded on its hind legs, he made for his regiment at a dead run. A French bayonet nearly took off an ear, and Gabriel kicked the soldier in the face as he passed. With the chaos around him, he might as well have been a wolf trying to catch the moon's attention by howling, but even so he could feel rhythmic thuds reverberating in his chest, deep and primal and growing louder. *The French cavalry.* With another hard kick he leveled a boot into a second blue-coated chest and veered left, cutting a swath through a tangle of blue and red coats.

Lieutenant James Humphreys had made a bloody poor choice strategically, and it wasn't just about the Sixty-eighth, either. If the allied army's left flank collapsed, the casualties would number in the thousands. Earl Wellington's plans to retake Madrid would fall into the privy, as well. To prevent that, he didn't doubt at all that the earl would risk crushing some of his own soldiers caught in the center.

And now that included him. The observation hill on his left, the one manned by Wellington and his prissy, aristocratic officers, remained the only landmark still visible in the smoke and dust and sea of heaving bodies. The hill where he was supposed to be waiting, watching to see if his own men lived or died.

Something white-hot grazed his left arm. His fingers could still flex, so with a curse he ignored it. Finally Humphreys and his officer's shako came into view, a French fusilier four feet behind him and drawing a bead on the lieutenant's head.

Gabriel drew his saber and slashed. "Humphreys!" he bellowed again. "You've cavalry riding down on you, damn it all!"

"Major?" the lieutenant stammered, stepping backward as the fusilier collapsed at his feet. "What —"

Gabriel stood in his stirrups. "Sixty-eighth! Left face! Form ranks and fix bayonets! Now! The French ponies mean to break our flank!" Regimental ranks would look grand, but at the same time he'd seen enough war to know the foot soldiers would barely slow the horsemen. And he needed to alter that arithmetic — quickly. Skidding out of the saddle, he grabbed hold of an abandoned French light cannon. "Humphreys! Davis!"

A twelve-pounder wouldn't do much damage, but he wouldn't want one pointed at him from ten yards away. Together he and Lieutenant Humphreys pivoted the cannon to face east, hauling it up directly behind his assembling regiment, while Sergeant Davis hopped onto the makeshift cart that carried it and shoved powder and a lead ball down its throat. "This is the only gunpowder cartridge and cannonball, Major," the sergeant grunted in his Highland Scots accent, hanging on as they set the heavy tail end of the tripod back into the mud again. "It's nae enough."

No, it wasn't. The Sixty-eighth Foot regiment readied themselves, the front line going down on one knee and the back one standing, bayonets at the ready. They'd get off one round before two hundred heavy horses smashed through them like paper. "Buttons," he snapped, and began tearing them off his uniform. "Musket balls. Flasks. Whatever you have in your damned pockets."

Smoke curled away, parting to reveal the French cavalry charging directly at them. Gabriel's mouth curved in a grim smile. He didn't need to stop the charge, but he did need to make the front line falter. It would cost him men, regardless, but at least they would be fighting back instead of slaughtered. And he would be in the middle of it, as he preferred. Drawing his pistol, Gabriel stepped up as Davis leaped to the ground. "Center line, down!" he bellowed.

The men directly in front of him went flat onto their bellies. Holding the pistol against the breech, Gabriel fired. The flash sparked, and he held his breath. Three hard heartbeats later the cannon went off with a thunderous blast. For a second he couldn't hear anything but the concussion thudding about in his skull. All at the same time, his troops surged to their feet and fired in ragged unison, the riders at the front of the cavalry seemed to explode in dirt and blood and sparks as they stumbled and veered away, smashing into their fellows on either side, and the cannon came careening backward.

Gabriel grabbed Humphreys by the collar and threw him sideways a split second before the rolling cannon could crush them both. Then he climbed to his feet, drew his saber again, and charged into the middle of the melee. "Jack!" he yelled, giving a sharp, two-toned whistle.

The bay appeared beside him a moment later, and Gabriel swung into the saddle. Robbed of its fastenings his jacket flapped open, tangling into his arm. He shrugged out of it and threw the red coat at a French horse's head, then sliced into the rider as the man struggled to keep his seat. The rest became a chaos of slashing and shooting and kicking and punching, muscle against muscle, French eyes widening in mute surprise and horror as he cut down one soldier after another. This — this was what he'd been made for. Anyone who thought to force him to go stand on a hill and watch was a madman. And a fool.

His arm began to feel weighted as if by lead, and Union Jack stumbled on the torn-up, bloody ground. Then he heard the French calling *replions-nous* — retreat. A moment later familiar red uniforms with their green collars and cuffs charged into the fray to encourage the Frogs' flight. The Eleventh Foot. Better late than never, he supposed.

"Major Forrester!" A messenger skidded to a halt beside him, saluting with one hand as he held out a missive in the other.

Gabriel lowered his saber. "Next time you ride up on me, you declare yourself first," he ordered, wiping a blood-smeared hand across his forehead. "Unless you care to have that arm lopped off."

The messenger paled. "No, sir. I mean, yes, sir." He lifted the paper again. "It's from Earl Wellington, sir."

Gabriel nodded, taking the note and for the first time feeling the pull of pain in his left arm, and the cuts and scrapes and bruises he'd acquired over the past hours. "Six o'clock this evening, my command tent," was all it said, but that was a plentitude. Either he was about to be promoted, or more likely, court-martialed for swearing at and then galloping away from his commanding officer at the beginning of a battle.

Lieutenant Humphreys, pale but for a streak of dirt and blood up the right side of his face, approached as Gabriel pulled Jack up and jumped to the ground. "Gabriel . . . Major Forrester, I —"

"It's done, James," Gabriel grunted. He wanted to punch the young man, pummel some sense into him, and he clenched his fingers against the urge. Fists didn't cure stupidity, and he didn't know that any cure at all had been found for ambition. "Don't you dare apologize — and bloody well not to me."

"I know. I couldn't see the signal flags, and I moved too quickly. The —"

"You lost men," Gabriel countered. "You're an officer. You will lose men again. For God's sake, make certain it's for a better reason than you couldn't see, or sell out your damned commission and go home."

The lieutenant swallowed, drawing in an audible breath through his nose. Gabriel half expected to be reminded that while he outranked James Humphries in the army, if they ever encountered each other on the streets of London *he* would be the one bowing. Not that he made a habit of bowing to anyone. Bowing was all about who someone's parents happened to be. Saluting could be the same, but at least there was the slim chance that a man's position had been earned rather than purchased.

The insult didn't come, though, and with a curt nod Gabriel turned on his heel and went to assist the stretcher bearers. Bowing

— losing sight of an opponent and exposing the top of one's bared head at the same time — was idiotic, anyway. If the custom had been up to him, he would have outlawed it. At least he didn't have to worry about anyone bowing to him. Whether his boots trod the rutted roads of Spain or the cobbled streets of London, he remained simply Major Gabriel Forrester. And thank God for that.

He'd earned every ounce of what he had, and he damned well preferred it that way. No one would ever comment behind their hands that his father or his uncle or brother had purchased him a commission to which he was completely unsuited. Fellow officers had long ago stopped asking who his family was, who he was, because the answer, quite simply, was that he was a soldier.

Or, if he listened to the men hurrying about and sending him salutes and nods as they passed, he was the Beast of Bussaco. Evidently setting fire to French munitions wagons and sending them rolling through the middle of the blue-coats' advance had made him legendary. All that concerned him was that the Bussaco attack had done what it was supposed to and kept the French from taking Lisbon. Whatever it was that made the difference between a hero and someone doing their duty, he would leave to others to figure out.

When he finally looked up to notice the sun lowering behind the hills to the west, accompanied by the wailing sound of some Scotsman apparently stepping on his bagpipes, Gabriel made his way across the sprawling encampment to his tent. He ducked inside and lowered himself onto the single, canvas-slung chair. His arm ached, and he ripped open the bloody remains of his shirtsleeve to expose a lead-ball-sized entrance wound . . . and thankfully a matching exit wound, high on his upper arm.

The tent flap lifted again. "I found your coat, Major," a gruff voice announced.

Held by two fingers, the formerly red coat with green facings entered the small tent, followed by the short, stout man who gripped it. Gabriel had no idea how his aide-de-camp could know it was his; any rank or insignia had been either torn away or obscured beneath a substantial layering of mud, blood, and horse shit.

"Just bury it with the rest of the casualties, Kelgrove," he returned. "After you help me bandage this. I'm to be dressed down by our lieutenant general, and I don't want to bleed on his boots."

"You're to meet with Wellington? In

what?" Sergeant Adam Kelgrove responded, dropping the ruined coat into a corner. "Your dress coat, I suppose, little as his lordship approves seeing those out in the field."

"I doubt my choice of wardrobe will sway him in one direction over another after I told him where he could stash his fucking orders."

With a snort, Kelgrove walked the two feet over to where Gabriel's battered trunk squatted at the foot of his cot. Abruptly he straightened. "You didn't actually say that."

"I did. Right before I charged down the hill."

"I wonder if Captain Newbury needs a new aide," the sergeant mused.

"He's too prissy for you. Have you seen the shine on his boots?"

"Boots or buttons. It's all the same to me." Kelgrove lifted the dress coat out of the trunk. "Speaking of which, promise me you won't tear the buttons off this one."

Gabriel stifled a brief grin. "So the button reference wasn't random. You heard about it."

"Everyone has. There may be a song about it already."

Hellfire. One nickname per war was plenty. "If I become the Beast of Buttons, I'm killing someone."

"I doubt anyone would dare. Aside from that, the burning munitions wagons at Bussaco were much more spectacular to view than some flying buttons."

"Tell that to the Frenchies who got hit by my epaulets."

"Even so, I would appreciate if you didn't make a habit of stripping decorations off your coat."

"I imagine the odds of me needing to fire off a cannon between here and Wellington's tent to be fairly small, but I can't promise anything," Gabriel returned.

"Well, I'm pleased as pie this amuses you, Major. Imagine my feelings when I rode up the hill to deliver a report to you, only to see my commander galloping hell-bent through the valley and cutting down Frogs like a lumberjack. When you decide to take on Bonaparte's army single-handedly, I'm supposed to ride with you."

"Then I wouldn't be lumberjacking single-handedly, would I?" Gabriel handed his aide-de-camp a strip of gauze and set a half-empty bottle of whisky on the table. "The ball went clean through, but take a look, anyway. I may have lost a piece of my shirt in there."

Sergeant Kelgrove immediately turned up

the lamp and pulled over a footstool to sit. "Don't even jest about that." Frowning, he picked up a magnifying glass. Peering through it, his right green eye enormous and bloodshot, he bent over Gabriel's arm.

Refusing to wince as Kelgrove wrenched the wound about, Gabriel took a swallow of the whisky, instead. They'd all been lucky today, and in more ways than one. They'd lost men, and some of them needlessly, but Salamanca would count as a victory. And with that victory, the push to retake Madrid remained in sight. If the price for him was a musket ball to the arm — or even through his skull — then so be it.

"I don't see anything," the sergeant finally concluded, setting aside the magnifier to splash whisky on the holes and then bind up the wound. "You can wager I'll be keeping a close eye on it, though. Soldiers wouldn't like it if an officer they bothered to name something ferocious like the Beast of Bussaco drops dead of blood poisoning. Hurts morale."

Silently Gabriel wondered if having that officer court-martialed for disobeying his commander's orders would have the same effect. "I appreciate your concern, Adam," he said after a moment. "Henceforth I will try to expire in a more heroic manner."

The aide-de-camp straightened and brought over the crisp red dress uniform. "See that you do."

After Gabriel pulled on a fresh shirt he stripped out of his mud-and-blood-caked trousers and boots, then dressed all over again in his heavy, stiff dress uniform. He would have preferred a quick jump into the river first, or at least a bucket of water over his head, but he wasn't about to keep Wellington waiting for him. Not after a written invitation — or order, or whatever the note had been.

Finally Kelgrove stepped back. "You'll do," the sergeant said, his expression glum. "Still too dashing, which Wellington don't like, but nothing I can do about that but hope you get your nose broken next time, Major. Or a saber cut across the bridge, at least. The one down your cheek just makes you look gallant."

"I'll add my prayers to yours."

"Aye," Kelgrove returned, evidently not hearing the sarcasm. "While you're up the hill I'll see if I can find some spare uniform buttons and let the washerwomen have a go at turning that lump back into a proper coat."

"And remind damned Humphreys that I want his written account of the battle and

20

his actions by morning. I want him to think it all through again and remember what an idiot he was."

"I'll do that. I think you'll find him a humbled man, this evening."

Fitting his black officer's shako over his head, Gabriel ducked out through the tent's flaps. "He'd best be, if he knows what's good for him."

Even with the sounds of battle practically still ringing through the valley and the village of Salamanca itself, the vast camp of the allied English, Portuguese, and Spanish armies had already settled into its usual state of controlled chaos. He made his way among the tents and wagons and horse paddocks, heading for the slight rise on the northern edge.

"Major Forrester," one of the lads in a group around a fire called, "I flatten out my buttons to pass them off as English coins. Never thought to use them as cannonballs!"

Amid the laughter, his fellows rose to toast him with their tin cups. "To the Beast of Bussaco, who saved all our arses again today! Huzzah! The Beast!"

Gabriel grinned, nodding. A few drunken toasts, he could manage. The first man who referred to him as Major Buttons, though, was definitely going to get knocked on his

21

arse. "Thank you, lads. And if you have any spare buttons you haven't hammered out yet, Sergeant Kelgrove has need of about eight of them. He'll pay a shilling apiece."

Wellington had been offered a villa on the far edge of Salamanca for his use, but as usual he kept to his large, plain tent where he could have ready access to his officers and men. The man lived as much on information as he did on beef and bread. When Gabriel reached the lieutenant general's lodgings, a slender young man looking no older than twelve saluted. "Major Forrester."

Gabriel returned the gesture. "Evans."

"Lord Wellington is about to sit for dinner, sir."

Stifling a sigh at how long he was likely to have to wear his heavy wool coat now, Gabriel nodded. "I'll await his convenience, then. Please send me word when he's avail —"

"Lord Wellington asks that you join him, sir." Taking a step back, Corporal Evans pulled the tent flap aside and gestured him to enter.

Blast it all. He'd sat for officers' dinners with Wellington before, and had on occasion joined the earl and other officers for drinks — and once, for a painful trio of hours at some local lordling's house to listen to all the young misses in the area sing and play the harp and the pianoforte. There'd always been a distraction, or other, more clever-tongued people to carry on the conversation. This was different. Still, he supposed, it would be more agreeable to be dressed down over dinner than with naught to show for it.

The tent had been partitioned into several sections, to give the appearance that those inside had at least a degree of privacy. In the middle sat a table with room for a dozen or so officers, though at present only two chairs and two settings were visible. A private approached to take his hat and gloves, while another one pulled a chair out from the table.

Perhaps he'd been killed this afternoon, after all; with the candlelit gloom of the command tent and the prospect of carrying on a prolonged conversation with his famously reticent commanding officer, this was shaping nicely into his idea of hell. When the chair-holding private cleared his throat, Gabriel blew out his breath and sat.

In the next heartbeat Wellington stepped into sight, and Gabriel stood again. "General."

"Major. You are going to remain for the

meal, I trust? Not gallop off halfway through the roast mutton to go fling buttons at enemy soldiers?"

Damnation. Gabriel brushed at the front of his uniform. "My aide-de-camp asked that I not do so, my lord. He worries the army will run short of buttons and we'll look too shabby to ride into Madrid."

"And I second his very wise request. And his worry. Sit down, Major. Redding, wine."

One of the privates scurried over to the tent's liquor cabinet and unlocked the large mahogany tantalus. Wellington might scoff at soft beds and other luxuries, but the man knew his liquor. Personally Gabriel would have preferred something stronger than wine, especially if he was about to be reassigned to a desk in the Horse Guards, but he was very clearly in Rome, so to speak. Tonight he would drink wine.

Once Private Redding poured, the tent seemed to empty of all staff. It must have been prearranged, because accustomed as Gabriel was to looking for subtle signs, shifts in the battlefield, he hadn't detected anything at all. The deep red drink was too sweet by far for his taste, but that meant it was likely more expensive than anything he could have afforded on his own, so he sipped at it and tried to look mildly impressed.

"I had a plan for the battle today," Wellington said into the silence, his own glass sitting untouched. "A feint by my center to lure in the French cavalry, with cannons to smash them to bits while my foot soldiers ground theirs into paste."

"Yes, sir. I'm aware of that."

"And you informed your Lieutenant Humphreys of this, as well, I assume?"

"I did." Gabriel took a breath. The lad didn't deserve defending, but if he had truly learned his lesson today, he had the makings of a competent officer. "The smoke obscured the flags. Humphreys knew if he lagged that he would leave an opening for the cavalry to escape. In his . . . inexperience, he rushed forward instead of looking for confirmation."

"So if you'd been there as you'd intended, you would still have all your uniform buttons?" Finally sitting back, the earl lifted his glass and took a long, slow drink.

"In theory, I suppose, though I have no way of knowing in what condition my uniform might have ended."

"I won't say you single-handedly won the battle of Salamanca," the lieutenant general mused a moment later, "but I will say that you single-handedly kept us from losing it,

Major. If they weren't already praising your actions at Bussaco, you'd be the Savior of Salamanca after today."

That didn't precisely sound like a drumming-down. Yet, anyway. "I am a soldier, sir. I do what is required to win."

"Just as well. Nicknames are tricky things to live up to."

Gabriel nodded. "I don't care what anyone calls me, as long as I'm permitted to do my duty."

"Mm. Very humble of you. And now that I consider it, rather ironic."

A frown pulled at Gabriel's face. "Beg pardon? I know you ordered me to the command hill, General, but I have never sought personal glory from the blood of my men. That —"

"A great many officers serve under me, Major Forrester," Wellington cut in. "Do you imagine that the loss of one from my side — even a competent, capable one — would cause me to surrender?"

"Of course not." And there was the boot he'd been expecting.

"It irritated me when you galloped off. Not because I required your counsel, but because I know you ride pell-mell into battle, and I had reason to wish you kept from harm." He reached into one of the pockets of his blue coat and produced a much folded letter, which he set down and slid across the table. "This arrived by special messenger before dawn. A second note is inside, addressed to you."

Frowning, Gabriel leaned forward and picked up the thick note. "I don't —"

Wellington took a breath. "I have written letters to lords, informing them that their precious thirdborn sons — not as precious as their firstborn sons, of course — have been killed in battle. This one" — and he gestured at the missive — "is out of even my experience. I invited you here tonight because it seems the sort of news one should hear from a sympathetic soul rather than read on one's own in the middle of a foreign country and a damned war."

"I . . . Are you certain this is meant for me? My parents are long dead, and I have but one sibling. A younger sister, living in London." His heart thudded. "Has something happened to Marjorie?"

"No." Wellington tilted his head. "You have no cousins, either, I presume."

"No. What —"

"You do have an uncle. A second uncle, rather. Or is it third? I can never keep the distant ones numbered correctly."

Gabriel opened his mouth, then closed it

27

again. "I remember my mother talking about a great-uncle she detested, and I know there was bad blood in the family . . ." He cleared his throat. "I wouldn't take up your time with my boyhood recollections, sir. This has something to do with the — my — second or third uncle, I presume? If he's died and left me some debt, I would appreciate if you simply told me. Any creditors will find it difficult to squeeze blood from this turnip."

"He has died, but he has not left you any debt. Rather, you have something of an inheritance coming to you."

For a moment the look in Wellington's steely blue eyes was almost sympathetic, and Gabriel's gut tightened. Whatever could make a battle-hardened general feel pity couldn't be good. He wanted to look at the missive, but Wellington had made it clear that he wanted to deliver the news, himself. Since he'd already disobeyed his general once today, doing so again seemed ill-advised. "My lord," he finally said, when the earl seemed content to allow the moment to draw out to the horizon, "first the offer of dinner and now this . . . reluctance of yours to deliver me the information you possess is rather alarming."

"Yes, I would imagine it is." Wellington

paused. "You've proven yourself a damned fine, ferocious officer, Gabriel Forrester, and not just by your actions today. I — and the British army — shall miss your service." Finally he sat forward and tapped the paper Gabriel held clenched in one hand. "Your distant uncle was the Duke of Lattimer, owner of several small estates in England and one exceedingly large one in Scotland. They, and the title, are now yours, Your Grace."

CHAPTER ONE

"For God's sake!" Gabriel exploded, momentarily mollified at seeing the quartet of wig-wearing fellows seated across from him jump. "Stop talking!"

"But Your Grace, this is all necess—"

Jabbing a finger at the one still making sounds, Gabriel stood, sending the ornate chair behind him over backward. "Stop talking," he repeated. Once the man subsided, Gabriel turned to his one ally, seated in the far corner of the room. "Kelgrove, what do you make of all this claptrap?"

The sergeant cleared his throat. "It's like walking through briars, but I make out that you've three estates, Major. Your Grace. The one in Devon, Langley Park, is being overseen by a Mr. Martin Graves, who's a fine and honest fellow. The one in Cornwall, Hawthorne, is just as well taken care of, by a Mr. George Pointer, who's also a fine and honest fellow."

"And the third one, Sergeant?" Gabriel urged, grateful all over again for his aide-de-camp, who after eight years in his company practically knew his thoughts before he had them and who also stood ready to assist with thrashing foes as necessary. Today, Kelgrove was very close to deciding that events definitely called for some thrashing.

"That would be Lattimer Castle, Your Grace. Your seat, I believe they call it, being that you're the Duke of Lattimer."

Gabriel pinned the lead solicitor with his gaze. "You were the one charged with keeping my uncle's affairs in order during his illness." Never mind that referring to the late duke as his uncle still felt odd on his tongue, much less in his mind. These were his circumstances, and he would deal with them as they stood — doing anything else would be pointless, no matter what he preferred.

"I . . . Yes, I was, Your Grace. Lattimer, though, is — well, it's in Scotland. In the Highlands."

Evidently that one word explained everything, though Gabriel couldn't see what difference it made. He knew Scottish soldiers, and they were damned fine warriors. "Yes, I saw it on the map, Mr. Blething. With the other estates you've told me the annual income, expenses, number of servants and livestock. You've said nothing about Lattimer, and have altered the subject every time I asked you about it. That makes me suspicious, and no amount of your prattling will make me forget it. The problem can't merely be that it's in the Highlands."

The paper man exchanged a look with his fellows, and Gabriel mentally leaned forward. For the devil's sake, he'd practically made a profession out of hearing all the words that went unsaid. Those carefully not-uttered words frequently ended up saving both his life and the lives of his men.

"I'm waiting," he prompted after another moment of silence.

"Well, some of it is pure nonsense, of course." Blething cleared his throat, his Adam's apple bobbing like a bird trying to swallow a worm. "The Lattimer estate used to be known as MacKittrick Castle, up until about a hundred years ago. That was when King George — the first one — tired of the Earl of MacKittrick and his family's very vocal Jacobite leanings. He had the patriarch hanged and handed the castle and property over to an ally he wished to promote. The first Duke of Lattimer."

Gabriel waited for more, but that seemed to be the end of the story. "That's well and good, but what makes it nonsense?"

Another of the paper men grimaced. "There's a legend, or a rumor, that when MacKittrick stepped up onto the gallows, he cursed the newly minted Lattimer title and everything that went with it."

"What's the curse?" Gabriel asked, folding his arms over his chest. If it was something about contented soldiers being pulled away from their duties for no good reason other than to listen to scrawny men who refused to give straight answers about anything, it was time for a drink.

"It's the nonsense of which I was speaking, Your Grace. The curse is merely an excuse for the steward to use every time something goes wrong."

"Mr. Blething, the four of you have been throwing figures and papers at me for three days with the relentlessness of an invading army. In that time you have regaled me with every useless bit of inane information at your disposal." Gabriel took a slow breath, trying to keep hold of his temper. "Tell me something useful."

In all likelihood the Lattimer curse *was* a basketful of idiocy, but the reluctance of the solicitors to discuss it made it more interesting than anything else he'd heard since he'd left Spain, and far more intriguing than deciding whether to sell Ronald Leeds's collection of rooster portraits or use them for target practice.

The second paper man found an old, stained piece of vellum. "Evidently while frothing at the mouth in either madness or fury, Malcolm MacKittrick declared that in English hands the land would turn to ruin, that any who allied with the English usurper would perish, and that the Lattimer line would fail."

"Considering it took you and the Crown better than six months to find an heir for Ronald Leeds," Kelgrove noted, "it seems like part of that might've come true."

"Nonsense," Blething stated again. It seemed to be the solicitor's favorite word. That and "income." "The new Duke of Lattimer is here. The line hasn't ended."

"The line took a ball through the arm the day your letter reached him."

"What about the rest of it?" Gabriel asked, figuring Kelgrove had won that argument. "The ruined land and the dead allies?"

"I'm certain no one's perished because of a curse, Your Grace."

"You're certain, are you? And the ruin?"

"Your Grace, you must understand that —"

"I understand that I'm beginning to lose

35

my sense of humor."

The solicitor grimaced. "It is a complicated matter. I have, over the past eight or nine months, since the duke's — the former duke's — illness, sent correspondence to Mr. Kieran Blackstock, Lattimer's steward. The first four letters went unanswered. The fifth letter, which I couched in sterner language because of His Grace's death, was returned to me five months ago. Inside, over my writing, I found scrawled the words 'Threaten me again and you'll find a dirk through your gizzard, English.' " He cleared his throat.

Ah, battle. Gabriel didn't bother hiding his amusement. "Let's see it."

"Beg pardon?"

"You said the letter was returned five months ago. Show it to me."

These men thought him an idiot best suited to shooting and punching, he knew, but they still did what he ordered them to do. Not out of respect or a sense of duty, but because he now controlled that flimsy thing known as purse strings. These paper men clung to those like a babe to its mother's teat.

As the solicitor on the far left nodded at his fellows and then bent down to dig through a file of papers, Gabriel clenched his jaw. He knew all about paper men. Paper men far away from war decided how many deaths were an "acceptable" loss and whether ten or a dozen lead balls would be sufficient per soldier to win a battle. They saw numbers and profit, not sweat and death. Generally he stayed as far away from accountants and solicitors as he could manage, and now here four of them were bowing to him and employed by him — four being, he assumed, the correct number required to tell him what he now owned.

Finally the missive appeared. He grabbed it out of the paper man's soft hand before any of them could decide he was incapable of reading all the words himself. The solicitor's letter was of course many-syllabic and fairly threatening, with words like "legal action," "required by law," and "easily replaceable" sprinkled throughout. Crossways over the neat lines of words, and written in a large, bold script, sprawled the gizzard threat in heavy black ink.

"Kieran Blackstock, you said?" he commented, handing the letter over his shoulder to Kelgrove. A large part of him wished he'd made that same response when they'd sent the letter naming him a duke.

"Yes, Your Grace. A Scotsman, who inherited the position from his father, I believe."

37

Blething's tone implied that the fellow's employment hadn't been his doing.

Gabriel stood. "Then we have our orders, don't we, Sergeant?"

"That we do, Major. Your Grace."

The paper men all scrambled to their feet. "I assure you, Your Grace, we have been overseeing the Lattimer finances for decades. This Blackstock barbarian will be replaced, as soon as we receive your approval, by someone more reasonable and duty-minded. We will have a report on the financial status of the estate by . . . by the end of the month."

"No."

"I . . . No?"

"No," Gabriel repeated. "You go on putting your numbers in columns and rows. *I* will see to Lattimer Castle, Mr. Blackstock, and to finding a replacement steward who better knows his duty. And it won't take me a damned month." He settled his officer's shako over his head. "Good day, gentlemen."

"But we haven't yet settled on your monthly allowance, or where you wish to set up residence, the hiring of new staff — a valet, for goodness' sake — or —"

"I've given you three days already. If you fling another figure at me, I will suffer an apoplexy. And then you'll lose Lattimer and your income from it to the Crown, after all. Send whatever else you think I require today to the Regimental Tavern in Knightsbridge. I'm leaving for the Highlands in the morning. You know that address, I assume."

"But as we told you three days ago, you have an estate here in London. Leeds H—"

"Leeds House. Yes, you did mention that. Several times. I'll be at the Regimental." Stuffing Blething's letter and its response into his glove, he made for the door. Now that a path had revealed itself, not a damned thing was going to keep him in this tastefully appointed room for another bloody minute. He had a destination, a task, and from the numbers being flung at him by the paper men, the monetary means with which to accomplish it.

Kelgrove pulled open the door as he reached it, then followed him down the short hallway and out to the noisy, dirty streets of London. Gabriel collected Union Jack, then headed southwest toward Knightsbridge where he'd taken a room above the Regimental Tavern. Whatever title they'd thrown at him, he felt far more comfortable seeing it as words — endless words — on paper. If he walked into Leeds House in Mayfair, all this insanity became real. Aside from that, moving his two trunks there for one night would be pointless. That, at least, sounded completely plausible and not at all like he was worried he'd piss himself if he thought hard enough about what had been laid before his scuffed boots.

"So you have a grand home in Mayfair and you don't even want to gaze upon it before you leave London?" the sergeant asked, interrupting his mental calisthenics.

With a sigh, Gabriel slowed Jack to a walk. "I'm hoping it'll go away. Along with all the solicitors, the estates, and the ache in my skull."

"No disrespect, but I imagine there are multitudes all around us at this moment who would give a limb for what you've had thrown at you, Your Grace."

And they could have it. Unfortunately, it remained his cross to bear. "So I sound ungrateful," he said, guiding his bay around a hay cart.

"Some would say so. Not me, of course."

"I'm fairly certain you're meant to be more respectful."

The sergeant snorted. "You do recall when they assigned me to your service? You ordered me to always give you an honest opinion, because firstly doing otherwise could get one of us killed, and secondly any flattery was wasted because you had no rich relations who could reward my bootlicking. You are the rich relation now, Your Grace, but I'm assuming your previous orders still stand."

After the sycophants of this morning, that seemed refreshing. "For God's sake, yes. And 'Major' will do. I don't intend to be 'Your Graced' enough to become accustomed to it."

"I know you said you meant to return to duty after you have this mess straightened out, but . . ." Kelgrove said, then let the sentence trail off. "You should do as you wish, of course."

"I've put a lifetime of sweat and blood into the army, Adam. I'm good at it. I'm too old and too stubborn to take on something this grand, and too plainspoken to want anything this frivolous. As you said, it was thrown at me. I should have ducked."

"I'll second that. As I am four-and-thirty and four years your senior, however, I'm willing to go a few rounds arguing that you're old."

Despite the quick change of subject, Gabriel heard the hesitation in his aide's voice, and he damned well knew from whence it came. A duke in combat would be nearly unprecedented, at least in this century. But

41

he would find a way. He couldn't imagine any other alternative. "Damnation," he muttered aloud. Every damned man who had a duke for a father should be obligated to marry and procreate well before he inherited, just to be certain the title had an heir. Otherwise, dirt-beneath-their-nails men like him found their own lives ruined for no damned bloody reason but that wealth needed an owner.

"Scotland, eh?" Kelgrove went on. "I've never been to Scotland. Been to India, Portugal, Spain, and bits of France, but not to Scotland."

"I've never been, either," Gabriel replied, lifting his gaze but unable to see the horizon for all the buildings. "A few weeks there, and I'll have Lattimer Castle set right and a new steward put in place to oversee it."

And then back to the Continent, the sooner the better. He'd asked for — and been given, with an absurd amount of ceremony — six weeks' leave, which at least indicated that the army did want him back. Whatever plotting and planning his military superiors might be up to with regard to his new title, the thought of returning to Spain and the war was the only thing keeping him from pummeling everyone in his path and fleeing to the Colonies. At least they didn't have dukes in America.

"Have you thought about what you'll tell your sister?" Kelgrove asked, pitching a shilling to an orange girl and catching one of the fruits in return.

Devil take it. Gabriel drew Jack to an abrupt halt. He'd been sending half his salary to his sister since he'd joined the army at age seventeen. Nine years his junior, Marjorie had always seemed so . . . young, and far too delicate for a rough-hewn man like him to be raising. He'd seen her sent to the best boarding schools he could afford, because that had seemed far more helpful than his presence. That, though, was no excuse for not even thinking about her now. Neither was the unexpected timing of his trip to London. If his circumstances had altered, so had hers. And someone needed to tell her that.

According to the papers he'd spent the past three days signing, she'd just become the sister of a duke. At the least she needed to know that her monthly income would be increasing by a number he couldn't even fathom.

"You wouldn't happen to have her address to hand, would you?" he asked, wheeling to face his aide and refusing to admit that he had no idea where in London she resided.

43

"I would, Major. She's in South Kensington."

"Well, aren't you efficient?" Gabriel returned dryly, trying to decide if that was censure he heard in Adam's voice. If it was, he deserved it.

"I thought you might wish to send her a note and then call on her this evening. You haven't seen her for some time."

"No, I haven't," he agreed. "But we're heading north in the morning. I'll see her now, or I'll have to send one of those paper men to talk to her until her ears bleed. I wouldn't wish that on Bonaparte." He blew out his breath. "I had Wellington tell *me*. I have a signet ring the size of a cannonball. Perhaps she'll appreciate it more than I do."

As they headed south toward the bank of the Thames the crowds of carts and pedestrians seemed endless, and his shoulders stiffened. Chaos and noise and bustle were nothing new, but in the army it carried with it an overall purpose and direction. On the main thoroughfares of London, with hundreds of people each concerned only with their own needs, chaos became a completely inadequate word.

"There, Major."

Kelgrove indicated a small, narrow town house on the right, sharing common walls with the dwellings on either side. A rose trellis crawled up the left side of the door and up around the window, while a low hedge of some kind of pink flowers ran along the bottom of the walls on either side of the front trio of steps. "It looks . . . quaint," he said, swinging down from Union Jack and somewhat surprised she could afford the rental of such a house with what he sent her, but she evidently spent wisely.

"It does," the sergeant agreed. "Shall I wait for you?"

"Come with me. You're more pleasant than I am." Taking a deep breath, he swung the brass boar's-head knocker against the dark green door. The French cavalry didn't unsettle him. Talking to a young lady with whom he had nothing in common but a set of parents — that was something else entirely.

A moment later the door opened, and he found himself looking at an older, round woman with her hair tucked into a maid's cap. "May I help you?" she asked, looking his red and white uniform up and down. "Sir?"

Marjorie had a maid? Gabriel cleared his throat. He needed to remember to be polite and civilized. This wasn't a battlefield. "Is Miss Forrester in?"

45

The maid held out her hand, palm up. "Your card, sir, and I shall inquire."

His card? "I don't have a card." If he did, he would only have to reprint it after today, anyway. "I'm Major Gabriel Forrester. Her brother."

Her small eyes narrowed a little. "Wait here, then. I shall inquire, Major." The door closed on his face.

"Rude woman," Kelgrove commented from behind him. "She would have been falling all over herself if you'd told her you were the Duke of Lattimer."

"But then Marjorie wouldn't know who the devil was calling on her." He didn't give a damn what some maid thought of him in the meantime.

The door opened again. "This way, Major Forrester. Miss Forrester will be down in a moment." Without waiting for a response the maid motioned him into the room directly off the foyer. Two chairs, a couch, and an end table sat in the center of the small, spare room, with a writing desk shoved against the near wall, a few shelves above it, and nearly every available space covered with bouquets of large, yellow daisies. Even with the fresh flowers, though, the room smelled musty, the closed-in sensation somehow made worse by the pervading scent of lemon verbena.

"This is very . . . cozy," Kelgrove muttered under his breath. "Smells like a funeral, though."

Gabriel nodded. The flowers, the scattering of books and baubles about the room, fit his nightmare of domesticity. None of it, though, felt like his memories of Marjorie. Had she changed that much? Or had he known her that little?

"Gabriel? Oh, good heavens, it *is* you!"

He faced the doorway. Marjorie was taller and slimmer at one-and-twenty than she'd been at seventeen, but that wasn't what struck him first. Rather, it was the careful bun in her dark hair, the simple, modest gown of green muslin beneath a green and yellow pelisse, the straight shoulders and level, blue-eyed gaze — somewhere over the past four years since he'd last seen her she'd grown into a pretty, clear-eyed woman.

"You look very well, Ree," he said, smiling as he walked forward to take both her hands in his. "And you've done nicely for yourself." Gabriel kissed her on the cheek.

She freed her fingers, stepping into the small room and shutting the door behind her. "I'm glad to see you, but what are you doing here? I thought you were in Spain."

"I was, until just under a fortnight ago."

47

He gestured at Kelgrove, standing before the window like a stout, red-coated paperweight. "Ree, my aide-de-camp, Sergeant Adam Kelgrove. Adam, my sister, Marjorie."

"Ma'am," Kelgrove responded, bowing.

"You brought your sergeant? Is this something official, then?" she asked, frowning.

"Yes, and no." He scowled. Fighting was so much easier than polite conversation. "Kelgrove said I should have sent word first. I apologize for not doing so. The past handful of days have been . . . interesting."

Marjorie put a hand on his forearm. "You never need to apologize for visiting me, Gabriel." She cocked an eyebrow. "Perhaps for doing it so rarely, but not for the act itself."

He inclined his head. She'd learned polish, and that was good. Manners and refinement were better weapons than a pistol in London Society. "To it, then. It seems we had a great-great-uncle. Ronald Leeds. The Duke of Lattimer."

A small furrow appeared between her delicate brows and then vanished again. "I heard about him. He passed away, didn't he? Five or six months ago. It was in the newspapers. They couldn't find any heirs, and speculation was that the Crown would end up with the property." She tilted her head. "Did you inherit something? Because

48

you already send me more than you should, Gabriel. I don't expect any more."

"I did inherit something." He pulled the signet ring from his pocket and handed it to her. "Actually, I inherited everything."

Her fair cheeks paled as she stared at the absurdly large ruby in its heavy, ornate gold setting. "*What?* You — If this is a jest, it isn't the least bit amusing."

"It isn't a jest. I had no idea, either. I've taken a leave from the army and just this morning finished three days of signing papers and answering questions about Mother and her family, to see if they matched answers they already had. It was ridiculous, but at the end they handed me that ring and a great deal more paperwork — and in essence the deeds to three estates, a large house here in London, and another one in Inverness. I need to go to Scotland to have a look at the Lattimer property, but I wanted to tell you that you won't have to rely on my salary any longer, as . . ." Gabriel trailed off as his sister let out a sob and sank onto the couch, the ring clutched to her chest.

"It's true?" she quavered, wiping at the stream of tears running down her cheeks. "Truly true?"

Gabriel frowned. Tears? For the devil's

sake, he didn't know how to deal with tears. "It's true. But what's wrong? You've managed all this on your own," he said, gesturing at the small house around them. "An increased income will only make keeping it up that much easier. And you'll be able to have —"

"Keeping it up?" she repeated, glancing toward the door and lowering her voice. "Do you . . . Why would I want to keep up this moldy, outdated rabbit hole?"

"But Kelgrove said this was your address. Your house."

The sergeant shifted. "I never said —"

"This isn't my house. Haven't you read *any* of my letters?"

"I haven't received any letters from you in months. What are you talking about?"

She sank down on the arm of one of the chairs. "When I left boarding school, I found myself . . . I wanted to live in London, Gabriel. I'm an unmarried woman with . . . very limited resources, and so I had a choice. I could either work in a shop, or become a governess or a lady's companion." She took a short, unsteady breath. "Eight months ago I accepted a position here, as the companion to Lady Sarah Jeffers. It gives me a roof, and food, and a gentry address, but she smells like wet wool and cats, and I . . . I thought I would be here forever, and then move on to sit with the next old woman who needed to purchase a friend she could order to fluff pillows against her backside."

For a long moment Gabriel looked at his sister. For the first time it occurred to him that if for some reason he'd decided to leave the army, how limited his own choices would have been. He wasn't fit for the priesthood, for damned certain, nor could he be a law clerk or — heaven forfend — a solicitior. For a young lady with good schooling and very limited income, the choices were even fewer. Why the devil had that never occurred to him before this moment? "I'm sorry," he said aloud. "I didn't —"

"I don't blame you, Gabriel, for goodness' sake," she interrupted, wiping her eyes and standing again. "And I'm not complaining."

Gabriel tilted his head. "You have every right to do so. Or rather, you did. Kelgrove, find some paper."

The sergeant began digging through his pockets, until Marjorie directed him to the writing table. "Over there. Take what you want. If what you say is true, I can repay her for the pages, now."

"I'm not lying to you, Ree. Not even I'm

that cruel. Sergeant, write out the address of Leeds House in Mayfair, and then another note to Mr. Blething ordering him to give Marjorie whatever she requires." He returned his attention to his sister. "I haven't seen Leeds House, but I've been told it's quite grand. It's yours. Blething is the solicitor who's been overseeing the Lattimer properties. He'll see that you have a monthly income requisite with your . . . new status. Hire yourself a staff, or keep whoever's there. No more cat dander or lemon verbena. Whatever else happens, I promise you that."

This time she choked back a laugh, still mingled with tears. "Thank you, brother."

When she flung her arms around his neck he patted her back, then extricated himself as quickly as he could. "I've done nothing. I *am* glad that one of us, at least, can benefit. As I said, I'm leaving for Scotland in the morning, but I will make an attempt to correspond with you more frequently from now on. And I will call on you before I return to the Continent."

Before another torrent of tears or hugging could begin, he headed for the door. Battles were easy. Family was much more difficult.

"Gabriel, I —"

"You're much better suited for life in

Mayfair than I am, Ree. Or rather, Lady Marjorie, now. Make good use of it."

Before he could put his hand on the door handle she seized his fingers again. "You did the best you could by me, Gabriel. You don't owe me anything. Least of all an apology."

He squeezed her hand and then pulled free of her grip. Being grabbed, hung onto, constricted his movement, and even in a musty house it left him uneasy. "Yes, I think I do," he returned, and cleared his throat. "If you like, I'll leave Kelgrove here to help you remove your things from this mildewed house." It should be him, he knew, but for the devil's sake, he needed some air before he choked on the injustice of it all. Because *he* hadn't put this right for her. That credit went entirely to luck, to a simple stroke of fate. And however little he needed it, however much he'd complained about it over the past days, to his sister this dukedom and what it represented made all the difference in the world. Damn him for not realizing that sooner.

"No, thank you," she replied. "I shall relish doing this on my own." She sketched a shallow curtsy. "Or perhaps I shall hire someone to assist me." Unexpectedly she rose up onto her tiptoes and kissed him on the cheek. "I hold you to your word, Gabriel. You *will* come see me before you return to your wars. And you *will* be careful in the meantime. Your Grace." She chuckled. "My goodness. You're a duke!"

With Kelgrove on his heels, Gabriel left the room, stepped around the nosy maid, and headed back out to the street. Yes, he had a title. And it was just as well that Marjorie could benefit from it, because he didn't know how to do so. Not without losing who he was. A soldier who believed for a moment that he was entitled to something — safety, luxury, privilege — was a dead soldier.

CHAPTER TWO

Fiona leaned her elbows on the railing of the graying, weather-worn fence. "What say we put in to buy a pint fer whoever finds Brian's cow?" she suggested.

The very large man standing a few feet from her snorted. "I'm nae paying a penny to find Brian Maxwell's damned cow. It's the third time this month the red's gone missing."

The farmer in question folded his arms across his chest. "I told ye, I gave her a fine pile of hay last night. She was in the pen with the other two when I turned in."

"When ye left fer the tavern, you mean," Fiona broke in. "I spoke with Abraham Dinwoddie, and he said ye drank half the beer in the tavern last night."

She'd never understood how someone could own three cows and only be able to keep track of two of them. It wasn't as if Brian Maxwell had an entire herd wandering the wilds. Two fields of wheat, three cows, a pair of hogs, and some chickens seemed fairly reasonable for a man, his wife, and their fourteen-year-old son to manage.

"I didnae!" the farmer protested. "I had but two beers, and then Tormod came in and I had to buy him a pint, and he had to buy me a pint." He leaned around her to point a finger at the broad-shouldered blacksmith. "Ye tell her, Tormod Mac-Dorry."

"I may have had a drink or two with ye, but I didnae lose track of my forge, ye lout. And I've two horses to shoe this morning, with nae time to spare hunting doon yer blasted cow."

The other four men present grumbled their agreement. Aye, they all had other things to do today, herself included. But if they left to go back to their tasks, finding the red heifer would be up to her and Brian. And Fiona doubted Brian could find his own two hands once he had a pint in him. She tucked her cold fingers into her coat pockets, and found a piece of leather that had peeled off an old pair of reins.

"I'll tell ye what, lads," she said, pulling it free and holding the scrap up so they could see it. "I meant to send this to Inverness to have it set into a locket, but I'll give it to the one of ye who finds that cow."

"Ye'd give us what?" Tormod asked, furrowing his brow. "Scrap leather?"

"This here is off the grip of a Cameron sword," she said. "The very sword that split Laird Robert Kerr betwixt the eyes at Culloden." As the only ranking Englishman to have been killed at the Battle of Culloden, Lord Robert had a certain degree of fame here that he'd likely never earned south of Hadrian's Wall. His death had become the one victory any Highlander could find in the whole disaster. And a relic from what had killed him — well, they were everywhere, and she'd yet to set eyes on one she believed to be the genuine article.

"That's nae off any sword, Miss Fiona," young Diarmid protested.

Tormod cuffed the footman on the back of the head. "Dunnae ever accuse a lass of lying," he grunted. "Especially nae this one."

"I apologize to ye, Miss Fiona," the servant said, scowling. "Ye ken I meant ye nae offense."

"None taken. But even if I cannae prove it to ye," she continued, "think of the bragging rights and the free beers ye'd earn fer producing this at the Fair-Haired Lass. And ye've walked all the way oot here, anyway."

The lads from the village and the castle

muttered together for another few moments, before Tormod nodded. "We've an agreement, then. Whoever finds the cow, gets the leather. But ye're paired with Brian Maxwell, Miss Fiona. Ye're the one least likely to knock him on his arse."

She nodded, not surprised. "Let's get moving, then."

As the others split off to search, Fiona straightened her green muslin skirt and tromped off south toward the edge of the bogs. "Thank ye, Miss Fiona," Brian said after a few minutes of scanning the muddy ground for tracks. "I swear the gate was latched last night."

"The gate's nearly a hundred years old. It wouldnae hurt ye to replace the ropes holding it shut. Ye cannae let her wander, Brian. The next time she eats Mrs. Garretson's onions, someone's likely to turn her into a beef stew."

As Brian grumbled again that the red was a good cow and he'd done as he'd said, his son Brady came trotting up from the direction of Strouth. "I came all the way up along the river," he reported, matching pace with his stouter father. "She's nae in the village, Da'. And I went through the MacKittrick gardens on the way back here just to be certain she hadnae wandered in after the flowers again." The boy grimaced. "I saw the blacksmith oot searching to the west. I'm thinking ye've enough peepers trying to find her. I should go back to Strouth, to keep a lookout."

Fiona stifled a grin. "Tessa Dinwoddie's oot riding this morning, I hear. Though with the fog coming in, I reckon she'll have to go back home before long." Half the stable boys at the castle had suddenly needed something that could only be found in the village this morning, and she could swear some of the footmen had vanished, as well. That was why she'd only been able to round up five men to help her find Brian's cow. Tessa Dinwoddie's bouncing bosom was a powerful draw.

Brian cuffed his son on the back of the head. "Ye've better things to do than ogle a lass's bosom, ye half-wit."

"I've a cracked millstone to inspect," Fiona said, "so if I'm looking fer the red, Brady, ye're to do the same."

"It *is* cracked, then," Brian put in. "I heard a rumor aboot sacks of grain piling up again." He spat over his shoulder. "Bad luck, it is. The third stone in two years."

"It's a blasted drunk stone dresser who didnae file doon the stones evenly his last visit. Nae poor luck. He'll mend it fer free

59

this time, or I'll try the stones on his skull." Fiona topped the low rise overlooking the edge of the waterlogged expanse with its dead trees and leaf-covered bogs below, and stopped. Faint mooing came to her ears. "Do ye hear that?" she asked, gathering her skirt and hurrying down the rugged hillside.

"It could be an owl," Brian stated, descending more gingerly behind her. "The red's nae foolish; she wouldnae wander oot here."

As Fiona trotted forward, careful to stay on the path, she pointed at a clear set of hoofprints edging one of the mudholes. "Then what's that?" she retorted.

A moment later the heifer came into view. She'd stumbled directly into a large mudhole, and stood up to her chest in the thick, dark goo. Her face was muddy, her long red fur caked in the smelly stuff and sticking out in every direction. As Fiona approached, the big animal lurched forward, lowing, and managed to sink another few inches.

"Brady, go fetch us a rope," she instructed, "and be quick aboot it."

The lad ran off toward the village. With a scowl at where Brian Maxwell stood lamenting the heifer's eminent demise from the safety of the bank, Fiona stepped out of her heavy work shoes and waded into the mud.

The stuff was cold — much colder than she'd expected even in the foggy weather, and she gasped in a breath. The bottom sloped steeply downward, and in a moment she was in up to her waist with another ten feet to go before she reached the struggling animal.

She finally stretched out to grab a handful of heavy fur and pull herself forward. "Dunnae fret, girl," she cooed, patting the cow on the rump. "We'll get ye free of this mess."

"Miss Fiona, are ye mad? Get oot of there before ye get kicked!"

"Ye might have said that before I waded in." Fiona wiped the back of her hand across her forehead, trying to move the pesky tangle of brown curls out of her eyes without depositing more mud in their place. "I'll climb oot when ye climb in, ye lazy oaf," she retorted, grabbing the heifer's tail and pulling sideways. The cold and wet of the mud sucking around her removed the last of her amusement. "No wonder the other lads didnae want to come help ye. This is yer doing, ye ken, because ye couldnae stay away from the tavern long enough to see yer own damned fence mended. I dunnae care who ye thought needed to be bought a drink."

With an annoyed moo the cow lifted a few

inches, managed a half step forward, then sank down to her chest again. Good Lord, this muck was thicker than Aunt Dolidh's gravy. Mentally she cursed the downpour of the past three days. To her the weather bore more weight than any foul words long-dead MacKittrick could aim at his own tenants, the arrogant, selfish man.

"My Brady'll be back in a quick minute," Brian countered, stomping a thin film of mud from the bottom of his boots. "And she isnae going anywhere in the meantime."

"She's sinking, ye *amadan.* She'll be off her milk for a week as it is, and another six inches'll drown her if she panics."

"Then stop yanking on her tail, woman!"

Narrowing her eyes, Fiona waded deeper into the mudhole. "Dunnae ye 'woman' me, old man. Get in front of her and help keep her head up. I'll nae let ye lose a prime milk cow because ye dunnae want yer boots muddy."

The heifer settled deeper on the tail of Fiona's words, and the animal's lowing took on an edge of fear. Cursing, Fiona dug both hands into the mud, leaned in, and shoved at the animal's hindquarters. Sucking cold mud slid up her shoulders to her neck, but the cow lurched forward a foot or so — before she gave up and sank again.

Today *would* be the day Tessa chose to go riding. Fiona glanced down at her mud-covered chest. Nae, she wasn't as amply proportioned as Miss Tessa Dinwoddie, but neither was she daft enough to risk complete ruin by trotting about in a ridiculously low-cut riding habit. Those mighty bosoms could spring loose at any moment, and then who knew what might befall?

"Brian, I'm nae telling ye again," she snapped, losing her footing and nearly submerging. "Either get in here and help me or go fetch Tormod and the others. This is yer damned cow."

The farmer looked back over the clearing as if he heard his lad returning. "There's nae need fer two of us to be trapped in the mud. And the blacksmith's likely all the way to the loch, by now."

"Ye did notice that Brady trotted off to Strouth, when MacKittrick's closer. Ye ken he means to get a good look at Tessa Dinwoddie's bosom before he returns, aye?" The boy was fourteen. They'd likely never see him again if he got an eyeful of Tessa's breasts.

"What does th—"

"Remain calm!" a male, decidedly un-Scottish voice bellowed. "If you struggle, you'll only sink faster!"

Straining against the sucking pull of the mud, Fiona turned around. A tall, broad-shouldered man in the crisp red coat of the British army skidded down the bank toward her, one arm outstretched for balance. Black hair cut not quite short enough to disguise its wave, a flash of pale gray eyes, a hard mouth, and a thin scar running down the left side of his face — her heart jumped into her throat, and not entirely from surprise. Ares, she decided instantly. The god of war. And he'd appeared out of thin air to claim her for his queen.

"Go away!" she yelled belatedly, backing up against the cow's rump. For Boudicca's sake, an Englishman in uniform charging at her should have been the stuff of night-mares. *Was* the stuff of nightmares, she corrected herself, no matter how instantly . . . compelling he looked. And upended by his arrival or not, Sassenach or not, she had to admit that he was toe-curlingly magnificent. Where the devil had he come from? And what in the world was he doing here?

He paused just long enough to catch the end of a rope thrown by a second soldier farther up the bank and still on horseback. "You're in distress. I'm here to rescue you," he returned, cocking his head at her as if she were the one who'd lost her mind.

If she was imagining English soldiers to be gods of war, perhaps she *had* gone mad. Fiona shook herself. "I'm nae in distress." She did have a sudden flash of the sight she must be, up to her armpits in mud, more muck likely spattered on her face and in her hair. Glancing up at the far bank to send a glare at Brian Maxwell, she caught sight of the farmer's backside as he ran off in the direction of the village. *Damnation.* He'd left her alone to deal with a Sassenach. A military one whose mere appearance seemed to have turned her brains to mush.

She scowled as he waded closer, his white trousers disappearing into the dark brown muck. "Go away," she repeated, and turned back to shove at the heifer again. If she could get the red beastie out of the mud, he'd have no reason to come any closer. Because if he touched her, bad things would happen. She was abruptly certain of that.

The first sign of anything resembling civilization in over two hours, and it came in the form of a woman in mud up to her tits. "Kelgrove, back Union Jack on my order," Gabriel Forrester continued, wading deeper into the cold muck as he knotted a loop into the rope he carried.

She'd returned to shoving at the cow's backside, though why she thought a slip of a female like her could budge the big animal, he had no idea. For God's sake, he imagined she barely came to his chin. "Stay still, miss," he ordered, tossing the loop over her head and down her shoulders.

"Ye bastard!" she exclaimed. "Dunnae —"

"My apologies," he interrupted, stepping closer to her before she could lose her balance and fall. A woman wriggling against him was nothing new, but he abruptly realized that it had been a while. As he reached around her to lower the rope to her waist, his hand brushed across one breast, leaving a muddy handprint. Eyes darker than fine, melted chocolate glared daggers at him as she twisted, and he fought the unexpected, heady urge to bend down and kiss her on those fine, full lips currently scowling at him.

Gabriel shook himself. Most of the rescues he performed involved weapons, and there was nothing soft and warm about them. He had no time for lust in the middle of a mud hole. "Slow and steady, Sergeant. Pull."

"Stay clear of the rope, Major," Adam returned from up on the bank.

"Don't fret, miss. I'll have you out in a moment," he said, as calmly as he could. Then the rope went taut, pulling her back hard against him. With a grunt he lost his footing and nearly went in over his head. Grabbing onto her, he steadied himself, then had to deal with her squirming in his arms like a landed catfish.

If all rescues resulted in him having a woman in his arms, he wouldn't mind performing more of them. Even the thrashing felt . . . invigorating. She might claim not to need a rescue, but any damned fool could see that she required help. He hoped that once they got out of the mud she'd be grateful for the assistance. That dark, dusky hair needed fingers run through it, and someone would have to peel her out of that clinging, muddy gown.

"Damn ye," she snapped, catching him with a flailing smack to the shoulder, but the rope held as Jack dragged the two of them backward toward the bank.

She stumbled again, and he swept both arms around her ribs. Her breasts seemed magnets to his hands, but that was hardly his fault. And he refused to feel guilty for enjoying it. He was performing a good deed, after all. "All safe now, miss," he said in her ear, setting her upright again. Abruptly she jabbed her elbow backward into his ribs. "Damnation," he grunted, pinning her folded arms against her chest in a hard bear hug and beginning to think she might be partly insane — a shame considering how pretty she was.

"I didnae ask fer yer aid, Sassanach," she retorted, staggering free as soon as they reached the bank and he half tossed her to solid ground. She loosened the rope enough that she could lift it over her head, then whipped around to face him again. "Now I have to go back in for the beastie, ye *amadan.*"

She had a surprisingly delicate face, he decided, especially considering the curses spewing from her attractive mouth. "The cow?" He'd half forgotten Sergeant Kelgrove, much less the heifer.

The lass shook mud from her arms. "Aye, the cow," she stated, still not sounding the least bit grateful. "Why the devil do ye ken I went wading in the first place? Fer a bath?"

"I'll see to the animal." Her black gaze held his for a heartbeat, then he wrenched his attention away to take the rope from her hands and push past her.

"I dunnae ken what's so amusing, Sassenach," she shot after him, annoyance and affront in every slender ounce of her.

Amusing? He was grinning, he realized. "I didn't expect my day to include rescuing lasses or cows," he returned, wading back into the muck. "Does she have a name?" he

68

asked, dropping the modified noose around the animal's wide-spaced horns. The beast had a definite quizzical look to her, with one horn curved up and the other turned down. Poor thing. Likely no one took her seriously with a permanent jester's hat on her head.

"We call her 'Cow.' Because she's a cow," the young woman returned, in the same biting tone she'd used before. "Do the Sassenach name their milk cows, then? Or is it that ye think all Highlanders have quaint names for their beasts? Ye already think us fools and idiots and baby eaters, so why nae that?"

"I only asked if she had a name." He knew they were fairly close to Lattimer Castle, but this woman would clearly be safe from the part of the curse that said death waited for English allies. He had the distinct impression that she wouldn't bat an eye if he went headfirst into the muck and stayed there. Gabriel sent her a brief, assessing look that upped the quotient of his lust even if it didn't give him any additional insight into her character, then went back to tightening the knot. "That should do it. Sergeant, get back around the tree there and use it for leverage. And you" — and he jabbed a finger at her — "toss some stones and branches in here between the cow and the bank, so she'll have some purchase for her feet."

"I would have done that before, if I'd had some decent help," she grumbled, but went to do as he suggested, wading back in up to her knees to place the debris. Slender and delicate as she appeared, clearly she wasn't a timid female, and that was for damned certain. Most of the women who followed the military camps had an edge of roughness to them, a toughness that he imagined came with knowing that the lad with whom they spent an hour might the next day end up dead in a ditch. In her he didn't sense that hardness, but rather something that teased at him even when he wasn't looking in her direction. Something . . . light.

"That man you were with. The one who ran away when I arrived. Was that your husband?"

She snorted. "If he was, I'd be a widow by sunset."

With him pushing from behind and the horse pulling from the front, the sucking mud reluctantly gave way, and Fiona had to admit — to herself — that this man didn't seem to be a complete idiot. And the way he moved, as if he were completely unaware of the splendid figure he cut, was in itself far more compelling than she wanted to acknowledge. His appearance didn't mean anything, of course. The Bible said Lucifer had been a handsome angel, after all, and look what he'd become.

The heifer lowed as she swung slowly around and began lunging halfheartedly toward firmer ground. She must have been towing a hundred pounds of mud along with her, but once she felt hard soil beneath her hoofs she lifted her head and surged forward. The Sassenach slapped her on the rump and sent her up the bank.

For a moment Fiona wondered if she'd be the next one to get her arse slapped. He'd already put muddy handprints on her bosom. The soldier — an officer, by his epaulets — though, only plowed back to where she stood knee-deep in the mud. "Now let's get you out of here," he said, and offered an arm.

Ha. She'd gaped at him enough already, and she was not going to grab onto him so she could make a bigger fool of herself. Damn all Englishmen, anyway, thinking they could waltz in and do . . . everything better than anyone else, simply because they'd been born south of Hadrian's Wall. Gathering her sodden skirts in her hands, Fiona slogged around him and up the bank.

"I didnae ask ye fer help," she stated again, shoving heavy mud from the front of her gown before striding over to pull the rope off the heifer.

"You *needed* my help, whether you asked for it, or not," he returned, from closer behind her than she expected. "And now that it's done, I think it's only fair that you return the favor firstly by giving me your name, and secondly by pointing me in the direction of Lattimer Castle."

"Lattimer?" she repeated, her voice gulping the word. "What do the likes of ye bright red Sassenach want with old Lattimer?" She forced a grin. If he thought her some dim female who didn't know better than to go slogging about in mud, then she'd be one. For the moment. "Though ye're nae so bright red, now. More brownish, with some green algae."

"You're wearing the same attire, miss," the major said coolly, his gaze drifting down the length of her and back up to her face again. "And my business is between Mr. Kieran Blackstock and me." He swung onto the bay and, despite the mud and water clinging to him, made the motion look both graceful and deadly.

For the briefest of moments she looked up at him, considering her answer. More than likely old Lattimer's damned solicitors had sent him to chase down the estate's ledger books, but if they'd resorted to using the military . . . Well, that wouldn't do at all. Cooperation, though? With the English army? That went against everything for which she stood, and more so because she liked his looks. She didn't like any Sassenach. Especially one who'd manhandled her and told her it was for her own good. They treated all of the Scottish Highlands the same way.

Steeling herself, she met his gaze, past that hard mouth and a straight, statue-perfect nose, to his pale gray eyes. The thin, straight scar that ran through his left eyebrow, skipped over the eye, and shallowed and disappeared down his cheek, made him look rakish, the sort of man who'd steal a lass's heart with nothing but a smile.

Fiona lifted one arm, gesturing northwest beyond the heather-covered hillside. "That way, aboot two miles. Keep the stream on yer right. And now we're even. Dunnae expect any more help than that."

"And your name?"

"Ye'd have that if I asked ye fer yer help. I didnae."

He gave a half salute as he wheeled the bay about. "You're a stubborn lass. I like

73

that." His precise mouth curved a little at the corners. "You should take a bath. If you change your mind and want my company, you'll find me at Lattimer Castle."

Debating whether she felt more aggravated or more flustered, Fiona lifted her chin. "I intend to take a bath. Nae with the likes of ye aboot, though."

"We'll see about that." With a nod of his chin he and his companion rode off toward the sloping hillside, arrogant man. Fiona bent down to collect a handful of mud and throw it at him. Evidently he had eyes in the back of his head, because at the last possible moment he shifted sharply sideways. The mud ball hurtled past his shoulder and thudded into the lavender-colored heather beyond. As the two men trotted out of sight, she swore she could hear them chuckling.

"Laugh while ye can, Sassenach," she murmured, "because ye'll nae be amused fer long."

She gazed after them for a time, trying to shove her worry aside. Lord knew there would be a plentitude of time for it later, when the pretty Sassenach eventually found his way to his destination. Unless he simply vanished into the bog toward which she'd sent him. That would be a fine conclusion to the day — though not for the muddy officer, of course. Still swiping mud off her skin and clothes and refusing to feel any guilt for sending such a fine-featured man into harm's way, she collected her shoes and headed off quickly northeast, keeping the stream on her left.

"If there ever was a castle here, it sank into the bog long ago," Adam Kelgrove observed, as they made their way around yet another deceptively shallow-looking pool.

With a noncommittal grunt, Gabriel pulled up Union Jack. Clearly the woman had lied to him; a foul repayment for a rescue. Of course even before he'd waded into the mud he'd known that she hadn't wanted his assistance, but firstly she'd needed it, and secondly, she'd looked as enchanting as a mud mermaid. Most people, friend or enemy, didn't attempt to lie to him, and he supposed he'd assumed she would be no different. He wouldn't make that mistake again. The question then became whether she'd merely attempted to send them away, or whether she'd meant to see them drowned in this damned bog.

He'd been a great many places in his thirty years, and he couldn't recall one that felt as utterly . . . desolate as the wide, shallow valley that surrounded them. No trees, no birds, no wildlife of any kind touched his sight. The overcast sky had begun to sink into the mountaintops, blending into the bog and surrounding moor to form an endless, gray nothingness. The hair at the back of his neck pricked, but he couldn't be certain whether it was the emptiness, or the sensation that it wasn't as empty as it appeared.

"What do you say, Major? Do we keep following the stream until we reach the sea?"

"No, we do not," he returned. "We turn around and find the cow's mud puddle again, and then we head northeast from there."

The sergeant followed as Gabriel wheeled Jack about. "Why northeast? It could be any direction but due south, since we came up that way."

"Because she lied. And when she lied, she faced squarely southwest, as if she were protecting whatever lay directly behind her. And I imagine it was close enough that she figured she could get there and warn Kieran Blackstock of our arrival before we discovered her ruse and turned back."

He felt his aide's glance. "You're being circumspect about all this, considering where she sent us."

"I'm not being circumspect," Gabriel

countered, tightening his dirt-coated fingers around the reins. With most of the mud dry, he felt more like a statue than a man. But not on the inside. On the inside he seethed, both with anger and with something more primal. While he'd been admiring her backside and other attributes, the petite lass had looked him in the eye and lied to him. That required a response. And the one he wanted to give had more to do with sweat and sex than asking for an apology. "I'm being patient," he said aloud. "Being reckless here would be both useless and unsatisfying, and potentially dangerous."

"You do mean to get angry, though — when the situation presents itself."

"As you know, Sergeant, no one makes a habit of lying to me. Nor do I approve of having my time wasted." Adding to that the matter of not even being thanked for his efforts and having a clump of mud thrown at his head, and perhaps he could admit, just to himself, that he was as angry at himself for being duped as he was at the black-eyed woman for attempting the deed. Successfully managing the deed, actually. If she hadn't had mud plastering her dress against her skin and showing every curve like some erotic chocolate statue, he likely wouldn't have been as willing to believe her — and that rankled, too. He didn't make a habit of thinking with his cock.

"I imagine this would not be a good time, then, to point out that I only just got the last of the bloodstains out of that coat you're wearing," Kelgrove said after a moment.

"No, it wouldn't be."

"I didn't think so."

The heavy clouds continued to settle lower as fog rose to meet them, reducing visibility with every passing minute. If the weather continued to worsen, the two of them would have to camp overnight or risk wandering directly into a deep bog. Gabriel cursed the black-eyed woman again. He'd expected trouble at Lattimer, but for the devil's sake, he hadn't even set eyes on the place yet.

Finally they spied the churned-up mudhole by nearly walking straight into it. With no sun, determining north from east had become a task all in itself. Gabriel paused, re-creating the scene, the position in which the woman had stood, and then kicked Union Jack into a trot again. He might be mistaken, but he'd learned long ago to trust his instincts. The error earlier — when he'd believed her in the first place — well, he wouldn't be repeating that.

"This fog's beginning to make me nervous," Kelgrove noted, after a half mile of silence. "I keep thinking we're being watched."

"We *are* being watched, I reckon," Gabriel returned. "Lobsterbacks in the middle of the Highlands? They'd be fools if they weren't keeping an eye on us." He felt it, too, the unseen, hostile eyes through the drifts of fog and mist. The rifle in his saddle, the pistol on his belt, and the saber at his hip — they would suffice, though certainly not against a coward's shot from hiding. But then death loomed everywhere he went. The prospect didn't trouble him. The idea of failing before he'd even begun, did.

Adam Kelgrove cursed under his breath, but Gabriel ignored it. The soldier knew what they were likely to be in for, and he'd been given the choice to remain in London to argue with the paper men. The Highlanders in the British army had a reputation for being fierce, fearless, proud, and supremely suspicious of their English comrades. At the moment, he happened to be banking on that pride to keep a ball from between his shoulder blades. A true Highlander, according to Highlanders, preferred a straight-up fight to a knife in the shadows.

Still, keeping a close watch had never

done a man harm. Halfway up the grassy, shallow slope, though, something else caught his attention. "There," he said, pointing at a deep gray spire that seemed to appear and disappear in the fog like a faerie's castle.

"I don't see . . . Ah. Thank God. And your sharp eyes."

Gabriel leaned a little sideways to loosen the rifle in its scabbard. Then he deliberately straightened again, his hands empty. "My sharp eyes also see two men on the hill to the left," he said quietly. "Just behind that cluster of trees. We won't begin any trouble here, but we will be ready to meet it."

"Us, not beginning trouble? You've gone soft, Major."

With a grim smile Gabriel slowed Jack to a walk. "This is my first time being in hostile territory that I actually own. But don't fret; my saber's ready to rattle."

"I wouldn't call that comforting."

Keeping his back straight, Gabriel led the way to the medieval monstrosity that slowly emerged from the gloom. In the damp air the slick stone walls looked almost black, with ivy crawling up the old stone all the way to the roof in places. No windows decorated the bottommost floor, which likely meant the castle had once served as a fortress, a bastion against the English and other clans, in the past.

Higher up the gleaming walls, though, tall, narrow rectangles covered by thick glass appeared at regular intervals. If the fog ever lifted, the view through them would likely be spectacular. Today, though, the dark stone with its twisting ivy tentacles seemed like a living, malevolent beast. Gabriel narrowed his eyes. He'd been called something similar, himself.

"I'm getting the shivers," Kelgrove commented, on the tail of those thoughts. "As the new owner, you might consider tearing the place down and starting over with something a bit . . . friendlier."

Though he'd spoken about Lattimer several times over the past few days, for the first time it felt like more than words on paper. He did own the castle. He likely owned the cow's mud puddle and the bog, as well, and quite possibly the cow, too. The paper men had said Lattimer and its surrounding ten thousand acres were his, but until now it had just been another number being spat at him. "Keep your voice down," he ordered. "I imagine Sassenach who suggest razing ancient castles don't live long."

"But you —"

"Halt and declare yerselves, Sassenach!" a

voice bellowed from somewhere in front of them.

Gabriel squared his shoulders but continued his approach. "I'll declare myself and my business to Kieran Blackstock, and no one else," he called back. No sense leaving room for cleverly worded misunderstandings.

"Shit," Kelgrove muttered beside him, but continued forward, as well.

"Well?" he pushed, into the silence. "You'd best decide whether to murder me or not, because I'll be at the front door in two minutes."

"You didn't need to suggest murder," the sergeant whispered.

"Yes I did. Murder implies a cowardly act. I'm certain they'd much rather kill me in a fair fight."

"I do not feel reassured."

In the fog-dampened silence he could practically hear the Highlanders thinking, wondering what to do with an English officer who didn't threaten or attack, but persisted in his advance. Mentally he counted down, from twenty to three, two, o—

"Approach, then," rang out as the count reached zero. "But keep yer hands well away from yer weapons or ye'll find a hole in yer chest."

"I don't mean to begin trouble," Gabriel returned. "But I will answer it in kind."

The castle's massive double doors, twice the height of a man, came into view. Seeing them, he was half surprised there was no iron portcullis to slam closed from above for additional security against invaders. This afternoon, though, the security consisted of a half-dozen men, four of them with bristling beards, all of them in kilts of green and red and black plaid, and most significantly, all of them armed.

The weapons varied, and he made note of that as he swung down from the saddle. A nasty-looking blunderbuss, two muskets, a rifle, a two-handed greatsword, and a pitchfork. From the bits of straw clinging to the last fellow's coat, Gabriel presumed he either worked in the stables or was a farmer — which didn't make him any less a warrior. Not up here.

With Kelgrove three feet behind him and slightly to his right, giving them both a good field of fire if necessary, Gabriel advanced to the doorway. The mud had stiffened his trousers and sleeves, and considering both his appearance and the additional trouble the black-eyed woman had caused him, he should have left both her and the cow to wallow about while he rode directly on to

Lattimer. No one would have been able to run ahead and warn the castle of his approach, and he would likely only be facing one or two startled men. The ungrateful female hadn't done him any favors, and he dearly hoped he would run across her again to repay her for the ill turn. He'd repay her several times, if fortune favored him.

"What do ye want with Blackstock then, Sassenach?" the largest fellow, the one with the blunderbuss, demanded.

"Are you Blackstock?"

"Me? Nae."

"Then what I want isn't any of your affair. Produce Blackstock, or stand aside."

The big man grunted, muttering something in Gaelic that sounded insulting and had the other men chuckling, then half turned to rap three times on the massive door. "The muddy English wants Blackstock or he'll break doon the door," he called out. "I reckon he's nae a threat, except to the clean floor."

Gabriel didn't feel disposed to correct anyone about the level of threat he posed. Rather, he listened to the distinctive sound of an iron bolt sliding free, followed by the deep-set groan of one of the doors swinging slowly inward.

With such perfect timing he might almost

be watching a play, a figure emerged from the gloom of the hallway. No kilt for this fellow, but rather a gray jacket, black trousers, and a lighter gray waistcoat flecked with yellow embroidered flowers — attire that Gabriel imagined would have served the man perfectly well in any of the finer houses of London.

The salt-and-pepper dark hair marked him as too old to be one of Wellington's tagalong, sycophantic lordlings, but he had that look about him — someone who thought himself just a little better than his fellows, not because of anything in particular he'd done, but because of who he was. Or thought he was. Gabriel had an inch or two on him, but they both still managed to be dwarfed by the Highlander with the blunderbuss.

"You're Blackstock, I presume?" Gabriel prodded, when the other seemed content to regard him from light brown eyes beneath straight black brows.

"Nae," a female voice took up, and the black-eyed woman stepped out from the shadow of the doorway, put her hands on her hips, and gazed at him levelly. "I'm Blackstock. Surprise."

CHAPTER THREE

She'd upended him, the overconfident redcoat. Fiona Blackstock kept her shoulders straight and glided forward, glad she'd washed and changed into a clean gown. And yes, it was one of her finest, a deep green muslin with light green and yellow flowers throughout, because she'd known this soldier would eventually find MacKittrick — Lattimer — Castle. She had no intention of showing a single damned spot of weakness in front of a Sassenach. Even one covered in mud but otherwise not much the worse for his adventure through the bog.

"You are not Kieran Blackstock," he stated, his low voice accusing.

She met his light gray gaze, wishing again that he wasn't as tall as he was. And that he looked foul instead of so devilishly handsome. "I'm Fiona Blackstock. Kieran's dead." Dead, or fled the Highlands. Either way, she was finished with him.

"You're his widow, then."

Fiona lifted an eyebrow. No condolences? Straightforward and brusque. But then she'd yet to meet an English soldier with anything resembling a heart, so she couldn't claim to be surprised, either. "I'm his sister. And who the devil are ye, Sassenach, to ride in here and make demands? This is clan Maxwell land, and I'll nae have anyone here threatened by a lobster-back."

"I haven't threatened anyone," he replied, clearly finding his footing again. That hadn't taken long. "Who is Lattimer's steward, then, if your brother is dead?"

"I am."

"Another jest?" he retorted. "The one where you sent me into a bog wasn't amusing, either."

"Ye think I'm nae capable of managing an estate?" she flared, before she could rein in her temper. *Blast it all.* Of all the things she'd expected today, being challenged by a nameless English officer hadn't been on the list.

"I have no idea what you're capable of. All I know of you is that you're a fair liar and that you know how to bathe." His gaze traveled the length of her again. "Alone, regrettably."

"I'm nae lying aboot this, *amadan.*"

"I'll not have ye insulting any lass, much less my own niece," her uncle Hamish finally said, when she'd begun to think he'd turned into a statue. And that after all his swaggering comments thirty minutes ago about keeping the English away from Maxwell territory by force, if necessary. "I suggest we continue this conversation inside, before ye stir up the lads," he continued.

The redcoat inclined his head, somehow making it look as if he had a choice in the matter. She didn't want him inside Lattimer; the old duke hadn't set foot there in twenty years, and he'd been the last Englishman to do so. This was her place, now.

Her uncle did make a point, however; the lads required only the smallest of slights to give them an excuse to begin a brawl, or worse, with the English soldiers. The deed wouldn't trouble her in the slightest, but the ramifications of beating in the Sassenach's pretty face did. More soldiers would come, because more always did, and it would be clan Maxwell that paid the price, no matter who'd provoked whom.

The officer brushed past her, carrying with him the smell of damp soil and fresh pine needles. He *was* tall, too, only lacking half a handspan on Tormod himself, though he was far leaner than the barrel-chested blacksmith. Up this close she had to admit that "pretty" was the wrong word for him, even in jest. With that scar running down the left side of his face — and the fine lines at the corners of his eyes from squinting in bright sunlight, that hard, precise mouth, and most especially the . . . direct, assessing eyes, she could call him handsome, striking even, but not pretty. That was if she'd cared to call him anything all, which she certainly did not.

She started back through the door, but the head groom caught her arm. "Lass," Oscar Ritchie muttered, "watch yerself."

"I will," she returned, scowling a little as she pulled free. If Oscar could point out one moment where she'd ever been foolish, she'd like to hear about it.

"Ye ken who that is? I saw him when I fought at Badajoz. The Beast of Bussaco, they call him. Major Gabriel Forrester. They say the Frenchies piss themselves when the Sixty-eighth Foot marches onto the field with him at the head."

Fiona stopped her retreat, uneasy alarm running through her. " 'The Beast of Bussaco'?" she repeated.

The groom nodded. "Aye. He's been stabbed, shot, and near blown to the devil by cannonfire, but nae a man's been able to stop him. I dunnae ken why he's here, but he's nae some fancy fellow parading aboot in a uniform."

"Thank ye, Oscar. I'll be cautious, but ye do recall I'm nae a man."

His mouth twitched. "I'd nae go up against either of ye, Miss Fiona."

Major Gabriel Forrester. Having a name to go with the face shouldn't have mattered, but it did. And now she knew a little of his reputation, as well. Whether that would give her an advantage when he told them whatever it was he wanted, she had no idea, but at least she no longer felt completely blind. And she knew something of what lurked behind that pleasing countenance of his. Things that didn't surprise her. Not when she looked into those eyes.

"The day room is up the stairs and first door on yer right," Uncle Hamish was saying, as if it weren't a very bad idea to invite a dangerous foreigner, an enemy, to join them for tea and biscuits. As she topped the stairs her mother's brother snagged her elbow, drawing her up against him. "Be polite, lass," he murmured. "We dunnae need the army deciding Lattimer would make a fine post for a hundred of their soldiers."

That actually troubled her even more than

the way men kept grabbing at her today. They'd gotten word that old Lattimer had died, back when the solicitors had been sending their insulting letters — as if she and the Maxwells had been cheating them or something. But no heir had been found. Did that mean Lattimer had gone to the English Crown? That they could indeed use it however they saw fit? "I'll behave," she agreed. "But he cannae set up a military post if nae a man ever sets eyes on him again."

"We'll worry aboot that later, Fiona." He released her and strolled into the room. "I'm Sir Hamish Paulk. My home, Glennoch Abbey, is a mile west of here. And ye've met my niece, Fiona Blackstock."

She folded her arms across her chest, waiting for the major to introduce himself. Would he refer to himself as the Beast of Bussaco? He'd asked for — demanded to see, rather — Kieran, and as far as she was concerned, that meant whoever he was, he could deal with her. If he wouldn't lower himself to speak with a woman, then he could go drown himself. She certainly wouldn't weep any tears to see him gone.

He remained standing close by the window, which, she supposed, given the filthy state of his uniform, could be out of concern for the furniture. Or perhaps he didn't feel comfortable sitting in the company of Highlanders. The other fellow, the stocky, short one who looked several years older than his commander, had placed himself on the other side of the room by the hearth. Strategy? Or was *he* simply chilled by the fine Scottish summer day?

"Lattimer's solicitor wrote you several times, asking for a report of the estate's earnings," Major Forrester said, his gaze on her. "Your response was not diplomatic."

So he *was* here because of that. Fiona kept her chin high. "His questions werenae diplomatic. But I'm nae saying another word to ye until ye introduce yerself and tell us why ye're here. I ken who ye are, Major Gabriel Forrester."

He paused for the barest of moments. "And how do you know that?" he asked levelly.

"Ye're nae the only man here to have served in the army," she retorted, not about to single out Oscar Ritchie for attention from someone his own people called the beast of anything. "But whoever ye are, I'm nae impressed by any man who gets himself lost, then thinks he can order us aboot because he wears a red coat."

His bisected left eyebrow lifted. "Got

myself lost, did I? Very well, then." Brushing off his dirty fingers, he dug into his coat and produced a folded paper. It was nice, heavy paper; vellum, unless she was mistaken. Whatever was written on it was likely important, damn it all. Keeping his gaze on her, he handed the missive to her uncle. "As your niece so astutely noted, I am Major Gabriel Forrester, commander of the Sixty-eighth Foot division, which is presently in Spain."

Uncle Hamish unfolded the paper and read through it. His craggy face went gray, his gaze lifting, wide-eyed, to Major Forrester. He took an abrupt seat on the arm of the couch. "I — this — ye dunnae expect me simply to believe this, do ye?" He clenched the heavy vellum hard in his hands.

"No, I don't. Kelgrove?" The major inclined his head in his companion's direction, and that soldier stepped forward to deliver a leather-covered bundle of still more papers to her uncle.

Whatever was afoot, just seeing Hamish Paulk unsettled gave Fiona uneasy shivers down her spine. She wanted to yank the vellum out of his hand and read it for herself, but she had the distinct feeling that that wouldn't reassure her. The last thing she wanted confirmed was that her nightmares were coming true, that the English Crown was taking possession of Lattimer.

"Uncle?" she finally urged, as he read through the additional pages with an increasingly grim expression on his hard-featured face.

Slowly he looked up. "Well. This isnae what I expected today." His dark eyes glanced from her to their unwanted guest. "Fiona, it seems Major Forrester here is the great-nephew once removed of Ronald Leeds." As she was absorbing that bit of information, he took a deep breath. "What that means," he said, and motioned with the papers he still held in one hand, "what *this* means, is that — according to a great many solicitors and members of the English Parliament and Prince George — he's the new Duke of Lattimer."

Fiona's heart went ice-cold and fell all the way to her toes. *Him?* Not just another power-hungry Sassenach, here to claim ancestral Maxwell land just like the old Lattimer and his father before him, but all that *and* a soldier. She looked over at him, to find his light gray gaze still on her.

"Surprise," he said, in the same tone she'd used on him earlier.

Well. If they were playing a game of who had the bigger secret, she supposed he'd

94

won this round. But putting a name on paper and claiming what came with it were two very different things, and bits of paper and vellum had never much impressed Highlanders, anyway. So aye, he could surprise her today. But by the end of this he would be the one running back south with his tail between his legs, and she would be the one laughing at his red-coated backside as he fled.

She shook herself back to the present just in time to hear Uncle Hamish ordering Fleming, Lattimer's longtime butler, to open one of the room suites on the south end of the castle for His Grace's use. "Nae," she interrupted. "The Duke of Lattimer should have the lord's chambers. Fleming, open the master suite."

Hamish sent her a glance, brow lowering. "Fiona, ye ken Lattimer's old rooms have-nae —"

"Because His Grace hasnae been here for two decades," she cut in. "Ye can see he's here now, and he should have the laird's bedchamber." As she spoke, she kept her level gaze on her uncle, daring him to countermand her orders. He might be the chieftain of this bit of clan Maxwell, but the running of this estate was hers. He didn't even lay his head here. And however polite he might be now, he couldn't like having an English duke about when for the past twenty years men had bowed only to him and the other clan leaders who came calling.

As she'd expected, he finally nodded. "Aye. Ye've the right of it, Fiona. The master's chambers fer the master of the house."

With a nod and a suspicious look at their new employer and his companion, Fleming galloped off to air out the quartet of rooms and see fresh linens laid. She would have to go up there herself later to make certain everything had been seen to. Thankfully a handful of hours of daylight remained; going into the master suite after dark was a task no one in his right mind wanted under the best of circumstances.

"Thank you," the duke said. "Do as you will, but I'm accustomed to sleeping on a cot with a stretch of canvas for a roof. Any bed will do."

"We're nae as primitive as that," she returned. "And we'll see to it ye have yer due." *Oh, that they would.*

"While ye wait, would ye care fer some tea, or perhaps someaught more substantial?" Hamish asked. "Mrs. Ritchie's the finest cook in these parts, and Fiona's seen to it that the larder's full."

"I'd rather take a walk through the house and about the grounds," the black-haired demon said. "I like to know my surroundings."

"Of course," her uncle replied. "I'll summon one of the men to take ye aboot."

"I have a steward to do that," the duke countered. "Unless you have an objection to accompanying me, Miss Blackstock."

"I have nae objection, Yer Grace." None that she had any intention of discussing with him, anyway.

A slight smile touched his mouth, but not his eyes. "It's Major Forrester, or Gabriel, if you please."

"Fer Saint Andrew's sake," she burst out, before she could stop herself. "I'm nae calling ye either one of those. Ye can be Yer Grace, or Lattimer. I'll nae have ye back in London telling all yer pretty friends how ignorant Highlanders are of proper custom."

He laughed, though she didn't see anything the least bit amusing in the entire conversation. But then she hadn't just inherited ten thousand acres of land that should have belonged to native Highlanders. "What's so amusing?" she demanded aloud.

"I don't have any pretty friends," he

returned, "and I doubt any of them are in London, either. Most of them are still in Spain, fighting Bonaparte."

She wished *he* still was. "A shame ye had to leave them."

"I'll agree with that, Miss Blackstock. And 'Lattimer' suits me better than 'Your Grace,' " he continued, his eyes dancing now. "I'll attempt to remember to answer to it." The duke gestured her toward the hallway door. "Shall we?"

"Dunnae ye wish to clean up first?" she returned, sending his stiff, filthy red attire a pointed glance. "And nae look so much like an English soldier, perhaps?"

He followed her gaze. "I have nothing else to wear. We'll begin outside, and I'll stomp off some of the mud."

"Ye might've done that before," she muttered under her breath.

"What was that?"

Fiona took a quick breath. "I said I'll have a bath drawn fer ye," she said aloud. "Fer after yer inspection."

"It's not an insp—"

"The weather's getting worse. We'd best be off." She pretended not to hear his protest, and instead led the way back into the hallway and toward the front door.

The idea that he had nothing to wear but

his uniform surprised her, and she couldn't push that aside as she led him out to the garden and the landscaped part of the grounds. He'd jumped into the mud without hesitation, even though she hadn't needed saving. But what self-respecting duke with at least three estates and thousands of pounds of income annually didn't even own a second coat? The Beast of Bussaco, apparently.

She wasn't fooled by the way he pretended to be straightforward and direct, either. Officers didn't do anything but give orders, finding ways to gain clever nicknames without actually earning them. Whatever the head groom said, Major Forrester couldn't possibly be any different. It wouldn't be long before he'd begin ordering her people about and sending for his military friends, and more than likely hiring a man to take her place. Well, then. She would make certain he was well gone before any of that could happen.

"What do you make of this?" Gabriel asked, submerging in the copper bathtub and then resurfacing to shake out his wet hair. He'd lived in dirty uniforms when necessary, but it felt odd and barbaric to do so in such lavish surroundings. And none of the servants had been particularly happy to see him eat dinner in the mud-caked uniform, but he hadn't had much choice. He'd asked for an old blanket to throw over the dining room chair, at least.

Across the ridiculously large and stiflingly opulent bedchamber, Adam Kelgrove unpacked the saddlebag he'd brought and set the simple shaving accoutrements on the carved mahogany dressing table. "The castle looks in need of some repairs, but it seems to be well cared for, and the gardens are simple, but well maintained. Animals look healthy, and no one's in rags. I didn't spy any silver candlesticks, but from the state of your welcome I'd say they chose not to set them out for you."

His aide paid attention; that boded well for Kelgrove's future as the likely next steward of Lattimer. Because pretty and petite or not, Fiona Blackstock was not a steward. Females didn't become stewards. It didn't take any London bronze to know that. "I agree," he said aloud. "So did Miss Blackstock refuse to send the estate books to the solicitors because there's no money in this place, or because she's stubborn and devious?"

"Or because she's a half-wild Highlander?" Kelgrove added with a brief grin.

Jest or not, that could well be the answer. She simply didn't want to be dictated to by any Englishman. She clearly didn't want *him* there. Gabriel remained unsure, though, whether her hostility came from her dislike of the Sassenach, or because she knew she'd been caught out pretending to be her brother for God knows how long and that now she was very likely to be replaced by a man. *Very* likely.

Considering that on first meeting him she'd sent him into a bog, she had reason to be worried. Generally people who tried to kill him didn't live long enough to make a second attempt, but this was so-called civilization. If he wanted to be rid of Fiona Blackstock he would have to explain himself to her, probably making her cry, and hand her her papers — if she had papers. Since she'd taken over the duties of her late brother without bothering to inform old Lattimer or his solicitors, he doubted she had anything but an almost admirable amount of mettle. If sending her away left her in need of consolation, he'd be more than happy to see to that before she went, too.

Outside the curtained windows came a low moaning, the tone rising and sinking in time with the sputtering of the fire in the stone and marble fireplace. "Wind's picking up," Kelgrove noted unhelpfully, walking over to collect the last bits of Gabriel's uniform and dump them into a basket.

"It should drive off the fog, anyway. I want a better look at the land and how it's being used."

"Well, you'll be doing that naked," his aide noted. "Your trunk won't be here for another three days."

Gabriel rolled his left shoulder, the arm still a little stiff from the rifle shot he'd taken. "I've been told that I'm wealthy now. Send a requisition for a second uniform tomorrow. And see if there's a tailor in that village — Strouth, isn't it? — in the meantime. Just my being here has the locals spinning. If I go about naked people could die."

Adam snorted. "With your permission, Major, I'm going to send for two uniforms. And when they arrive, I'm going to burn this one." He hefted the basket, heading for the door. "I'll see if I can at least save the boots. Pull that rope on the wall there if you need me," he said, gesturing at a heavy, tasseled pull by the bed. "It'll ring in the servants' quarters. I'll be in the kitchen seeing if I can render any of this wearable again, and I'll more than likely be weeping."

With a chuckle, Gabriel settled lower in the blessedly warm water. "Find yourself a bed, not in the servants' quarters. You're not a servant. Wake me at six, and locate some damned trousers for me."

A moment later he found himself alone. Lined with interspersed panels of heavy wood paneling and burgundy and gold wallpaper, and liberally decorated with large, stuffed animal heads, the room seemed close despite its size. Two sets of three tall, rectangular windows, presently closed tight behind dark curtains the color of wet pine needles, allowed a view of the world outside. Dominated by a large oak bed that practically required a ladder to mount, the bedchamber clearly belonged to a wealthy, powerful man who liked to be reminded of what he owned. Except that that man now happened to be him, and he didn't feel nearly as comfortable with his possessions.

Even with three days spent fencing with the late Ronald Leeds's solicitors to learn about the late duke's investments and his holdings, he hadn't felt the slightest connection to the man or his . . . things. In fact, he'd mostly felt annoyance — though perhaps fury was a better word — at his great-uncle once removed, for upending a simple, orderly life. The fact that his sister could benefit from his altered circumstances seemed the only positive turn in any of this.

Here, however, surrounded by echoes of the man and his ancestors — the ones who'd evidently taken the land and MacKittrick Castle from clan Maxwell in the first place — he had his first real sense of who the former Duke of Lattimer actually was. If this room truly was an indication of the man's character, Gabriel didn't much like the late Ronald Leeds and his exaggerated sense of self-importance.

The wind's moaning resumed, the sound cold and mournful. The fire sputtered again, turning the room into a cave of deep, flickering shadows. He'd have to bank the fire before he retired for the night, or risk the wind pushing hot coals off the hearth and onto the old Persian rug set before it. Black-eyed Fiona wouldn't weep any tears at his demise, but he was loath to make things that easy for her.

While the bathwater had been hot he hadn't minded the dirt so much, but now that it had begun to cool he became very aware of the layer of mud settling beneath his arse. With a sigh he stood, stepping onto the chill stone floor and knotting the coarse linen towel around his hips.

He emptied the glass Kelgrove had left beside the bath of its generous pour of whisky, and walked barefoot across yet another dark, moth-eaten Persian rug to refill it. Three weeks ago imagining anything beyond how he meant to keep his men and himself alive beyond the next day, how he meant to win his next battle, had seemed a waste of time. If he ever *had* indulged in daydreams, he would never have been able to conjure anything as absurd as this. Even as a holiday. Him, the Duke of Lattimer, standing in a grand room in an ancient house set on more land than some of the American Colonies could claim for themselves.

The painting of a dog and yet more damned roosters that hung on one side of the chimney banged and set itself off kilter by a good two inches. *Hm.* Stepping up to the wall, he nudged the painting back to level. A gap or two in the chimney wouldn't surprise him in the least, given the state of the rest of the building, but that could be dangerous. He'd have to look into it in the morning.

On the other side of the chimney a book jumped, and three tomes shot out and fell to the floor four feet away from where they'd begun. "Ah," he said aloud, squatting down to retrieve the books. "You're a ghost." Gabriel turned the books over in his hands. "A ghost who doesn't care for poetry. Well, I'm not fond of it, either."

The idea of spirits wandering about the old castle — or anywhere, for that matter — didn't particularly surprise him. In twelve years of fighting he'd seen too many things that neither logic nor the church could explain. The idea of some spook here in the room with him actually felt . . . not quite comforting, but almost fortunate. At the least, books flying off shelves kept him from dwelling on why he'd come here and what the devil he was supposed to do about it. He'd be more comfortable if someone would just point a gun a him.

"You make a fucking ridiculous duke, Gabriel," he muttered, downing half the whisky in the glass and setting the rest aside for the ghost. The sooner he made Kelgrove's new position official and returned to his own duties, the better.

He needed to leave as soon as possible, to go back to his command before he could lose the edge that kept his men and himself alive. Because while this might be a proper setting for a duke, it was too much, too opulent, and too frivolous for Major Gabriel Forrester — and that was the only person he knew how to be.

Someone knocked at his door, and he walked over to pull it open. Black eyes widened, and Fiona took a quick step backward. "I — Where's yer damned valet?"

Gabriel allowed himself a grin, both at her discomfiture and because she'd stopped his mind from traversing a road he had no wish to explore. Yes, she'd caused him to jump into a mudhole, and then get lost in a bog for nearly three hours, but at this moment he felt grateful. "Adam Kelgrove isn't a valet. He's my aide-de-camp. And I sent him off to bed. Is there something you required?"

"I — Nae. I dunnae require a thing from ye." She looked down at his hands. "Ye like poetry, do ye?"

For a bare moment he'd hoped she would say yes, she did require something, and that it was sex. That was what he wanted of her. The chill from the hallway began to wash into the room and swirl up his legs beneath the towel. "No. I don't read poetry. Evidently there's a ghost in here."

"Aye? I'm nae surprised. There are nasty spirits all aboot the castle."

Gabriel nodded. "No doubt. I'm getting cold standing here, so either come in or go away," he said, turning his back to head for the fireplace where it was warmer, and setting the books down on the mantel. "And I assume you wanted me in this room because of the wind stirring up the fireplace and that attractive moaning sound it makes? And the ghost, of course."

She followed him into the room, closing the door behind her. The hairs on his arms lifted; perhaps she did want something, after all. He damned well hoped so. Gabriel took a slow breath.

"I wanted ye in here because it's the laird's bedchamber," she retorted, hefting the bundled material she carried against her chest. "Do the ghosties and the wind trouble ye, Lattimer? I can give ye a different room. It willnae be as grand, of course."

"Don't bother. It's out of the weather, which puts it above most places I've spent the night." He faced her again, and caught her quick gaze lifting from his torso back to his face again. From her expression, though, he couldn't tell whether the patchwork of scars that decorated his back and chest intrigued or horrified her. He was accustomed to both reactions from the fairer sex.

"Dead Highlanders looking fer bloody vengeance against an English soldier dunnae trouble ye, either?"

Faint suspicion over the ghostly events and her timing in coming to call on him touched him, but he set it aside for later. Instead he chuckled. "Dead enemies don't trouble me much at all, Miss Blackstock. Not nearly as much as live ones."

Her scowl deepened. "Well, then. Suit yerself." She tossed the bundle of cloth at his bare chest. "Ye said ye had naught else to wear. Seems foolish to me that ye'd ride all the way to the Highlands withoot a change of clothes, but mayhap that's the way of Sassenach these days. Those" — and she gestured at the bundle — "belonged to my brother. Ye're of a height, I reckon."

"Thank you." He wouldn't put it past her to have sprinkled them with pepper, but he did appreciate the gesture. "And I do have clothes; my trunk should be arriving via mail coach by the end of the week."

She folded her arms across her rather modest bosom. "Mail coach? Ye're the mighty Duke of Lattimer. Ye can purchase a dozen coaches, ye ken."

When had it happened, that other people understood his life better than he did? "I suppose so. I've recently been handed an entirely new set of rules. I'm still learning them."

"Ye admit to that?" She sounded surprised.

Did admitting that he didn't know how to be a duke equate with some sort of weakness? It didn't feel that way. Nothing he'd said would prevent him from doing his duty. "Why shouldn't I?" he asked aloud. "I'm a plainspoken fellow, and I don't feel the need to lie about who or what I am, Miss Blackstock."

"Ach, I didnae lie, either. Nae a man asked if I was still Kieran, and I didnae volunteer the information. So ye keep yer high horse oot in the stable."

He grinned. "A sensitive subject, is it? I don't have a high horse, but I'd be willing to commiserate with you here in private." Deliberately he sent his gaze down the length of her and up again. Moving up to her, Gabriel hooked his finger into the lace neck of her gray gown. She smelled of heather. He'd never found that arousing before, but he did now.

When she lifted her face to look up at him, those soft-looking lips parted, his cock jumped. He tugged her up against his chest, very aware that only a thin muslin gown and a towel separated them.

"So ye mean to have me, do ye?" she

murmured, chocolate-colored eyes meeting his.

"I'm a man with an appetite," he returned in the same tone. "You sent me into a bog, and the entire time I couldn't stop imagining you peeling yourself out of that muddy gown." He leaned down, capturing her mouth in a hard, heated kiss. Her mouth was just as he'd imagined, soft, warm, and molding against his. When her hand dug into his damp hair, the tight rein he held on himself loosened just a little. Three weeks of his world spun off its axis, but this, *this,* he knew how to do.

Her mouth retreated from his just a little. "I'll have to do as ye demand, Yer Grace," she stated. "I suppose it's better me than one of the maids."

Gabriel scowled. "I'm not 'demanding' a damned thing. You kissed me back. I felt it. A man and a woman. You and me."

Her gaze remained on his mouth. "A duke and an employee," she corrected.

"What? So now I can't have a woman if I outrank her? That's ridiculous. And you're not my employee, anyway."

Finally she met his gaze. "I'm yer employee until ye dismiss me."

Fuck. "That's a fine use of strategy, Miss Blackstock," he countered, "but your hand's still in my hair."

Swiftly she withdrew it, her fair cheeks flushing a pretty pink. "I was trying to keep my balance."

"No you weren't. And now you know for certain what I want. I believe you want it, as well."

She opened and closed her mouth, then belatedly shoved away from him. "I most certainly dunnae yearn fer your touch, Lattimer."

And yet she remained alone with him in his laird's bedchamber. Reminding her of that fact wouldn't benefit him, however, so he didn't mention it. She'd used some sound strategy, even if it did rely on him being of good character. He couldn't count that as a compliment, but it was close to one. If she wanted this to be a game of wills and wits, she was welcome to try to stand against him. "We'll see about that," he said aloud. "I'm not often wrong."

"Well, ye are this time. I dunnae even want ye here in Scotland. This isnae the place fer anyone to be fumbling aboot like a wee infant. I ken ye have a bushel of other properties south of Hadrian's Wall, and I wish ye'd gone to one of them to learn how to be an aristocrat."

"And yet I'm here because of you, Miss

Blackstock," he returned, noting just to himself that she still stood close enough to touch. Gabriel curled his hands into fists, but that did nothing for the warm rush of lust still humming just beneath his skin.

"Me?" she retorted. "How the devil could ye be here because of me when the first time ye knew aboot me was when ye dragged me oot of the mud?"

"Because old Lattimer's solicitors wrote you five times asking for the estate's financial report before you finally answered — and that was only to threaten them. I am now responsible for this property. The 'knife in the gizzard' reply didn't give me much of an idea of what might be amiss here, but it did suggest something was wrong." Nor did having a hot-tempered female as a steward satisfy his requirement for a responsible leader who could stand in his stead.

"Ye'll have all yer facts and figures, then. But ye willnae have me." She turned on her heel. "Good night."

The view of her swaying backside nearly made him consider suggesting once again that she stay. For the devil's sake, he hadn't had a woman in . . . weeks. And tonight that seemed like a very long time. He caught her arm, twirling her around to face him and dragging her up against his chest.

113

"Good night, *Your Grace,*" he murmured, brushing the pad of his thumb along her lower lip. So soft, so free of the tired cynicism that marked most women of his acquaintance. If he was the Beast of Bussaco, she was some sort of sharp-tongued angel. He'd never met her like. Leaving her be, unless she expressly ordered him to do so, was out of the question. And he'd spent better than a decade assessing people at a glance. She might claim not to be interested, but everything about her said she was lying. And so until he figured her out, until he had her, he'd sooner give up breathing than this hunt.

Her shoulders squared. "Good night, *Yer Grace,*" she enunciated, glancing at him and then away as he released her. Taking two quick steps, she opened the door and then very firmly pulled it closed behind her.

Gabriel eyed the door for a moment after she left, weighing whether to go after her or not. Strategically it made more sense to give her the night to think about him, to remember that kiss. He couldn't be the only one to think it had been rather spectacular. The bulge in the front of his towel certainly agreed.

As for the ghost of MacKittrick and his curse, he had a feeling that at least one of those things had more to do with Miss Blackstock than a dead Jacobite after revenge. And if any Highlander tried to slip in and kill him tonight, they would serve as a warning against anyone else attempting it again.

Blowing out his breath, he finished toweling off and then pulled a clean shirt over his head. At least Kelgrove had stuffed an extra shirt into his travel bag. Once he'd blown out the candles and banked the sputtering fire, he climbed the trio of wooden steps pushed up against the side of the bed and rolled beneath the heavy, soft covers. With every movement he seemed to sink farther into the plump mattress beneath him, until he began to feel as if he were about to drown in satin and feathers. Despite the chill in the air and the wind whistling down the fireplace, the heat from his own body surrounded him, closing him in a baking, goose-down coffin.

"Damnation," he swore, sitting upright and flinging sheets and quilts and pillows off the side of the bed. He tried lying back again, but immediately began to sink into the mattress once more. "Bloody hell."

After ten minutes of hot, wallowing torture he sat up again, swam his way to the edge of the behemoth, and slid to the floor.

Christ. He'd fought Frenchmen who put up less of a fight than that damned bed. Breathing hard, he lay down on the pile of blankets he'd shoved onto the stone floor. "You can take the bed, MacKittrick," he muttered aloud.

So this was his first night as a duke in his own castle. As he contemplated his situation, he couldn't deny one thing — parts of it felt familiar. A foreign land, surrounded by hostile forces who wanted him either gone or dead and didn't much care which one it was, and him with the assignment to bring order out of chaos. And the fact that the opposing forces were led by a supremely desirable black-eyed female with dusky hair? He would manage her just as he'd managed every other obstacle in his path before now. This was about sex and it was about war, and he was a damned expert in both.

CHAPTER FOUR

"Did he piss himself, Miss Fiona?" Fleming the butler asked in a hushed whisper, his hands brushing lovingly across a half-dozen of the strings that traveled through the usually hidden passageway in which he stood, through the wall, and out to the backs of a trio of paintings — among other things — in the bedchamber beyond.

"I tied off one of those dusty old books on the top shelf, too," the young footman just beyond him breathed. "They sent half the bookshelf onto the floor, I reckon."

"Aye. Has he run yet?" the butler took up again.

That had been the plan, of course. Her father and Uncle Hamish had run the original strings themselves, some twenty years ago. Their experiment marked the last night the old duke had laid his head at Lattimer, as a matter of fact, and no one believed that had been a coincidence. And what worked for one duke would work just as well on another. Or it should have.

But this duke was young — younger by some fifteen years than Lattimer had been at the time of his last visit, she reckoned. And this duke bore scars, not just of an unlucky brawl or a fall from a horse, but of war. A war he'd fought, rather than standing at the back and ordering other men to die. And he'd kissed her like he was drowning and she was air. She'd protested, of course; an arrogant, invading Sassenach had no right to lay a finger on her, much less his mouth. She hadn't noticed the heat and the solid strength of him, and she certainly hadn't appreciated any of those things. Yes, he looked like the personification of Ares, and yes, that and his self-confidence might be attractive to some English lass, but she wasn't English.

"Did he run, Miss Fiona?" Fleming repeated.

She blinked. "Nae," she said absently.

"Nae? But we put him in there especially," Hugh, one of Lattimer's two dozen footmen, protested, as he sent a longing look at the additional strings in his hands. "And I tested it during dinner. It should've worked."

"It did," Fiona conceded. "He'd just

picked up the books when I knocked. He said the living frighten him more than the dead." Well, that hadn't been precisely what he'd said, and she had the feeling that nothing much did frighten him.

"This should've turned his hair white," Hugh protested. "It would've done that fer me."

"Well, it didnae trouble him a whit," she snapped back, still trying to dispel the image of that hard-muscled chest. For God's sake, he'd been shot at least thrice, and it looked like someone had gone after him with a saber on more than one occasion. Oscar had mentioned cannonfire, as well. And he'd made it clear what he wanted of her. Had she convinced him that she wanted nothing to do with him? *Damnation.* She hadn't even convinced herself.

"Nae a whit?"

"He's got the wind crying through those holes in the chimney, too, but that didnae seem to bother him, either." At the disappointed looks on the servants' faces, she relented a little. "Tell the rest of the staff to go on with spreading the ghostly tales, but dunnae be so obvious aboot it that he catches onto the idea we're trying to drive him off. The only way he'll stay gone is if he doesnae *want* to come back."

"We'll see to it, Miss Fiona."

As the butler slipped out of the dark passageway and back into the storage room where she stood, she caught his arm. "Did Ian come by fer supper?"

Fleming nodded. "Aye. He's got only half a dozen men watching the road tonight, because of the weather."

"He should've kept them all oot. We dunnae need more troubles right now to add to the ones we already have."

"Seems to me it's the other way round. It's *him* we dunnae need adding to *our* troubles." The butler jabbed a finger toward the passageway and the master bedchamber beyond.

Oh, she agreed with that. "Either way, one calamity at a time is more than enough fer me. Send Ian to see me when he gets back in the morning. And keep him clear of His Grace."

After the two men had gone, she shut and locked the storage room door behind her and the hidden passageway beyond that. The last thing she needed was for someone to decide to take matters into his or her own hands and spoil the game entirely. Of course, if one of the castle's actual old ghosties went for a walk about the master bedchamber, she had no objection at all. It was a popular room for the spooks, after all. As she'd told the duke, there were several old Maxwells who had no reason to want a Sassenach back in the castle and claiming it for himself.

For the past twenty years Uncle Hamish, as both a clan chieftain and a local aristocrat, had been the closest they had to someone of the new Lattimer's rank — though Gabriel Forrester seemed closer to a groom than a duke, truth be told. Never in her wildest imaginings had she thought the major who'd jumped into the mudhole to rescue her, whether she'd required assistance or not, would be the new Duke of Lattimer. If he hadn't been in a uniform, she would even have enjoyed his attention. If he hadn't been wearing anything at all, she would have appreciated him even more.

Fiona clenched her jaw. *That was enough of that, damn it all.* She didn't appreciate him. She wanted him gone. Getting rid of him now wouldn't be as simple as misdirecting him or even convincing him that his presence was both unnecessary and unwise. The man had a piece of paper proving that he had the right to be at Lattimer and to claim it for himself. Further, he had the right to see all of them — those who'd been living and working on this land for generations — gone, if he chose to do so.

An English soldier, for God's sake. His ilk had been hated and feared in the Highlands for better than four hundred years before the battle at Culloden. While he was far too young to have fought on that field, he hadn't come to Scotland simply to view the scenery. He'd come because he had questions about the property's finances. Questions she'd stupidly refused to answer. She might have lied and kept him away for a time, if she'd known they'd found an heir for the property, if she'd known that heir was Major Gabriel Forrester. But now he was here, and he no doubt wanted to know how much money he could shake out of Lattimer. Nor would he be the only Sassenach ever to bleed the Highlands to pay for a luxurious life in the soft south.

For a moment she considered going back into the storage room and pulling some more of the strings, after all. Something was bound to frighten him. She'd like nothing better than to see him fleeing shirtless into the night — and only because shirtless meant he'd panicked. Not because he looked fit and muscular and she hadn't minded at all taking a gander at him, scars and all. No, that would be ridiculous. Her, thinking carnal thoughts about a Sassenach simply because he thought them about her.

As she'd said, they needed to make certain that this duke would leave of his own accord and, just as importantly, never wish to return. His arrival had set the household — and the countryside — on its ear, and yes, that seemed to be her fault. She'd decided not to let a nose-in-the-air solicitor order her about, and apparently that had consequences. She should have known better, but no one had bothered to be concerned about Lattimer until the old duke's death had revealed that his own solicitors hadn't done their jobs. Her lack of cooperation, though, meant that no one had felt it necessary to inform her either that a new duke had been found, or that he was heading north for a visit.

First thing in the morning she needed to go speak with Oscar Ritchie. The head groom at least knew of Major Forrester, which was more than she or anyone else she'd encountered could claim. The more information she had, the easier it would be to form a strategy to be rid of the new duke before he could make things worse than they already were. Before he could kiss her again and she forgot how much she was supposed to dislike him.

Finally she shut herself inside her own

bedchamber and sank into the chair set before the fireplace. The room sat only four doors down from Lattimer's, and while she would have preferred to be farther away, this room had been hers since her second birthday — which had coincided with old Lattimer's exit. Aside from that, she wanted to be close enough to hear if any trouble should raise its head.

Her mind centered on how to best be rid of this large, troublesome Englishman, and her drifting thoughts swirled about a fresh bullet scar on a muscular arm, an assessing pair of light gray eyes, and a mouth that seemed almost cruel until he grinned. And when he kissed her . . . Now she didn't know whether to fall asleep and dream about him, or stay awake to think about him all night. *Blast it all.*

Gabriel pushed aside the heavy curtains, then stilled with his hands gripping the green, linen-lined silk. "Good God," he breathed, his bare feet, the chill in the air, the rumbling hunger in his stomach all forgotten.

Before him, stretching out over perhaps half a hundred miles, lay the Scottish Highlands. The land directly beyond Lattimer's formal gardens sloped off gently to the shore of a vast blue lake that curved to the east out of sight beyond a cluster of tumbled ruins on the rocky bank. Trees edged down to the western shore and up the hill beyond, with patches of purple heather and thistle carpeting open meadows. Beyond the lake, rough, rock-tumbled hills lifted into craggy white mountains that stood starkly silhouetted by the rising sun.

Of all the places he'd been in the world, of all the things he'd seen, this . . . humbled him. Belatedly two things occurred to him: he didn't know the name of the lake, and most of what he could see belonged to him.

He'd known since he'd first donned a uniform that he was made for war. The idea of people trying to kill him, the violence, the cold and the heat, the long days of battle and the longer nights of waiting for the battle to come — he relished the things that broke other men. He was accustomed to responsibility and command, but owning land, being responsible for people who carried rakes and hoes rather than muskets and rifles, fell so far out of his realm of expertise he couldn't even sight it over the horizon.

Gabriel took a slow breath. He knew battle. And Lattimer had just become his battleground. If he looked at it that way, the castle was his command tent. The Highlands was his battlefield, and the Highlanders were either his troops, or the enemy's. In the next few days he would have to decide which, and then act based on that fact.

As he turned to finish dressing, he caught sight of a lone figure strolling through the garden in the direction of the stables. Even with a heavy coat and a sturdy hat jammed low on her dusky hair, he recognized Fiona Blackstock. From that attire she was either dressed to go riding, or to rob a mail coach. Though the latter would certainly be an interesting twist, he had to assume she meant to trot off somewhere out of his reach.

Every good victory came with a prize, and she would be his. That didn't mean, however, that he was going to let her make more trouble while she was here. If she thought riding out early would keep her clear of him or give her the opportunity to gather re-inforcements, she didn't know him at all. In addition, somewhere between the mudhole and the drawing room she'd learned his name, and before he'd given it to her. Someone here knew him, and he needed to figure out who that was. Not because he had anything to hide, but because this campaign looked to be about strategy and leverage. He needed to know who stood on the field of battle.

Swiftly he finished buttoning his donated trousers, but that still left him without boots or a coat or jacket. He checked outside his door, but either Kelgrove hadn't yet risen, or the sergeant hadn't been able to chisel the mud off his Hessians.

Pulling the bell seemed too regal, but as far as he knew people didn't walk about half naked in proper houses. Scowling, he grabbed hold of the thing and yanked it down a half-dozen times, then went digging through the chest and wardrobe to find them empty of everything but an old, yellowed cravat.

His door slammed open. "Major!" Kelgrove panted, diving into the room pistol first.

"Put that down, Adam," Gabriel ordered, sidestepping out of range.

"But . . ." Kelgrove straightened. "From the way you were slamming that bell about, I thought you were being strangled with the rope."

"I didn't know how emphatic to be. I need my boots. And a coat."

"I still have your coat soaking. The boots are wearable, but you'd never pass inspection with them."

"The boots, Sergeant. And any coat will

do, as long as it's warm. I'll meet you at the stable."

"Are we leaving?" Kelgrove looked hopeful at that idea.

"No," he returned, though he could damned well sympathize. "Our task here isn't finished. I'm going for a ride."

"I . . . Of course, sir."

The lord of the manor was more than likely expected to use the grand staircase at the front of the house, but Gabriel opted for the more direct route of the servants' stairs at the back. Even indoors the wood and stone beneath his bare feet felt half frozen, but Fiona already had a head start on him. He wasn't going to wait about for perfectly shined shoes.

"Yer Grace," a redheaded young lady announced as he reached the bottom floor, giving him a deep curtsy and nearly dropping the stack of linens she carried.

"Good morning," he replied, settling for a polite nod as he moved past her. Perhaps he should have paid more attention to how Wellington and his lordling flock addressed their servants, but most of them were men he didn't care to emulate in war, which gave him no desire to do so in peace.

"Ye've nae shoes on, Yer Grace," the woman noted, the tone of her voice alone telling him that she thought him mad.

"Yes, I'm aware of that. Thank you."

He'd thought most everyone in the household would be out in the main part of the house, likely looking for a glimpse of him, but servants still seemed to be everywhere. By the time he reached the door past the kitchen he'd been made aware at least a dozen times that he was barefoot. These Highlanders were a helpful lot. His feet were numb with cold by the time he reached the stable on the far side of the garden. If he didn't catch up with Miss Blackstock, he wasn't going to be amused. He dodged a clump of horseshit and put his hand on the stable door.

". . . called Beast doesnae fill my heart with hope," Fiona's honeyed voice came, and he lowered his hand again.

"I wasnae in the Sixty-eighth regiment," a male voice returned, "so I can only tell ye what all of us saw and heard. And that was how Major Forrester made his way past the Frenchies' cannons to their munitions wagons, set fire to 'em, and sent 'em rolling doon the hill into the middle of the French troops. They scattered like cockroaches, Miss Fiona, instead of marching on us."

"Well." Silence. "That doesn't sound beastly, Oscar."

Gabriel nodded to himself. He hadn't thought so, either. The act had been meant to disrupt France's advance and to save English lives, and in that he'd succeeded. The rest, the nickname and the absurd amount of notoriety and praise it had gained him, was ridiculous.

"They say he's unstoppable," the Oscar fellow continued in his thick brogue. "And fearless. Nae a man I'd like as an enemy."

"I suppose if he'd stayed in Spain or in England I'd like him just fine," she returned. "But he came here, and I'll nae have any Sassenach dictating to me, whatever papers he brings with him."

"I'd nae wish to go against either of ye."

"I'll take that as a compliment. If he comes looking fer me, tell him I've gone to the mill or someaught."

The large stable doors rattled, and almost without thinking Gabriel ducked around the side of the building. A horse headed away from him down the hill at a canter, and the doors closed again. So she rode places alone. He couldn't imagine any London lady doing that, but he had very limited personal experience with anything proper.

He waited long enough for her to be reasonably out of sight, then strode back around and pulled open the stable door.

"Good morning, gentlemen," he said to the large group of grooms and stable boys measuring out hay and oats for the dozen horses in residence, and pulled his saddle off its post.

"Yer Grace," the oldest of them exclaimed, and trotted over to grab hold of the other side of the saddle. "I'll see to this."

Gabriel recognized him as yesterday's guard with the pitchfork, and now he knew the voice, as well. "And you are?" he asked, releasing his grip.

The man bowed, walking backward toward where Union Jack stuck his head over the stall door and nickered. "Oscar Ritchie, Yer Grace. Lattimer's head groom, if ye please."

"Ritchie. Are you related to Mrs. Ritchie, the cook?"

He grinned. "Aye. My good wife, she is. Ye want yer Jack saddled, do ye?"

"If you please."

"Ye ken ye've nae shoes on, Yer Grace."

Gabriel sighed. "Yes."

"Rollie over there'll lend ye his boots."

The youngest of the stable boys, a lad with bright red hair and cheeks to match, frowned. "I willnae. My ma gave me these boots."

"I'll worry about my own boots," Gabriel

broke in, trying to decide how to broach the subject of military service without sounding like he'd been eavesdropping, but then deciding that holding on to that piece of information might be wiser for the moment. Despite his reputation to the contrary, he did know something about patience.

The groom bent in another bow. "As ye say, Yer Grace."

While he slipped the bridle on over Jack's head, Kelgrove skidded into the stable. "I did what I could, Major," he panted, squatting in front of where Gabriel seated himself to pull on the boots, "but you shouldn't ever wear them to see Wellington again."

"For the devil's sake, Kelgrove, they're boots," he retorted, stomping into the left one. "They serve a purpose. I don't give a damn if I can see my reflection in them or not."

"Of course not, sir. But *I* do." The sergeant stood, shaking out a heavy brown woolen coat. "I found this in the attic, with a selection of your predecessor's clothes. Most are too small and more fit for a costume party, but a few of them are passable. Thank God you found trousers, though, because no one's been willing to lend you anything but kilts."

Gabriel shrugged into the coat, then took

hold of Jack's bridle. "Thank you. I'll be back shortly."

Kelgrove stepped in front of him. "Major, you cannot go riding by yourself. It isn't . . ." And he sent a look at the interested grooms surrounding them. "It isn't safe."

Swinging into the saddle, Gabriel inclined his head. " 'Safe' hasn't concerned me in quite a long time, Adam. And find me a harder mattress, will you? I nearly drowned in that one."

Without bothering to wait for an answer, he ducked beneath the stable door and sent Union Jack galloping down the slope toward the lake. It felt like an hour since he'd heard his quarry depart in that direction, but it couldn't have been more than ten minutes at most. Still, given the dense clusters of trees, with narrow streams and pathways leading up through the shallow hills all along the shore, she could be anywhere. Except the mill, of course.

Slowing Jack to a canter, he considered. She had no idea he rode behind her, so she wouldn't be hiding or trying to cover her tracks. He reckoned that she had a specific destination in mind, especially given that his pocket watch read barely six-thirty in the morning.

The trail forked in three different directions ahead, and he pulled Jack to a halt and hopped to the ground. With the damp and then the wind yesterday, the myriad tracks were faint and dulled at the edges — with the exception of a quartet of deer and a horse with metal shoes. "There you are," he murmured, mounting Jack again and heading away from the lake and up the trail that paralleled a stream toward the top of the hill.

A few minutes later the trail topped a rise, opening out to a heather-filled meadow split by the curving stream. On either side of the water, and joined by a stone bridge that looked Roman, was a village of perhaps three dozen small stone and wattle houses, a blacksmith, a tavern, a church, and a shop or two. He knew at least one village lay on Lattimer land, so he supposed this could be it — Strouth. More buildings and people for whom he was responsible. More weight to sit upon his shoulders — because while he was accustomed to holding lives in his hands, those were soldiers, men who for the most part had signed up to face danger and death. Here there were undoubtedly women and children, babies and grandparents, all people with whom he had little experience — and no idea how to protect.

"Were ye following me, then, Lattimer?"

Gabriel shook himself out of the tangled cobweb of his thoughts as Fiona Blackstock appeared at the far end of the bridge to put her hands on her hips and glare at him. Somehow she managed to look both formidable and enticing at the same time. "Yes, I was," he returned coolly, sending Jack clopping onto the bridge. "You mentioned several times yesterday that the Highlands was a dangerous place. I'm here to protect you." *And to see what the devil you're up to,* he added silently.

"I meant that the Highlands arenae safe fer *ye,* Sassenach. I'm perfectly well, thank ye. Go back to Lattimer before ye frighten the wee bairns. Or all the way to London, and spare the lot of us."

"Bairns. Those are children, yes?" he persisted, ignoring the verbal jabs as he swung out of the saddle.

As he moved up to keep pace beside her, Miss Blackstock lifted an artfully curved eyebrow. "Aye. Bairns are children. And that's a cow, and that's a wagon," she said, imitating his accent as she pointed.

Her unrelenting hostility amused him. He much preferred a female who handed out clever barbs to someone who pretended friendship while sharpening a knife for his

135

spine. "Are you this foul-tempered every morning, or did I unsettle you last night?"

"Ye didnae unsettle me." Her shoulders squared. "Ye're nae the first ham-fisted man to try pawing at me."

While he didn't appreciate the "pawing" description — because pawing implied a lack of skill or finesse — the way his gut tightened and his jaw clenched in reaction to her statement actually surprised him more. He didn't want to hear that other men had been after her, regardless of the fact that he'd only known her for two days and kissed her once. The fact that men had pursued her made sense; her looks and her sharp, clever tongue made her very nearly irresistible. But even though he could barely call the two of them acquainted, her presence left him distracted and keenly focused all at the same time.

The camp women he knew were anything but exclusive. He knew that; he was accustomed to it. This was different. And the fact that other men pawed at her, with a degree of finesse or not . . . Well, he didn't like it. At all.

"Nae answer to that?" she prompted.

Damnation. "I've been accused of many things, but being ham-fisted isn't one of them. You —"

He glanced past her to see the end of a long metal tube rounding a corner in their direction, and abruptly he was in battle again. "Get back," he ordered sharptly, grabbing Miss Blackstock's arm and hauling her behind him.

Gabriel felt the startled flex of muscles beneath his hand, and then she jerked away from him. "William MacDorry, ye carry that musket pointed at the ground," she ordered, pushing in front of him again.

"It's fer rabbits, Miss Fiona," the older man protested, though he immediately lowered the muzzle. "Mrs. MacDorry said she'd use it on me, if I didnae dispatch the vermin eating her garden flowers." He grinned, a gap where one front tooth was missing. "Did I scare ye, lad?"

Fiona's shoulders lifted. Ah. He was about to be introduced as the Sassenach duke interloper. "You startled me," he amended, before she could begin her speech. "No harm done."

MacDorry narrowed one watery eye. "Sassenach, are ye? Nae the one Miss Fiona sent off into the bogs, yesterday."

"Yes, that very same one. Gabriel Forrester. Good hunting to you, sir."

The old man doffed his cap. "Thank ye kindly, Gabriel."

Fiona made a strangling sound. "He's —"

"I'm joining Miss Blackstock on her errands this morning," Gabriel finished, beginning to enjoy the idea that he'd quashed her plans to reveal his identity. She frustrated the devil out of him; now he could return the favor.

"Well, good day to ye then, lad. And to ye, Miss Fiona."

She rounded on him as MacDorry shuffled off. "Ye ken he'll be mortified when he realizes he spoke so familiar to a duke," she snapped.

"Do I seem offended?" he retorted. "I reckon he'll recall what a pleasant lad that Sassenach was, and how he didn't put on any airs."

"Ye arenae pleasant." With that she turned on her heel to march up the gravel path between the cottages.

He followed her. "Very well. 'Pleasant' is the wrong word. But tell me, Miss Blackstock, have you thought about our kiss? Did you dream about it? I did."

"If I'd done such a thing, which I didnae, I'd call it a nightmare. Nae a dream."

"I might believe you," he returned, not bothering to hide his grin, "if you hadn't brought me trousers last night."

"And how is that, precisely?"

"Me being unable to dress and leave the bedchamber would have benefited you, according to the nonsense you've been spitting in my direction. You did something counter to your own best interest, and in favor of mine."

"I gave ye the clothes before ye kissed me, if ye'll recall."

"I recall every moment. Do you?"

"What do ye —"

"I jumped into the mud to save your life. In return, you sent me into a bog," Gabriel stated. "And I only came up here in the first place because you threatened murder. I have two other estates with stewards whose letters and accounts seemed perfectly reasonable. I let them be."

She glanced over her shoulder at him. "I told ye that ye'd have yer figures."

Most of the women of his acquaintance were camp followers — the occasional officer's wife, but mainly washerwomen, seamstresses, and the lightskirts who made a living off frightened young lads away from home and facing death. She was nothing like any of them. Every time he set eyes on her he recalled how she'd looked with her muddy muslin clinging to her curves, and he could taste her mouth again.

"You have me interested in different

figures," he returned. "You're a conundrum."

"Because I brought ye trousers and I tried to kill ye in a bog? Ye're a madman."

Now *that* amused him. "I don't mean to insult you, but people far more skilled than you have attempted to murder me, and in far more lethal ways."

"Aye? What ways?" This time a twinkle danced in her black eyes.

Almost before his mind could grasp the fact that she'd just jested with him, Gabriel stepped forward, nudging her back against the rough cottage wall directly behind her, and held her there with his forearm across her chest. He took her mouth, warm and soft and tasting of tea. And this time he was certain she kissed him back. "You seem more lethal already," he murmured, teasing at her lips again, then stepping back before she could shove him away. Strategy.

Her gaze remained focused on his mouth, until finally she cleared her throat, looked up, and poked a finger into his chest. "Enough nonsense, Sassenach. Ye wanted to follow me, and here we are. Do ye mean to go inside with me?"

Putting aside the way she'd just accused him of nonsense — a word he'd never heard associated with himself before this moment, he glanced toward the small cottage's door. "Yes, I do," he decided. Not many people — none, in fact — made a habit of poking him, either. For a woman who barely came to his chin to do so was oddly arousing. Of course he found everything about her arousing, even if that was counter to every considerable bit of common sense he possessed. She'd called him a madman; perhaps he was.

She nodded. "Through this door, this isnae aboot ye. Or me. Ye keep yer mouth shut, or ye wait ootside."

Gabriel lifted an eyebrow at the orders, but she'd intrigued him again, damn it all. In a matter of two days she'd proven she wasn't like any other woman of his experience, and she continued to do so almost by the minute. "Agreed."

With a last warning look at him, she moved sideways to rap on the simple oak door, put a smile on her face, and pushed it open without waiting for an answer. Gabriel gave her a second, then followed her inside and closed the door behind them.

The first thing he noticed was the dark; it overwhelmed everything. The cottage had no windows at all, with the only light coming from a small fire in a tiny fireplace. His well-honed instinct for survival kept him with his back to the door while he waited for his vision to adjust to the dimness.

Then the smell touched him; dead, rotting flesh combined with an odd mix of tea and herbs. He recognized it immediately from his years in the army — gangrene, which someone was trying to treat with poultices. Fiona had moved across the tiny space to sit in a chair by its single bed. As she produced a thick slice of bread from the small sack she carried, she began speaking softly in Gaelic.

Gabriel didn't understand a word of it, but the roll and lilt of her voice mesmerized him. The smell, the cottage, the world itself faded away on the soft rise of her words. He wanted to move closer, but this time sternly resisted the impulse. She'd made it clear that this wasn't about him, and he had no wish to disturb any of it.

As she spoke, she tore off small pieces of the bread, dipped them in a cup of water, and fed them to the withered figure on the bed. A woman, he decided, only because of the length of the gray hair piled about her head.

A second figure stirred from right beside him. It took every ounce of his training not to jump. Eyes that reflected the firelight stared at him as she scurried over to the bed. Pulling the thin blanket aside, she removed the heavy bandage on the old woman's left foot, washed the wound, and put on fresh wrappings.

When Fiona stood to put her arms beneath the old woman's shoulders, clearly meaning to lift the figure off the bed, he stepped forward. Putting a hand on Fiona's hip, he nudged her aside and slid his arms beneath the invalid's shoulders and knees, then lifted.

It was like lifting a doll, he imagined, though he'd never had occasion to hold one. The old woman seemed more dust and cloth than flesh, and he held her as carefully as he could. In front of him Fiona and the other woman stripped the blanket from the bed, carried out the top layer of straw beneath it, and brought in armloads of fresh, sweet-smelling stuff to replace it.

Once they'd put down a blanket and secured it over the straw, he laid the old woman down again and stepped back. Fiona tucked her in, still talking quietly, then kissed the woman on the forehead and backed away. She gestured at Gabriel, and he pulled open the door and followed her back outside into the sunlight.

"That woman needs light and fresh air," he said with a scowl as soon as he closed the door behind them. "And maggots to clean out the corruption. The damp in there will finish her off more quickly than the gangrene."

"Aye," Fiona answered, walking back to the edge of the stream, where she knelt and washed off her hands and arms.

"You have a castle with fifty rooms sitting a mile away. Why haven't you —"

"Oh, my goodness!" she exclaimed, straightening again. "Why didnae I ever think of that? Thank heaven ye came along when ye did!"

Gabriel narrowed his eyes, and declined to offer her an arm as they made their way back to the path. "And yet despite your sarcasm, she's still lying there in the dark."

Fiona bent to pick up a fallen shovel and set it back against a cottage's stone wall. "A hundred years ago, yer castle was the seat of Laird MacKittrick, a clan Maxwell chieftain. This corner of the clan gathered there every year to arrange marriages and feast and celebrate. Then Laird MacKittrick stood up fer the Jacobites and against the Crown. He lost his head, and the Crown gave his estate to a Sassenach duke."

"Lattimer," he finished, wondering what in the world this had to do with an old woman suffering from an infected foot. "I've

144

heard the story."

"It's nae a story," she retorted. "It's true history. And it means yers is a Sassenach hoose now, whether the Duke of Lattimer resides here or nae. And Mrs. Ailios Eylar willnae set foot in it. And before ye suggest we carry her to Lattimer whether she likes it or nae, I'll tell ye she'd rather die in her own wee cottage than leave it fer an English castle. Because taking her inside Lattimer would be akin to dragging her oot of the Highlands."

He'd encountered that level of hatred before, though previously it had been on the battlefield, over the point of a weapon, or as he and his men marched through a village that might have preferred not to be liberated. The idea that the frail woman he'd lifted in his arms hated him because some dead king had given a gift to some ancestor whose name he didn't even know, unsettled him. He'd never had a lineage to even speak of before now. And he'd apparently inherited its burdens, as well. "That's why you told me to be silent, then. So she wouldn't know I was English."

"Aye."

By now word of his presence had obviously spread through the village, because everywhere he turned Gabriel caught glimpses of faces — peering at him from around corners, from behind wagons, out of half-closed doorways and through shop windows. Did they know he was the Duke of Lattimer? Or did his simply being English make him a feared curiosity?

"The old duke," he said aloud, stopping while Fiona untied her black mare from the hitching post. "Was he a cruel man? Or did you just hate him for being English?"

"I only set eyes on him once," she responded, stepping into the stirrup and mounting astride, and giving him a tantalizing glimpse of bare calf before she settled her skirts again. "I was but two years old. A wee bairn. I've nae heard that he was a cruel man. Why? Are *ye* a cruel man?"

No sidesaddle for Fiona Blackstock. She sat in the saddle well, completely comfortable. "That depends on who you ask." Gabriel put his fingers to his mouth and whistled for Union Jack.

"Ye're a violent man, though. I dunnae need to ask anyone aboot that." At least she hadn't tried to ride off without him.

"I'm a soldier." Jack trotted up, and Gabriel swung into the saddle. "A farmer milks cows, and I kill enemies of the state."

"Ha. That's very practical of ye," she noted, leading the way as they trotted back over the bridge. If she had any other visits to make it seemed she'd decided to postpone them until he was elsewhere.

"I'm a practical man," he agreed with a half smile, settling into a comfortable canter beside her. Glancing down, he again took in the sight of her bare calf above men's work boots. How the devil was he supposed to see to Lattimer when he couldn't conjure anything but how her soft-looking skin would feel against his? "Are you a practical woman?"

She pursed her lips, and he nearly brained himself on a tree branch. "I reckon I am. That doesnae make us the same."

This time he grinned over at her. "I may not be a Highlander, lass, but I do know the difference between a man and a woman. I have an almost artistic appreciation for those differences, you might say."

Fiona snorted. "Do ye? I'd nae noticed."

No, they didn't have much at all in common, but he was fairly certain that this was flirtation. And it was a damned fine beginning.

CHAPTER FIVE

What sort of man kissed a woman twice within two days of being introduced? Certainly not a gentleman. Fiona glanced sideways at the six-foot man and a trained warhorse, walking two feet away from her.

And what sort of woman encouraged that behavior? Because while the first kiss last night had truly surprised her, she could make no such claim for the second. Yes, it had been partly curiosity; what lass wouldn't want to be certain if a kiss had been as fine as she remembered it, or if her imagination had given it merits it didn't deserve? Now she knew that if anything, her recollections hadn't given that kiss enough credit. Good heavens.

"You just admitted to being practical," he said abruptly. "If you pretend now to be overwhelmed with shyness I'll simply keep making statements until you feel compelled to respond."

"I'm nae being shy," she retorted. "I was thinking that old coat and those trousers might've fooled Ailios into thinking ye were a visiting Maxwell farmer or someaught, but they didnae fool me. Nae fer a second."

"I wasn't trying to fool anyone. I'm not a spy. I am precisely what you see."

Perhaps that was so, but what *did* she see when she looked at him? Not quite the same thing she'd noted when he'd first jumped into the mudhole. Fiona clenched her jaw. Why was she even contemplating the question? "Why did ye follow me?" she blurted, to change the subject before she could begin mooning at him or something equally outrageous.

"I saw you heading for the stable," he returned promptly in his deep English tones. "You owe me a look at the ledgers, and I didn't want you escaping somewhere."

" 'Escaping'?" she repeated, scoffing. "That would make me a coward, which I amnae. And I dunnae call me attending to my duties escaping."

"Nor do I." She felt rather than saw his gaze on her, because she deliberately looked elsewhere. His gray eyes seemed far keener than they should have, and she absolutely didn't want him thinking that she found him . . . interesting. That might lead to more kissing. "But strictly speaking," he continued, "they aren't *your* duties, are they?"

Back to that again. Damn her for being too stubborn to answer one of the solicitor's bloody letters, anyway, and bringing this mess down on her own head. "They were my father's duties, they were my brother's, and now they're mine," she stated, with every bit of confidence and disdain that she could muster. "If the old duke didnae like my ways, he had nearly four years to tell me so."

"Ah. So he knew you'd assumed the position of estate manager?"

"He knew Lattimer was being run well and fairly," she retorted, though privately she doubted old Ronald Leeds had given Lattimer Castle more than a passing thought in twenty years. "We'd nae earned him much of a profit, but he didnae have a complaint that reached my ears." As far as she could tell he'd tried to forget the place altogether. And that suited her quite well.

"I shouldn't have bothered coming here, then," he said, guiding his big bay gelding around a fallen tree. Whatever she thought of him, she had to admit — to herself, at least — that this Major Gabriel Forrester knew how to ride. He sat straight-backed but completely at ease, his fingers loosely

150

gripping the reins as he guided his mount with pressure from his heels and knees more than anything else. That was likely so he could ride and shoot or slash at the same time, but the why of his skill didn't make it any less impressive. The Beast of Bussaco, indeed.

"Nae, ye shouldnae have," she agreed belatedly, after he lifted one curved eyebrow at her, the expression rendered more quizzical by the scar that bisected the left side of his face. "I cannae even imagine all the trouble the French must be causing in Spain without ye there to stop them."

"Neither can I," he returned, his voice clipped. "But as this property belongs to me," he continued, ducking beneath a branch, "I require more than the word of a damned gizzard-threatening female to convince me that Lattimer is running as it should."

"And that's the mouth ye kissed me with?" she retorted, before she could stop herself.

His lips curved upward. "Not kissed. Kiss. Present tense. Will kiss again. Future tense."

"I dunnae need a damned grammar lesson, ye annoying man. And ye'll have the books," she said as evenly as she could manage. "I'm nae carrying them in my pockets,

151

though, so ye'll have to wait until I can hand them to ye."

"And I'll remain by your side until you do so." He tilted his head. "Very close by your side."

She scowled. "I think mayhap ye saw someaught in yer bedchamber last night that scared ye, after all. Or was it the banshees in the bog?"

He laughed. The sound had more than an edge of cynicism to it, which didn't surprise her. What *did* surprise her was the way the sound made a pleasant shiver run up her spine.

"What's so damned amusing aboot that?" she demanded, reminding herself how much trouble he represented. If anything, his strikingly handsome appearance made it even worse. "Do ye nae believe in fairies or banshees or spirits, at all? Ye say they dunnae trouble ye, but I ken ye trouble them, Lattimer. And they dunnae much care to see a Sassenach army officer in these parts."

"The only bit that stays with me from last night is the way you looked me up and down, and how you tasted."

Christ in a kilt. "I'm nae talking aboot me," she tried again. "I'm saying ye arenae in Spain or England or anywhere else in the wide world. Ye're in Scotland. And if ye

dunnae believe in the magic of the Highlands, Lattimer, I can only feel sorry fer ye."

The duke glanced at her again. "I believe
that lead can solve a disagreement more
definitively than words. I believe that nothing sobers a man faster than the sight of his
own blood. I believe that the sensation of
winning a fight is equaled only by sex with
a warm, willing woman. If you believe in
magic, Miss Blackstock, that's your choice.
But I suggest you let me show you something more tangible."

She swallowed, shivers running delicious
fingers along her muscles. Tightening her
fingers on Brèaghad's reins, she decided it
might be wiser — and safer — to stop talking to him altogether. Fiona set her tongue
hard against her teeth and sent the mare
into a trot. A second later he caught up to
her, chuckling.

As they trotted up past the garden and
along the east wall of the castle she was
fairly certain half the occupants had pressed
themselves against the upper windows to
stare, but she did her best not to notice. Of
course they were curious, and of course they
would all want to know everything Lattimer
had said to her. Some of it, though, she
would never repeat. And some of it she
needed more time to consider. Not only

153

their second kiss — and why, oh why was she counting them? — but his genuine concern over Mrs. Ailios Eylar. And his genuine surprise that they hadn't moved the old lass into Lattimer, as if bringing ill cotters into the grand house was something dukes did all the time. Clearly he had no idea how to be an aristocrat. For the first time, though, she wondered if that might be an unasked-for, unexpected opportunity.

As a soldier he would have seen gangrene before, but as an officer she'd assumed he'd taken pains to keep as much distance from the dirt and disease of battlefields as possible. But he hadn't even hesitated to step forward and lift Ailios into his arms as if she'd weighed no more than a feather. He hadn't flinched at the smell, or at allowing illness and disease to touch him. In fact, it hadn't troubled him at all that she could tell. And that did impress her.

At the stable she dismounted and smoothed her long green skirt down again. "If ye trust me enough to give me an hour or two," she said, walking away toward the house as soon as Oscar Ritchie took Brèaghad's bridle from her, "I'll meet ye in the doonstairs office and have all yer wee numbers lined up nice and proper fer ye."

"Meet me in the breakfast room in ten

minutes," he countered. "I haven't eaten yet. Have you?"

If he was asking, then at least he hadn't heard her stomach rumbling. "Nae," she said over her shoulder. "I havenae. But the ledgers arenae —"

"I'll review the books on Friday. In the meantime I'll continue familiarizing myself . . ." His gaze took her in from her toes to her head. "With Lattimer."

And he continued to spin her about. Clearly he didn't think much of her — or of any lass, more likely — having a go at managing an estate. But that didn't preclude him from lusting after her. Most of the men on MacKittrick — Lattimer — land treated her more like a sister or a daughter, and his bold gaze and bolder kisses both affected her more than she cared to admit even to herself. All that when he still obviously meant to dismiss her from his service.

Ha. He could go about making demands and saying and doing things to make her heart race, but she knew the facts. Employed by him or not, she would be remaining in the Highlands long after he'd dipped his toes into being an estate owner and left for the Continent again. Mad, confounding, enticing Englishman. Perhaps that was what it was; she'd never understand, because he made no sense. Because he was a damned Sassenach.

She'd barely made it through the servants' area and up the stairs when a hand grabbed her arm and pulled her into one of the small sitting rooms off the main hallway. Fiona yanked her arm free and spun around. "What the devil do ye think ye're aboot, Ian Maxwell?" she demanded, just remembering to keep her voice down as she closed the door behind them.

Just what she needed this morning, another of the few men who didn't treat her like a family member. She had more than enough distraction to fill her cup already. The gamekeeper sent her a lopsided grin and sagged back against the wall. "Ye said ye wanted to see me early, and that I should avoid yer new master," he returned, folding his arms over his chest, his damp red hair glinting in the light through the east window.

"He's nae my master. He's my employer. And yers too, by the way." Perhaps he wouldn't be her employer for long, but for the moment it suited her argument.

"Are ye saying I should show him some respect?" Ian asked, lifting a ginger eyebrow. "A Sassenach lobsterback?"

"Nae. I'm saying ye're to show *me* some

respect. Show him whatever ye choose." It was on the tip of her tongue to warn Ian not to underestimate Lattimer, but she kept her mouth shut. She hadn't figured the duke out yet, and until she did, she didn't feel comfortable giving her opinion about him.

"But ye dunnae want him knowing aboot the missing sheep."

She shook her head. "That's fer us to deal with. I dunnae care to give a Sassenach soldier an excuse to ride aboot the Highlands hunting for trouble." Nor did she want Lattimer to think he might be needed, because he wasn't, or that she couldn't do her job, which she could.

"Seems to me the easiest way to see to that would be to get rid of him."

"And that is my plan," she returned, wishing Ian had neglected to come by, after all. She had a very formidable, very compelling man to meet in the breakfast room. "We cannae kill him or half the king's army will be on our doorstep. He has to want to leave — which is why we're nae to pique his curiosity aboot anything." She crossed the room to open the narrow door that led to the corridor along the back of the common rooms, some previous duke's way of keeping the servants as unnoticed and unseen as possible. "Which is why ye're to go back oot to the overlook with the other lads and stop the thieving."

Ian straightened, sending her a jaunty grin as he started to stroll by her. As he drew even, though, he stopped. "Dunnae ye worry yer pretty head, Fiona. I'll find whoever's stealing from us, and I'll see to him the Highlands way — withoot any damned Englishman trying to put his own rules onto us."

"*I'll* see to our thief," she countered. "Once ye've caught him. So go catch him."

"I'll go. But ye cannae send a lad oot to battle withoot a kiss." With that he took a step forward and pressed his lips against hers.

The act stopped her for a moment — not because she didn't generally enjoy a bit of fun with the gamekeeper, but because for all his self-confidence, she definitely noted some flaws now. Hm. Lattimer had said he wasn't ham-fisted. Now she had some proof that his skills didn't end on the battlefield. "Ye're kissed, then," she returned aloud. "Off with ye."

Fiona closed the door on him before he could respond to that. It would only be something manly about how he'd bring her the moon itself if she asked him for it, or some such nonsense. *Men.* All she required from him was the damned sheep. The rest of the bragging and swaggering was just wasting her time when she couldn't afford to be late to the breakfast room.

Frowning, she walked back to the sitting room's main door. Ian was a handsome lad for certain, but lately he'd become a bit smug. And without much reason, as she'd discovered now that she had someone else's kiss with which to compare his. And that line of thought led her back to a six-foot Englishman who refused to relinquish her attention despite her best efforts.

As she left the sitting room, she ran straight into the Englishman's hard, muscled chest. Before she could stop herself she'd grabbed his arm — and then nearly fell over anyway when he twisted faster than lightning to shove her backward against the wall and hold her there with a hard left forearm across her throat.

For a bare second the look in his eyes — dangerous, deadly, and very, very calm — actually frightened her. Then with a blink he became the cynical, sexy thorn in her side once again. "I beg your pardon," he said, relaxing his arm but not moving away from her. "Did I hurt you?"

"N . . . No. Of course not."

"I'm sorry, Miss Blackstock," he murmured, not sounding particularly sorry at all. "I expected you to be in the breakfast room."

Fiona kept her head lowered; if she looked up at him, with his face so close to hers, she might — he might . . . She should have been frightened, she supposed. He looked like a soldier, but just there for a moment she'd seen it. The whip-fast reflexes, the immediate assumption that his life was being threatened, and his very swift, decisive reaction. But she didn't feel afraid. Startled, yes, but mostly she wanted him to kiss her again.

"I needed a word with one of the maids," she improvised, freeing a hand to gesture down the hallway toward the breakfast room.

He caught that hand with his free one, folding his fingers around hers. "Did you?" he returned, his hold more gentle than she expected. "You weren't hiding?"

"Of course I wasnae hiding," she retorted. "Now let go, before someone sees ye and drags ye oot fer a hanging."

His mouth curved. "Still tempted," he whispered, then straightened. "After you," he returned in a more normal tone, releasing her and stepping back.

She refused to smooth her gown or give

160

any other evidence that she felt the least bit . . . disappointed. He'd mauled her an hour ago, and now nothing? Humph. Turning her back, she strode for the breakfast room. Mrs. Ritchie the cook apparently thought the duke needed to eat a great quantity of Scottish fare, because as Fiona swept into the room the sideboard practically groaned with the weight of all the food — everything from haggis to porridge and toast to black pudding and bread-and-pork sausages and boiled eggs. It would either make him fall in love with the Highlands, or flee at top speed. She had a feeling it wouldn't be the latter.

"Do ye need me to explain what's here?" she asked him.

"I'll manage," he returned, his voice a bit flat. "One of you send for Kelgrove, will you?" he continued, glancing at the quartet of footmen who'd been lounging in the corner and sprang upright upon their arrival.

"I'll fetch him," she said quickly. God knew she could use a moment to pull her thoughts back together again.

Fiona wasn't surprised that Lattimer wanted his sergeant to join them for breakfast. Kelgrove clearly wasn't any typical manservant. In fact, she'd thought since yesterday that the duke meant for Sergeant Kelgrove to replace her as estate manager. Well, if the sergeant had as little experience with managing a property as his commander seemed to, she would make certain his ignorance showed. No Sassenach was allowed to replace her simply by virtue of the fact that the new prospect was English, and a man.

She turned down the next hallway, then slowed as she caught a few words of conversation from the first-floor linen closet. ". . . doesnae even ken how to sleep in a proper bed," one of the maids, Tilly, was saying.

"And the Sassenach call *us* barbarians. *Amadans,* the lot of them. The sooner Miss Fiona boots him oot on his arse, the better, I say."

"Do ye reckon it's the curse bringing him here? He couldnae have come at a worse time."

"Aye, he could've," Dolidh's voice returned. "What if he'd ridden up three springs ago when all the fields flooded?"

"That would've been the old duke. And that *would've* been worse. At least this one's handsome." Tilly giggled. "My mama said the old one had a face like a bowl of porridge."

Fiona pushed the door open the rest of

the way. "Keep yer tongue-wagging confined to below stairs," she said, eyeing Tilly and Dolidh as they gathered sheets and towels to go upstairs. "I might've been him, and then where would we be?"

Tilly dipped a shallow curtsy. "We'll be more cautious. Even if he wasnae a Sassenach, having a duke aboot will take some getting used to."

"Aye, that it will," she agreed. "Though hopefully he'll be gone before we have a chance to get accustomed to him." And before she could begin to be tempted by his very carnal line of thought. She slipped in, shutting the door of the small room behind her. "Did I hear ye say Lattimer didnae sleep well?" If the room *had* unnerved him despite his dismissal of specters, that could make removing him from the property considerably easier. The sooner, the better, as far as she was concerned.

"I couldnae say if he slept well or nae," Tilly returned, and giggled again. "It would be improper to call on his bedchamber while he was in there. After he walked doonstairs I went in to tidy the room. He'd pulled the pillows and blankets onto the floor and slept there, like a hound. I didnae know if I should leave him a nest there, or nae."

He'd slept on the floor? She could attempt to put that to ignorance of the proper ways of dukes, but she couldn't believe that he didn't know how to use a bed. Englishman or not, Gabriel Forrester demonstrated less . . . refinement than she'd expected. She'd always had a vision of the English as delicate, civilized tea drinkers who preferred words to action. He didn't fit any of her preconceived notions, which made him difficult to dismiss. All she knew at the moment was that he wasn't civilized, or delicate. Hard and heated seemed a much better description.

"Isnae that odd, Miss Fiona?" Dolidh said, lifting an eyebrow.

Fiona shook herself. "Aye. To be certain. I'd wager the Duke of York doesnae sleep on the floor."

The two maids exchanged a look. "We were saying, too, it was odd that he claims his valet, that Mr. Kelgrove, isnae a valet and has him sleep in a proper bedchamber like a gentleman."

It made sense if Sergeant Kelgrove had plans to be Lattimer's next estate manager. "Oh. Aye. Odd," she said aloud. Taking a breath, she backed out of the room again. "Remember, keep yer voices doon." She started down the hall, then remembered

Lattimer's request and had to return to the linen closet. "Tilly, fetch Sergeant Kelgrove and send him to the breakfast room, will ye? His Grace requests his presence."

"I'll fetch him right away, miss. I suppose he'll be eating with ye, as well?"

Fiona shrugged. "Who the devil knows what these Sassenach are aboot?"

She certainly didn't. Because she thought she'd figured out Lattimer and his entire character within two minutes after they'd officially met — and yet every time she'd expected a particular response from him, he'd surprised her. Every blasted time. She needed to do better, needed to figure out what motivated him other than lust for her, if she ever hoped to be rid of him. For heaven's sake, she'd spent far too much time thinking about him already.

"I've seen it on a map, Miss Blackstock," Gabriel said, refusing to be led into the stiflingly book-bound library. "I'm asking you to ride some of the paths with me and point out anything of significance."

She stayed just inside the doorway, as if she thought it was some magical force rather than a dislike of the musty smell of the old, old books that kept him in the hallway. "And I told ye that I have tasks to see to, and those ledger books to organize fer yer inspection. I'll nae have ye dragging me aboot the countryside and then accusing me of neglecting my duties."

Thus far her duties seemed to consist of blocking him at every turn, and she was damned good at that. "You don't have duties, because no one hired you to work here. But you go about your day, and I'll allow you to drag me about the countryside or linen closet or wherever it may be. In fact, I recommend that we begin in the linen closet."

He watched for her reaction; if she gave a single sign that she truly found his attention offensive or unwelcome, he would swallow his bloody pride and step back. In none of their previous encounters had she seemed the least bit reluctant, but neither would he have guessed that she'd been kissing some other man directly after leaving him at the stable until he'd overheard her doing so.

Miss Blackstock, however, merely blew out her breath and straightened her shoulders, which he'd already come to recognize as a sign that an argument would be forthcoming — not that it took much skill to realize that.

"It's nae use," she returned. "Ye'll frighten the bairns and the lasses everywhere ye go.

We have some excellent maps showing the topography of the property. And the oldest and most recent floor plans of the castle itself. I imagine a soldier would find those things more useful than he would a trudge doon to the church to carry bread to the poor."

No one argued with him like she did, countered his every move with a quick verbal jab or a withering look. If she'd been a soldier under his command, she would have been dressed down and sent to dig holes by now. But he'd never viewed any soldier the way he looked at her, and being aware of that didn't make it any less frustrating. He wanted to put his hands on her, and he wanted to hear her moan with pleasure. Finesse and he weren't friends, but he could give it a go, he supposed. If nothing else, he had to acknowledge that she wasn't some camp lightskirt he could use for an hour and send away.

"According to the — my — very loud solicitors in London, what little money Lattimer brings in comes from a combination of wool, textiles, ceramics, and whisky. Show me where these things are done. Please." That was a word he didn't use often; he hoped she appreciated it.

Rather than giving in, though, she gestured deeper into the library where maps galore lay on a table, no doubt set out for him during the oddly lengthy luncheon in which he'd been forced to partake. He'd never eaten so much in his entire life as he had today. "I can point oot —"

"Not on the damned maps," he cut in. Gabriel folded his arms over his chest, ignoring the way the weight of his borrowed coat felt wrong. Soldier or not, the moment he'd arrived it had become clear that wearing a uniform here wouldn't gain him any cooperation from anyone. "Either you escort me on your errands, or I'll have a groom show me the property. And he may not be aware of whatever it is you don't wish me to know."

She opened her mouth, then snapped it closed again, which only drew his attention again to her soft-looking lips. He was surprised her sharp tongue didn't cut them. "I've nae secrets," she finally retorted.

Considering what he'd overheard earlier, he didn't believe that for a damned minute. And if she was kissing two men without mentioning either to the other, she wasn't as prim as she made out, either — though "prim" didn't fit. Fiery, perhaps. Lithe and enticing but stubborn as hell suited her better. And his, whether she knew it yet or not.

"And?" he prompted. "Will it be you, or the groom?"

With an exaggerated sigh that returned his attention to her tits, she pushed past him back into the hallway and proceeded to stomp toward the main staircase. "At least old Lattimer had the good sense to stay away and let us do our work," she grumbled.

"I can't imagine why he didn't spend more time here," he returned, falling in behind her. "You've all been so welcoming to me."

Her shoulders stiffened, but she kept walking. Turning her back was likely meant to insult him, but it gave him an unmatched view of her swaying hips. He liked gazing at her arse, at least until he could manage something more intimate. And he would do so, because whatever his mind told him about entanglements with possible enemy opponents, his body wanted her more badly with each passing moment.

Gabriel expected to be riding Union Jack again, but as they left the castle and approached the stable, Miss Blackstock called for the hay wagon. A coach and a phaeton sat unused at the rear of the large building, but if she meant to unsettle him with poor transportation, she'd badly underestimated him. "Are we going to be hauling hay?" he

169

asked. "A hay wagon isn't very intimate. Cushioned, though, at least."

Her cheeks darkened. "I'll show ye aboot because ye ordered me to, Lattimer," she returned, stepping back as two stable boys brought out a big pair of sturdy gray Highlands ponies. "I'm seeing to my duties, whether ye think they're mine or nae. So aye, we'll be transporting someaught. It will-nae be hay."

He started to ask what they would be transporting, but that proved unnecessary the moment the next group of stable boys appeared. Pitchforks in hand, they dumped generous plops of horseshit into the burlap-lined back of the wagon. A procession of grooms and more stable boys followed, round and around, each one adding to the load — and the smell.

"Is this for my benefit?" he muttered, facing Miss Blackstock and immediately distracted by the sight of her pulling on a pair of work gloves. She had long, elegant fingers, better suited for an artist than for someone waiting for a shit-piled wagon. He wanted those fingers on his bare skin.

"Nae. This is part of being Lattimer's estate manager." She cocked her head at him. "Ye still wish to follow me aboot, do ye, Lattimer?"

"I don't mind traveling in the company of shit, if that's what you're asking, Miss Blackstock. My only objection would be if you're taking these men away from their duties just to see if I'll hold a handkerchief to my nose or flee to the garden to whimper and breathe in the scent of the roses."

Her soft lips clamped hard together. "Ye said ye'd allow me to continue my duties. I've been driving this wagon once a week fer the past month, Yer Grace. It's nae fer my amusement. Or fer yers."

She seemed to be in earnest, and he couldn't quite imagine any female volunteering to sit with shit for a jest. "Good," he returned. "Then I shall join you." Once the servants finished loading the wagon, he climbed up to the hard wooden seat and leaned over to offer her a hand.

Her fingers balled into a fist, then straightened, and she grabbed his wrist solidly. Even through the work glove, her elegant fingers had strength. Gabriel half lifted her as she scrambled to find a foothold. If not for the grooms and stable boys, he would have dragged her onto his lap. The pitchforks looked sharp, though, and he didn't intend to die over a chit. Not unless her name began with "Queen" and ended with "of England."

"Ye can let me go now," she muttered, just before he could realize he still held her wrist, but after he felt the fast burr of her pulse beneath his fingertips.

"You smell better than what's behind us," he returned, belatedly opening his hand.

"That isnae much of a compliment."

Gabriel tilted his head. More flirting? "Do you want a better one?"

Fiona hid her scowl, though she didn't bother to deny to herself that her lowering mood had nothing to do with his sexual advances or accusations of frivolousness. It was becoming clear that Gabriel Forrester wasn't a fool. Nor was he going to make it easy for her to cast him as one. She supposed, though, if it had been too easy then she wouldn't so keenly enjoy the thought of seeing him run when she succeeded.

"Nae. I dunnae want a thing from ye," she muttered, sitting down beside him. "Come along, lads," she ordered, taking up the reins and bracing her feet to hold the horses as she released the brake. "Four of ye should do today, since we'll have His Grace to help." There. He wouldn't be able to wiggle out of that without looking proud — or at least delicate.

For once she had a plentitude of volunteers; evidently the lads expected more excitement today. Four of them climbed up to sit along the narrow sides of the wagon, six pitchforks driven like grave markers into the smelly mound in the middle.

"Hup," she called, flicking the reins and nearly losing young Andrew overboard as the wagon lurched into motion. Unfortunately Major His Grace Forrester kept his seat as if he'd ridden on a wagon a hundred times. Perhaps he had, though.

"Where are we going?" he asked, turning slightly away from her as they took the rutted dirt road that curved parallel to Loch Sibhreach heading west. Given the way his attention had been focused on her from the moment they met, Fiona wondered what had happened. He'd avoided kissing her before breakfast, but just a few minutes ago had suggested a rendezvous in the linen closet. She thought he'd forgotten whatever it was that had annoyed him, but perhaps not. The moment she began mentally reviewing her actions, though, she sternly stopped herself. *Idiot.* She didn't *want* his attention.

Just then, though, she realized he wasn't slighting her — not consciously, anyway — but that he'd shifted to keep his gaze on the trees to their right. Highlanders always had a mind toward potential enemies, but this duke had elevated alertness to an art form.

"We had a rock slide during the rain a few weeks ago," she explained, refusing to be pleased when he faced her again, "and it halved the downslope pasture we use fer our largest flock of sheep. They overgrazed the pasture they could reach before we knew it, and left most of the ground bare. Now that we've moved the flock higher up into the foothills and cleared the boulders, we're replanting the field. The horse shit makes fer a fair fertilizer. Winter here comes hard and early, and we dunnae want what's left of the good soil washing away with naught to hold it in place come spring." That wasn't the entire story, but that was all he needed to know about it.

He studied her face in that unsettling way of his. "And you decided this should be a task that you personally oversee?"

Fiona clenched her jaw. "Considering that ye'd lose the other half of yer spring grazing next year and then half yer yield of wool the year after, aye, I ken I should see to things personally. Do ye disagree, then? Do ye reckon I should sit and embroider ye an apology letter while the pasture lies bare?"

The low, rumbling laugh coming from deep in his chest made her grin before she could stop herself. "An embroidered apology would at least demonstrate sincerity, considering how much work you'd have to put into it."

"I'll keep in mind how much effort it takes to convince ye of anything, then," she retorted, doing her best not to be amused. "It all comes doon to one fact: good grazing pasture makes fer healthy sheep, which makes fer good-quality wool and meat, which makes fer more blunt in yer pockets, Yer Grace."

"I wasn't disputing your decision, Miss Blackstock. I only asked you to explain your reasoning."

Fiona rolled her shoulders. Uncle Hamish would be advising her to stop letting the Sassenach needle her, to spend her time smiling and convincing him they had things well in hand so he could go back to his war or to one of his other estates in England and leave anything north of Hadrian's Wall be.

The Duke of Lattimer wasn't kissing Uncle Hamish, though. Instead he kissed *her.* And jumped into mudholes to rescue cows and lasses — whether they needed it or not — and rode on wagons full of horse-shit without so much as batting an eye. There had to be something about Lattimer Castle or the Highlands he would think too hard, too gloomy or unpleasant, too frightening or exasperating to justify his continued presence. She would merely have to find it.

When they reached the edge of the bare area of pasture, the sight of sprouting grass where they'd spread seed and manure last week eased her mind a little. It didn't have to be pretty, and it would likely produce as much thistle as it did grass and sweet heather, but the ground wasn't bare. It would hold the soil against the coming rains.

"Last week's work?" the duke asked, hopping to the ground and walking around to offer his hand to her. "You've covered what, a quarter of the pasture over the past month?"

"Aye." Ignoring his hand, Fiona climbed down the wheel to the spongy ground. "In a few weeks we'll work back across anywhere the grass didnae take."

One of the lads, Michael, handed her a shovel. This was far from her favorite task, but she wasn't about to stand back and watch while others labored to finish a plan she'd devised. Oh, she was certain a London lady wouldn't step her dainty toes within a mile of the stinking field, but she wasn't any blasted hothouse flower.

Lattimer took the spare shovel, which

didn't surprise her. She hadn't given him the chance to wiggle out of some shoveling, at least. After five or ten minutes he would no doubt throw down the tool and demand to be returned to the castle. Or so she hoped.

Instead he stood shoulder to shoulder with the lads, asking for and taking advice on how thickly to spread the manure, how many seeds to use, and whether to work uphill or downhill. Then he stripped off his coat and tossed it onto the wagon seat, and rolled up his shirtsleeves.

She'd briefly seen what lay beneath the thin linen shirt, the well-toned muscle and collage of scars. Her skin heated, and with a stifled curse she turned her back and moved around to the far side of the wagon from where he worked. Aye, he was a striking man, and a fit one, with cat-quick reflexes and an evidently agile mind. But he was also English, a British army officer, and an invader at a time when she already had enough about which to worry — not that *any* time would have been opportune for his appearance in the Highlands. And she did *not* feel an attraction to him, whatever he and her body kept trying to tell her.

The goal remained; she needed to find a way to be rid of him. Manure and shoveling might not have worked, but she would figure out something. The sooner, the better.

CHAPTER SIX

Now he knew what hell looked like. As he'd anticipated, it was filled with numbers. Gabriel shoved away from the table to pace to the tall library window. "Who the devil decided that success could only be rated by equations on pieces of paper?" he demanded.

"Because if everything had to be decided on a battlefield, you would rule the world."

Gabriel turned around, lifting an eyebrow at Sergeant Kelgrove. The man still sat with his face buried in ledger books, and likely hadn't even realized he'd spoken aloud. With a grin, Gabriel strode over to pour himself another glass of whisky. "And that would be a poor idea, I suppose?" he mused.

Finally Adam sat back to rub at his eyes. "I would hate to see young ladies coming to blows over who'd worn the finest gown at one of your combat soirees." Furrowing his brow, he closed one of the books. "Though that does have some merits, now that I consider it."

The moment his aide mentioned females, the unbidden image of Fiona Blackstock strolled into his thoughts again and put her hands on her hips to glare at him. If a lady measured the success of her gown by taking on all comers, he would put his money on his temporary estate manager. The woman didn't back down from anything, including him.

"Agreed," he said aloud. "Now, without causing my brain to explode, what's afoot here?"

"Three things that I can see, Major. Firstly, you own a huge property that's somehow managed to earn a profit of seven quid — over the last three years."

Gabriel cocked an eyebrow. "That seems . . . small."

"That's likely why she didn't want to send the ledgers to those paper men of yours."

With a nod, he sat one haunch on the deep windowsill. "What's the second thing?"

"Well," Kelgrove began, sitting back and tapping a pencil against his chin, "I'm no expert in aristocratic households, but until two days ago, and for twenty years previous to that, Lattimer has had no owner in residence. Despite that, your Miss Black-

180

stock has been hiring servants like a mad-woman. If you include the gardeners and stable boys, you have ninety staff at this house alone."

"No wonder I haven't been able to turn around without having fifty people trying to bring me tea or fluff my pillows." Ninety servants. Ninety people to serve a house full of employers, family, and guests, plus the residence itself, seemed a little excessive but not unreasonable, at least to someone who had no experience with such things. Even to him, though, ninety staff to see to the maintenance of an empty house seemed extreme. Especially with two thirds of the rooms closed, their furniture sheeted, and the fireplaces cold and dark. "Is that where the profit is going? To pay the servants?"

"Some of it. The rest is beyond me. Some of the expenses don't sound plausible, which leads me to the third thing. Three millstones over the past two years, a large amount of lumber, several repairs to the castle that I'm not convinced were actually made, the —"

"She isn't stealing," Gabriel cut in. He knew dishonesty, and while he believed Fiona Blackstock to be hiding a great many things from him, she wasn't a thief.

"That isn't for me to say, sir." The sergeant

cleared his throat. "And . . . while I know you ordered me to refer to you as my commanding officer rather than as the Duke of Lattimer, I'm beginning to worry that these Scots will firstly think me an idiot, and secondly imitate my apparent lack of respect for you."

"So you want to call me 'Your Grace'?" Gabriel said, sighing. The reasoning was sound, whether he liked it or not. "Fine. But for God's sake don't begin thinking I'm delicate."

Kelgrove snorted. "I don't believe that'll be a problem, Your Grace. Miss Blackstock, however, already is a problem, and will continue to be one until you get rid of her."

As Adam went about closing the rest of the ledgers and almanacs, Gabriel watched him. Almost from the moment he'd learned about Kieran Blackstock's lack of cooperation, he'd decided that Kelgrove would be the ideal replacement. This would be the perfect moment to make that official, but even as he considered it, he knew he wasn't about to say a word. Not yet.

And it wasn't only because he wanted to see Fiona out of her gown and spread beneath him, though that would have been reason enough. It felt most comfortable to put it to his curiosity about the bits of conversation he'd overheard in the small sitting room, involving some thievery and a mysterious man he hadn't been meant to see, but who had kissed her.

He clenched his jaw. Yes, the thievery bothered him — Lattimer and all its troubles were his responsibility, and someone either needed to tell him about it, or he would take steps to make certain he found out officially. The kiss, though, the idea that another man had put his hands on a woman he meant to claim for himself, made his blood boil. For two days he'd pretended he knew nothing about it, and for two days it had taken every ounce of self-control he possessed to keep from finding the bastard and pounding him senseless, then kissing Fiona again and erasing whatever thoughts she had of this interloper.

And the only reason he'd bothered to restrain himself was because of the very, *very* slight chance that *he* was the interloper. Nothing he'd discovered since then answered that question one way or the other, damn it all. The marble female carved into one side of his ridiculous fireplace was beginning to look attractive, if he didn't mind getting his cock burned off.

Kelgrove continued to look at him expectantly, and Gabriel shook himself. "We are in the middle of hostile territory, Sergeant. I agree that not everything is supposed to be a battle, but if I dismiss her too quickly we'll have one on our hands. In addition, she has knowledge of these people and of Lattimer that I do not." And working alongside her would hopefully reduce the time it would take the sergeant to find his footing. It added time to his own stay when he'd anticipated remaining no more than a week at most, but when he'd set that goal for himself he'd had no idea he'd be dealing with Fiona rather than her brother. If bedding her meant remaining in the Highlands a few more days than he'd planned, then so be it.

"I can't argue with that," the sergeant returned, obviously not reading Gabriel's thoughts. "But it's still my duty to tell you that in my opinion these Scots are trying to get rid of us. A footman and Mrs. Ritchie the cook spent nearly an hour this morning regaling each other with bloody tales of hauntings at Lattimer — those in the master bedchamber in particular. And they made damned certain I could overhear them."

"I'm not surprised to hear that. I've been haunted for four nights, now."

The sergeant didn't seem to know what to make of that. "You have? You never said. I'd have been on my horse and riding south before I finished screaming."

Gabriel shrugged. "It's nothing I can shoot or that can shoot me, so I didn't see the point." And after the third night of nonsense he'd pulled the paintings off the wall, found the strings, and cut them. Last night had been much quieter, but he didn't mean to bring up anything about the subterfuge. His so-called steward could do that, if she wished to know whether he'd begun to feel spooked or not.

"You're a braver man than I am. But you do know if they can't frighten us away, they'll likely attempt something more forceful, next."

Gabriel agreed. "It seems to be my luck that I'm pulled away from a war straight into a rebellion."

The sergeant sent him a quizzical glance. "Do you think they're Jacobites?"

"Probably." Even as he sighed he couldn't help but find that amusing; not only had he landed in the middle of a conflict, but it had to be one that had been settled decisively — and exceedingly brutally — sixty years ago.

"We could send for troops," Adam suggested. "God knows most men would give an arm to serve under the Beast of Bussaco, even in Scotland, and even with a title added onto his rank."

"I'm not sending for an army." Just the idea of bringing redcoats into the middle of this powder keg made him shiver. And not because he could already imagine the "I knew it" look on Fiona's face. When Ronald Leeds died, the battle of the Highlands had become Gabriel's. Calling in reinforcements after less than a week would be admitting defeat before he'd barely begun.

"But —"

A knock sounded at the door. Before he had time to respond, the heavy oak swung open. Sir Hamish Paulk, Fiona's uncle and, as he'd discovered, a clan Maxwell chieftain, strolled into the library. Not only was Paulk dressed for a grand ball, but he swung an ivory-tipped cane in one hand. Gabriel would have wagered a month's pay that the thing sheathed a rapier.

"Good afternoon, Your Grace," Hamish said grandly, bowing.

"Come in," Gabriel returned belatedly, and Kelgrove coughed.

"I . . . Oh. Aye," Fiona's uncle rejoined with a chuckle. "If I've interrupted ye, I do apologize."

Hm. The Maxwell chieftain was much friendlier today, in a too grand, completely

186

insincere way. Too grand, in fact, for Hamish to think anyone would fall for it — which made it a very poorly veiled threat. *Good.* That removed any reason for him to be polite in return. "I expected you three days ago."

Sir Hamish hesitated for a bare moment, then resumed his stroll forward. Taking the seat opposite Kelgrove, he settled back and crossed a calf over the opposite knee. "I did mean to be here, Yer Grace, to greet ye properly now that we all ken who ye are," he drawled, flicking an imaginary piece of lint from his dark blue coat sleeve. "But yer arrival has stirred things up some. I spent all afternoon yesterday, fer example, convincing Father Jamie Wansley that yer being at Lattimer didnae mean the king's army was marching up behind ye."

This damned business that he somehow meant to murder everyone in their beds hadn't been amusing to begin with. Yes, he knew how to fight, but he was a soldier, not a brawler and not a damned murderer. For God's sake, he'd been wearing civilian clothes since that first day, and he'd only snarled at Fiona — and only after she'd snapped at him first. His familial duty had brought him here, damn it all, not his military one. "I hadn't realized Highlanders panicked so easily," he returned aloud.

The Scot's left eye twitched. He'd scored a hit, then. Good. The Highlanders certainly spoke their minds, and he saw no reason why he shouldn't. He always had before now.

"We dunnae panic," Paulk countered, his tone more brittle. "We arenae accustomed to having a duke in residence. And we arenae accustomed to having an English soldier aboot. When ye combine —"

"Of course you are," Gabriel interrupted.

"We are what?"

"Accustomed to having English soldiers about. That's been your complaint since well before Culloden. Too many redcoats tramping across the Highlands."

Sir Hamish's face turned scarlet. "I'll nae have a Sassenach speak of that place in my hoose," he growled, gripping his cane.

"This isn't your house," Gabriel returned crisply. "And yes, I *am* a soldier. I was born in 1783, thirty-five years after Culloden. I've killed a great many men, but never yet a Scotsman." He sat forward, holding Maxwell's gaze. "I want to make that perfectly clear, Paulk."

"I told ye that I reassured Father Jamie."

"So you did." Gabriel straightened from the windowsill. "How many other people have you reassured that I don't mean to murder them or drive them out of their homes?" They had a word in the army for a man who promised friendship and stirred hate. Calling Hamish Paulk a traitor, though, or a spy, would begin them down a path he'd wanted to avoid.

Maxwell's fist tightened around the ivory handle of his cane. In response, Gabriel pushed one booted foot into the floor. Perhaps he didn't need to resort to name-calling. He would allow the Scotsman to move first, only because that would answer several of his own questions. But neither would he be standing there if and when the blow landed.

"I dunnae take yer meaning, Yer Grace," Maxwell said through clenched teeth, which made Gabriel think he understood it quite well. "I'm a Maxwell chieftain; I've a duty to look after my clan. At this moment ye cannae dispute that ye're a large disturbance. And the people on this land are skittish when it comes to change."

According to what he'd been overhearing he wasn't the only disturbance in the area, but he wasn't supposed to know about the thievery — unless he could twist up Sir Hamish enough to get the chieftain to mention it in his presence. Then he could jump on the information without having to reveal that he'd been eavesdropping on Fiona.

"If it's a disturbance to bring a bit of order to land I own, particularly when I was brought here because of your own niece's lack of cooperation, then so be it. And the people on this land, who evidently look to you for reassurance, are going to have to accept that some change is inevitable. And you are not —"

The door swung open again, accompanied by a swirl of soft green and the scent of heather. "Uncle Hamish!" Fiona exclaimed. "Nae a soul told me ye were here! I'd nae have interrupted if I'd known, but I thought His Grace might care to drive oot to see his whisky distillery today."

She'd been listening to the conversation, then, and had also come to the conclusion that her uncle could be maneuvered into wagging his tongue about the sheep thefts. Clever chit. But she'd given him another opening, and he wouldn't pass it by. He sorted out problems for a living, after all. And Miss Blackstock happened to be a very stubborn, very attractive problem.

"Thank you, Miss Blackstock," he said aloud. "I'd be very interested to see my distillery. I wish you'd offered earlier."

Her mouth twitched in a forced smile.

"There's been a great deal to do."

"And a great many obstacles to overcome." Her, chief among them.

This time the amusement in her eyes looked genuine. "This is the Highlands. Some obstacles will nae ever be overcome."

Now *this* seemed like progress. "I don't know about that, Fiona," he returned, using her given name intentionally and liking the way it felt on his tongue. "I'm a very determined man."

"Ye cannae proceed here like this is one of yer military campaigns, Yer Grace," Paulk interjected, clearly misreading the true topic of conversation. "It'll serve ye best to have some patience. Because yer —"

"My mere presence is disruptive," Gabriel finished. "I'm not convinced that's a bad thing. It seems to me the lot of you could use some disruption."

Fiona scowled to herself. There he went, digging at her uncle again. Och, the man was relentless, and worse, clever. He knew something was amiss, and he knew no one would be likely to answer his queries directly. And so he threw hot stones into the pot and waited for it to boil over. "Uncle Hamish," she said with a too grand smile, trying to put out the fire before Lattimer found a reason to stay on in the Highlands.

Because while she'd only known Lattimer for a handful of days, she did know that he would immediately decide the thievery business was his. He was an army major. Nothing was allowed to happen without his permission. "Did ye see the price of wool has gone up? That's some fair news fer a fine morning."

"I did," her uncle said, a touch too sharply. "And that reminds me of someaught. Might I have a quick word with ye? I've a letter from the Duke of Dunncraigh."

She nodded. Anything to separate the two men before something happened. "I'll be back in a moment, Lattimer."

Her uncle didn't stop until they were halfway down the hall and deep into the billiards room. "What the devil are ye aboot?" he demanded, his voice hushed but his eyes fierce.

"What do ye —"

"Ye were flirting with him!"

Her cheeks darkened. "I wasnae!" She stepped closer to him. "The way the two of ye were sparring, I had to step in and distract him. I half expected ye to challenge him to do better than we have with finding the sheep thieves. And that would be unfortunate."

The chieftain narrowed his eyes. "I've yet

to need ye to advise me on what's best fer the clan, Fiona. Ye mind yer own troubles. Ye may've done a fair job of keeping up an empty hoose, lass, but it isnae empty any longer. And if ye keep throwing yerself at him, ye'll find yerself disgraced *and* replaced by that Sergeant Kelgrove when he goes. Now *that* would be unfortunate."

Fiona blinked. After Kieran had vanished into the bog, she'd insisted that she could manage Lattimer in her brother's stead. Hamish hadn't liked the idea of a nineteen-year-old lass overseeing a castle and its accompanying ten thousand acres, but he'd disliked the idea of arousing the old Lattimer's attention even more. The last thing they'd wanted was for the duke to send some Sassenach up to the Highlands to take over running the estate. With his own house and all the Maxwells in the valley to see to, Hamish Paulk couldn't have managed it himself. But he'd helped her figure it out, helped her organize the books after the disaster her brother had made of them. And now, it seemed, he was finished with helping.

Of course she *had* just implied that he had a wagging tongue. Perhaps she'd hurt his feelings, and he'd simply struck back. She could blame her complete lack of finesse on

Lattimer — in four days he'd upended everything, including her own common sense.

"Aye," she replied, deciding he expected an answer. "I ken. But ye said we should be friendly. I think he meant to anger ye, Uncle. I wanted to help keep the peace."

For a moment he regarded her. "I've nae doubt aboot that, lass. But I didnae say to be friendly. I said to be polite."

Fiona nodded. Whatever the reason for his sharpness a moment ago, they seemed to still be allies, anyway. "Have ye truly a letter from Dunncraigh? He couldnae possibly know already that we've the new Duke of Lattimer here."

"I've a letter, but nae, he doesnae know London found some soldier to take Lattimer from us again. I've sent word to him aboot that. I imagine he'll want to make Gabriel Forrester's acquaintance fer himself."

Fiona began to feel light-headed. She'd been introduced to Domhnull Maxwell, the Duke of Dunncraigh, at a clan gathering when she'd been eleven or twelve. The chief of clan Maxwell had even spoken to her a few times since then, not that she felt entirely comfortable at being noticed by him or his circle. Dunncraigh always had an eye toward making alliances, expanding the clan's influence. As the niece of a chieftain she had some status in the clan, and she did not want to be married off at someone else's whim. "How fares His Grace?"

"Well." Hamish sighed. "He's ordered me to make the acquaintance of Viscount Harendell's sisters. Seems I've been a widower long enough."

She allowed herself a muffled sigh of relief that the letter hadn't been about her. She wasn't nineteen any longer, after all. Not for four years. "Ye have my sympathy," she returned. "Do ye wish to remarry? Ye've nae spoken aboot it. Nae to me, anyway."

Her uncle shrugged. "Ye ken yer aunt and I didnae see eye to eye. I'll nae have another shrew, but I hear Morag Harendell's pleasant enough."

A shrew. Was that Agnes Paulk's only epitaph? Fiona had always thought of her late aunt as being spirited, and she'd enjoyed the woman's straightforward ways, so different from her own mother's. In truth, in some ways she'd felt closer to Agnes than to Muran Paulk Blackstock.

"I dunnae know either of the Harendell lasses well," she offered, stepping back toward the door, "but they both seem pleasant from a distance. And I ken the family's wealthy as Midas."

He gave a slight smile. "There is that. Before ye return to the Sassenach, Fiona, I need to know fer certain that ye understand what's afoot here. He's nae yer friend, and he's nae wanted or needed here. If we can be rid of him before Dunncraigh arrives, all the better fer us."

Oh, she didn't need to be reminded about that. She nodded. "I ken." Even if one of the men didn't annoy her and the other one make her nervous, two dukes under the same roof was two too many. And with word already sent to Dunncraigh, she could find herself in precisely that situation within weeks, damn it all.

"Make my excuses, will ye?" Hamish said, apparently satisfied that she understood his warnings. "I find I've nae much more politeness to give the Sassenach today."

If she knew Hamish Paulk as well as she thought she did, his involvement wouldn't end at a letter. He would continue to smile in English and spread dissension in Gaelic. Fiona supposed she generally wouldn't mind, except that while she wanted to be rid of Lattimer, she certainly didn't want to see him — or anyone else — injured. Or worse. And that had nothing to do with the way she'd felt this morning seeing a lock of his raven-black hair fall across his temple despite his proper, precise haircut. Or that when Tilly the maid had asked the duke's eye color she'd been tempted to describe the sky at dawn instead of simply saying "gray." That was ridiculous.

Especially when they still had other avenues available to be rid of him.

Remaining in the billiards room for another moment to give her uncle time to vanish, she then squared her shoulders and strolled back into the library. Sergeant Kelgrove had moved to the bookcase nearest the door, no doubt so he could conduct an inventory of all the books in the collection. Soldiers did like to count things. Lattimer, though, remained at the worktable, his palms flat on its surface as he leaned over the current ledger. He hadn't put on his uniform since his arrival at the castle; either it had been ruined in the mud, or he'd realized that wearing the red was akin to jumping out into the middle of the lane during a horse race. For a single moment she allowed herself to speculate over what a fine figure he would likely cut in a proper Maxwell kilt, but of course that was worse than utter nonsense. He would never wear the plaid. He wasn't a Highlander.

CHAPTER SEVEN

"Did your uncle slink away, then?" the Duke of Lattimer asked, lifting his head.

"Uncle Hamish doesnae slink anywhere," she retorted, wondering if anyone else — if he — thought she'd been flirting with him. Ridiculous. It made her words harsher than she would otherwise have intended. "And ye shouldnae have spoken to him that way."

"I'm not polished," he returned, and gestured for her to take the seat across the table from where he stood. "Do you think he dislikes me now?" His tone was serious, belied only by one lifted eyebrow and a twinkle in his light gray eyes. "I had such high hopes after our first meeting."

Fiona snorted. "Ye're a strange one."

"I've been called far worse than that, and by allies. Sit."

The doorway seemed much safer, but with an exaggerated sigh she pulled out the chair and perched on the edge of it. "I have duties to see to."

"So you've said. Who's Dunncraigh?"

The question didn't surprise her as much as did his directness. But then he'd just admitted to a lack of polish. "Domhnull Maxwell, the Duke of Dunncraigh. The chief of clan Maxwell."

"And does Sir Hamish often inform you when he has a letter from the Duke of Dunncraigh?"

She frowned. "I dunnae see how that's any of yer affair. And if I'm to sit, then ye sit, as well. I dunnae like ye glaring doon at me like a great gargoyle."

Never in a hundred, hundred years would she have dared to speak to Dunncraigh so rudely. This duke, though, gave her a half smile and sat down opposite her. "Do you actually mean to guide me through the distillery, or was that an excuse to interrupt my argument with dear Uncle Hamish?"

"Uncle Hamish would flop aboot like a landed fish if he heard ye calling him 'dear' anything."

"Noted. Are you going to answer my question? Or if you prefer, I could ask what you were worried he might say, and you could answer that one."

"I came to take ye to the distillery," she stated, meeting his gaze and daring him to contradict her.

He continued to look at her, leaving her with the unsettling feeling that he could hear both what she said and what she didn't say. She, however, was not some captured Frenchman in fear for her life and ready to begin spilling secrets just because he wanted her to.

"Kelgrove, find me some paper, will you?"

Wordlessly the door behind her opened and closed again. Finally the duke lowered his gaze to the ledger and flipped a page. "And you may as well go see to your duties, Miss Blackstock. If you're going to lie to me, I've no use for you."

And now he sounded like a duke, when she'd half thought he'd banished Kelgrove so he could kiss her again. Not for a rebuke. She shoved back to her feet, angry despite the fact that his assessment happened to be correct. "Ye need yer aide to tell ye if my figures are correct or nae, so dunnae ye climb up on yer high horse to me, Lattimer."

He looked up at her, but stayed seated. "Back to figures again, are we?" His gaze lowered, taking her in from the hips, lingering on her chest, and then lifting to her face again. "Yours looks very fine to me."

Her cheeks heated, damn it all. Maddening, arrogant Sassanach. Didn't he know the difference between her doing her duty, and creating more, unnecessary problems for her — his — tenants? And why did some stupid, unreasonable part of her like the way he looked at her as if he wanted to eat her? With a growl at her own reaction as much as at his unexpected high-handedness, she turned on her heel and stalked through the doorway. "Insufferable," she muttered.

Steel clamped down on her shoulder and wrenched her around. Off balance, Fiona struck out with her fist, only to have her wrist caught by the same steel grip. Her nose came up against the middle of Lattimer's chest as he dragged her up against him.

"What the devil are ye —"

"Let me make something clear," he said in a low voice, the sound sinking into her with a swirl of ice and fire. "I'm not a man to be trifled with. Nor am I an idiot. A few weeks ago I was fighting Frenchmen in Spain. I had no idea that I had a duke for a great-uncle once removed, or that I was his only heir. But I was, and here I am. Lattimer is both my property and my responsibility. It now has my protection, and my attention. I will see to it that it's running properly, and I don't particularly care if some neighboring landowner thinks he has a say in what I do."

Fiona lifted her chin. He might loom over her, but she bloody well wasn't afraid of him. "I can see it has yer attention, Lattimer. We dunnae require that, or yer protection, or yer stomping aboot bellowing orders. We didnae have the old duke's attention fer two decades, and ye can see all the walls still standing. Ye —"

"Stop talking."

Oh, that was enough of that. "I willnae! Just because ye dunnae want to hear someaught doesnae mean it isnae true."

Light gray eyes narrowed. "And you are annoyingly defiant for a woman who stole her brother's job."

"I didnae steal it!" she retorted. "Kieran . . . was here one day, and the next he wasnae. Nae letter, nae good-bye, nae clothes taken from his wardrobe. His horse came back withoot him. And aye, we searched for him, too. He either fell into a bog and drowned, or he abandoned me. I prefer to believe the former. But either way, I inherited this position. I didnae steal a damned thing."

"And I inherited *this* position. I didn't steal it from you, or anyone else. Don't assume, though, that I have no interest here, or that I have nothing to offer, simply because I'm unexpected."

"Well, that's very clever," she snapped, and jabbed a finger into his hard chest. "I'm supposed to see that we're alike now, aye? I'll tell ye straight, Sassenach. Ye and I are-nae anything alike. And ye can stop kiss—"

His mouth lowered over hers, hard and hot and tasting of strong American coffee. Hunger, want, lust — she could taste those, too, feel them in the way his mouth molded against hers. Fiona put her hands on his shoulders, pretending that if she kept her fingers clenched into fists it didn't count as holding on to him. She was angry with him, after all, even if this didn't feel as much like anger as it did mutual need. The heat of him surrounded her, making her want to lean up along his chest and put her hands on his bare skin. God, he was so . . . male, sure of himself, confident that she felt attracted to him, and every time he kissed her she wanted . . . Blast it, she didn't know what she wanted any longer. But it had everything to do with him.

Abruptly he lifted her off her feet, backed her a half-dozen steps, and set her down again. "If you won't answer my questions, you force me to find another way to proceed. Consider that, Fiona." A heartbeat later the library door closed in her face.

Fiona stood there in the middle of the hallway. She wouldn't have been at all surprised to find her mouth hanging open. *Well.* He'd certainly shut her up, if that had truly been his intention. Arrogant Sassenach soldier, now she couldn't decide if she wanted to throw herself on him again, or punch him in the nose.

At least no one else had seen them groping each other. Fiona couldn't imagine any excuse clever enough to explain why she'd permitted a Sassenach to kiss her, much less why she'd halfway thrown her arms around him. And why she continued to stand there gawping like a beached fish.

Smoothing her skirt, she marched for the stairs. Lattimer could bloody well threaten whatever he wished, because she had other things to see to. Actual things that benefited the estate and its tenants. Well, mostly they benefited the tenants, but if nothing else broke or went missing this year he'd see some profit, too. Hopefully. She hadn't managed that for any of the past four years, what with the sheep thefts and the grain sacks getting wet, and the grinding stone in the mill cracking. Aye, she could blame it on the curse, but there was no column for curse-caused misfortune in the ledger books. Only for profit and loss. And Lattimer Castle had seen increasing numbers in the loss column for years.

"Miss Fiona," Fleming the butler said, as she descended to the foyer, "Niall Garretson at the mill says the new grindstone won't turn. I didnae understand it all, but the runner stone's too flat, or someaught."

She swore under her breath. Having the blasted thing shipped from Derbyshire had cost a fortune. If it hadn't been carved correctly, it could take another week to pull it off and regrind it — if Tormod the blacksmith had the tools for the job. "I'll ride doon and take a look," she said aloud.

"Blasted MacKittrick curse," Fleming grunted, crossing his fingers. At least he didn't spit over his shoulder; she frowned on that when they were inside the house. "The laird might've settled fer cursing the English, and nae the property where his own kin were settled."

"Aye," she returned absently, still trying to brush Gabriel Forrester from her mind. "Have someone keep a watch over the duke while I'm away." She walked outside, then paused on the front gravel walk. "And dunnae tell him where I've gone. The last thing I need is fer His Grace to be crushed by a millstone."

Hamish had been correct about one thing — even if Lattimer avoided death, his mere presence in the Highlands was distracting enough to cause them all trouble. Her, especially. Because however loudly she denied it, she *had* been flirting with him. And not only was she still counting their kisses, she looked forward to them.

"Your paper, Your Grace," Kelgrove said, slipping back into the library with a short stack of what looked like stationery. "Though I do assume you know you have a plentitude of pages at your elbow there."

"Yes, I know. I wanted to get rid of you."

"As I thought."

Gabriel closed the damned ledger again before he could have a seizure from trying to figure it out. "What did you overhear?"

"The Duke of Dunncraigh wants Sir Hamish to remarry, evidently into a very wealthy family, and His Grace has been notified that you're here and will likely come by for a visit, something they don't expect you to enjoy." Kelgrove ticked off the points with his fingers. "One mention of the thievery, and there seems to be a clash of wills between the two of them."

That last bit didn't surprise him in the least. The woman could drive a saint to drink — and he was no damned saint. She could also make a saint at least consider some sinning, because he doubted any man dead or alive wouldn't have some carnal thoughts in the face of those flashing dark eyes, the curve of those lips, and the way she seemed to burn from the inside out. He imagined not even an infamous Highlands winter could stand against her.

He hadn't been able to do so. Whatever excuse he gave, whatever strategy he pretended to be following, the fact remained that he thought of little but her face, her mouth, her voice, her curves, from the moment he opened his eyes in the morning to beyond when he closed them at night. He would do more than kiss her, despite the way she seemed determined to thwart his every move — and despite the fact that he'd overheard her kissing someone else just a few days ago. All of which made him a madman, he supposed.

"Do you have any idea what all this means for you, Your Grace?"

Gabriel shook himself. There was a larger game afoot here than what he meant to do with Fiona Blackstock. "Beyond the obvious point that none of the Scots want me here? I'm not certain." He straightened, moving to the window where a glorious afternoon waited beyond. "I do know that I'll see it all straightened out before I depart."

The sergeant nodded. "If I may suggest something?"

"Of course. That's why you're here." Any interest Kelgrove took in Lattimer Castle was a good thing, considering.

"The chit. Miss Blackstock. I know you said she has her uses, but aside from the fact that no one hired her, her . . . stubbornness and lack of cooperation is doing nothing but hindering you. In short, however much information she has about the estate and its people, you can find those things elsewhere."

Just a few days ago the woman had tried to send him to sink into a bog, for the devil's sake. One where her own brother had apparently drowned. And he was not letting her get away from him. Not even if that proved counter to his own campaign here. "I'll sack her once I find out what it is she's keeping from me," he returned aloud. "She's a game piece, and I don't think I can put this puzzle together without her."

There. That at least sounded logical. As for whether he meant it or not, he could figure that out at a time when his subordinate wasn't eyeing him with cautious curiosity.

Movement outside the window caught his attention, and he stepped closer to see the tail end of a large, red cow wandering up the carriage drive below. "See if you can decipher anything else," he said, and headed for the door. "She wouldn't have handed these over if she had a choice."

One of his five hundred footmen stood in the foyer as he arrived downstairs. "Yer Grace," he squeaked, bowing, and held out a greatcoat. Gabriel turned around, and the servant helped him put it on.

"What's your name?"

The boy's Adam's apple bobbed up and down. "Diarmid, Yer Grace."

"Diarmid. Thank you."

"I . . . Ye're welcome, Yer Grace."

Gabriel stepped outside into the cool, fresh air of a Highlands summer afternoon. He took a deep breath, trying to clear the clutter of his thoughts, and turned up the side of the house.

The shaggy beast had one horn that turned up while the other angled down, giving her a comic, tragic visage. Apparently the farmer Brian Maxwell wasn't having any better luck keeping track of her today than he had when she'd wandered into that damned mudhole.

"Hello, Cow," he drawled, moving between her and the tall ferns bordering the estate's formal gardens. Of course Fiona had been jesting about her name, but he didn't have a better one to call her, so Cow would have to do. "Let's find you some hay, shall we?"

The cow stopped, lowering her head to nibble at the long grass to one side of the drive. Hoping he hadn't miscalculated the animal's willfulness and that he wasn't about to make himself look foolish in front of a household that already thought him the devil, Gabriel pulled up a large handful of the sweet grass and waved it under the bovine's nose.

"This way, Cow," he said, and stepped sideways.

The beast stood where she was for a moment, eyeing him through long, red strands of fur hanging over her face, then swiped across her nose with her tongue and swung around to face him. Evidently the possibility of fresh hay outweighed the colorful enticements of the garden.

He half expected Fiona to come charging into view and chastise him for coddling or some such nonsense, but he and the beastie made their way slowly to the stable without incident. "Oscar," he called, "have one of your lads see to the animal here."

A handful of his eighty stable boys trotted into view and herded Cow into a pen. Gabriel dropped the grass he'd picked and waited for the head groom to appear. "Well caught, Yer Grace," Oscar Ritchie drawled. "That blasted cow's a menace to every garden in the valley."

"Send for Brian Maxwell, if you would," Gabriel returned. "If the man can't manage a cow or two, I can find him employment cutting peat or drying seaweed."

Those were the two most menial tasks that came to his mind, and he wasn't surprised to see the groom's amusement flatten. "Aye, Yer Grace. I'll send a lad to fetch him fer ye."

This endeavor had been idiotic, now that he considered it. In his position he couldn't afford to look foolish, and the reward for keeping a single cow out of the garden when the locals were likely accustomed to the nuisance couldn't possibly have been worth the risk.

At least it had succeeded, and Fiona Blackstock hadn't charged out to reprimand him in front of everyone. Which made him wonder where, precisely, Fiona might be. After all, his first thought when he'd seen

211

the cow had been to show his would-be steward that he could manage the beast without having to resort to jumping into the mud, allowing the garden to be devoured, or shooting it. A half-witted, pride-driven tactical error of the sort he thought he had outgrown within six months of putting on his first uniform. The kind of mistake that in his world could get both him and his men killed.

"Have you seen Miss Blackstock?" he asked Oscar, as the groomsman ordered one of the stable boys to deliver a pitchfork of hay to Cow.

"She rode off with Ian Maxwell some twenty minutes ago," the groom returned. "Shall I fetch her fer ye, Yer Grace?"

"No. Have her see me when she returns." So she hadn't intended to show him the whisky factory today, after all. If she'd been gone for twenty minutes, she'd left within two of his shutting the library door on her. That, at least, hadn't been a mistake. And it had been for her sake as much as his. He liked her, enjoyed her, but he didn't trust her. And while he couldn't stop himself from kissing her, he could remind himself that he wasn't the only man she'd kissed this week.

Gabriel clenched his jaw. Whoever the

devil that other man had been, they needed to have a conversation. With their fists.

He was tempted to have Union Jack saddled just to get him out of the house, but after yesterday he had a letter to write. His solicitors in London might have thought him incapable of functioning without their constant yelping, but he remembered the important bits. He remembered that he had more money than he and his sister together could ever hope to spend, and he remembered that he wanted to show Fiona he could be a duke.

Two hours later he'd franked two letters and sent them off to Strouth and the Fair-Haired Lass tavern there, where he'd been assured the next mail coach headed south would collect them for delivery to London. He'd sent word to the overseers at the textile mill, the porcelain works, and the whisky distillery that he wanted to see them first thing tomorrow morning. As he'd warned her, if he couldn't get Miss Black-stone to cooperate, he would simply go around her. And then, if she was as concerned with her secrets as he thought her to be, he had no doubt she would change her defiant tune.

"What the devil are ye aboot?" Her voice came on the heels of that thought, and she stomped into the upstairs sitting room where he'd gone to find what he suspected was a secret door leading down a hidden corridor cutting across the center of the second floor of the castle. The old building seemed to be rife with them.

Gabriel rapped his knuckles against the next section of wall, hearing solid stone behind the paneling. "I'm looking for a passageway."

"I'm nae talking aboot that. Ye threatened to take a man's cattle and send him to cut peat? Ye damned Sassenach, that's how ye find yerself with a lead ball in yer skull."

The deep lilt of her voice distracted him, and he pushed back against it. Moving on, he kept knocking against the wall. "If a man isn't capable of doing his job, I'll find him one he *can* manage. It's as simple as that."

"It isnae. Nae here in the Highlands." Even with his back turned he could practically see her hands going onto her hips. "And if ye're set on being rid of men who cannae do the job they've been given, ye should begin by looking in the mirror."

And there it was again. How unfit he was to be a duke, to be in charge of setting this place to rights — not that he could do so until she decided to tell him precisely what was wrong with it. He turned around to face her. "So I'm not fit for this duty?" he ground out, stalking up and grabbing her by the hand even when he knew he'd be better off not touching her. "In your estimable opinion, then, who *is* suited to be the Duke of Lattimer? You, I suppose, Duchess?"

She tried to yank her arm free, but he'd finished with the way she snapped insults at him and flitted away. After a heartbeat or two she stopped pulling and settled for glaring up at him. "At least I ken Highlands ways, Lattimer. At least I wouldnae ever insult a man oot of his own presence and tell the world he's a failure at the work his father's father's father's father passed all the way doon to him, and all without ye ever speaking more than a half-dozen words to him, if that."

Well, that cut close to the spine. With a deep breath he bit back the retort he'd been ready to make. "I'll make you a bargain," he snapped. "I will meet with Brian Maxwell and see for myself whether he's lazy or merely unlucky. If it's the latter, I will do what I can to help him keep Cow wherever it is she belongs."

Her black gaze lowered to his mouth and lifted again, making his pulse speed in return. For God's sake, somewhere over the past few days she'd become a siren, and he a sailor who'd been at sea for a very, very long time and couldn't resist her even when he knew he should. "I cannae argue with that, I suppose, but how is it a bargain?"

With her hand in his grip, he drew her up against him. "In return," he said, working not to lean toward her, " 'Sassenach,' 'major,' 'soldier,' and 'English' all leave your vocabulary, at your peril. If you mean to continue to insult me, you'll have to be more clever than that."

She swallowed. "And what peril is that?"

"I'll think of something."

Fiona searched his face, but Lattimer didn't seem to be jesting in the slightest. Never in a hundred years would she have expected a duke to request a meeting with a tenant farmer and then offer to help him, if need be. And yes, Brian Maxwell *was* lazy, but she'd always reckoned that was because of his consistently poor luck. He claimed to have been struck with ill fortune thanks to the curse, because evidently one day twenty years ago he'd tipped his hat to the old Duke of Lattimer. She didn't believe in such things, of course, but she supposed it mattered more that Brian *did*. "I agree to yer bargain, Lattimer," she said, and stuck out her free hand since she couldn't seem to wrench the other one free.

"Gabriel," he corrected. "I'm removing 'Lattimer,' as well. I've heard you use it against me."

Still holding her hand out, she cocked her head at him and hoped he couldn't see that the idea of using his given name made her think thoughts that had no business being in her brain. "Everyone'll think I'm being too familiar with ye. That we're . . . friends, or someaught."

He lifted an eyebrow. "Will they, then?" he said, a half grin curving his mouth.

Clearly he was daring her to back down. And she was a Blackstock of clan Maxwell. She'd yet to come across a thing that could stop her. Not even the MacKittrick curse stood a chance. "Shake my blasted hand then, Gabriel, unless ye've changed yer mind." There. And by saying it quickly, his name didn't pause long enough to linger on her tongue, not the way it did when she said it to herself.

He took a deep breath. "I'm not shaking your damned hand," he rumbled, and captured her mouth with his. Heat speared through her again, sharper this time. Fiona put her hands on his shoulders, unable to keep herself from molding her lips against his as he tilted her head up with his fingers.

Their fourth kiss. A very fine one, indeed.

Slowly he lifted away from her, releasing her in the same motion. They had their bargain, then, for whatever good he thought it would do. "Are all Sassenach soldiers as mad as ye?" she asked, dismayed that her voice frayed a little at the edges.

"I very much doubt that, Fiona."

"Well. Fine, then. I'll send fer Brian."

"I already have. I believe by now he should be waiting in the front sitting room. Would you care to join me?"

"So ye meant to talk to him anyway, and ye nae said anything? Ye cheated, ye big . . . Gabriel."

"If you'd asked Oscar Ritchie, you would have known precisely what I did. I've hidden nothing from you." Gray eyes met hers. "I doubt you can say the same." He gestured toward the door. "After you."

There he went again, accusing her of lying. He wasn't supposed to have realized anything was amiss, and she had no idea how he'd discovered . . . whatever it was he'd found out. Or perhaps he hadn't realized anything, and he simply had a suspicious nature. However it had come about, he didn't seem the sort to let his questions lie unanswered.

She hadn't actually lied, yet. Not really.

Not saying anything one way or the other wasn't lying. That tactic had little to do with the truth either, however, and with him suspecting subterfuge she couldn't keep it up much longer.

Which gave her a choice. An outright lie, or at least a partial truth. A truth that would more than likely see him extending his stay until he'd beaten the problem it represented into submission. Fiona paused just short of the sitting room doorway. Yes, the castle had a curse on it. But a curse didn't steal things. People did that. And Lattim— Gabriel — might actually be more help than her finger-crossing, over-the-shoulder-spitting fellows who'd evidently decided that the castle's deepening ill fortune was both to be expected and inescapable.

"I couldn't say for certain," the duke drawled from so close behind her that the hair on the back of her neck lifted, "but I think you may have something on your mind. I hope it's me."

Fiona turned around, put both hands on his hard chest, and shoved him into the empty breakfast room opposite. He didn't resist, which surprised her, but it seemed entirely possible that he thought she meant to kiss him again. Which she wouldn't. Certainly not now that it had occurred to her to do so.

Shutting the door, she hauled him all the way over to the window. A little truth, a bit of truth, just enough to ease his suspicions and to aid her with catching the culprit. Then he could leave feeling he'd accomplished something, Lattimer or MacKittrick or whatever the British Crown said it should be called today would no longer be losing sheep, and then she could manage the rest once Gabriel was gone.

"If this is a seduction," he murmured, "you don't have to work this hard."

Fiona stared at him, half thinking she must have slipped into another daydream. "I'm nae seducing ye. I wanted to tell ye someaught."

He bent his head toward her. "You smell like heather."

A slight, pleasant shiver went through her. If he hadn't been English, and a soldier, they would likely have been naked together by now. As it was, every time she so much as glanced in his direction she thought of kissing. And kissing him only led to her wanting to kiss him more.

"Stop spouting yer nonsense," she stated, taking half a step backward and hoping he couldn't tell that she'd hesitated to do so.

His bisected eyebrow lifted as he relented.

"Enlighten me, then. What did you want to tell me?"

"We're missing sheep," she said in a low voice. "It began with a few at a time, then a hundred at once. Now that they're up in the hills, we're losing some nearly every day. There's nae pattern we can sort oot, and nae trace of attacks from wildcats or anything else that could be harassing them." She scowled. "Everyone blames it on the MacKittrick curse, but I'm nae going to accept losing livestock to superstition."

He searched her gaze, clearly trying to decipher if she was telling him the truth or not. Which she was. Just not all of it. "I'm assuming you kept this from me because you're afraid I'll go charging after the culprits and get myself killed." Gabriel lowered his eyebrows. "No? Perhaps you're worried that I would take on the task of finding the thieves and, by so doing, lengthen my stay at Lattimer."

Well, wasn't he the clever one? She narrowed her eyes. "Ye're so certain of yer answer, I willnae bother with offering my own." It certainly wouldn't do for him to begin thinking he had everything figured out, anyway. "I will say that there's nae a Maxwell in the Highlands who would approve of me telling ye what I just did. If ye go aboot flapping yer gobber and saying it was me who told ye, well . . . just dunnae do any such thing."

As she watched, the expression on his face altered. She couldn't quite say how, but she knew he wasn't amused any longer, and he wasn't going to make one of his cynical jests. For this moment, she had his complete, undivided attention. It felt like she'd stepped too close to a hungry, wild lion — or so she imagined, anyway. At the same time, that scar running down his face — she abruptly wanted to run her fingers along it.

"Whether you're actually in my employ or not, Fiona," he finally said, his low, precise voice quiet, "and regardless of whether we're allies or not, your confidences are safe with me. I will protect you, with my life if necessary."

The idea of a duke — any duke — purposely laying down his life for a castle's steward, an estate manager, was utterly ridiculous. And yet, as she gazed into his dawn-colored eyes, she absolutely believed that he meant what he said. "Well, ye're a madman then, Gabriel Forrester. I told ye what ye asked; do with it as ye will. I've nae idea who's been doing it, and I've been looking. Dunnae get yerself thrown over a cliff fer some sheep." Even though that would make things easier on her, she couldn't say that was what she wanted, any longer. In fact, she still wanted to touch him even when she knew she shouldn't. She settled for poking a finger into his shoulder. "And dunnae go aboot accusing the tenants or frightening the bairns. I reckon there's nae a soul at MacKittrick who wants ye here as it is."

"Nae a soul?" he repeated, mimicking her.

Fiona lowered her hand and took a long step backward. "Nae a soul," she repeated, though she couldn't muster quite as much heat as she'd intended.

"Mm-hm."

"Dunnae push yer luck, ye demon. Ye're nae as charming as ye think."

"Yes I am."

Charming didn't quite seem the correct word; perhaps compelling, or mesmerizing, fit him better. When he walked into a room, all eyes went to him and remained there. Hers certainly did, despite her best efforts to ignore, detest, and be rid of him. On the battlefield he must have been the devil himself, tall and straight-backed and leading from the front, cutting a bloody path to victory. No, Gabriel Forrester wasn't a Highlander. He was, however, the very definition of a man. And Fiona had no idea how much longer she would be able to resist him, or if she even cared to try.

CHAPTER EIGHT

"Miss Fiona," Brian Maxwell said, rising from his perch at the very front edge of one of the chairs in the sitting room, as if he'd worried he might dirty the thing. The farmer held his tam in his hands, his hair dampened and combed and his old coat buttoned.

"Good afternoon, Brian."

"I've nae been summoned to parlay with a duke before," he went on, his hat spinning a slow circle in his restless fingers. "Do ye ken what he's after? Because my cottage has been on this land fer more than a hundred years, and I'd nae see it burned doon and my wife and bairns left to the cold because of a cow, or because he's a yen fer grazing more sheep."

Oh, dear. "Brian, ye —"

"I have no intention of turning you out of your home, Mr. Maxwell," Gabriel said, stepping around her and into the room.

"You have a fence problem and a wandering cow, both of which have been pointed out to you before. Why haven't you remedied the situation?"

Brian's face reddened. Before she even realized she was moving, Fiona had put a hand on the cotter's shoulder and nudged him toward the table where the liquor tantalus stood. "A whisky fer ye, Brian?"

Beneath her hand she felt his shoulders lift. "Aye, Miss Fiona. That'd be grand. The walk up the hill here does make my old knees creak like a witch's cackle."

She unlocked the tantalus and poured him a generous glass, glowering past him at Lattimer as she did so. "Did ye hear we found the red heifer almost to the laird's garden this morning?"

"Aye. One of the stable lads told me. And he told me what the laird said." He glanced back at Gabriel, then faced her again. "I thought she might have trekked oot toward the river after those onions. Ye ken she's partial to wild onions."

"So ye've said. I dunnae suppose Brady and ye have managed to cut the new fence posts yet."

The farmer shook his head. "Brady's forever getting his chores tended before dawn, then disappearing until nearly dark.

He's but fifteen, or I'd swear it was a lass twisting his head aboot. Flighty lad he is, just like his mother."

The rotund Mrs. Maxwell was the least flighty person Fiona could imagine, but that was neither here nor there. Brian had long ago convinced himself that he was surrounded by creatures who only wanted to be elsewhere. And perhaps he had a point. "Drink up now," she urged, "and we'll put our heads together to find the best way to keep the cows where they belong."

He took his drink, sent the duke another cautious look, and wandered over to look at the trio of prize-winning cows immortalized in oil paints on the wall. "So he can't manage his cows *and* he's drinking my whisky?" a deep voice murmured in her ear a moment later.

Heaven's sake, he was stealthy. Fiona turned around, looking up to meet his gaze. "Ye're the grandest man he's ever met," she whispered back, "in the grandest place he'll ever see. He's already been knocked off his feet by ye summoning him, and then ye begin ordering him to give ye answers. He's nae one of yer soldiers, Gabriel. He's a small man who lives on the same patch of ground where he was born, and who fully intends to die on that same spot. And in his thinking, ye're the one man able to take it away from him."

The look he gave her was unlike anything she'd seen from him before. She had no right, of course, to speak to him like that; the only other duke of her acquaintance would have cuffed her just for speaking out of turn. Gabriel Forrester, however, didn't look angry. More than anything else, he seemed . . . surprised. Stunned, even. And she didn't think that was because she'd given Brian Maxwell a glass of whisky.

"He is incompetent," Gabriel breathed, lifting his eyes momentarily to glance at Brian. "Is he not?"

"Aye, he is. I dunnae believe that to be his fault. He owns three cows and grows wheat. That's what he is."

Whatever he'd looked for on her face he seemed to have found, because a hard heartbeat later he strolled over to stand beside Brian. Fiona started forward as well, not certain what he meant to attempt next or how much additional trouble it might cause. Abruptly he put out an arm to stop her, unless she cared to walk her bosom straight into his palm.

"Mr. Maxwell. As I was saying earlier, how many men and supplies should I send over tomorrow to see that your fence is repaired

228

to your satisfaction?"

Fiona blinked. That . . . that truly surprised her. Brian nearly dropped his glass, clearly as stunned as she was. Had Gabriel not only just listened to her unasked-for advice, but followed it? Next, pigs would be jumping over the castle.

"How do I know ye arenae offering to fix my hoose so ye can rent it to someone else and make yerself a profit?"

"Bri—"

"Because there's a greater profit in the wheat and the . . ." He glanced at Fiona, and she quickly made a churning motion. "And the butter you provide for the household."

The farmer's chest seemed to puff up like a robin's. "Well. I always feed my girls the sweetest grasses. If it wasn't fer the red one and those onions, I'd nae have to have a pen at all."

"I'll send Rory back with ye," Fiona put in, naming one of the gardeners. "He can read and write. He'll make a list of the supplies ye need, and we'll —"

"We'll have men down there in the morning to repair that fence," Gabriel finished.

He'd said "we," which felt different than it did when she said it. She, of course, meant the other inhabitants of the property,

the Maxwells and the Paulks and the Din-
woddies and all the others who formed clan
Maxwell. Coming from him, well, she
wasn't entirely sure what it meant. But it
did seem to include her. Her uncle Hamish
seemed certain she was about to be sacked
by Lattimer, but that "we" didn't make it
sound that way.

"Well, thank ye, Laird Lattimer. Yer Grace,
I mean. I . . ." Brian finished off the whisky,
started to set the glass aside, then changed
his mind and handed it to her, all the while
bobbing his head like a chicken. "I'll be off,
then. I can fetch Rory myself, if it pleases
ye."

"Aye. Thank ye, Brian."

The farmer left the room, two footmen
joining him as they headed outside to find
Rory. Fiona set the empty glass down by
the tantalus. There she was, alone in a room
again with the Sassenach. If she did something foolish like look at him, she might
grab him by his village-sewn lapels and kiss
him, for heaven's sake. Taking a breath, she
made a show of snapping her fingers as if
she'd just remembered something and hurried for the door.

"I know how to interrogate a soldier," he
said from behind her.

For a second she contemplated pretending she hadn't heard anything and making a run for it. "Brian Maxwell isnae a soldier," she said anyway, still moving for the door.

"Exactly. I would have made things worse. Thank you, Fiona."

That slowed her down. "Ye're welcome, Gabriel."

"Are you with anyone?"

That stopped her in her tracks. "I beg yer pardon?" She turned around. "Why have ye been kissing me if ye think I'm with someone else?"

For a moment his expression didn't seem at all amused. "Because if there is someone, you might want to warn him."

"Aboot what?"

"That I don't share. That's me, being civilized."

"Impossible man."

His grim smile looked at least as frustrated as it did amused. "You have no idea."

And now perhaps he might be able to use his soldierly ways and point her toward an invisible sheep thief, and then he could go away before she forgot why his presence and his kisses and why having someone here who could cut through clan pride and solve problems was such a very terrible idea.

"Missing sheep," Kelgrove muttered, kicking his gelding into a canter to match Union Jack's pace. "We rode all the way to the middle of the Scottish Highlands because Miss Blackstock didn't want to admit she can't find some bloody sheep?"

"She didn't say they were missing. She said they'd been stolen," Gabriel returned, sending Jack toward the overgrazed pasture. Considering Lattimer boasted three large flocks and a dozen smaller ones, this wasn't much of a starting point. At the moment, though, it was the only one he had.

"I could lose my pocket watch and say it was stolen, just as easily," the sergeant replied. "That doesn't make it so."

That was the second time Kelgrove had implied — or rather, suggested — that Fiona had lied about something. Gabriel didn't think she had done so, though he still believed she hadn't told him everything. All the same, Kelgrove's statement annoyed him. "I'm not easily fooled. Would you agree with that?"

"I would emphatically agree with that, Your Grace. As I recall, it took you less than a minute to work out that Private Simmons had gone off to meet some lightskirt, and he had not, in fact, fallen asleep on watch as he'd claimed."

Gabriel had never understood why Simmons had put forward the lie, since leaving his post and falling asleep on watch were both hanging offenses. The only thing he could figure was that the private had preferred to be remembered as a laggard rather than as a rogue. The lad's mother had been Irish Catholic, as he recalled. He'd needed to know, though, whether he'd had a spy or an ill-fated fool on his hands. In the end, Simmons had died because he was a weak-willed idiot who couldn't resist a twopenny whore.

That, though, was years past and far too long ago for him to even bother with wishing there had been a different ending to the tale. "When you're agreeing with a point I make," he commented, "you don't need to bring up examples where I ordered a man's death. My point is that Miss Blackstock wasn't lying. Someone's stealing sheep. *My* sheep. I'd wager a year's salary that something else is afoot, as well, but this starts me on the hunt, at least."

The overgrazed pasture came into view, and he slowed Union Jack to a walk. Adam drew up beside him. "That's a generous amount of shit," he noted, as they rode through the newly sprouting grass toward the narrow center of the valley.

"Yes, it is. The rock slide that separated

the flock came from up there," he said, gesturing at the steep slope to the left where darker soil and rock not yet blasted by the weather carved a raw wound all the way to the top of the gorge.

Whether it looked natural or not, the placement was so perfect that he had to suspect the slide had been started intentionally. Twenty feet to the left or the right, and the sheep and their shepherds would have been able to navigate past the tumbled boulders. The best way to determine for certain whether the mess had been ill luck or encouraged misfortune would be to climb up to the top of the cliff and take a look at where it had begun. Gabriel swung out of the saddle, did a quick survey of the rock on either side, then headed up the firmer-looking left edge of the slide.

"Your Grace," Kelgrove called, his voice breaking at the edge, "that is not a good idea. Come down and I'll take a look."

"You don't even like to climb ladders," Gabriel replied, grabbing for handholds as he ascended.

The slide had occurred well over a month ago. In that space it had rained several times, and he knew from personal experience that the wind had been active, as well. There might well be nothing to see even if someone *had* helped the slide along. If he was going to find anything, however, the odds were better today than they would be tomorrow or any day thereafter.

"But Your Grace, you —"

"Shut up and look for anything down there that could point to this being intentional," he grunted.

"I . . . Yes, sir."

While his sergeant continued to complain about having a commanding officer who took far too many chances, Gabriel continued upward. Fiona hadn't known precisely when the slide had happened, but from the look of both the slope and the wide swath of torn-up ground below it had been large, sudden, and violent. Any sheep on the far side would have been fairly easy to snatch, and no one would have been able to climb across the unstable debris for days after it fell, lowering the odds of anyone finding tracks that didn't belong.

A rock broke loose from beneath his foot, sending him scrambling and another trail of debris clattering downward. "Look out below!" he called, digging the toe of his boot into a narrow crack and twisting to watch the miniature slide. It picked up some loose earth and a few smaller rocks, but nothing to match the size of the one he'd knocked loose. Something big would have had to dislodge at the top, then. Something that had been there for a long while in rough conditions.

Finally he reached the steep section above the slide. Edging sideways, he moved across it, looking for signs that anything other than nature had caused the fall.

Three quarters of the way across, he found it. A trio of straight-edged gouges marked the center section at the top of the slide. He ran his fingers along the remaining side, feeling smoothed earth that would have dug at least a foot into the ground. Any footprints would have been washed away, but nothing in nature had ever made a cut so straight that even after a month he could make it out. Shovel marks. They couldn't be anything else that he could conjure.

"What the devil are ye doing perched up there like a great owl?" Fiona's familiar voice called from below.

The sound nearly had him losing his balance again. Turning his head, he dug his fingertips into the rock face. "Inspecting," he returned.

She stood almost directly below him, her hands on her hips and her face lifted to see him. "I told ye aboot the sheep so ye'd stop badgering me aboot hiding things from ye. Nae so ye could go clambering up the mountainside like a great goat."

He'd been called far worse than that. And by her. "Your rock slide was no accident," he called down. "How long did it keep you from getting to the far side of the pasture?"

"Aboot a fortnight, I reckon. With the ill weather it took some time to settle, and then we had to bring in the heavy horse and wagons to clear a safe path."

In two weeks he could have moved Wellington's entire army a good hundred miles, set up camp, and fought a battle or two. A hundred sheep could be anywhere — with or without help. The information left him with more questions, but shouting them down the side of the gorge didn't make much sense. Leaping sideways to reach a handhold over a smoother section of the collapse, Gabriel began a controlled backslide all the way down to the valley floor.

"— allow the damned Laird of MacKittrick Castle to go off and break his bloody neck?"

"I didn't 'allow' a damned thing, Miss Blackstock," Sergeant Kelgrove grunted. "I learned a long time ago that Major Forrester — the Duke of Lattimer to you — will see a problem solved in the most expedient way possible. Even if that means putting himself in harm's way."

"Bollocks," Fiona retorted, and Gabriel grinned. She and the landslide had some things in common. At the least they were both unstoppable once they got started.

"Say 'bollocks' all you like," Adam returned, "but I was given an order. In the king's army we follow orders, whether we approve of them, or not."

"Then I do say 'bollocks' again, English. He isnae yer commanding officer any longer. He's yer liege lord. Ye dunnae merely agree to die with him leading ye into bloody battle. Ye make certain ye keep him from harm, even at the cost of yer own blood."

Gabriel scowled. No. That was wrong. He wasn't some precious . . . thing. He didn't lead his men from some safe hill far away from the battlefield. And he was no one's liege lord, and certainly not the Laird of MacKittrick Castle. He was the Duke of Lattimer, and he only required his tenants and servants to do the work to which they'd agreed. His duty was to see Lattimer safe and well managed, and then to return to a war that needed to be won.

"I can keep myself from harm," he stated, jumping the last few feet to the valley floor. "And I recall you saying that while I might have been named the Duke of Lattimer, I would never be the Laird of MacKittrick." He lifted an eyebrow for emphasis.

"Ye arenae," Fiona retorted. "But if ye die stupidly, ye'll have everyone worried aboot the MacKittrick curse rearing its blasted head again. I've enough to manage withoot ye doing that."

"*You* have enough to manage, do you?"

Her shoulders squared. "Ye've nae tried to send me away, so aye, *I* have enough to manage."

"If you're in my employ, then, and if you don't like the way I've done something, Fiona, tell *me.* Don't blather on about it to any fool who'll listen."

"Sir!" Kelgrove protested.

"Not you," Gabriel amended.

"That's one command I'm pleased to follow," Fiona put in.

"I don't doubt that. Now. I found shovel marks up there. Was that from your men cleaning up the slide?"

She looked toward the top of the gorge. "Nae. Are ye certain?"

"Yes."

Her eyes narrowed, her gaze moving from the slide to the far field. "Well, now. That would be a handy way to separate half the flock and do away with them, wouldnae?"

"I thought so. But it doesn't tell me who did it. As for why, how much would a hundred sheep be worth?"

Fiona shrugged. "They were all ewes, so I'd say aboot two pounds each. Two hundred pounds. That's a fine profit fer the effort of a rock slide."

"Where might they sell a hundred head all at once?"

"We've drovers all over the Highlands, paid to drive herds of cattle or flocks of sheep to market. It could have been as far as Aberdeen or Fort William. Or both. That would look less suspicious, I reckon — dividing up the flock."

This was getting more interesting — not because of her ready answers, but because this quest wasn't some ploy manufactured to keep him occupied. She didn't know who'd done this — and he meant to give her the answers she wanted. "In other words," he said, "anyone could have taken them, and sold them anywhere."

"Aye."

"That's not helpful."

Her arms crossed over her pert chest. "Ye asked me what was amiss, and I told ye. Sheep are missing. We lost another four yesterday. I didnae say ye'd be able to discover who stole that hundred head." She

240

tilted her head, the dark hair that caressed her temples drifting across her face in the breeze. "As backward as we Highlanders are, even we might've been able to find the thieves if they'd kept the flock in their garden."

"You should address His Grace more respectfully," Sergeant Kelgrove stated, his expression annoyed.

Gabriel had nearly forgotten his aide was even present. "I'm already accustomed to Miss Blackstock's direct manner of speaking."

"It's her between your tenants, your servants, and you, sir. The way she addresses you will be imitated by others."

"Dunnae speak aboot me as if I'm nae here," Fiona protested. "And I reckon if *Gabriel* doesnae like how I address him, he can tell me so."

Adam looked like he'd swallowed a bug. Gabriel, though, didn't feel nearly as annoyed as his aide looked; she'd called him by his given name in front of someone else. It shouldn't have mattered in the slightest, but it did. Covering his abrupt urge to smile by turning his back to collect Jack, he couldn't explain even to himself what seemed to be happening, except that in the midst of this chaos and frustration at the

241

stubborn nonsense keeping him from his duties, he felt . . . easier. Not quite relaxed, because God knew he'd stepped from one battle direction into another, but lighter. Because of her, and her relentless pushing at his well-established sensibilities. It would never serve him in Spain, but here humor seemed to be an essential part of dealing with Highlanders and the Highlands. And it felt like it had been a very long time since he'd laughed.

"Are ye finished, then?" Fiona asked.

He mounted Jack and swung the bay around to face her. "Here? Yes. The trail's too old. Why don't you take me to see my gamekeeper? I imagine he would have noticed any odd comings and goings."

Even if he hadn't been watching for it, he would have seen the widening of her dark eyes, the way she checked her advance for just a heartbeat. His hunch had been correct, then; it had been Ian Maxwell who'd kissed her. It was therefore time that they meet. Past damned time.

"Sergeant, return to Lattimer and send people out to give me a head count of the stock I have left. Employ some additional shepherds to help keep watch."

"Some of them have sons and daughters who know what they're aboot," Fiona put

242

in, still being unexpectedly helpful.

"Your Grace, it isn't . . . proper for me to leave you out here alone with Miss Bla—"

"Och, I promise ye I willnae ravish yer commander," she broke in. "Dunnae be such a lass."

Kelgrove flushed. "Once again, I am trying to do my duty. Insult me all you like, but the fact remains that —"

"The fact remains that I can't be in two places at once, and so you're going back," Gabriel finished. "I want to know where we stand, and I want to move a few steps ahead of our thieves. You'll provide me with accurate information, and she knows where to find this Ian Maxwell. Go."

With a curt nod Kelgrove dug his heels into his mount's ribs and galloped back toward Lattimer. Or MacKittrick, or whatever the castle wanted to be known as today. The old manse could be more fickle than a woman, it seemed.

"If ye wanted to be alone with me, ye should have told me where ye were headed this morning," Fiona commented, swinging up as easily as any man to sit astride her mare.

"I frequently want to put my head through a door after a conversation with you, Fiona, but I think I've made it clear what I want of you. And since you followed me out here, I conclude that you want me in return."

"Mayhap I'm only being neighborly," she returned, moving into a trot beside him.

He snorted. "You? Neighborly?"

Her eyebrows lifted. "I'm very neighborly. Ask anyone."

"Anyone but me, you mean," Gabriel said, kneeing Jack to send the bay a touch closer to Fiona and her black mare. "While I happen to find your antagonism charming, I wouldn't call it neighborly."

"My antagonism's yer fault," she retorted with a half grin, "because ye're hard-hearted *and* trying to give yer sergeant *my* job. I'll nae give the stewardship up withoot a fight, ye ken."

"Good. I like to fight."

"I've noti—"

He reached out, caught Fiona beneath the arms, and dragged her out of her saddle. Pulling her across his thighs, using her flailing grab around his shoulders as she tried to steady herself to draw her still closer, he took her mouth in a deep, hard kiss.

Her fingers tightened across his shoulders, her legs curling against his thigh. Gabriel teased at her until her lips parted. He tangled his tongue with hers, forgetting to breathe, as he pulled her against his chest.

His cock jumped at the weight of her across him. He hoped she felt it, felt that he wanted her. His fingers wanted to tear at her clothes, bare her skin to his gaze and his touch. Gabriel caught the bottom of her dress, drawing it along as he ran his palm and splayed fingers up her thigh.

"Stop," she whispered against his mouth, turning her grip on his shoulders into a push.

Damnation. His blood high, lust and battle pounding together in his chest along with the desire — the need — to claim her as his own, and she'd said the one word that he'd sworn he'd listen to. Clenching his jaw so hard he could practically hear the muscles creak, he lifted her away from him and set her onto her feet in the middle of the shit-covered field. He wanted to bellow a protest, to demand to know who he needed to bloody in order to have her remove that word that kept her from him. Ian Maxwell seemed the most likely opponent, and luckily he was close by.

Fiona stood with her back to him for a moment. Abruptly, though, she turned around. "Well," she panted, putting a hand on his boot and lifting her face to look up at him, "that's definitely a fine beginning, I reckon. But I'll take more convincing than that."

The world righted itself. "It's to be war, then," he murmured, taking her chin in his hand and leaning down to kiss her sweet, soft mouth again.

Her black eyes danced as he straightened. "Oh, aye. Come and get me if ye dare." Releasing his boot, she collected her mare and mounted again. "I recommend ye find a better battlefield than one that's covered with shite. And that's the only help ye'll get from me, Beast of Bussaco."

He hadn't put that nickname on the list of forbidden epithets, damn it all. "I have an idea or two," he countered. "But you should know one thing."

"And what might that be?"

"I never lose."

CHAPTER NINE

"Ian!" Fiona called, hoping that the game-keeper would be out shooting rabbits and not sleeping the morning away in his cot-tage. Aye, he was notoriously charming, and aye, the two of them had a bit of fun from time to time, but it hadn't been anything to merit that deadly look in Gabriel's eyes when she'd told him to stop undressing her. He'd done so, at once, but if he did suspect her connection to Ian, and if he thought her hesitation had been because of the game-keeper . . . She shut her eyes for just a moment. *Please let him be elsewhere.* "Ian Maxwell!"

A moment later the door rattled and pulled open, and Ian's shock of tousled red hair emerged into the sunlight. "Fiona, my lovely," he drawled. "If ye wanted to see me, I told ye I'd —"

Before she could cut him off, Gabriel stepped into view, and Ian snapped his mouth shut. Immediately he straightened, tucking in his shirt as he stepped onto the packed dirt and oyster shells at the front of the small cottage. With a quick glare at her, he ran a hand through his hair and made a half bow. "Yer Grace."

"You told Miss Blackstock you'd what?" Gabriel asked, his tone flat and hard. She sent the duke a glance, alarmed. Telling him about the sheep had made her feel like a traitor. Admitting her interest in him as a man had gone against every logical bone she possessed. He was not allowed to do any battling because of her.

"He told me he'd be by first thing tomorrow morning," she cut in.

"Aye," Ian seconded. "I didnae expect her to bring ye by to call on me is all I meant, Yer Grace. And why are ye here? Is someaught amiss?"

"My flocks of sheep are thinning," the duke returned. "You, I assume, are a competent tracker. What have you noticed?"

At least Gabriel hadn't named her as the one who'd given away the secret she'd asked everyone else to keep. Ian would likely ask her outright later, but when she considered it, it really wasn't any of the gamekeeper's affair how she worked to stop the thefts, as long as they did stop.

"Surely a duke has larger worries than where a few sheep have wandered off to."

"I do not," Gabriel stated, still brusque. "This property relies on sheep for a good portion of its income. Income that filters down to the salaries of my employees and the upkeep of their homes, and mine. Aside from that, I cannot abide thieves. So instead of telling me where my attention should lie, why don't you answer my question?"

"Yer question?" Ian repeated, his fair skin darkening. Likely no one had spoken to the redheaded charmer in that tone for a very long time, if ever.

"Have you noticed anything?" the duke repeated, his tone saying he wouldn't be doing so again.

"Nae. I've nae noticed anything aboot missing sheep," Ian stated, starting to fold his arms across his chest and then evidently changing his mind.

"And why is that? You travel more of this property than anyone else in my employ. Hasn't Miss Blackstock asked you to look into the matter?"

"Aye, she has." The gamekeeper regarded her with narrowed eyes. "But sheep trample all over the territory. I cannae look at a track and tell if this one's been stolen or that one's wandered off on its own."

Gabriel tilted his head, his continued aggression making her wonder if he'd overheard her talking to Ian earlier in the week. And good God, the gamekeeper had kissed her that morning. If he *had* heard, that explained him asking if she was seeing anyone, and his suggestion she warn them away. Whatever he'd heard certainly hadn't made him stop pursuing her. Fiona shivered. No one had ever desired her like that. If she allowed herself to dwell on it — on him — well, it could be very intoxicating.

"Doing that very thing, Mr. Maxwell, is now your one and only task. You are to look for any tracks apart from the main flock and follow them until you either find the sheep and return it to pasture, or find where it's been taken. How many men do you command?"

Ian snorted. " 'Command'? I dunnae command a soul, because I'm nae a bloody sol—"

"How many men work with you?" Gabriel amended. "Stop dancing about and answer my questions."

"Gabriel," Fiona murmured beneath her breath, trying not to move her lips. "Dunnae make an enemy fer nae good reason."

"I have a reason," he returned, sharp and nearly silent.

"Nae. Ye dunnae."

He shifted a little. "I looked at the ledger books, Mr. Maxwell. This thievery has been going on for some time. I would hazard a guess that the resulting reduced income concerns you and your fellows more than it does me. For one last time, then, what have you found, and who is helping you?"

Ian eyed him for another moment. Only when he nodded did Fiona let out the breath she'd been holding. "I have three lads who help me regular," the gamekeeper said. "Fiona gave me four more. We have been looking, but I've nae run across anything yet that makes me willing to accuse anyone."

"Hire ten more," Gabriel said. "Or borrow them from elsewhere in the household. And don't accuse anyone. Find me the evidence. I'll see to the rest."

"I'll do as ye say, then. All the locals will know ye're searching fer the thieves, though. The thieves will hear it, as well, and lie low."

"Then one way or another, the thefts will stop."

They left Ian standing there outside his cottage. Fiona could almost feel the heat from the curses he was likely sending after her. If having Lattimer stir up the cotters was indeed enough to stop the thefts, however, her shoulders were strong enough to hold against Ian Maxwell's ire. Her companion's ire, though, concerned her more.

"Why did you protect him?" Gabriel said after a moment, keeping his bay to a walk beside her and Brèaghad.

"Fer exactly why I said. Dunnae ye reckon ye have enough enemies withoot making more fer nae good reason?" She cleared her throat as his gray eyes shifted to study her. "Highlanders like to know why we're doing a thing, rather than going in blind. That's why he balked."

"No it isn't."

"Then enlighten me, Gabriel."

"Why don't you enlighten me?" he retorted.

"Christ in a kilt," she grumbled. "Nae, I willnae. Ye had a life before ye rode into the Highlands, and so did I. There's nae amount of whitewash or scrubbing that can make it otherwise. And I told ye I liked yer kisses. That doesnae make us friends or allies."

Light gray eyes swept across her. "You, Fiona, are a difficult woman to decipher."

"I reckon I'll take that as a compliment."

"You should."

Something had happened between them, something more than their fifth kiss. Now she couldn't seem to stop flirting with him, talking with him, teasing with him. It was an odd, electric sort of connection, a heightened awareness, almost like the moment at the starting line of a horse race when every nerve and muscle was gathered in and alert, waiting for the pistol to go off. If he hadn't realized how drawn to him she felt, he would see it soon enough — but she wasn't going to say it aloud. Not for all the tea in China.

"Ian Maxwell," he resumed, turning his gaze toward the snow-topped peaks on the horizon. "I don't like him. He thinks he has a claim on you *now*. Not in your undiscussable past. Tell me he's wrong."

For heaven's sake, what was she being coy for? Her pride, she supposed it was, could cause someone harm. "I'm nae involved with Ian Maxwell. Nae fer some time. And he knows that, as well."

"Good. And thank you for telling me. I'm a man made for war, Fiona. I don't jest about the things — or the people — I require."

The hairs on her arms lifted, and she was glad she'd donned an old spencer jacket with long sleeves. "Then ye can stop interrogating me aboot it."

"Agreed." He paused. "I do have another

question, though. If most of the tenants aren't aware of the thefts, how have you been investigating?"

Finally, something she could answer without blushing. "Very carefully," she returned. "I'm related in some way to most of the people in the valley, and I share a clan with all of 'em, regardless. I have to tread carefully."

"I didn't set out to make the situation more difficult for you." His wry smile warmed her insides even though she knew better.

"Honestly, I've been subtle through nearly two years of thievery. Ye've nae made any friends fer either of us, but if yer way works, I'll owe ye my thanks."

"Friends," he repeated, his tone unexpectedly thoughtful for a man who compared sex to battle. "Friends are a tricky concept. If you have them, I envy you."

She frowned. "Ye have friends, surely. Kelgrove's yer friend."

"I'm fond of him; I'll concede that. For most of my life I've been surrounded by people, and I've been alone in the middle of them all. It's difficult to befriend men when I have to order them into battle, and I have to watch them die. You make me think of other things, and as long as you do, I'm going to be after you. It's a powerful attraction, seeing something other than death. You're a powerful attraction, Fiona Blackstock. And kissing isn't enough."

Heat swirled down her spine. No one had the right to be as . . . compelling as he was. No flowery words, no poetry, and over a matter of a few days. The way he described his life — not the sending men to die, but the being responsible for their well-being, for their safety — felt very close to her own experience. Surrounded, but alone. Even Kieran, her own brother, had become so distant and so neglectful before he finally vanished that she would never have considered confiding in him.

Could she confide in this man? That, she didn't know. But she could certainly find pleasure and solace with him. If she dared. "How do ye know I even like ye?" she asked aloud.

For the second time today that rare, fleeting grin touched his mouth. Without a noticeable motion from him, his bay accelerated into a smooth canter. "You do. You would have told me otherwise."

"Ye're devoting a great many men to this, Gabriel," Fiona noted, as she wrote out a ledger page to be devoted solely to a daily sheep count.

"I have a great many men at my disposal, thanks to your liberal hiring," he returned, pacing to the door, leaning out into the hallway, and returning to her side again.

"If a man's employed, he's nae oot poaching or thieving." That had been the theory, anyway. The estate still suffered from both, but it would have been much, much worse.

"Is that how you fight the curse?" he asked, finally taking a seat opposite her.

Technically this was his office, but no one had bothered to tell him that. She liked the view over the gardens and the morning sun through the window, so she wouldn't be volunteering that information, either. "It's how I look after my kin," Fiona corrected.

"I want you to know, if I had someone taking a sheep or two, here and there, I'd let it go. But we aren't missing a dozen head this year, are we?"

She didn't need to look at the ledger to know the answer to that question. "Nae."

"Three hundred seventy-one sheep, Fiona. That's not some poacher trying to feed his family. And I'm not going to spit over my shoulder and blame it on some curse. This needs to stop, and I will stop it. And I don't particularly care who I might anger in the process. They aren't *my* kin."

"And ye willnae be here fer the conse-quences, anyway." A week ago the idea of him leaving the Highlands would have delighted her. It would still definitely make things easier to have him gone. Most things, certainly. Fiona forced a shrug. "That's bonny. The thieves' kin can curse ye, but since it wasnae *my* doing, I can blame the damned interfering Sassenach and go on with my day."

"As you should."

He'd actually considered that, she realized. And it didn't give her as much comfort as it was likely supposed to. "Does that mean ye arenae going to leave Sergeant Kelgrove here to take my place?"

"I have one goal at Lattimer — to see that this estate is managed profitably and that nothing underhanded is taking place. And the concern over profit isn't on my own behalf, so stop wrinkling your nose."

Fiona reached up to touch her face. She *did* seem to be wrinkling her nose. Until he'd said something, she thought her dis-approval had been internal. "Ye're a duke," she returned aloud. "How are ye to attend all the grand soirees in London if ye dun-nae make a profit on yer lands?"

"I won't be in London." Reaching for-ward, he closed the ledger and pushed it aside. "And I have other properties. I also have a younger sister. Have I mentioned that?"

"Nae, ye havenae." And something about the information surprised her. The image of the solitary commander felt such a part of him that it almost seemed he should have sprung from the ground fully formed and armed, like Athena from Zeus's skull.

"I could have gone into business and provided her with a better life, but I didn't. I chose to fight, which left her both alone and with considerably fewer choices in her own life. She . . . spent the last few years as a lady's companion, and I didn't even know — not that that would have made any difference. Once I got the news about the Lattimer inheritance, I gave her the old duke's house in London, and I mean to see to it that she never has to worry about money or a damned roof over her head for the rest of her life."

It sounded noble, a man making amends to his family for something that actually hadn't been his fault. Fiona had spent a great deal of the past few days studying this man, though. She'd spent too much time thinking about him, really, but he *had* stated, several times, that he meant to bed her. Even with all the sheep-centered activity she'd scarcely been able to think of anything else. She needed to keep in mind, though, that his original plans hadn't altered a whit. "Ye're still Major Gabriel Forrester after all, aren't ye?" she said aloud.

His brows dove together. "Why wouldn't I be?"

"What I mean is that this — Lattimer Castle — is just another passing duty fer ye. Wellington says to go win a battle over there," she said, gesturing vaguely southeast, "and so ye do. Then ye move on to the next fight. Ye realized yer sister wasnae happy, so ye fixed it. I didnae answer yer Sassenach solicitors, so ye came to sort me oot and replace me with someone more reliable. Now ye're fighting the battle of the sheep. When ye finish with that, ye'll go on and find the next fight, and the next one."

His light gray eyes cooled. "Considering that I'm solving a sheep problem you've been failing at for nearly two years, and that I seem to be ranking lust over practicality in allowing you to stay on here, what, precisely, is your complaint?"

She could see it, clear as daylight. When the next battle came he would leave this one behind, forgotten. Finished with. He'd do the same with her, most likely.

"Little by little this place, this land, has

been failing," she offered. "Everyone blames it on the MacKittrick curse. My *athair* — my father — pushed against the fall, then Kieran, and now me, but it's been like trying to stop water from running downstream." Her brother had actually begun well, better than her father, even, but she could understand the slide back into chaos; there were days when she very nearly decided to simply let the dam burst, herself.

"That isn't the story you told me when I arrived."

"I reckoned we'd be better off with ye elsewhere." Fiona met his gaze. "So ye solve our sheep troubles and go. We'll nae have another difficulty here once ye stop the thievery."

"That's sarcasm," he announced. "What have I done to merit that?"

"Ha. It's what ye havenae done. But yer uncle didnae care what happened up here, so I dunnae see why ye should. Leave it to us. We *have* to be here." With that she stood, heading around his chair and out the hallway door.

She advanced three steps toward the stairs, and then something snagged her gown, stopping her in her tracks. Then she began sliding backward, bunching up the carpet runner against her feet.

"I'm not finished arguing," Gabriel stated from behind her.

She refused to turn around, digging her feet in harder. "I am. Stop manhandling me, ye brute!"

"No." Hands wrapped around her waist, and then her feet left the floor entirely.

"And ye English call *us* heathens!" she snapped, twisting to swing a fist at him.

He dodged the blow, and she struck empty air. Hoisting her up, he carried her back into the office and slammed the door closed with one foot. Only then did he set her down onto the edge of the desk. "Now," he said, grabbing both her wrists in one of his big hands, "where were we?"

Fiona kept her mouth clamped shut and glared at him. She'd spent her life surrounded by men who were bigger and stronger than she was, and she'd never given an inch. She wasn't about to begin doing so today, even if it cost her the stewardship at MacKittrick.

"Very well. I'm not much for talking, anyway." Without another word he took her face in his palms and kissed her.

She tried to keep her mouth closed, to not kiss him back. The heat of him, though, seared straight through her skin and into her muscles and bones.

All of her logical, annoyed thoughts about the trouble he meant to leave behind for her to deal with, the way he thought *this* would win him the argument, melted in a steamy haze of openmouthed kisses. The force of his embrace tilted her head back, and she grabbed onto his lapels to keep from losing her balance. Sharp, heady desire swirled down her spine, making her fingers clench.

When he stepped between her knees, she could feel his arousal pushing at her even with his trousers and her skirt between them. *Saints above.* She'd laid out his strategy, clearly stated that she knew he wouldn't be staying — that he *couldn't* be staying, not with his thoughts already shifting to his next, faraway battle. Gabriel hadn't bothered to disagree with her, either, because how could he? They both knew it to be the truth.

And yet she still couldn't stop herself from kissing him back. She wanted every ounce of his attention. She wanted to feel his hard, fit body on hers, to trace his scars with her fingers and learn what he'd done to earn them. And he had earned them, every one of them. Someone with his drive and ferocity wouldn't have been wounded foolishly. He'd been set on his task, his duty, and someone — *someones* — had gotten in his way. She had no doubt they'd paid an even higher price than he had.

"Tell me you want me," he whispered against her mouth, running a hand up her thigh and drawing her skirt with it.

It was entirely possible she'd become another challenge for him, another battle for him to win. She was no one's damned prize, and he would never conquer her. But however he saw her, she had her own wants. And he was one of them. "I do want ye," she returned, pushing off his coat and then pulling his plain shirt free of his trousers so she could run her hands up his bare chest. "Ye're naught but bad fer me, but I want ye."

"Unbutton my trousers," he ordered, his mouth drifting down to her throat. He tugged down one side of her muslin gown and took her left breast into his mouth.

Fiona gasped, pleasure spearing through her. He knew what he was about, thank all the saints and sinners. "I'm nae one of yer soldiers," she managed in between moans, rocking against him. "Ye cannae order me aboot."

His fingers continued their trail up her thigh, dancing through her curls until he spread her open and dipped inside. "You're wet for me, Fiona," he murmured, and flicked his tongue across her taut nipple. "Open my trousers."

With an unsteady sigh, dragging her fingers through his hair to keep his mouth pressed to her breast, she decided arguing with him now would be counterproductive. The buttons were stubborn, but she managed to open the trio of them and shove his trousers down past his thighs.

"Put your hands —"

"Shut up," she interrupted, and wrapped one hand around his girth to stroke the length of him. *Mmm.* Another electric shiver settled between her thighs.

His fingers jumped and then returned to his intimate stroking. They could likely make a contest over who would come first, but she wanted that warm, generously sized cock inside her before he let loose.

"You've done this before," he commented in a low moan, half closing his eyes as she stroked him again.

"And do ye have an objection to that?" she asked, breathing hard as his entire body shivered beneath her ministrations.

"I do not."

"Wise words, Sassenach."

Tugging her arms free of her dress, he pushed the material down to her waist, then dipped to tease at both her breasts with his mouth and one free hand. At the same time he slid the fingers of his other hand deeper, pressing his palm against her mound.

"God's sake, Gabriel, get to it before I faint dead away, will ye?"

He took her mouth again, tangling his tongue with hers, then shifted his hands to shove her skirt up over her hips. She lifted against him, and he freed the material from beneath her bottom, leaving her entire gown bunched about her waist.

"Miss Fiona!" Fleming the butler's frantic-sounding voice came from the direction of the stairs. Fleetingly she wondered how long he'd been calling for her. "Fiona! Where are ye, lass? It's urgent, it is!"

Gabriel lowered his head against her shoulder. "Fuck," he said, very quietly and very forcefully.

Then before she could make her mind work enough to say that she needed to answer the butler, he took her sleeves and helped her shove her arms back into them. His cock still jutting out from beneath the hem of his shirt, he lifted her off the desk to the floor and brushed at her skirt to settle it back down past her ankles.

"Go," he whispered, and nudged her toward the door.

Fiona wasn't certain she could walk in a straight line. Taking a deep breath and trying to shake the lust from her skin, she stepped forward and pulled open the door, making it into the hallway just as Fleming reached her. "Were ye calling fer me?" she asked, brushing at her eyes and making herself yawn. "I think I fell asleep on the ledger. Do I have ink on my forehead?"

That should have elicited at least a smile from the butler, but it only earned her a quick glance and a head shake. "I didnae want to say anything to the laird until I spoke to ye," he said, his voice low and tense, "but I feared I'd have to go to him when I couldnae find ye."

Her annoyance began to shift to alarm. "Ye did find me, Fleming. What the devil's afoot, then?"

"A coach and four just came over the hill. Three more and yer uncle Hamish are with it. I cannae say fer certain, but I'd wager it's the Duke of Dunncraigh. The Maxwell's come to see the new laird."

CHAPTER TEN

By the time Gabriel tucked his shirt back into his trousers and retrieved his coat from the floor, the entire castle practically reverberated with excitement. This Dunncraigh was the man they all wanted here. The Maxwell had their trust and their allegiance in ways a Sassenach soldier could never hope to accomplish — and not after only ten days in residence.

Another general had arrived on the field. At best that meant a shift of strategy, a reassessment of troops and the fragile, tentative loyalties he'd been cultivating. At worst, he would have a full-blown rebellion on his hands. Through all that, however, one thought stuck in his mind and refused to be dislodged — Fiona wanted him, and nothing this Dunncraigh said or did was allowed to interfere with that.

Before he left Fiona's office, he replaced the ledgers in their drawer, then locked the desk and pocketed the key. Theoretically Dunncraigh could be a jovial, dim-witted drunkard who'd gained his position only because he'd been born into it. He supposed that happened as often in the aristocracy as it did in the army. But Gabriel had never planned a battle strategy with the idea that his foe would be incompetent. Or that his opponent would be alone and without allies — or in this case, that Dunncraigh couldn't recruit them from his own damned household.

The side door of the office opened into a sitting room, which in turn opened either to the hallway or to a small gallery. From the gallery Gabriel made his way through another sitting room and what he assumed was supposed to be the steward's office, since it was smaller and much more plainly appointed than the office Fiona currently used. He exited into the hallway at the foot of the servants' stairs and made his way quickly and quietly up to his own bedchamber. Apparently all of the ten thousand servants he employed had made for the windows at the front of the house, hoping for a glimpse of their beloved duke.

Shoving aside the cot he'd had brought in, he grabbed the bellpull and yanked on it, then dug into his wardrobe. Thank God for Kelgrove and his obsession with clean, presentable attire.

"Dunncraigh — the duke, that is — just walked into your foyer." Adam shoved open the door and swiftly closed it behind him. "You'd almost swear he owned the place."

"Almost." Gabriel stomped into his second boot. "Help me with this, will you?"

The sergeant hesitated, then hurried up to help him into his fresh crimson coat with its emerald facings. "I thought you'd decided that wearing this was a bad idea, Your Grace."

"If I'm about to meet the man I expect to find downstairs, he'll make certain everyone remembers who and what I am. This way I can greet a fellow duke in dress attire and cut him off at the knees at the same time." He glanced at Kelgrove. "You got a look at him, then? I don't suppose he was a drooling simpleton?"

"I saw him through a window. Then someone started shouting that you were shaking the bell off its hinges. I didn't notice any drooling."

Gabriel nodded. "I'll forgo the shako and the side-arms," he decided. "I'll leave it to you whether you want to be a civilian or a soldier."

"I'll have to be a civilian, then, because

I'm not leaving your side until I know no one's going to try to put a broadsword through you."

"Or a knife in my gizzard?"

"That, too."

For the first time in ten days, Gabriel felt like himself. He had no sheep thefts or other domestic problems to solve, no woman to chase, no worry that some fake ghost would begin lobbing books at his head in the night. The heavy, close-fitting wool coat, snug white trousers — he could barely remember a time when he hadn't worn them. As for Fiona, the day he based his actions on whether she approved them or not, that would be his last damned day. She knew who he was in the uniform or out of it, and they'd been a literal inch away from having sex on what was probably *his* desk.

With Kelgrove on his heels, he walked to the head of the main staircase. He could hear them below, voices he didn't recognize mingled with that of Hamish Paulk and the sweeter tones of Fiona. They spoke in Gaelic, which brought his level of alertness even higher. It might have been habit, or it might be the Highlanders attempting to keep something from the two Englishmen residing in the house. Either way, it would stop. Nobody got to plot against him in his own bloody house. Even if he'd never owned one before.

For the second time that afternoon he felt the tensing of his muscles, the deep, slow breathing, the sense that the world around him, the unnecessary objects and sounds, faded while the goal before him became more clear, more vibrant. Fiona had done it to him the first time, as unexpected as it had been. This time, it was his old companion, war. If this wasn't a battle, he would be disappointed. His body, his mind, were certainly ready for one. And the devil knew he had some excess frustration wound into it all.

Black eyes caught his and widened as he reached the landing. Gabriel wanted to keep his attention on her; she was by far the brightest object in the room. It took more willpower than he expected to look away and refocus. Sir Hamish had donned a crisply pleated kilt of red and green and black, the Maxwell colors. He'd known, then, that the duke was coming. Perhaps Dunncraigh had even stopped at Glennoch before arriving at Lattimer.

A trio of younger men stood ranged just outside the inner circle. Two wore plainer versions of the Maxwell plaid, while the third had dressed more like an English

271

gentleman. What they wore didn't matter, though; at this moment they were there to guard the duke, and he would keep an eye on all of them.

The man at the center of the gathering stood a little over six feet in height, his shoulders broadened by silver epaulets that adorned his black jacket. Like Paulk he wore a dress kilt, long white stockings, and ghillie brogues. Unlike Paulk's, they were fine but not as crisp, as if he lived in them for longer than an afternoon. Deep green eyes beneath thick, neatly trimmed hair the color of bleached bones looked up at him, the mouth below thin and straight.

Gabriel added the new information in, filling the empty bits of his knowledge. The duke wielded power, and was accustomed to doing so. He expected reverence, but prepared for enemies. Unless he was greatly mistaken, the Maxwell was nobody's fool.

"The Duke of Dunncraigh, I presume," he said aloud, stopping at the bottom of the stairs.

"Aye. And ye would be Lattimer." Dunncraigh said the last word like an insult, which wasn't surprising. None of the Highlanders liked the name the English king had given to the castle. To them it would always be MacKittrick.

"Gabriel Forrester. I've been looking forward to meeting you."

"Have ye, now? Then offer me a whisky and we can get acquainted."

Gabriel inclined his head. "Fleming, have someone fetch a bottle, if you please. One of the hidden ones; not the newborn piss you generally serve. We'll be in the drawing room."

Hamish didn't like that, but Hamish Paulk wasn't his main concern. This was about sharing information he wanted known, and acquiring more than the other side realized they were giving.

"I've lads outside who'll need beds," Dunncraigh stated, not moving.

"And I have enough footmen to see them all to rooms," Gabriel returned. He was outnumbered already; hell, he had been from the moment he'd first arrived. "They can leave their weapons in the stable; I don't like armed men in my home." Unless they were him, of course.

"Ye heard His Grace, Artur. See to it."

"Aye, m'laird." The well-dressed man sketched a bow and then exited out the front door.

Fiona cleared her throat. "This way then, Yer Grace. Yer Graces," she said, stepping well around Gabriel and heading up the stairs. As she passed, he could practically feel the air vibrating around her. Whether it was from worry or from anger, he couldn't say. Not without giving her more of his attention than he dared at the moment. That didn't make him want to do it any less, however.

It was an odd duality. Nothing distracted him from battle. His life, the lives of his regiment, the entire allied army might depend on his insight and concentration. He didn't waver in his attention. Ever. Being in Fiona's company, though, listening to her, touching her, had shifted from being a challenge with a very pleasant reward to an obsession that wouldn't end with them naked together. At the moment he couldn't reconcile the two halves of his desire — wanting her now and wanting her always — with his life and career, but he would have to do so. Soon. She pushed at his thoughts, set him afire. But he couldn't give in to that. Not now.

The duke and Hamish followed her, while he fell in behind them. The two men now at his back were likely still armed, but Kelgrove would be behind them. Most men, he knew, hesitated before striking a blow. It was a huge gap, the divide between contemplating an action and taking one. For him that space didn't exist. If anyone moved, he would be there first. The mobile chess game topped the stairs and proceeded into the drawing room, and the sergeant closed them in.

"Your Grace," Gabriel said, gesturing at the most comfortable of the plush, over-stuffed chairs in the room. Without waiting for a response he turned to hold a chair for Fiona, then moved to claim one that backed against a wall.

"Hamish says ye've a plan to stop the sheep thefts that've been plaguing ye," Dunncraigh offered, pulling a pipe from his sporran. He lit a spill on the lamp beside him and held the burning roll of paper to the pipe's bowl and puffed until it began to glow red.

Someone had told Hamish about the sheep situation, then. He wondered who that might have been. "I haven't been here long enough to be plagued by anything," he returned, "but yes, I believe diverting another thirty men to overseeing the flocks will discourage the thieves. Likely some local poachers or brigands. Hopefully they'll move on by the end of the week to find easier prey." Or more likely they would be lured out by his apparent stupidity and arrogance and strike again, and he would have

275

them at a time he could plan and predict.

"Aye, nae doubt that'll end it. Ye've put the fear of English soldiers into 'em, anyway."

Ah, the "insulting through pleasantries" portion of the conversation. Well and good, but Gabriel was more curious about *why* Dunncraigh felt the need to insult him. The duke was the undisputed power here; as far as he knew, every Highlander on Lattimer land owed the Maxwell fealty. Even the uncharacteristically quiet one sitting halfway across the room. Everything she did was for the Maxwell, or for clan Maxwell, anyway. If there was a difference between the two, he hadn't yet seen it.

"I'm glad to hear that you've taken an interest in my sheep woes," he said aloud, clenching his jaw to remind himself not to look at Fiona. He sat forward. "Have *you* had any thefts?"

Dunncraigh gave a short laugh. "There's nae a soul would dare steal from me," he commented through a haze of pipe smoke.

"But someone *has,*" Gabriel countered. "The people here are all part of clan Maxwell, Miss Blackstock informs me. My sheep and the income they bring are vital to them. You knew about these thefts, and they've been going on for two years. I have to conclude that you've deliberately chosen to do nothing to help your own clansmen." More a straight-up insult than a gentle poke, but he was only a soldier.

"That's uncalled fer, Lattimer," Sir Hamish put in from his own seat, close by his precious laird.

"I disagree."

"That's because ye know naught of Highland ways, Lattimer," Dunncraigh took up. "Of course this is my clan, but this bit of it lies on yer land. Before King George — the first one, ye ken — stepped in, Lattimer — MacKittrick, rather — was Maxwell property. MacKittrick was a Maxwell chieftain. These people were his responsibility, and he answered to Dunncraigh. My great-grandfather Dunncraigh." He took another long draw from his pipe. "Now these people are fer ye to look after. I cannae change their birthright fer the convenience of the Lattimer line, and they were born part of my clan, but the responsibility goes to ye."

"I'm aware of that," Gabriel returned evenly. He might prefer pistols to saber-rattling, but that didn't mean he had no skill at fencing. "But old Lattimer died just under a year ago. As far as you were aware, this place had no laird at all for most of that time. And little prospect of finding one."

"It still doesnae have a laird. It has a Sassenach duke." The Scottish duke pointed his pipe stem at Gabriel. "And before ye say someaught that I might find insulting, I did try to step in after old Lattimer died with nae an heir anyone knew of. I petitioned the English Crown to return the land to Maxwell hands. I offered to purchase this old wreck outright. But they had Lattimer's mess, all his properties and holdings, to untangle, and so I had to sit on my arse and wait until they declared Ronald Leeds to be withoot issue or heirs. And then they found ye."

When Dunncraigh gestured for Fleming to refill his glass of whisky, Gabriel risked a glance at Fiona. Her sun-kissed face had grown pale, her gaze and her attention flitting between her uncle and the duke. No one in London had bothered to tell him that Dunncraigh had tried to reclaim Lattimer, and he supposed at the time it wouldn't have mattered to him. It felt significant now, as did the fact that Fiona hadn't mentioned it to him. Then again, she was part of clan Maxwell. And while they had a mutual attraction, not by any stretch of the imagination would he say they had mutual trust.

Sir Hamish polished off his own whisky in time with the duke. They likely shat at the same time, as well. "Even while old Lattimer was alive and this property was his responsibility, he mostly couldnae be bothered to take an interest," Paulk commented. "It's old land, Lattimer. Roofs leak, millstones crack, and people claim untended property fer themselves. Missing sheep, I'm afraid, is only the latest trouble here. This place has a curse on it, ye ken."

That nonsense again. "It is an old place," he agreed. "And after becoming acquainted with it and its 'troubles,' as you call them, I have to commend Miss Blackstock for the care she's taken of it."

Hamish looked over at her. "Aye. She's done a fine job, untried lass that she is. Better than we expected."

Abruptly Fiona stood. "Thank ye fer saying so. And speaking of which, I need a word with Fleming and the cook, or it'll be boiled potatoes fer dinner."

Gabriel wanted to leave with her, and not just because of the unfinished business between them. That could wait, he reminded himself, and stayed seated. This match wasn't finished yet.

"So the lass has been helpful to ye?" Dunncraigh asked, crossing his ankles.

"Not particularly." Whatever her loyalties, he wasn't about to cause trouble — more trouble — for her with her clan. "She clearly cares for Lattimer and the people here, and as I said, she's done a fine job with what she's had." He paused, abruptly realizing that he'd already decided who Lattimer's next steward would be. Replacing her would do her harm, and he'd rather cut off his own arm than injure Fiona. He sent a quick mental apology to Kelgrove both for dragging the sergeant into the Highlands and for putting him into the middle of this without warning him first. "I found her lack of cooperation damned annoying. In fact, I brought my own man in to take over her duties, once we've learned the routines."

Green eyes turned to find Kelgrove standing silently beside the closed door. "Another Englishman, aye?"

"Yes," Gabriel answered. "Sergeant Adam Kelgrove. My aide-de-camp."

"Ye dunnae mean to take on Lattimer yerself, then?"

"I haven't resigned my commission, Your Grace. And there is still a war being fought on the Continent." And men who relied on him to keep them alive.

At the moment, though, he was more interested in tonight. Dinner would likely be another chess game, another contest of insults and diplomacy of the sort he detested. But the game he truly looked forward to was the one that would take place when the rest of them had gone off to bed. He meant to call on Fiona Blackstock. And no one was allowed to interrupt, this time.

"Why didnae ye tell me that Dunncraigh tried to purchase MacKittrick?" Fiona whispered, as she brought her uncle a glass of port. She wanted one herself, after the longest and most silent dinner in the history of the Highlands.

"What concern is it of yers?" Hamish returned, his gaze squarely on Gabriel's red-coated back as the duke poured himself a glass of something from the liquor tantalus. "Bloody lobsterback."

"Because if the Maxwells took it back, I assume ye or one of Dunncraigh's sons or nephews would move in here. None of ye would require a steward." Aye, she was being selfish. And she was equally certain that she *would* have been nudged out of her employment. Even so, she wasn't certain why no one had bothered to say anything. Wanting to take back an old holding back didn't seem like it needed to be a secret, and she'd been the Maxwell overseeing it for the past four years.

"Clearing the Sassenach oot of the middle

of the Highlands would be a boon fer all the clan. So stop yer whining over who told ye what."

"I'm nae whining. I'm asking ye a question," she retorted, thankfully remembering to keep her voice down. "And as fer being good fer us all, well, the clan hasnae been doing a damned thing to help me with anything here. I've arranged it so the hoose employs nearly a hundred servants. *That's* aiding the clan. If MacKittrick sinks into the mud, that's a hundred more mouths fer the rest of ye to feed, and that doesnae include Strouth or the fishermen and their families, or anyone at the textile and porcelain works."

That seemed to earn his full attention. He faced her, eyes narrowed. "Dunnae ye go dictating to me, lass. I convinced His Grace to let ye have a go at running MacKittrick in the first place. And that wasnae an easy thing, with the example yer own brother set." Glancing away again, no doubt to see if Gabriel had wandered within earshot, he turned back to point a forefinger in her face. "Ye may work here, but ye're a Maxwell first and last. Yer duty is to me and to Dunncraigh. Nae to that Sassenach. Ye'd best remember that."

"Of course I remember that." Trying to

explain that what Gabriel was doing to stop the thefts was also in the best interests of clan Maxwell would likely only get her a cuffed ear. But by all the saints, she'd spent years trying to keep the people here fed and clothed and protected, and for most of that time she'd had no support at all. A man who took action wasn't supposed to be a rarity in the Highlands, but it had been here at Lattimer — until Gabriel had arrived. She likely should have seen that earlier, and certainly she should have noticed how unacceptable it was.

"Keep it in mind, the next time ye're tempted to tell him aboot missing sheep or where we hide the whisky. Now go away. If Lattimer asks ye what we've been discussing, ye can tell him I was admiring the way he stepped in to stop the thievery. Arrogant *amadan*." With that last grumble he turned away and walked off to stand with Dunncraigh and the Maxwell's nephew, Artur. Evidently the duke's son and heir, Donnach Maxwell, was too precious to risk this close to a Sassenach.

"That looked pleasant," Gabriel's voice came, and she started. He'd moved to gaze out the window behind where she sat, but she'd never heard him approach.

The hair on her arms lifted, and with an

annoyed cluck she briskly rubbed her fore-
arms and picked up her cup of tea. "Family
business," she returned, from behind the
cup.

"You do recall that you work for me, I
hope," he said, humor touching his low
voice.

"Do I? I seem to recall a contrary opinion
or two about that."

"Not from me. Not tonight."

She wanted to turn around and look at
him. For Boudicca's sake, she'd been spinning for days. And now he'd twisted her
about again. Acceptance? Appreciation? Or
was this some sort of ploy to make her a
spy against her own? "Do ye wish me to
bow to ye, then?" she asked, trying not to
show that he'd ruffled her.

"I've never asked anyone to bow to me,
and I certainly wouldn't make the mistake
of suggesting that you be the first."

She took a breath. His expressions were
difficult enough to read when she could see
them, and she was beginning to think she
might be dreaming. Otherwise she couldn't
conjure a reason why he would suddenly
decide she could keep the job for which
she'd been fighting. "Ye expected
someaught from someone, or ye wouldnae
be wearing that damned uniform."

"Ah, that," he mused. "It's what I am, as you've so often pointed out."

"Ye didnae wear it fer me. Ye wanted Dunncraigh to see it."

"Clever lass." He took a swallow of something; whisky, she presumed, since his scowl at the after-dinner port had practically turned the contents of the bottle to vinegar. "Any idea how long my uninvited guests will be staying?"

"I dunnae imagine they'll be here long. The duke wanted a look at ye, to size ye up."

Another pause. "So I've been measured now, have I?"

If she kept talking to him, she was going to float away, given the amount of tea she was having to consume to conceal her mouth from the other men in the room. "I reckon ye have been. And thanks to that stuffy nonsense ye spouted aboot scaring away the thieves, I imagine he thinks ye just above an imbecile."

"Good."

Fiona nearly did look over her shoulder at him then. "Why is it good that the Duke of Dunncraigh thinks ye're an idiot?"

"Because I'm not one."

"That doesnae make any damned sense. And stop talking to me."

"No. I have more questions for you. And I like the sound of your voice."

Port or brandy would have been a *much* better choice than tea, she decided. There he went, looking for trouble. If he found some, if the sheep or whatever came next made him stay on for an additional week or a month, would he consider that to be good or bad news? And what would it be for her? A pleasant romp beneath the bedsheets was one thing — especially when she knew his thoughts and his heart lay on the Continent with his regiment. Bedding him even let her thumb her nose a little at her uncle and the Maxwell; they'd both likely turn up their toes and fall into their own graves if they knew she'd been naked with — or rather, would be naked with — the Sassenach duke.

If he continued to find reasons to stay, though, the entire equation changed. The question of her loyalties, of her . . . affections would cause all kinds of additional trouble. Not for him, because he would always have the next horizon on his mind, but for her, because she would never be going anywhere.

"I dunnae want to answer yer questions," she finally whispered back, when she realized she'd been silent for too long. "They always mean trouble fer me."

"I could say the same about you. I'd be happy not to talk, if you'd excuse yourself and join me somewhere more private. I'm not finished with you, Fiona."

Oh, she should just tell him that that had been a mistake, and that they were lucky Dunncraigh's arrival had interrupted them when it had. But the sensations and the memory were too fresh, and for God's sake she'd been hard-pressed not to stare at the front of his close-fitting white breeches all night. But it hadn't been a mistake. It had been a risk, and one she remained willing to take. Once they had the house to themselves again, that was. "The Duke of Dunncraigh and his men are staying here, Gabriel. Ye ken they'd string ye up by yer bollocks if they caught ye with me."

He cleared his throat, obviously finding the threat amusing. "They could try," he returned.

"Fiona, ye're quiet this evening."

She just managed to keep from jumping as Artur Maxwell dropped onto the couch beside her. "Am I? I'll admit, I didnae wake this morning with the thought that the Duke of Dunncraigh would come calling."

Where most of the Maxwell's inner circle wore more traditional Highlands garb, the duke's nephew had always preferred English attire. It made him stand out, she supposed, just as the crimson coat Gabriel wore set him apart from the crowd. The difference, though, lay in the why: the gentleman's clothes were a costume for Artur, a way to gain attention. For Gabriel, they were simply the outer skin of who he was. And who she'd begun to wish he wasn't.

"We do make a stir, I suppose," Artur returned with a charming grin. He glanced over his shoulder. She followed suit, expecting to find Gabriel looming, but he'd strolled over to converse with the other duke in the room. "Uncle Domhnull wanted to surprise the Sassenach," he went on. "We didnae want to have to listen to any pretty speeches aboot the English saving Highlanders from ourselves."

"I dunnae think Lattimer knows any pretty speeches." If he did, he'd never attempted to regale her with one. No, he clearly preferred directness with a touch of sarcasm. Veiled threats and pretty words hiding lies — those were tricks for other men.

Light green eyes assessed her bosom. "And how are ye faring here, with a murdering brute fer a master?"

Answering that question today was far more complicated than it would have been a week ago. She didn't want to seem flippant, because evidently Dunncraigh had had a say in allowing her to take on Kieran's job. On the other hand, too much dedication, too much praise for her new employer, and she'd be seen as a traitor to her clan. Fiona sighed. All this because she loved what she did and wanted to continue doing it.

"He worries aboot the missing sheep, and I see to everything else. Nae much different from before we even knew he existed, if a mite louder."

Artur chuckled. "Lattimer doesnae mean to stay, I hear, so ye've nae much longer to listen to him." He glanced toward the ceiling. "It's a shame the way this place has been falling to rubble. Hopefully its fortune — and yers — will alter soon."

She smiled. "It willnae, according to the curse. I dunnae think Lattimer's likely to wake up as a Highlander."

Brushing his fingers along her forearm, Artur stood again. "Aye, but he *is* the last of his line."

A sudden shiver ran up her spine. "But fer his younger sister, aye," she blurted, not certain what had made her want to be certain everyone knew that Gabriel was not entirely alone in the world, but convinced it was vital that she do so.

"A sister? Well. I suppose even the devil had parents."

As accustomed as she was to danger in her everyday life, for a moment Fiona couldn't help wondering if she hadn't just saved Gabriel Forrester's life. If so, she didn't feel even an ounce of regret. Sassenach or not, he was trying to help. And that was more than any of the other men in this room had attempted.

The drinking and sly insults continued until past midnight. As the clock in the foyer began chiming the quarter hour, Fiona set aside her teacup and stood. "If Yer Graces have nae objection, I'm off to bed. We've a count of the sheep to make at sunrise."

Gabriel was the only one who even acknowledged her, giving her a brief nod from where he stood between Dunncraigh and Sergeant Kelgrove. She wouldn't want to be Kelgrove tonight, a southern commoner caught between an English and a Scots duke. Of course she didn't precisely envy her own situation tonight, either.

The hallway outside the sitting room had a chill to it, and she took a deep, grateful breath at the absence of both the heat and the tension. Immediately, though, the noise of more conversation hit her. Far too many servants milled up and down the hallway and spilled into the library and the billiards room where a handful of the Maxwell's men had retreated to play.

She caught the arm of a second footman as he walked by. "Lochie, Fleming's likely to be caught up till daybreak. I want ye and four others walking the floors all night. Make shifts if ye want, but five of ye are to be awake and alert at all times."

He tugged on his forelock. "I'll see to it. Are ye expecting trouble, Miss Fiona?"

"It does seem like it'd be a good time fer some," she returned, and left the noise behind to ascend the stairs to the third floor and the long hallways of bedchambers. The storage room next to where Gabriel slept remained locked, so at least no one would be trying to frighten him into leaving tonight. Though knowing him, he might welcome a few ghosties after the deadly and dull drama of the evening.

She stepped inside her own bedchamber and closed the door behind her, then leaned back against the old, polished wood. She knew MacKittrick was slowly failing, but she only felt it when her uncle and others were present to point out the old castle's flaws and cracks. For God's sake, at least she kept it running — and from losing money. That would have brought the London solicitors north to pound at the front door faster than anything else.

Making a profit would be easier if she didn't have so many employees to pay, but this was the only opportunity most of them would ever have to earn an honest income. Without that, the property would likely be missing far more than three hundred sheep and a few cattle. And it wasn't only about keeping thievery to a minimum; these people were her kin and her clan, and she would keep them safe and fed and with a roof over their heads even if the lairds were too occupied with arguing over who had the responsibility and the ownership of the place to do anything else.

The small fire in her hearth had dropped to nearly nothing, and she knelt down in front of it to add another log and stir the embers back to life. Immediately the room brightened and warmed, and she stood with a sigh. The men downstairs could come and make their proclamations and puff out their chests and then leave again. She remained. She was the one who'd put her blood and sweat and dreams into the old castle, and whoever claimed ownership today or tomorrow or the next day, she knew one thing deep in her soul — this place, these people, they belonged to her. And she belonged to them.

"When you stand in front of the fire like that," the low, precise, English voice came, "I can see the silhouette of your legs."

Fiona turned around as Gabriel silently closed the door behind him. "A gentleman firstly wouldnae be looking at my legs, and secondly wouldnae comment aboot them." Asking why he was there wouldn't serve any purpose; she knew the answer already. Goose bumps lifted on her arms.

"Is this gentleman of whom we're speaking blind, by any chance?" As he spoke he began unbuttoning his red coat.

"I didnae say ye were invited in here," she stated, mostly because that sounded like something she should be saying.

"Then tell me to leave." His fingers paused their descent down his chest.

Fiona regarded him for a moment. A handful of years ago a lass who found an English soldier in her bedchamber had exceedingly good cause to be alarmed. Even speaking to a soldier would have meant trouble for her and for her family. In other circumstances that likely still held true — but he wasn't just any soldier, and she supposed she wasn't just any lass. Not tonight, anyway. "I reckon ye can stay fer a time," she said aloud.

"It'll be more than a time," he returned with a grin that heated her all the way to her bones.

Oh, this was going to be very, very wicked.

CHAPTER ELEVEN

Gabriel hooked a finger into the low neckline of Fiona's gown and yanked her forward, lowering his face over hers and taking her mouth in a whisky-tasting kiss. Digging her fingertips into his shoulders, she lifted along his body to deepen the embrace. Whatever the devil about him it was that felt so intoxicating, she couldn't get enough. No damned interruptions this time, or someone was getting punched in the nose.

"Help me with my boots," he murmured, letting her go as he pulled his shirt off over his head.

This time she wasn't going to waste time arguing over who removed which piece of clothing for whom. Sinking onto her knees, she gripped one heel and pulled as he lifted his foot. Once the other one came free, she shifted her attention to his breeches. As she began unfastening them, his fingers dropped to her hair, pulling pins free and casting them aside.

Tiny shivers raced along her scalp and down her spine at his touch. It required all her concentration to open the last button, and then she took his trousers by the waist and drew them down. His very impressive cock made the degree of his lust unmistakable, and she closed her hand around it. When she deliberately ran her tongue from base to tip, his entire body jumped.

With a low, indecipherable curse he took her by the arms and lifted her to her feet again. "You are not some camp whore," he murmured, his voice very controlled and still ragged at the edges. "And I am not going to come in your hand like some untried schoolboy."

He kissed her again, openmouthed. Fiona ran her hands down his bare back, smooth skin with hard, toned muscle just beneath, crossed here and there by the different-textured scars with which war had decorated him. With sure fingers that said he'd done this sort of thing before, Gabriel untied the ribbon that ran beneath her breasts and then undid the single button at the nape of her neck.

"Arms up," he commanded, teasing at her mouth again.

She complied. "I'm nae surrendering, ye ken."

His laugh reverberated against her own ribs. "Just as well. I'm not ready to stop my advance yet."

He sank down in front of her, gathering the blue of her skirts in his hands and standing as he lifted, until the gown slipped over her head and she stood naked before him. Gabriel kicked off his breeches and lifted her into his arms.

Fiona squeaked and flung her arms around his shoulders as her feet left the floor. She was a fairly slender woman, and he a tall man, but even so he didn't seem to feel her weight. That in itself sent her heart speeding, and heat between her thighs.

Without ceremony Gabriel dumped her onto the middle of her bed, then climbed up after her. His knees on either side of her hips and his palms above her shoulders, he leaned down to take her mouth again. "I like your bed," he stated unexpectedly, lifting his head and experimentally bouncing on all fours.

An exasperated laugh burst from her chest. "Ye like my *bed*?" she repeated, wrapping her arms around his shoulders and pulling him down for another kiss. Hot and shivery delight twirled through her, beginning at every place they touched skin to skin.

"Mine's too soft. We'd have sunk out of sight by now."

She remembered the maids talking about the pile of blankets he'd made on the floor, and she knew he'd had a camp cot put into his bedchamber. Was simple luxury that foreign to him? "If ye knew how many geese gave their feathers fer that mattress, ye'd nae be complaining."

"It's too soft," he repeated, sliding lower to take one of her breasts in his mouth. "Yours is plump but firm. Much better."

Fiona tilted her chin up, moaning. "I'm nae a damned mattress."

He sucked, flicking her nipple with his tongue and then turning his attention to the other one. "I was talking about your bed, not you," he returned, his voice muffled and tickling against her skin. "I'm looking forward to sinking into you." Shifting his weight onto one arm, he trailed his free hand down to part her nether lips and slip inside. "Like this."

Well, she could play this game, too. She liked this game. Releasing his shoulders, Fiona stroked a hand down his hard, muscled abdomen and curled her fingers around him again. "With this?"

"Yes," he hissed, half closing his eyes.

Seeing his reaction to her touch felt heady. Fiona tightened her grip just a little, and he jumped again. "Then what are ye waiting for?" she whispered, sliding down the bed to meet his face and nibbling on his lip.

He drew in a hard breath between his teeth. "Put this on me. Now."

When he pushed a French condom against her hand she would have teased him again, but the predatory glint in his eyes stopped her. He seemed to be a man who'd been pushed just about as far as he could go. Swiftly she pulled the goat bladder over his girth, tying it around the base and glad she'd done enough embroidery as a lass to be able to make a bow. This man wanted her. Badly. And she briefly wondered how long it had been since he'd had a woman. That same part of her wanted to make him forget any other lass he'd ever bedded and only remember her. "Done," she managed shakily.

With a low growl Gabriel shoved her thighs apart, lifting one knee to open her further, and buried his cock inside her. Fiona groaned aloud, her eyes closing as she concentrated on the filling heat of him. *Good God.* Already ripples of convulsive pleasure shivered through her. And then he began to move.

He began a slow, deep rhythm, sinking onto his elbows so he could continue to fondle her breasts, lightly pinching her nipples. She could barely remember to breathe, all of her clinging against him, feeling the deep, tight, satisfying slide.

Almost immediately she climaxed, shivering in spasms of delight, moaning in time with his thrusts. Everything vanished but the two of them, heaving and sweating, entwined. Again and again he entered her, pushing her ecstasy past any coherent thought.

When he finally moaned and held himself inside her, she could only dig her fingers into his shoulders and gasp. He climaxed hard, then with a deep exhalation lowered his head to her shoulder. *Sweet saints and sinners.* Fiona didn't think she'd ever be able to move again. She didn't want to ever move again. Her heart pounded so hard and fast she couldn't count the beats. "That was very bonny," she finally sighed, half to herself.

Out of breath as he was, Gabriel chuckled at her words. "Very bonny," he echoed, kissing the soft skin of her shoulder and neck.

The silky softness of her surprised and intrigued him. Fiona Blackstock was outspoken, practical, and very willing to help mend fences, shovel manure, or do whatever else Lattimer — MacKittrick — required. On the inside she didn't seem to fear anything. At the same time, though, his slightest touch could make her shiver. She was soft and delicate and sensitive, and damned well gave as good as she got.

He could see himself protecting her, protecting this. In another life, this could be everything he wanted. Fiona could be everything he wanted. But twelve years ago he'd signed papers, sworn an oath, and donned a uniform. He fought when and where king and Crown needed him to fight, because that was his duty. There were people — and land and property — to be protected. This, here, at Lattimer, this was . . . a holiday. She was a holiday. Or so he'd thought. But nothing about this, about her, felt momentary.

Reluctant as he was to remove himself from her, neither did he want Fiona to begin pointing out again that she wasn't his mattress. Taking a breath, he pulled out and sat on the edge of the bed to clean himself off.

She sighed luxuriously. "I ken these are from rifle or musket balls," Fiona said, running her fingers up his back to brush the round scar just beneath his rib cage on the right side, and the new one on his forearm. "I reckon this long, straight one's from a sword or a saber, like the one on yer face." A finger traced the white line running down his left hip to his arse. "But what's this one?" She tapped his right shoulder blade.

"Which one is that?" he asked, so she would continue touching him.

Her finger made three, close-together, almost horizontal strokes. "It looks like a cat got ye, almost. A very large cat."

"Ah, that. My men and I chased some smugglers into an old fort. One of the bastards pulled an old iron mace off the wall and swung it at my head. He missed, mostly."

Her fingers stroked the scars again. "So ye've nearly been killed by weapons both modern and ancient."

"I suppose so. It keeps things interesting."

"What would ye have done, do ye reckon, if one of these holes had stopped yer soldiering?"

"I don't think about that."

She sat up behind him to drape her arms loosely about his shoulders. Joined together, comfortable — it felt . . . new, and yet somehow like he'd found the last missing piece to something he hadn't even realized he'd lacked until that moment.

"That's a mite foolish, isnae?" she suggested. "To nae consider the consequences?"

He shrugged against her, a deep part of him wishing this night would go on forever. "I consider the circumstances of failure, and I plan for things as best I can. Knowing what could go wrong is one thing; dwelling on it is counterproductive. It's . . . difficult to put into words. I move forward. An enemy tries to stop me or turn me aside. I stop them so I may continue forward."

"Do ye save people, or just kill enemies?"

"I make an effort to keep civilians from harm, if that's what you mean. I try not to send my men straight at a cannon when they could go around it — unless the task itself is to charge the cannon."

For a moment she remained silent, her fingers idly caressing his skin. "The people ye keep from harm. Do ye see them after? Do they thank ye?"

"By the time a village is safe enough to hold a parade I'm generally far away from it, taking back the next village." He twisted his head to look at her, her chin resting on his shoulder. "Why all the questions?"

"I was just wondering if ye'd ever stayed in one place long enough to see that what ye did somewhere made a difference. To see if any roots tried to sprout from the soles of yer boots."

"I don't need to see that. And roots, literal and figural, would slow me down."

"Then I dunnae think ye ken what ye're fighting fer," she returned. "Ye follow commands like a hunting dog, and ye never get to enjoy the meal ye've fetched fer someone else."

Whatever this conversation was becoming, he abruptly didn't like it. Kissing and sex was much simpler than conversation. "Have you ever set foot outside the Highlands, Fiona?" he countered. "Outside Maxwell land, even?"

Her brow furrowed, and she moved back away from him. "Nae, I havenae. But what does that —"

"Then stop trying to judge the motives of people with whom you have nothing in common," he suggested, standing to retrieve his breeches and shrug them on. She had no damned right to criticize how he lived his life. She knew nothing about it.

"I see what this is. Ye dunnae like what I'm saying, so ye dive in to counterattack. Sometimes a question's just a question, Gabriel. It's nae part of a battle."

"Everything is a battle," he retorted. Picking up his boots and the rest of his scattered clothes, he padded barefoot for the door. He wasn't finished with her yet by any means, but he knew her well enough to realize that she enjoyed poking and prodding at him. His hard travel cot would give him a better night's rest, though he doubted he would be doing much sleeping.

No, he hadn't quite decided what he wanted of her, what he needed of her, but he had more than a hunch that it wouldn't end with the capture of sheep thieves. But that wasn't anything he could decipher in her presence. Not tonight. First he needed to decide who, precisely, he was becoming and whether either of them could live with this new version of himself or not.

Gabriel unbolted the door to Fiona's bedchamber and inched it open — and was immediately grateful for the hard-learned lessons of caution. A figure strolled up the hallway, shadowed in the scant candlelight but silhouetted well enough that he could make out the frock coat and narrow-legged trousers. Silently he closed and bolted the door again.

"What is it?" she whispered from right behind him.

Gabriel nearly dropped a boot. Of course

she'd followed him; she wouldn't want him to escape with the last word. "Artur Maxwell," he murmured back, gesturing her away from the door and lowering his gaze to her naked backside as she retreated toward the bed.

"His room's on the other side of the stairs," she muttered, pausing to retrieve her night rail from the footboard and pulling it on over her head. "What the devil is he doing here?"

Her door handle dipped and righted itself again. "I can guess," Gabriel returned, his general annoyance with the arrogant fop deepening into a possessive hatred. Fiona belonged with him. His fingers balled into a fist. He'd been the one to bolt her door. If he hadn't, Maxwell would have been in her room by now.

"That snake," she exclaimed, her voice thankfully still hushed. Her tone mollified him a little, but didn't make him want Artur any less bloodied.

The handle lowered and lifted again, more emphatically this time. Fiona had been with other men before him. Was Artur Maxwell one of them? Did she call their encounters bonny, too? Scowling, he glared at her. "Is this his custom when he visits, then?"

"What? Nae. He makes my skin crawl."

306

Good. "You've been with other men, though."

"Aye. And ye've been with other women. Shut yer gobber, Gabriel, before ye get both of us hanged. Ye can go on aboot being jealous later."

Was that it? Jealousy? It felt far more . . . deadly than the word poets and novelists bandied about so readily. "What —"

A quiet knock sounded at the door. *The bastard.* Gabriel started forward, but stopped when Fiona grabbed his arm. "Nae. If ye answer that door, someone'll end up dead."

Gabriel narrowed his eyes. Nearly every encounter he had with people who counted themselves his enemies ended with someone dead. "It won't be you, and it won't be me."

"Go hide under the bed, ye lummox."

Under the bed. Him. "No."

"Then . . ." She glanced around the room, then padded over to the tapestry hanging on one side of the fireplace. Swiftly she pressed a pheasant design on the wood panel beside it, and the tapestry swung out on one side. "Come on with ye, Gabriel. Please."

He wouldn't have moved, except for that last word. Still frowning, he slipped through the hidden door and she pushed it closed

307

behind him. Damp, stale air settled around him, dust and wood chips and the devil knew what else rough beneath his bare feet. Even with the pitch-darkness he sensed space beside him, but moving now would mean making noise. And he had no intention of being caught half naked in a priest hole while holding his clothes in his arms. Letting her confront Artur alone went against every instinct he had, but she'd asked, and so he would wait. For the moment.

Distantly he heard her door click open. "Artur? What's amiss?" Fiona asked, sounding believably sleepy.

"Naught's amiss," the male voice answered. "Ye're a lovely lass, Fiona, and the night is long and cold."

Gabriel clenched his jaw. Damned bloody interloper.

"I dunnae accept visitors to my bedchamber in the middle of the night, Artur, no matter how cold it is. Go to bed."

"Ye're a lass alone, Fiona. Ye could benefit from having a man nearby who'd look after yer interests."

"I can look after my own interests, thank ye very much. Good night, Artur."

"Ye dunnae even ken what yer best interests are. How much longer do ye think ye'll be allowed to work here? Whatever pity anyone felt over ye being left on yer own is well faded by now."

On to threats, already. The charm and pleading hadn't lasted long. Gabriel didn't doubt that Fiona could stand up for herself; she did so with him constantly. But this was bullying, and he didn't like bullying. Not in general, and definitely not here and not tonight. Not when her scent still clung to his skin. How difficult would it be to dispose of Artur Maxwell, compared against the stir his disappearance was likely to cause, anyway? That was a very large lake — loch, rather, as Fiona kept reminding him — just beyond the garden. Adding secret passages to that, and this became a rather simple exercise.

"If I'm nae mistaken, my employment's up to the Duke of Lattimer now," she replied. "Dunnae make me say it again. Ye've had a bit much to drink, and ye need to be off to bed."

"I reckon I'll stay here tonight, lass."

At the sound of the door thudding and then something falling off the shelf beside the door, Gabriel reached forward to shove at the unfinished wall in front of him. He had no idea where the door release was, but he didn't much care. Breaking through it would serve just as well to get him into the room. Dropping his clothes, he angled his shoulder forward, tensing.

"I'm nae going to apologize fer busting yer beak," Fiona's voice came, and he froze in mid-charge. "Ye make a stir in here and Lattimer will hear ye, ye ken. He's just doon the hallway. Now go to bed, fer God's sake."

Her door closed, none too gently, just as Gabriel's questing fingers found the latch and turned it.

The firelight seemed bright as the sun after the hidden passageway, and Fiona's angry, upset expression was clearly visible as she turned to face him. "That man," she muttered, and then couldn't finish because Gabriel kissed her.

He likely shouldn't have, given the fact that he'd come calling in a manner nearly identical to Artur's, but he couldn't stop himself. She'd defended herself when he'd wanted to do it for her. She'd forced one man to leave her be, while he remained. With her.

Fiona kissed him back, her fingers digging hard into his bare back. She opened her mouth to him, tangling her tongue with his. "Thank ye," she mumbled against his mouth, pressing her body against his and making his cock throb all over again.

310

"For what? I didn't do a damned thing." Swiftly he unfastened his white soldier's breeches and freed himself, then hiked her night rail up around her waist and lifted her onto the edge of the dressing table. With another deep kiss he buried himself in her damp, tight heat.

With a groan she wrapped her ankles around his hips and braced her arms on the table behind her. "Exactly," she managed, flinging her head back as he rocked into her.

Gabriel didn't know what the devil that meant, but for the moment he didn't care. Only one thing mattered, and that was the woman splayed before him, around him. His, and not only for tonight, whether she realized it or not. Whether he knew how to accomplish that miraculous feat or not.

"I have no idea how you did this," Kelgrove said, taking a brush to Gabriel's dust-and-cobweb-covered dress uniform, "but I'm thinking you need a half-dozen spare uniforms from now on."

Gabriel looked at his aide's reflection in the full-length dressing mirror. "I made do with one for battle and one for parades for years, Adam."

"Yes, and I got the shivers every time you walked into your tent and out of it again. If you're going back to wearing your uniform here," he went on, "and since you have the blunt, it would be pleasant if you stopped shaving years off my life and purchased additional clothes, Your Grace. Because if this is how you look after one dinner, two coats isn't going to be enough."

"I'll consider it," Gabriel conceded, far more comfortable in his battle coat than he'd been last night in his dress uniform.

It had taken some doing to rise early enough to slip out of Fiona's room without being noticed by forty thousand servants and his unwanted guests, rumple his cot to make it look slept in, then wash and shave in the chill bowl of water on its stand so he could dress himself before Kelgrove came in at six o'clock to wake him. Fiona had left him with some new, temporary scars, and he had no intention of allowing anyone else to see them and speculate.

"Dunncraigh's man headed up just when I did," the sergeant offered. "Square-shaped little fellow. I think he might be a mute. He's at least very unfriendly."

"Noted. I won't attempt to tell him any jokes."

Abruptly Adam set aside the dirty coat, stood, and then sat down again. "I've done a fair job of assisting you, haven't I, Your

312

Grace? Major?"

"You've put up with uniform disasters that would have destroyed lesser men. Why?"

The sergeant stood again. "I'm being serious, sir."

Gabriel turned around. Kelgrove was four or five years older than he was, raised with two older sisters and three younger brothers somewhere in Surrey, as he recalled. They didn't chat much about things before the army, which suited him well enough. Adam liked to rage about dirty uniforms and bugs in the bread, but he'd only very rarely seen the sergeant genuinely upset. When Gabriel had staggered out of the smuggler's fort with that mace driven halfway through his shoulder blade, yes, and when a close friend didn't return to camp at all. But none of that had happened today that he knew of, and yet Kelgrove looked nearly in tears. "Take the burr from beneath your saddle and tell me what's amiss, then."

"Yesterday you told Dunncraigh and Sir Hamish that you meant to employ me as your steward. And in the next breath you said you would be returning to the Continent as soon as you could manage it. I . . . I am as much a soldier as you are, damn it all. And I know where I am most useful. That happens to be by your side. I hope that by now you know I do more than clean your uni—"

"Of course I do." Gabriel cleared his throat. "When we first rode up here I thought you would do well here. As far as I knew Kieran Blackstock was the steward, threatening solicitors for no damned good reason. Nothing here is what I expected, not the least of which is the fact that my property is populated by Highlanders. There . . . is a division here, clan Maxwell versus everyone else and, in particular, me. I criticized Fiona yesterday because I didn't want her clan chief or her uncle to think she was being too helpful. It was a feint."

"A ruse."

"Yes. A ruse." That sounded better than admitting he'd been thinking of little more than protecting her.

"Well." Adam let out a chuckle, then grimaced. "Thank the devil for that, then." Seating himself once more, Kelgrove resumed brushing at Gabriel's dress uniform. "Whatever command you end up with, I will be happy to continue to serve with you. The Horse Guards will be near enough my family that I can visit, without forcing me to spend all my holidays in Surrey."

"The Horse Guards is in London, Adam. The Sixty-eighth Foot is in Spain." He scowled at Kelgrove. "Did you find another barrel of that contraband whisky overnight?"

"Of course not, Your Grace. It's just that . . . Well, you're a duke now."

"Yes, and Wellington's a marquis. He's still my commanding officer."

The sergeant's face reddened. "I'll leave it to my betters to sort out. I would be honored to serve with you anywhere you're posted."

With that oddness echoing through his thoughts, Gabriel made his way down to the breakfast room. Yes, several of the commanders in the Horse Guards had noble titles, and a surprising number of them had never seen combat. He might have had a title forced on him, but he had no intention of spending his days pushing flags about on maps. The idea was both suffocating and ridiculous.

The Duke of Dunncraigh already sat at the breakfast table, working his way through a stack of thinly sliced ham and a thick piece of bread slathered in butter and apple jam. "Good morning, Dunncraigh," Gabriel said, opting for a pair of boiled eggs and some of Mrs. Ritchie's rather exceptional haggis.

"Lattimer. I'd like a few minutes of yer time this morning. I've something to discuss with ye."

Fiona would be going into Strouth this morning to see old Ailios Eylar, and he'd wanted to join her. If conversing with Dunncraigh convinced the duke to leave more quickly, though, it would definitely be worth the time spent speaking with him. Being a duke, he would have thought, should have put him in the position of not having to host people whom he disliked. Aristocrats were absurd creatures. "I have some time after breakfast," he said aloud.

"I'll meet ye in the garden at half-seven, then."

Something had evidently happened between last night and this morning, and not just to him. An entire exchange of dialogue without any sneering or insults. Next they'd be doing the Highland fling together. "I'll be there."

Up in the Highlands summer mornings came early, and light already danced through the room's four narrow windows and deepened the blue in the carpet. Another pretty day, though Gabriel enjoyed the rainy, foggy ones just as much. Highlands weather was like the Highlands itself — changeable, unpredictable, and extreme.

As for why he felt the need to dwell on the graces of sunlight this morning, he could thank the next figure to enter the breakfast room. Fiona wore pale yellow, with a darker yellow and red pelisse over the simple muslin of her gown. Her dusky hair was tied back in an artfully chaotic tangle atop her head, her black eyes bright and full of fire. His heart beat harder as she passed behind him. *Mine.*

"Yer Graces," she intoned, heading for the laden side table and making her breakfast selections. "I hope ye both slept well."

"Quite well, thank you," he returned, not surprised when she set down her plate several chairs away from him and across the table. "You?"

"Fer the most part, aye. And I've just added the head counts together; ye didnae lose a sheep yesterday."

"Good." He took a breath, remembering the part he'd decided to play. "I reckon we've taught those poachers that I won't be trifled with."

"Aye," Dunncraigh took up. "Ye've outsmarted them fer certain."

Ah, the morning's first sarcasm. At the moment Gabriel couldn't be certain whether the duke simply thought him an idiot, or if he knew something more about the thefts than he was letting on. His arrival could be read the same way — a co-

317

incidence, curiosity over meeting Lattimer's new owner, or an attempt to discover the strategy of sheep protection Gabriel had implemented. Though why the Maxwell would need to steal sheep, of all things, he had no idea. Still, he never assigned anything to coincidence until it had proved itself to be nothing more.

One by one Dunncraigh's men arrived for breakfast, including a dour-looking Hamish Paulk, who'd evidently left his home at Fennoch Abbey before dawn to make it to Lattimer in time for eggs. When Artur Maxwell strolled in, Gabriel looked up, and immediately had to stifle an unhelpful grin. "What the devil happened to you?" he intoned.

Artur swiped his hand gingerly across his swollen nose and black left eye. "I ran into a door in the dark," he muttered. "Ye might place a few more candles aboot, Lattimer."

"I'll see to it."

As he looked down he caught Fiona's amused glance. Were they allies now, finally? It felt like they were, especially after last night. That boded well, even if he was surrounded by a herd of hostile Highlanders.

"What are yer plans fer today, Yer Grace?" she asked Dunncraigh, with the cautious smile she'd adopted yesterday. "I'm happy to assist ye with whatever ye require."

Artur made a derisive noise at that, but continued eating. Dunncraigh, though, wiped his mouth and stood. "I've nae been here fer some time. I thought I might take a ride aboot the lake and down to Strouth, in a bit. And I'd like to see the textile mill, if ye've nae objection, Lattimer."

Gabriel wondered how Dunncraigh would react if their roles were reversed and the Sassenach had just stated that he meant to poke into the duke's holdings. "I may accompany you," he said aloud, more to prick at the Maxwell than because he meant to subject himself to more torture.

Of course the moment the Maxwell finished his breakfast all of his hangers-on did as well, and less than a minute after Dunncraigh swallowed his last bite of ham the only three people left in the breakfast room were Gabriel, Fiona, and Hugh the footman.

"They're very coordinated," Gabriel commented, inhaling the scent of his strong coffee one last time before he drained the cup. "Almost regimental."

"Ye shouldnae make fun; if one of 'em hears ye, they'll all know aboot it."

"Do you think they all know what happened to Artur's nose?"

Fiona's lips twitched. "They likely know his version of it, which I would imagine varies some from mine."

"I don't like the idea of you going anywhere alone while they're here, for that very reason. At least take Oscar with you when you ride into Strouth."

A slow smile touched that mobile mouth of hers. "And there ye are, nae trying to forbid me from going at all. Do ye have a fever?"

"I know better than to attempt to stop you." He gazed at her for a moment, then shook himself before Hugh could notice his employer was acting like a moonstruck puppy. "Dunncraigh wants to speak with me in the garden. Any idea what he might want?"

She shook her head. "They dunnae tell me anything. Just the two of ye?"

"That's what it sounded like. Perhaps he wants to apologize for not giving Lattimer more of his attention."

"I've nae wish fer more of his attention, thank ye very much. Nae if it comes with him and his men eating half the larder."

When Hugh turned away to pile some plates, Gabriel leaned across the table. "What about *my* attention?" he murmured.

Her smile deepened, color touching her

cheeks. "I reckon we can discuss that later," she returned in the same tone.

He felt those words all the way to his bones. "I look forward to it."

After he finished eating he debated whether to station Kelgrove at one of the upstairs windows that overlooked the garden, but decided against it. Dunncraigh didn't frighten him, and he saw no reason to give any indication otherwise. The knife in his boot should serve him well enough if any trouble did arise.

He found Dunncraigh standing beside the swan-adorned fountain in the center of the garden. Half the heads were broken off and the basin held only rainwater, but the view of the loch and the forest beyond was spectacular.

"Ye're prompt," the Maxwell said, his gaze remaining on the loch. "But in my experience military men generally are."

"What experience is that?"

"I was three years old when I lost my father, grandfather, three uncles, and two cousins at Culloden," Dunncraigh returned. "I've kept a careful eye on everything in a red coat since."

"And I wasn't born until several decades after Culloden, and I put on my red uniform twelve years ago. I've never fought a battle on British soil."

Finally the duke faced him. "That doesnae make us friends."

Gabriel took in the man's relaxed posture, his open hands, his straightforward stance. Fisticuffs didn't appear to be imminent, which was something, he supposed. "Does it make us enemies?"

"That depends, lad, on the next bit of this conversation. I told ye I inquired after purchasing Lattimer before the Crown tracked ye doon."

"Yes."

"Will ye sell it to me now?"

Even with the conversation headed in that direction, the blunt offer surprised Gabriel. This wasn't the dance he'd expected. "Why would I?" he asked aloud, seeking more information.

"Because ye dunnae want it. It was never entailed as part of the first Lattimer's properties; it's yers to do with as ye please."

"Did you have this conversation with my predecessor?"

"Aye, of a sort. He said the king put an English duke here to remind the Scots to behave, and he'd nae be the one to decide we'd been punished long enough." Dunncraigh looked at him assessingly, the same way Gabriel viewed an open field likely to be littered with hidden enemy soldiers. "Times have changed since then. The laws have changed in our favor. And ye said ye want to go back to the army."

"I do."

"Then ye cannae be laird here."

Gabriel lifted an eyebrow. Explanations were one thing. Orders were another. "I don't think that's up to you."

Dunncraigh gave a slight nod. "Let me tell ye what I see here, and then ye decide, lad."

This was becoming very interesting. "I'm listening."

"Lattimer, MacKittrick, whatever name it goes by, is falling apart. Losing sheep's the least of its troubles. Ye, yer old uncle, his father before him, nae a one of ye's given a damn aboot this place. I reckon ye've heard there's a curse."

"I have."

"Well, it's real. It's ye Sassenach killing this land. Too many fields have gone fallow, yer irrigation system's half rotted and clogged with roots and fallen trees. Ye had two sizable villages here, but one of 'em burned to the ground and the other's filled with cotters well past their prime because all the young folks have either taken employment here at the hoose or fled to Inverness.

Ye've sheep, cattle, fish, textiles, crops, whisky, and pottery that all need a plan, nae just someone to count them up."

That hardly sounded fair to Fiona, but Gabriel kept his objection to himself. Whether he agreed with the information being handed him or not, it still might prove useful.

Dunncraigh took a deep breath. "What does that all mean, ye may ask? Especially to a man nae accustomed to owning more than yer pistol and a hat? It means a man with his sights set on a different life has nae business keeping this property. It's nae a hobby. The people here arenae soldiers, and they cannae manage withoot help from a laird. Ye can only fight one war, and ye've already said this one doesnae interest ye. And this *is* a battlefield — a war against the weather, the price of wool, sickness, ill chance — it's a new fight every day, and ye never get to declare victory. Nae here. So ye go play soldier duke, lad, until ye realize ye cannae be both and ye cannae give away one of them. And then ye'll still have yer other, comfortable profitable properties in England, where the fight's much easier. Sell this one to me, and I'll be its general."

It was all just words, things he'd thought of in passing before. Lined up, piled together all at once, though . . . Gabriel pushed back against the sensation that he couldn't breathe. All the weight of Lattimer, of the smaller estates in Cornwall and Devon, of his regiment, the work he'd put into his career, the men he'd watched die, the lives he'd saved — it wanted to crush him. And not just because of the added weight of his new responsibilities. It finally occurred to him — he wasn't Major Gabriel Forrester any longer. He would never, could never, be that man ever again. Nothing, not a damned thing in his entire life, could be as it was. And there stood Dunncraigh, looking at him calmly, expecting an answer.

"I'll think about it," he grunted, and turned away.

He needed to move, to catch his breath, to give his mind a moment to churn his flashes of thought into something coherent. If there was anything coherent to consider.

Sense lay in there somewhere. Kelgrove couldn't help — the sergeant had already realized that no one would allow a duke onto the battlefield. Why hadn't *he* seen it? Because he simply couldn't imagine anything else? Because fighting, leading troops into battle, had taken up nearly half of his life?

He wanted to talk to someone. And only one countenance pushed its way through the muddle of his thoughts. Only one person he knew would be forthright and honest, without worrying over being insubordinate or losing employment or position.

Before he'd consciously decided his next step he found himself walking up to the outlying buildings of Strouth. His legs were tired, which made sense considering he'd walked mostly uphill for better than a mile.

"Yer Grace," a young lady carrying a milk pail squeaked, nearly dropping her load.

"Good morning," he said, almost reflexively. "Have you seen Fiona? Miss Blackstock?"

"Aye. She brought a sack of apples up to the church. I think she's still there, Yer Grace."

"Thank you."

The small stone-and-wood church lay at the highest end of the pathway that meandered among the cottages, with the inn, the smithy, and the handful of shops that made up the village ranged below that. The other inhabitants he encountered looked surprised to see him on foot, but otherwise went about their own tasks. They had their own lives to see to, and he had made it clear that he had no interest in them — whether that had been his intention or not.

He pushed open the faded gray door of the church and stepped inside. It smelled of roses and mildew, a heady and slightly nauseating combination. Only one of the pews sat occupied, by a rotund woman wearing a matron's cap who snored enthusiastically. It struck him that he didn't know her name, or her family, and yet at this moment her welfare was his responsibility.

Fiona sat in an alcove to one side of the altar, opposite the priest's vestry. Father Jamie Wansley, who evidently worried about an English army marching on Strouth, sat next to her. They both munched on apples and were chuckling over something.

Jealousy stabbed at him again, sharp and unexpected. Last night, and for days before that, he'd felt a connection. Was he the only one? Should he even have come here, or was he being an idiot twice over?

She turned her head and saw him. "Ga— Yer Grace. I didnae . . ." She trailed off, her expression shifting from amused to alarmed. "What's wrong?"

All he needed was for Father Jamie to begin a rumor that the Duke of Lattimer had lost his damned mind. Gabriel forced a smile. "Nothing. You'd mentioned something about new windows for the church,

327

and I wanted to take a look for myself." *And to see you,* he added silently, hoping he wasn't on the verge of making the worst mistake of his life. It didn't feel that way, but the time had long passed when he relied on feelings over facts. Or was that time gone, along with what he'd thought would be his future? And Fiona Blackstock was all that remained — if she remained. For him.

Chapter Twelve

Fiona blinked. She and Gabriel hadn't conversed about church windows that she could recall, but if he'd gone to the bother of conjuring an excuse to be there, something had clearly happened. Setting aside her half-eaten apple, she stood up. "Of course. Father, will ye excuse me? I'll show His Grace that cracked window. That's a good place to start, I reckon."

The parson stood to sketch a deep, too formal bow. "Of course. I'm honored by yer presence at our humble place of worship, Yer Grace. Any repairs ye can make fer us would be welcome."

As soon as the priest vanished into his vestry and closed the door behind him, no doubt to compose a list of all repairs he'd ever dreamed of, Fiona sat down again. "What is it, fer God's sake? Ye look like death shook ye and threw ye into a ditch."

He glanced over at her, briefly amused.

She wondered what he saw when he looked at her. This man who'd traveled the world and faulted her for not seeing enough of it, had for some reason set his sights on her. And now, when something had sent him here to her with an excuse on his lips — the first lie she'd ever heard him utter — she felt . . . Despite what she knew, what she'd been raised to believe about foreigners in general and English in particular, she wanted to see that troubled look gone from his face. And she felt worried. What in the world could upend a man who not only faced death every day, but went riding out looking for it?

"Dunncraigh offered to purchase Lattimer from me. Take it off my hands."

For a moment she couldn't breathe. Lattimer, actually returning to Maxwell hands again? That should have left her elated. Gabriel meant to leave anyway, so what did it matter? Except that he should have been elated, as well, and instead he looked almost angry. And he'd come to find her.

"When Wellington told me I'd inherited a dukedom," he said after a moment, his gaze on the pulpit, "he said he was sorry to have lost a fine officer. It never occurred to me that he knew what he was saying. That last day, when he knew about my title and I didn't, he pulled me out of the field to go stand on a hill and watch the battle from safety. I couldn't do it. I saw a mistake my lieutenant was making, one that would cost lives and perhaps even the battle, and I charged in to set things right. That's when I got this." He gestured at where the fresh scar on his forearm lay.

"Ye're a brave man, Gabriel. I've nae doubted that, from the moment we first met."

"It's not about that." He scowled. "I wasn't supposed to go. I should have sent a runner to order Lieutenant Humphreys to slow his advance and look for French cavalry on his flank. The runner would have taken too long, between receiving the message and delivering it, if he'd even survived the run through the middle of the battle, but that's what I should have done. Dukes don't lead from the front. They advise, or fund, or supervise drills and formations in their unblemished dress uniform."

"Ye're a duke. I imagine ye could do as ye like."

He shook his head, his expression becoming rueful. "I could, yes. And I'd be forced to surround myself with soldiers whose only duty was to protect me. I could charge into a fight, and they would all die. Because of

331

me. For me. Not in order to win a battle for Britain."

That made sense. She'd been surprised to hear that he meant to return to the war in the first place, but he'd been so certain of it that she hadn't questioned. "Ye've been too close to the trees to see the forest, I suppose," she mused.

"I didn't see the trees, either. God, what a fool I am."

She frowned. "Ye're a great many things, Gabriel, and I've called ye most of them, but I dunnae think ye're a fool." Fiona shook his sleeve. "Is that what Dunncraigh said to ye? That ye were a duke and didnae want to be saddled with Lattimer?"

"That's precisely what he said. No one told me, you know. Those damned solicitors spent hours detailing how much money I had at my disposal, the artworks I now owned, how many estates I'd inherited. Not one of them could say what owning property *meant.*" He slammed a fist into the base of the window.

Given the force of the blow, she was surprised the stone didn't give way. "Gabriel."

"These people here," he went on, ignoring her protest. "You look after them. You bring them apples, change their dirty bedding,

332

employ them at the house when they wouldn't be able to find food or a roof elsewhere. That's what a duke — a laird — is supposed to do."

"Aye, it is."

"Is this it?" he returned, more forcefully. "A fight . . . a fight that can't ever be won? Tilting at the same bloody windmill on the same bloody patch of land for the rest of your bloody life? What —"

"Then sell it," she interrupted, matching his volume. "If Lattimer is nothing but a chain holding ye doon, then sell it. Put it oot of yer mind."

Gabriel clamped his jaw closed. "Dunncraigh said I'm the curse. My ancestors and I. That we're the reason for this mess."

Later Fiona would have to give herself a stern talking-to over why she felt the need to be so damned honest with this man, when it might be easier, and it would certainly be much simpler, to let him think what he chose and keep her blasted mouth shut. "It isnae *you*," she said, emphasizing the word. "Or them. It's that there's been nae a man to see anything *but* that windmill. This place isnae a windmill, Gabriel. It's nae some broken princely manor, and it's nae a pile of muck withoot a speck of value.

333

It's nae a burden. But to know that, ye have to see it differently."

"See it how?"

She pursed her lips. Her clan chief wanted this property. For that to happen, Gabriel would have to sell it. Given that, she had no business encouraging him about anything. But he wasn't only asking her about Lattimer. He was asking how he was supposed to live the rest of his life.

Loyalty, kinship, clan — yesterday the Duke of Dunncraigh had admitted that he hadn't stepped in to help stop the sheep thefts. He said he'd stayed away because he was in the middle of arguing with the English government over whether he could purchase Lattimer outright. Strategically it made sense, given that the less profitable the property was the more eager the Crown would be to dispose of it. But this place wasn't just property. It was people. Her people, and even more directly, the Maxwell's people. As far as she was concerned, people should not be a strategy. And her clan chief should have known that.

"Come with me," she said, wrapping her fingers around Gabriel's and pulling.

If he hadn't wanted to go with her she would have had better luck pulling a boulder up a hill, but after two or three hard tugs his hand tightened around hers and he stood. He truly wanted an answer, then. And she would give him one, because in the last eleven days he'd done more for Lattimer than any Maxwell laird. What she didn't know was whether the answer she gave him would be the one he wanted to hear. Or what it would mean for her.

They left the church behind and headed down the slope toward the heart of the village. As they neared Ailios's cottage, though, Gabriel pulled his hand free of hers and stopped. "I don't want to see Ailios and be reminded that she hates Englishmen," he said. "I'm not in the mood for torture today." He turned, looking back in the direction of the castle. "What I *am* in the mood for is liquor. A large quantity of it."

"Eyes open and mouth closed," she said crisply. "And ye need a change of clothes, now that I look at ye, ye redcoat."

"Fiona, I —"

"Nae." She stepped around in front of him to make certain she had his attention. "Ye asked me a question. I think the answer is someaught ye have to see, and nae words I can say to ye. And if ye think I'm nae risking anything by being seen holding hands with ye, especially while ye're in that uniform, think again."

His shoulders lowered, though she wasn't certain if it was acquiescence to her argument, or overall defeat. "Then find me a blanket I can put over my shoulders."

"Mm-hm. This way."

She led him to the smithy. Tormod Mac-Dorry was the only man in the village of a size with Gabriel, though convincing him to lend out his clothes to a Sassenach, especially with the Maxwell wandering about, could be problematic. Luckily, though, Tormod didn't seem to be home.

Fiona knocked at the door of the cottage that backed up against the smithy, waited a moment, then knocked again. When no one answered she pushed open the door, tightening her grip on Gabriel's hand to pull him in after her.

"I'm not stealing another man's clothes," he stated.

Putting her hands on her hips, Fiona whirled around to face him. "Stop being a petulant boy and make a decision, then. Ye cannae stop being a duke, and that means ye cannae live yer life as ye intended. So ye can weep and stomp yer feet, or ye can choose a new life. Do ye have any idea how many people never get that chance?"

For a hard beat of her heart she thought he might strike her. And that would alter everything. His light gray eyes were ice and fury, and his right hand coiled into a fist. Abruptly he grabbed a pot off the small table and hurled it into the wall so hard it chipped the stone.

" 'Petulant?' " he snapped. "Tell me honestly that you would be laughing if someone walked up to you and informed you that you had to leave Lattimer and would only be allowed to bake bread for the rest of your life."

"That's precisely what I thought ye meant to do when ye arrived here." She lifted her chin as he took a step toward her. Aye, he was a violent man, but one with fierce control. If he lost those reins, though, they would all be in for it. Beginning with her.

Gabriel drew in a hard breath, his jaw clenched so hard she could practically hear his teeth grinding. Then with an audible growl he began stripping out of his red coat. "I have a shirt. I need trousers."

Letting out the breath she hadn't realized she'd been holding, Fiona hurried over to the small chest beside Tormod's bed and began digging through it. She found a neatly folded full kilt, but set it aside. Even if Gabriel agreed to wear one, which she didn't think he would, having him walk outside in Maxwell colors where Dunncraigh and his men could stumble across them would be a very poor idea, indeed.

"Here," she finally said, freeing an old, patched pair of brown trousers from the bottom corner of a drawer. "His winter clothes, I reckon."

Keeping his gaze squarely on her, he stripped out of his boots and trousers, the plain white shirt he'd worn beneath his coat hanging past his hips and just barely hiding his privates from her view. She swallowed. Neither of them was in the mood for sex, but that didn't stop her from thinking about it, or him, and the way he'd looked lying beside her in the bed. The way he'd felt inside her. And how much she wanted to repeat the experience.

He shrugged into the borrowed trousers and buttoned the front. "Tormod has more girth than I do," he commented, his voice easier but still too cold and precise for her to relax in his presence. Digging into the back of the waist, he tightened the gusset ties. "It'll do, as long as there's no running and jumping."

There. A bit of humor. "No running and jumping," she agreed. As he tucked in his shirt and stomped back into his boots she found an old turnip sack. Leaving his uniform there for Tormod MacDorry to find would never do, so she stuffed the red jacket and white trousers inside the sack and tucked the bundle under her arm. "Let's go, then."

Gabriel followed her, at least, but she'd already begun to worry. What he wanted, the opportunity to continue as he had been in the army, didn't exist. If she didn't know him as well as she felt like she'd begun to, she could well end up failing not just him, but herself — and thereby everyone for fifteen square miles. But he'd asked for help, and so she would try to give him an answer. He'd asked *her,* and that meant more than she felt comfortable even dwelling on today.

Outside Ailios Eylar's cottage she knocked, then pulled the rope latch and stepped inside. Behind her, Gabriel stopped halfway through the door.

"Madainn mhath, Fiona," Ailios greeted her, giving a slight nod from the mound of pillows propping her up in her new wooden bed. Well, not new, because it had come from one of Lattimer's myriad closed-up bedchambers, but it was clean and sturdy, and certainly new to Ailios.

"Good morning, Miss Ailios," she returned in English, for Gabriel's benefit. "Where's Eppie?"

The old woman's sharp eyes went from

her to Gabriel and back again. "My daughter's oot picking fresh flowers," she said, changing to English as well. "Now that we have windows, she says they pretty up the cottage." She set aside her knitting. "Is this him, then? The English?"

"I mean no offense," Gabriel said gruffly. "Fiona suggested I visit you."

"She's been telling me aboot ye, lad. How ye held me in yer arms, and how ye ordered me to be taken to the grand hoose fer air and medicine. And how when she said I'd nae set foot in the castle while it bore the name Lattimer, ye made workmen come and cut me windows for real glass that opens, bring me a new bed, and fix my chimney to stop it smoking."

"I'm glad to see you so much improved, ma'am." He walked to the side wall of the tiny house and tapped a knuckle against the glass of the half-open window. "I'd like to put down a wood floor as well, if you'll allow it. I think that would keep you warmer in the winter than dirt or even stone."

"And then what?" the old woman asked.

Fiona frowned. Ailios's conversation could be biting, but this was not the blasted time for it. "If ye —"

"I mean to say," the invalid interrupted, "my neighbor, Mrs. Dinwoddie, says ye're

340

only making improvements so ye can clear us oot and bring in English tenants. Or it's because ye pity us poor Scots, which is near as bad."

He shook his head. "This is your home, ma'am. And your daughter's. You know things about this land that I could never hope to learn on my own. If you'll allow me to ask you a question from time to time, I would consider myself more than repaid for some windows and a floor."

Ailios sat in silence for a moment. "Well, isn't that a surprise," she finally muttered almost to herself. "I suppose I'll wait to see what questions ye choose to ask, or if ye come calling to ask any at all."

With a relieved smile Fiona went to kiss the old woman on her paper-thin cheek. "Dunncraigh's aboot, so we must get back to Lattimer. I'll be back to call on ye on Thursday."

Outside, Fiona headed back toward the church where she'd left Brèaghad to graze among the tombstones. Gabriel walked behind her, but she didn't try to engage him in conversation. Whether she'd shown him anything useful or not, he had a decision to make — and it was one that would for better or worse impact her life nearly to the degree that it would his. Had she done the right thing? Her uncle wouldn't think so. Dunncraigh would likely banish her from the clan if he ever learned anything about it.

Then again, she hadn't precisely *said* anything. And even if for God knew what reason Gabriel decided to keep Lattimer, that didn't mean he would be a better landlord than the old duke had been. She supposed if he went about interfering in the wrong way, he could be a worse one. Or he could merely be absent. And she didn't think she would like that, either.

"Did ye ride here?" she asked belatedly, ducking under a tree branch to collect her mare.

"No. I walked." His palms settled on her shoulders, and he turned her to face him. "I didn't do those things for Ailios Eylar. That was you."

She shook her head. "It'd been a fortnight since she fell over that blasted hoe and cut her leg. I'd been going to see her daily. I knew she'd nae live with that infection, but I thought to make her comfortable. Ye were the one who bellowed that she should be at the castle, and that she needed fresh air and clean bedding." Fiona tapped her forefinger against his breastbone beneath his plain white shirt. "Ye made me mad, accusing me of being a half-wit, or so I told myself ye had, and so I had those things done to prove that it wouldnae have made any difference. And then she started to get better."

"Thank you for telling me."

Did he understand, then? Or was he still so occupied with looking for a way to change the impossible that he hadn't seen it? Fiona tilted her head, regarding him. At least he *looked* calmer. "Ye said when ye have a battle to fight, ye look at it as an obstacle and find a way past it. And when ye've done that, ye move on to the next battle."

"I'm not a complete idiot, Fiona," he returned, exasperation touching his voice. "You're suggesting there are battles here that I can win. And then stay on to see what victory looks like."

"And feels like. Aye. Here ye may have less use fer yer saber, though in the Highlands ye cannae be —"

He pulled her forward and kissed her. Tangling her hands into his thin shirt, she lifted on her toes to meet him more squarely. Heat speared through her, his touch flavored with both desperation and hope. Hope that she'd given him.

Finally he lifted his head again. "Your own clan chief wants me to sell Lattimer to him.

Do you truly not want me to do that?" Gray eyes seemed to gaze all the way into her soul, making her wonder what he saw there. "Do you want me to stay?"

And now it was all back on her shoulders again. She had only eleven days now by which to measure him, put against a lifetime of seeing how the leaders of her own clan regarded this castle with two names. How they regarded the cotters who lived on this land. "Aye," she said softly. "If ye mean to make a fight of it, then I want ye to stay." God help her, but it was an excuse, to say she wanted him there for the sake of the tenants. Because she couldn't say the other part, that she wanted him there for her.

Despite its name, Lattimer Castle didn't have turrets. What it did have was a widow's walk running around the perimeter of the main hall's roof, presumably so the MacKittrick females could keep watch for their men to return from battle. Like the rest of the nonessential parts of the house it was flimsy and rusting, ready to fall into the garden or the front drive at any moment.

Gabriel climbed up from the small door in the attic and made his way along the iron railing, then hiked up the peak of the roof at the center to stand at the highest point of

Lattimer. Over his head a scattering of clouds raced to join their fellows, trapped against the white peaks to the west.

All around him in every direction lay his land. The loch, the forest, the glens and valleys and ravines and foothills, the thin trails of smoke above the trees that marked the chimneys of Strouth — chance, luck, or some persistent clerk in some minister's cabinet who'd refused to let Lattimer revert to the Crown had decreed that it all belonged to him. If he wanted it.

Until the Duke of Dunncraigh had made him an offer for it, he'd never considered that he could be rid of Lattimer. The idea of being a titled landlord was so new to him, he'd just assumed that all the properties came with the title and were inseparable from it.

He turned a slow circle. The Maxwell had described a morass of never-ending trouble and despair, while Fiona wanted him to see happy, smiling tenants who came out to shake his hand every morning. The truth, of course, was somewhere in the middle. What it turned out to be, however, wasn't precisely the point.

"Am I to climb up there after you?" Kelgrove called from the walkway below. "I'm not dressed for mountaineering."

"Stay down there. It's safer. Marginally." Gabriel sat, resting his arse on the peak of the roof and bracing his feet against the sloped shingles. "I have a quandary, and I require your unfailing honesty."

"You don't want to serve at the Horse Guards," his aide commented, starting to lean against the railing and then settling for bracing his hands against it. "That's it, isn't it? I know you don't like the politics of it. And in my thinking, the first general you flattened would see your military career ended, anyway."

"You're counting on my flattening someone, then."

"I've been your aide for seven years, Your Grace," he returned, as if that explained everything. "Perhaps Wellington would give you a division. You've certainly earned one."

Brief hope touched him, but he shoved it away again. That was a part of his life he needed to give up. He already knew that. The question had become what to do next. "I'm a scrapper, Adam. I couldn't lead from some hilltop, sending notes to my regimental commanders about how to counter enemy movements. I would be miserable at it, and that would cost lives."

"You're a bloody fine strategist, sir," the sergeant said stoutly.

"Thank you, but two different people — three, counting you — have pointed something out to me today. I likely should have seen it weeks ago, but I don't think I wanted to." He kept his gaze on the loch, on the splinters of sunlight it reflected back into the sky. "I'm a duke, whether I want to be one or not. My duty here isn't to examine the ledgers and hire someone to give me accurate reports while I spend my time riding about Spain with Frenchies shooting at me."

"It isn't?"

"No. It isn't. My duty is missing sheep, sheep that are accounted for, broken fences, bare fields, sick tenants, churchyard luncheons, and a great many things I know I can't imagine. It's clearing boulders, chasing poachers, counting cattle, harvesting crops, and hosting bloody boring Society dinners, however the devil one does that."

"Begging your pardon, but that's what your steward is doing."

"That's what a steward has had to do for twenty years, because the Duke of Lattimer has been elsewhere and utterly uninterested. These people are protected by virtue of my life. It's . . . irresponsible of me to risk leaving them to fate because I have a gift for battle."

"I can't argue with that," Adam returned,

"though I will point out that you have three properties and three stewards. Why is your duty these sheep and these boulders, in particular?"

That was why he valued Adam Kelgrove's aid. If nothing else, the sergeant made him think things through, develop his argument and his strategy to fill whatever holes Kelgrove found in his line of thought. "You saw the reports on Hawthorne and Langley Park," he said aloud, naming his two more southerly estates. "In your opinion, do either of them require a change of course? Or my attention at all, for that matter?"

"In my opinion? No, they do not. They are old, stable properties, both being managed by men who have decades of experience. Which you do not." Kelgrove paused. "If you're asking whether you could take up residence at one or the other of them, of course you could, but you . . . wouldn't find it terribly challenging."

"I'd be bored out of my damned skull, you mean." In his nightmares he could imagine a softer life, sitting behind a desk and looking at figures someone else had written out, agreeing to everything his steward suggested because the man knew far more about the mechanics of the estate than he ever would. He would go riding and hunting and fishing, spend his nights drinking, and slowly go mad.

Here, though, it was different. Lattimer needed help. And it was already cursed and half ruined, which minimized the odds of him making things worse. Here had Fiona Blackstock. However much that one fact should have been weighted, to him it seemed . . . everything. It could measure against every other choice before him and still be the thing that mattered the most. But he'd never led with his heart before. Ordering men into battle, riding into cannonfire required hard resolve and logic. Why couldn't he make himself see this, see her, that same way?

"At this moment I have several reasons for wanting to remain here," he admitted, navigating through what he wanted to say as carefully as he knew how. "I have no idea if they're the right reasons."

His aide squinted one eye against the sunlight. "Miss Blackstock being one of them, I presume."

Well, he hadn't expected *that*. And if Kelgrove had figured out his obsession with his steward, others had, as well. *Fuck.* "What makes you say that?"

"You . . . look at her a great deal. And you smile. That frightened me at first, until I figured out the reason for it."

"Very amusing, Adam," he returned dryly. "Does anyone else suspect?"

"Some of the servants do. They reckon she's leading you on in exchange for more funds coming into Lattimer."

"And your opinion?"

Abruptly Kelgrove became fascinated with the rust on the railing. "She's very dedicated to this place," he finally said. "Is she aware that her clan chief wants to purchase it?"

"She is. She asked me not to sell it to him."

For the first time during the course of the conversation, Adam looked genuinely surprised. "That . . . doesn't make sense."

"It does, if you take into account my charm. And mainly, the lack of interest Dunncraigh's shown in aiding the situation here." He frowned. "That could change if he became the landlord of course, but . . ." Swearing, he dragged a hand through his hair. "I like it here, Adam. God knows I like the challenge of it. But it isn't just about me, and which assignment I want. Am I the one who can do the most good here? Or is it Dunncraigh?"

"I think that your asking the question, sir, answers it as well." Kelgrove sighed. "Despite the fact that I would rather continue to serve you someplace where the fighting is more straightforward and our foes wear uniforms, this place suits you. I've never seen you step into a situation that you didn't somehow improve by involving yourself in it. You would be dead if that were otherwise. And so would I. A hundred times over."

Gabriel looked up again, taking in the view once more. Contemplating things wasn't in his nature. He saw, assessed, and acted all within a heartbeat and with the deadliness of any finely honed weapon. If he could name the exact opposite of who and what nature had made him, this — being a duke — would be it.

Him, a duke. Not just in name, but in fact. For the rest of his life. The head of a line that at the moment had only one other member, and no heirs. And at the same time, a very, very large family of dependents in need of an effective leader. It should have terrified him. In some ways it did, but mostly when he considered the consequences of failure. And that was a familiar sensation, and one that almost felt . . . comforting.

Deciding to remain at Lattimer did provide him with an answer to the one question that had troubled him almost from the moment he'd set eyes on the dusky-haired

351

chit up to her armpits in mud. Stating, knowing Fiona belonged with him was one thing. Making it happen was another. But now, in this whirlwind of chaos, he might have just found a way.

"Well then," he said, standing to brush off his trousers and return to the precarious safety of the widow's walk. "Let's get started, shall we?"

As Fiona had said, in planning a battle he found the obstacle before him and looked for the most expedient way to go past, around, or preferably through it. In preparation for meeting with his next obstacle, Gabriel changed back into his uniform and sent word that he was to be informed as soon as Dunncraigh returned from surveying the land the duke expected he was about to own.

Before he left the bedchamber, *his* bedchamber even with that damned bed in which he couldn't sleep, Gabriel stopped to look at himself in the full-length dressing mirror. In the years since he'd put on his first uniform he'd gained some muscle and a few inches in height, and of course myriad scars both internal and external. The eager, naïve optimism had disappeared very quickly, but for the first time in over a decade he felt it again. Not as naïve, perhaps, but unmistakably hopeful. And that surprised him more than anything. Until he'd discovered *why* he felt so . . . hopeful, he meant to hold onto the sensation for dear life.

He brushed at his sleeve. This could well be the last time he wore any uniform. He didn't have to wear it *now,* but with a battle waiting on the horizon, it felt both appropriate and strategically sound. This was how Dunncraigh would see him, whatever he chose to wear. And this was how he dressed to begin a war — at least this one, last time.

The morning room gave him enough space to pace, and it was the first door at the top of the stairs. Fiona had vanished into her office, ostensibly to leave him to make his own decision, but neither of them could pretend she wasn't part of it. He wondered, though, if she'd realized just how large a role he meant for her to have in this. That would be the next battle, he imagined. He had them all lined up, ready for the saber.

"He's here," Sergeant Kelgrove said, leaning into the doorway. "Sir Hamish is still with him."

"They're connected, Hamish's lips to Dunncraigh's arse," Gabriel returned, rolling his shoulders. "Thank you."

The sergeant nodded, patting his coat pocket. "I'll be close by. Bellow if you need my pistol."

Gabriel paused at the top of the stairs to watch as the Maxwell and his entourage milled about in the foyer, commenting about profit and yield. *His* profit and yield, no doubt. "Your Grace," he said, and eight pairs of eyes lifted to look at him. "Might I have a private word with you?"

"Of course, lad."

He caught the congratulatory nod Sir Hamish sent his clan chief, but Gabriel kept his own expression neutral. Here, he was outnumbered. In the morning room the odds would be even, and he reckoned he had surprise on his side. Backing to the door, he waited until Dunncraigh joined him before shutting them in together.

"Ye've considered my offer, then," the duke began.

"I have. I didn't expect it, I have to admit."

"It's well past time MacKittrick returned to Maxwell hands," Dunncraigh said, clearly in an expansive mood. "I reckon ten thousand pounds will satisfy us both, aye?"

"That seems a low number," Gabriel returned, curious enough about Dunncraigh's strategy and motives to let the conversation play out a little. *Feint and parry, look for weaknesses.* Some things never changed, thank the devil.

"If the estate was in her prime, aye. But we both ken she's long past her glory days."

"I can't argue with that. With the textile and pottery works, though, you —"

"Lad, what ye have are two wee factories and a distillery that barely pay fer themselves, and thousands of empty acres fit fer naught but sheep. Sheep ye dunnae have. Just bringing the estate back to a profit will take time that ye dunnae want to spend here. And who knows when that curse could next cost ye still more time and money. Give her back to the Maxwells. Ye're a hero in the army, I hear. The Beast of Bussaco, or someaught. If ye want twelve thousand pounds, I'll give ye twelve thousand."

"I'm flattered," Gabriel lied, deciding the shite was deep enough. "But I'm going to have to decline."

"Wh— I didn't quite hearye."

"I'm keeping Lattimer."

He doubted Dunncraigh was rendered speechless very often, but that seemed to do it. The duke stood there in the middle of the room, staring, a hundred different emotions flitting across his face. Then anger settled in, and didn't budge.

"Is this a jest?"

"No."

"Ye've been a duke fer what, a month? And now ye decide ye're fit to manage a Scottish estate in the Highlands? Ye didnae strike me as being a madman, Lattimer. And I'm telling ye straight up — this place is too much fer ye."

"I have a steward," he returned coolly. "I'll manage."

"Ha. Yesterday ye said ye meant to replace her with yer own man. Now ye think ye can rely on her? We only allowed her to take on this job oot of pity after her brother up and vanished. She's running aboot here like a headless chicken, losing sheep, watching crops fail, and missing market dates fer wool and wheat. Aside from that, she's a Maxwell. She'll nae remain here if ye stay on."

She would damned well stay on, if he had to tie her to the bedpost. Defending her to this man would only make trouble for her — but that didn't mean Gabriel wasn't supremely tempted to begin bellowing about how much better she'd looked after the Maxwells here than Dunncraigh likely ever would. "Your plan for manufacturing and sheep doesn't leave much room for your clan here, anyway," he said instead.

Dunncraigh narrowed his eyes. "This place will break ye, Major Gabriel Forrester.

That's who ye truly are, isnae? Ye wear that red coat and ye keep my land from me, when ye havenae the faintest idea what to do with it. And a man in the Highlands who doesnae ken what he's aboot, that's a dead man."

Gabriel kept his arms loose by his sides, ready to move if Dunncraigh came after him. He hoped the old man would. "I've fought a great many battles with enemies who thought to end me, Dunncraigh. I'm still standing."

"Ye're a devil!"

"I've been called that before, too." He would have been content to leave it at that and send the duke and his party out on their arses. As he'd realized, however, this wasn't just about him. There were people to consider. People who would continue to look to Dunncraigh as their chief. "I'm not keeping Lattimer out of spite, Your Grace," he went on, trying to keep his jaw from clenching. Being magnanimous didn't suit him. "I have the means to make improvements here. Ones you might not be able to make, considering the amount you would be spending to gain it back." Ones Dunncraigh probably wouldn't make, if he meant to graze sheep.

"So ye mean to help the poor backward Highlanders where we cannae help ourselves. Damn ye, Sassenach."

"I will do what I can for my property's tenants, as is my duty," Gabriel countered. "And given what I've heard from you, I believe I have more concern for them than you do."

The Duke of Dunncraigh drew a hard breath in through his nose. "I'll tell ye what, Lattimer; ye do as ye will. We'll see how well ye fare when half yer tenants and yer steward and yer staff abandon ye. When the curse hits at ye again and again because MacKittrick doesnae want a Sassenach living here. And then I'll make ye another offer, and ye'll thank Christ fer my generosity and take it on bended knee. I know the Highlands. Ye dunnae. And the people here are mine. They arenae yers, and they nae will be."

After that last bit of vitriol the duke stalked past him to the door, yanked it open, and slammed it shut behind him. A vase near the door teetered off a shelf, and almost without thought Gabriel reached out to catch it and set it back in its place.

Perhaps Dunncraigh's threats and dire predictions would have intimidated some pampered English lordling. For him, though, the list of challenges and impossible disasters seemed more like a typical duty roster, even if the assignments themselves were different. It would have been much more dismaying to think he might be bored.

With a grin Gabriel went to inform Fleming that their guests were to be gone by sunset. And next he meant to find himself a bed he could actually sleep in. It needed to be large enough for two.

CHAPTER THIRTEEN

Fiona listened. The fate of Lattimer —
MacKittrick — Castle waited down the
hallway somewhere, decided between a man
who didn't want to be a duke and a duke
who'd been neglecting his own people.
She'd done what she could, what she hoped
was best for the tenants, but if she knew
one thing about Gabriel Forrester, it was
that he would make a decision swiftly, and
then act on it just as decisively. Which decision he would make, however, she had no
idea.

The hands of the small clock on the shelf
moved so slowly she could almost swear
they were creeping backward. An hour, then
two. No gunshots, no shouting, no bagpipes
calling men to battle — that should have
been a good sign, unless it meant that Gabriel had agreed to sell the estate to the
Maxwell. Or that one of them had murdered
the other one. "Oh, this is too much," she

muttered, and stomped for the door. Someone was going to tell her what had happened, or someone was going to get punched in the nose.

Out in the hallway the silence continued. With over a hundred people in the house, the lack of noise both surprised and unsettled her. The . . . aloneness of it, though, didn't have as much to do with absent servants as it did with the realization of how much she'd come to depend on the presence of Gabriel Forrester in her life. And however much she tried to twist the answer into concern over the land and the tenants, she had to admit, just to herself, that she wanted him there, and she wanted him with her.

A loud thud from the direction of the stairs made her jump. "Hello?" she called, making her way around the corner. And then she stopped, blinking. The house wasn't empty, after all. "What the devil are ye doing, Hugh?"

The footman looked up from the massive mattress he and three other servants wrestled down the main staircase like a great, floppy wall. "It wouldnae fit doon the back stairs, Miss Fiona," the footman grunted. "We'll have it cleared oot in a moment."

"But what are ye doing with it?"

"His Grace said to burn it. All those feathers'll make a great stink, but he said he didnae care aboot that and it was fit for neither man nor beast."

The meeting had finished, then. But what had come of it? Once the lads got past the landing with the behemoth, she headed up the stairs. Someone up there was hammering, and two maids laden with a large buck's head passed her on the way to the attic. Either a herd of elephants had found their way into Gabriel's bedchamber, or someone was taking an axe to the room. That didn't bode well. Her heart settled into a fast, worried tattoo.

Leaning cautiously into the doorway, she caught sight of Gabriel standing on a footstool and tearing the dark green hangings down from the skeleton of his four-poster bed. Behind him Kelgrove and three additional footmen dragged the massive wardrobe toward the door.

"What's all this?" she asked, straightening.

Gabriel hopped down from his perch and tossed the heavy wad of material onto the floor. He didn't seem angry; in fact, he looked . . . pleased. And she still had no idea what that meant, damn it all. The man likely smiled at cannonfire. "I'm turning this bed into kindling," he said.

"It looks like ye're turning the entire room into kindling. Any particular reason?"

"I'm making it more livable," he returned. "Speaking of which, did you know half the knickknacks on the shelves back there have strings tied to them? It's almost as if someone were planning to trick whoever might be sleeping in here into thinking the room was haunted."

"Hm. Fancy that." She eyed him. A half smile on his lean face, a plain shirt with the sleeves rolled to the elbows, and buckskin trousers stuffed into his worn boots, he looked more like a servant than a duke. But then he was like no other duke she'd ever met, anyway. He certainly had nothing in common with the Duke of Dunncraigh. She'd never expected that to be something she thought of as positive, but that was precisely how she saw it. Now, anyway. "There are a plentitude of other bedchambers up here, ye ken."

"Yes, but this is the master bedchamber. My bedchamber. Connected to my study. And the sound of the chimney moaning lulls me to sleep."

His bedchamber. There were only a very limited number of ways to interpret that statement, and she took a quick breath. Her gaze on him, she waved her fingers at the other men in the room. "Lads, give me a moment to discuss someaught with His Grace, will ye?"

Kelgrove stretched his back. "We need to take that other bed apart and haul it in here, anyway," he muttered, leading the way out the door.

Once the men were gone, Fiona shoved a chair out of the way and closed the door. "*Yer* bedchamber?" she repeated. "Ye've decided fer certain nae to sell it, then?"

"You make a very compelling argument." He walked up to her. "I hope you've thought this through."

Oh, thank goodness. "Me? Ye're the one giving up one life fer another, Gabriel."

Light gray eyes held hers. "I'm not the only one."

"Ye mean Kelgrove? Is he staying on?"

"If I can find something interesting enough to keep him occupied. But no, I don't mean Kelgrove."

Heat slid through her, but she wanted him to say the words. "What are ye talking aboot?"

He reached out, brushing a strand of hair out of her face. "I told Dunncraigh I would be keeping Lattimer, and he yelled a great deal. He assured me that I'll lose half my tenants, my entire staff, and my steward by sunset, being that he's the Maxwell and I'm an intruding Sassenach."

She hadn't considered that. Gabriel's presence was supposed to aid the tenants, not drive them away. Cold worry slid through her gut. "Is Dunncraigh still here?"

Both of his eyebrows lifted. "Are you suggesting I change my mind?"

Briefly she wondered if any threats not accompanied by a weapon ever troubled him at all. "Nae. But I do think I should gather the staff and speak with 'em before he begins spewing threats. Some of the folk here *will* listen to him, especially if ye dunnae counter his venom."

His amused expression darkened a little. Eventually he would realize that most men and women weren't fearless, weren't so assured they could make their own way in the world. "We'll both speak to the staff," he said after a moment. "I assume we can fit them all in the ballroom."

Fiona turned on her heel. "I'll see to it."

He caught her around the waist, pulling her back against him. "See to it in a moment."

"Gabriel, he could be causing all kinds of mayhem already. If he orders the clan to leave before we can speak to them, ye *could* lose most of them. I'm nae jesting aboot that."

His iron grip didn't loosen. "You didn't answer my question. You're not going anywhere until you do."

She gave up shoving at his arms and leaned her head back against his shoulder to look up at his face. If any other man had ever tried manhandling her like this, she would have kicked him right in the sensitive bits. When Gabriel held her, the world felt . . . slower, as if time stretched. She felt it even now, when heaven knew she had urgent matters to see to. Both of them did.

"What question, then?" she asked, trying to sound exasperated rather than infatuated. She didn't have time today to be infatuated.

"I asked if you've thought this through." His grip tightened a fraction. "You do everything you can to help the people around you. I admire you for that."

"Thank ye."

"I've just defied your clan chief. At sunset I'll set him outside on his arse if he hasn't left before then. He wants *you* to prove your loyalty to clan Maxwell by abandoning Lattimer." He lowered his face to her hair, his breath a warm, whispering caress. "Are you ready to stand against your own clan?"

Christ in a kilt. "I'm nae standing against

my clan. I'm standing against one man who happens to be my clan chief. A man who's done a piss-poor job of looking after his own."

"That's semantics, Fiona. Some of these people whom you've known all your life, people whom you've helped more than they'll ever realize, *will* call you a traitor and turn their backs on you."

Fiona started to protest that such a thing would never happen. As she considered it, though, she kept her silence. As much as she'd tried to provide for them, some of her neighbors and kin had little but the dirt beneath their feet. All they owned was pride — pride at being Maxwells of clan Maxwell.

Gabriel released her, moving around to face her. "I need to know that whatever happens," he said, taking her hands in his, "I'm not going to lose you." A quick scowl contorted his face. "Your support, I mean."

Her heart stuttered. He might have altered what he said, and clumsily at that, but she'd heard it. She would never forget it, and the keen yearning it made her feel. Being essential to anyone, much less a man as self-possessed as Gabriel Forrester — she couldn't remember ever feeling that before.

The question, though, remained — if she stayed on at Lattimer, she would likely lose her clan. She had a better reason than most to stay on, and even so the idea of not having that vast family at her back still gave her pause. How could she ask them to stay?

He continued to gaze at her, his expression unreadable. "Am I asking too much? We haven't known each other for long, after all. How does Shakespeare have Henry the Fifth say it? 'I speak to thee plain soldier.' I couldn't write you a rhyme to save my life. I'm not a master of the clever turn of phrase. If you —"

"Ye'll nae lose me," she whispered, lifting up on her toes. "Or my support."

Freeing her hands from his, she slipped them over his shoulders, drawing his face down for a deep slow kiss that stole her breath and eased her worry. They would think of something, because the alternative would be worse than failure. And neither of them could afford to fail.

Taken all together, the number of staff and servants Fiona had hired over the past four years was quite impressive, Gabriel decided, following her into the castle's huge ballroom. Nearly twice as many would fit in there and still have space to dance a jig, but as they all — the stable boys, the gardeners, cooks, footmen, maids, and men and women from half a hundred other positions he was certain Fiona had invented — finished shuffling around to look at him, it occurred to him that she'd been commanding nearly as many troops as he had.

"Good afternoon, everyone," Fiona said. "As ye know, the Duke of Dun—"

"Is it true, Miss Fiona," a male voice called out, "that anyone here after sunset will be exiled from clan Maxwell?"

That caused another burst of noise, much of it angry and directed at him. Good; none of this was allowed to fall on Fiona's shoulders. Not when she'd worked so hard to keep all these people — and all the others on the property — clothed and fed and employed. Putting his fingers to his mouth, he blew an earsplitting whistle.

The voices sputtered and died down to a low, concerned murmur. Once he had their attention, Gabriel dragged over a chair and stepped up onto it. "The Duke of Dunncraigh offered to purchase Lattimer from me today," he stated in a carrying voice. "I turned him down."

The voices erupted again, and he glimpsed Kelgrove by one of the doors, the sergeant's hand in his pocket. Gabriel had seen mobs before, seen what they could do to a man with nothing to wield but anger and their bare hands. He put his own hand up again.

"Dunncraigh likes the textile and pottery works, and the distillery, of course, and he likes all the glens and glades and open fields, because they're a fit place for him to graze his sheep."

"We dunnae need the fields," a woman's voice shouted. "He can do as he wants with 'em."

Fiona pulled a second chair over next to his, and reached a hand up to him. When she stood beside him, she faced the men and women, some of whom had likely been employed here since before she was born. "I asked my uncle Hamish once how many servants he employs at Fennoch Abbey. Eighteen, he told me. Now this hoose is bigger, but Dunncraigh has his own grand estate already. We'll suppose fer the sake of argument that if he owned this place and if he didnae tear it to the ground as nae better than a ruin, he would send his firstborn, the Marquis of Stapp, to live here. Do any of ye think Donnach Maxwell would be willing to pay the salaries fer a hundred of ye? Nae. Two thirds of ye would be turned away. And then ye *would* need the fields, or ye'd be off to the workhoose in Inverness. There are Maxwells there right now, ye ken — but nae a one who hails from Lattimer."

"For the past four years," Gabriel took up, fighting the growing urge to kiss her right there in front of everyone, "Miss Blackstock has been keeping two sets of ledgers; one for the old duke and his solicitors, to keep them away from here, and the other for all of you, the villagers at Strouth and scattered across the property, and the workers in the factories. *She* did this. Not Dunncraigh. In fact, the only thing I can find that the Maxwell has done for you is to collect his tithes."

"But he's our clan chief!"

"Withoot the Maxwell, we'd have nae protection from the English and their soldiers!"

"*I'm* English," he countered. "And a soldier. Or I was one until this morning, when I realized I had to choose between a war on the Continent and keeping peace here. With all of you. I'm not a clan chief. And I know most of you refuse to see me as this castle's laird because I'm not a Highlander. What I *am,* however, is here. If you'll allow it, I mean to stay."

"What aboot the MacKittrick curse?" someone else, Fleming, he thought, asked. "If the castle went to Dunncraigh, the curse and all its ill fortune would be finished!"

"Nae!" Fiona said loudly. "Whether ye

believe in the curse or nae, ye know the words of it. And there's nae a mention of it ending when a Maxwell takes MacKittrick back. Old MacKittrick said the land would be cursed until an Englishman becomes a Highlander, someaught every one of us always reckoned to be impossible." She put a hand on Gabriel's arm, her fingers warm even through his sleeve. "Here's an Englishman. I dunnae ken whether we can make him a true Highlander or nae, but we can damned well try."

"— I couldnae say," Hugh the footman commented as Fiona passed by one of the small sitting rooms, and she slowed to listen. "But if Miss Fiona thinks he could make a go of it, that's a damned sight better than watching MacKittrick crumble aboot my ears."

"Ye should keep yer voice doon, lad," Fleming's familiar voice returned. "Dunncraigh and his men havenae left yet. Oscar says Lattimer was oot shoveling shite with the rest of 'em trying to save the pasture. The Maxwell might at least have given us the seed, but he didnae. Miss Fiona had to go hat in hand to clan MacLawry to buy it."

She smiled. This, today, had actually been

the easy bit. Hope was fairly simple to spread. The next weeks, though, the first time something went awry, *that* would be the moment to watch for. Even knowing that, though, this afternoon she felt it, too. Gabriel — it made sense that he'd learned which words to use to inspire his troops, but no oath bound anyone to him here. And yet with him beside her, she didn't feel alone. She hadn't even realized how alone she'd been until he'd arrived to set everything on its ear. Of all the things she'd thought when he'd dragged her out of that mudhole, it hadn't been that she would find him a partner, a lover, and a friend.

And while of course Lattimer was his, and all of the ultimate decisions were his, she hadn't yet felt pushed aside, undervalued, or ignored. Perhaps it was because he had so little experience as a landowner, and she supposed it could change with time. But he listened to her opinion and asked her advice. By all the saints and sinners, she'd never before met *any* man who did that and didn't consider himself less because of it. It had certainly improved her opinion of him at the beginning.

Slowing again, she touched a hand to her lips. Through the hallway window she spied a herd of deer grazing along the crest of the hill, while below them a laden hay wagon rolled along the rutted front drive toward the stable, a dog running alongside, tongue out and tail wagging. Gazing out, she felt . . . content, and at the same time as if something unexpected and marvelous lay just beyond the horizon. Delight tingled through her at the oddest moments, making her grin. And it all centered around not the property, but the man. Gabriel Forrester.

"So now ye figure the Sassenach's the one to break the curse, do ye?" Hamish Paulk's voice drawled from down the hallway.

Her shoulders stiffened, the warmth of her insides cooling, as if she'd just been dumped into Loch Sìbhreach. "I figure he'll see that we have seed fer planting, that the irrigation trenches are repaired, and that the hoose keeps standing," she commented, turning around to face her uncle as he approached. "Whether that breaks the curse or nae, it's someaught."

"And ye reckon the Maxwell wouldnae have done the very same thing? And that his attention wouldnae have benefited every Maxwell fer a hundred square miles?"

"I dunnae care aboot a hundred miles. His sheep would have driven oot every Maxwell fer fifteen square miles," she returned, deliberately using the size of the

Lattimer estate. Fiona narrowed her eyes. Never in her life had she spoken like that to her uncle. Instead of being mortified, however, she felt . . . strong. Because even though Gabriel had closeted himself with Sergeant Kelgrove to draft letters to his London solicitors, she wasn't alone. "Ye and my grandfather and his grandfather have been the only chieftains here fer a hundred years, Uncle. Dunncraigh's lived quite well withoot a chieftain at MacKittrick Castle. And withoot paying us any heed at all, in fact, except to complain aboot who owns the property."

"A Sassenach owns th—"

"This property would be naught but grazing land fer Domhnull Maxwell's sheep, and ye know it. He could look well by nae displacing anyone else aboot Dunncraigh, and still have space to make his money. He looks after his own. That hasnae included us since the Crown took MacKittrick."

"But it would have included here again, if he owned MacKittrick. I've yet to meet anyone who can guess what the duke has up his sleeve, much less a female with but four years' experience managing a ruin of an estate. Ye're selfish, lass, convincing the major to stay on so ye dunnae lose yer own position. I'm ashamed of ye. Ye're nae better than yer brother, making a big noise when ye should keep yer damned mouth shut."

She blinked. "What 'noise' did Kieran make?" she asked, ice gripping her chest.

Her uncle leaned closer. "One nae as loud as the one ye made today, Fiona." He straightened. "Ye mark that while ye watch the Sassenach change everything, bring in his Sassenach staff and a highborn Sassenach wife to bear him the next Duke of Lattimer. In six months, lass, ye'll be nae more than a maid, if the duchess allows ye to stay at all. Ye'll clean his piss bowl and be his whore, and ye'll nae be a Maxwell ever again." He turned around to walk back up the hallway. "Never again."

Fiona stood where she was for a moment, her back to the tranquil view out in front of MacKittrick. Lattimer, rather. Hamish hadn't touched a hair on her head, but all the same she felt like she'd been slapped. She'd come to welcome the fact that Gabriel had the power to stand against Dunncraigh, but at the same time she'd forgotten something vital. Gabriel didn't talk like a duke or act like one, and she'd never heard of any aristocrat at all who insisted his steward call him by his Christian name.

But he *was* a duke. One of considerable wealth and property. And given both his strong sense of duty and the ramshackle way he'd inherited, he likely would decide to marry and have children, and do it fairly quickly. If nothing else, he wouldn't want to see Lattimer abandoned to the fates again. And of course she'd been the one to convince him of that.

Generally she appreciated irony. Not today, however. She didn't consider herself particularly naïve, either, but had she been? When she'd spoken to the staff earlier, she'd meant every word she said. She'd imagined the next months, the next years, and in her dreams it had been the two of them, Gabriel and her, together. They would reclaim MacKittrick together. But none of her daydreams had concerned themselves with English laws and proper aristocratic wives for the most aristocratic of titles.

A tear plopped onto the back of her hand. Shaking herself, she wiped the wet off on her skirt, then rubbed her arm across her face. What mattered was that the land and the people prospered. Who accomplished that deed didn't matter. Nothing else mattered.

"Miss Fiona?"

Jumping, she looked up. "Dolidh. Ye

startled me."

"I was just asking, miss," the maid said, while a trio of others waited a few feet away, "do ye truly believe His Grace — Lattimer, I mean — is the one to break the curse?"

"Aye. I truly believe he'll be the one to make MacKittrick a proud, grand place again."

The girl grinned. "And what of ye and His Grace?"

Fiona's cheeks warmed, despite her best effort to remain cool and collected. *Good glory.* They knew? "Beg pardon?"

The others giggled. "Dolidh says he's sweet on ye," Tilly took up. "And Niall Garretson told Oscar Ritchie he saw ye kissing oot by the mill."

"Well, I say ye shouldnae be spreading such idle gossip," Fiona managed, fighting against the renewed urge to cry. Tomorrow — or the next day, perhaps — she would have figured it out, how to turn away those questions with a smile. Today she wanted to stop thinking about anything.

"Och, well, then," Dolidh returned, still clearly amused. "He's a fit man all alone in the Highlands. I'd wager he's aching by now fer a willing lass to warm his bed."

Oh, now she wanted to begin pulling the maid's hair. For Boudicca's sake, she had no idea what to feel, except that she knew she hurt. Damn Uncle Hamish, anyway. He might have let her be a fool for a few more days. She was much happier being foolish.

Tilly abruptly gasped. A heartbeat later all four maids had scurried for the stairs. Fiona looked up the hallway, then ducked inside the music room and closed the door, pushing down on the handle as she did so to keep it from squeaking. *Damnation.*

She'd known the Duke of Dunncraigh was still at Lattimer. Somehow she'd expected, though, that he and his men would pack their things and stomp directly from their guest bedchambers to the front door. What had they been doing in the north wing, tramping the floor looking for any sympathetic souls?

The door's handle lowered, and she hurriedly backed deeper into the room. Hamish railing at her had been harrowing enough. She wasn't certain she could bear hearing the Duke of Dunncraigh hurling the same ugly arguments at her, particularly when they made so much sense. And what Hamish had said about Kieran and the "noise" her brother had made . . . She didn't even want to think about it.

To her surprise it was Artur Maxwell, though, who strolled into the room. Sending her a sideways glance made a bit comical because of his black eye, he wandered over to the pianoforte and pressed a few of the keys. High-pitched discord echoed into the room, oddly reminding her that she needed to have the instrument tuned.

"If ye're here to make threats and howl at me like a banshee, Hamish Paulk already gave me that speech." She folded her arms across her chest.

He sat down at the pianoforte, flipping the tail of his English coat out behind him, and began playing a jaunty Scots tune. The words, as she recalled, were exceedingly bawdy and rather insulting. Artur played well, better than she did, more than likely.

"So ye're here to serenade me?" she shot out. "I'm nae impressed."

The tune banged to a halt. "Hamish Paulk is a small-minded man who'd cut off his own feet if my uncle said he was too tall." He sighed. "That said, ye ken Uncle Domhnull knows it was ye who told the servants here they could trust Lattimer. Ye did a fair job of turning a Sassenach major from the scourge of MacKittrick into its bloody savior. And I think that'll be very interesting once yer English soldier takes a wrong step and the lot of ye realize he cannae walk across the surface of the loch."

"He'll do as any good landlord ought, and that's all any of us has the right to expect."

Artur laughed. "It may be all any of ye has the right to expect, but ye ken ye've made every lass and lad on his land think he'll be performing miracles." Standing, he sketched a bow before he turned back to the door. "Dunnae trouble yerself though, Fiona. When he falls, the Duke of Dunncraigh will be aboot to set things right again fer all the Maxwells."

"Fer all the Maxwells but me, ye mean. Go on and make yer threat; it'll itch at ye until ye scratch it."

"Ye're mistaken, lass. He'll set things right fer ye, certain as anything. The two of ye may find ye disagree aboot what that entails, though."

With that he slipped out the door again. After all the clever turns of phrase and sideways threats from Artur and Hamish, she almost wished now that it had been Dunncraigh stomping in and simply bellowing at her. At least Artur had only spat his venom about how Gabriel would eventually stumble. All in all, she would have to say that Hamish's words had cut more deeply.

If she wanted proof that she was no longer welcome in clan Maxwell, though, they'd provided it. However this went, she, at the least, could never go back. And if her uncle was right about what Gabriel would do next, and it certainly made logical sense, she *was* still alone. And always would be, now.

She could of course try telling herself that it didn't matter. The tenants and staff and workers here could call themselves whatever they wished — clan Maxwell, or not. As long as someone who cared about them remained on the premises, she'd far exceeded her own best expectations. So if Gabriel didn't care for her as much as she'd come to care for him, it didn't matter. Except that it did matter, but only to her.

CHAPTER FOURTEEN

The last thing Gabriel had ever expected to do when he set out to restore order to some unseen property in the Scottish Highlands was to set up a rebel encampment in the middle of enemy territory and then ask his former foes to join him in deposing their own ruler. What surprised him was that so many of them had agreed to do so. According to Kelgrove, less than a half-dozen of his hundred servants had slipped out the back way, belongings in hand. Generally he met traitors with the point of his sword, but he let them go without word or ceremony. If they chose to return by the end of the week, he would allow that, as well. This might well be battle, but it was the least straightforward one he'd ever fought. And the one with the most doubtful — and yet important — outcome.

The number of converts to his cause was likely why the trio of black coaches were on the front drive and stacked with luggage. If Dunncraigh hadn't been so masterfully outflanked by a slip of a lass who possessed a heart as big as the Highlands, it might well have been a different duke fleeing the premises. But there they were, the Scottish duke and his men, descending the main stairs to join him in the foyer.

But where was the lass? He'd assumed she would be somewhere in the background flitting about — though "flitting" didn't seem the right word for a woman with a tongue as sharp and nerves as steady as hers — to calm the worries of the staff, but Dunncraigh's exit would look much more definitive if Fiona stood beside him in the foyer to watch the Maxwell depart.

Just as the duke reached the main floor, though, Gabriel felt her arrive, a rush of warmth and electricity directly beside him. At that moment, it might have been damned Bonaparte himself standing there glaring at him from the foyer, and Gabriel wouldn't have so much as blinked. Confidence, ease — he was accustomed to feeling them, but not because someone else stood with him. Because *she* stood with him. Without looking back at her, he descended the stairs.

"I'll nae shake yer hand, Lattimer," Dunncraigh said, pausing as Hamish Paulk helped him on with his coat. "I consider ye and all who stand with ye to be scoundrels and traitors, none of ye worthy of —"

"Good-bye, Your Grace," Gabriel interrupted, to stop any further threats and insults to his servants. "Best of luck with your sheep."

Fiona's fingers brushed his, though he wasn't certain if it was out of appreciation or because he was pushing too hard. Despite her insistence that this was all about the good of his tenants, however, he knew it was also about strategy and positioning. And he damned well wanted to remind everyone in earshot about where the Maxwell's priorities lay.

He followed the men outside. Above him he had no doubt every window was filled with eyes gazing down at the drive. They would see their laird leaving, but they would also see him staying, Fiona beside him. And as far as he was concerned, that last bit was a sight to which they'd best become accustomed.

"Ye remember my offer, Lattimer," the duke said, pausing halfway inside his massive coach. "After ye've failed here I'll still purchase the land from ye. And any *loyal* Maxwells will be welcome to stay." His steely gaze flicked to Fiona and back again.

"Thank you for wishing us ill. I'm certain we'll all give your words the weight they deserve."

"Bah."

With a last glare Dunncraigh vanished inside the coach. Gabriel stepped forward and closed the vehicle's door himself, so the footman wouldn't have to do it.

As the coaches rolled away down the rutted drive, he turned his back on them to face Fiona. The sarcastic comment he'd been about to make faded as he took her in. She'd been crying. And that was unacceptable. "A word with you, Miss Blackstock?" he said, motioning her toward the castle's massive front doors.

"Of course."

She led the way into one of the dark, windowless storage rooms directly off the foyer. Gabriel took a candle from a hallway sconce and followed her inside, shutting the door behind him. The room was littered with rolled carpets and chairs badly in need of new upholstery. He set the candle on a frayed seat beside the door and faced her.

"What's wrong?"

Her responding laugh had an edge of hysteria to it. " 'What's wrong'?" she repeated. "Ye — we — just threw my clan chief oot the door."

Gabriel scowled. "And?"

"And what?"

"You knew what we were doing." A thought abruptly occurred to him, and he snapped his mouth shut over what he'd been about to say. Something inside his chest wrenched, painfully. He didn't like the sensation. "You think you made a mistake."

With a scowl she rushed forward to put a hand over his mouth. The candle flickered wildly. "Nae, I dunnae think I made a mistake," she hissed. "And keep yer voice doon, or ye'll open that door to find everyone's fled the hoose."

Taking her hand, he lowered it from his mouth to his chest. Touching her was always better than not doing so. "Then why were you crying?"

She tried to tug her hand away, but he held it there. "What in the world makes ye think I was weeping?"

Gabriel tilted his head, wishing he had more light with which to study her face. "I may not be an expert in female behavior," he retorted, "but I know what the aftermath of crying looks like. And since you're dancing about the question, I have to assume it's either something I've done, or something you think you've done. Or haven't done."

"Well, ye're wrong. So ye ken even less than ye thought ye did."

"By God, you're exasperating. Just tell me, will you?"

She met his gaze, briefly, then looked away again. With a clearly irritated sigh she jerked at her hand again, and this time he let her go. When she started for the door, though, he shifted around her to block her escape. Fiona shoved at his shoulder, but he refused to budge. Whatever troubled her, he was beginning to feel quite alarmed. Wounds, he could manage. But she wasn't physically injured.

"I cannae talk to ye with ye looking at me like that," she burst out.

He didn't know what it was about his gaze that was so distressing, but he did know how to remedy it. Licking his thumb and forefinger, he reached over and snuffed out the candle. "Then talk to me now," he said into the darkness.

And it *was* dark. He couldn't even make out his hand in front of his face. He could hear Fiona, though, her surprised breath as blackness enveloped them, the fumble of her hand as she brushed against a chair back and then gripped it.

"Ye're a madman, Sassenach," she muttered, the veriest touch of amusement in

388

her voice.

Well. He considered that to be progress. "I asked you a question, Fiona. Why were you crying?"

"Dunnae ye have more pressing matters to worry over?"

"Other matters, yes. More pressing ones, no."

"Fer God's sake." She took a breath. "Fine. Uncle Hamish had words with me. They cut a wee bit deeper than I expected."

Ah, good. A target. "How so?"

He was quite certain she growled. "He's a widower. Did ye know that?"

"No." But he did make note of it. Hamish Paulk wouldn't leave anyone behind when Gabriel killed him.

"Dunncraigh's after him to remarry. The duke gave him a choice of three sisters. They're from a good family, and the marriage will strengthen the bonds of the clan."

Clearly she was on her way somewhere, so he kept his silence, his face turned to where he knew she stood even if he couldn't see her there. He could still conjure her, though, every curve, the soft, curling dusk of her hair, her eyes as black as the darkness around them. The warmth of her skin, the delight of her laughter — the Fiona Blackstock he saw in his mind stood as vibrant

389

and compelling as the actual lass before him.

"Ye're from good family, whether ye knew it or nae," she finally went on. "Old Lattimer's line was nearly snuffed oot. Ye cannae let that happen again, or who knows what'll happen nae just here, but at yer other properties, too. Ye're the beginning of a new dynasty, Gabriel. Ye need to find yerself a lass from a respected family, an aristocratic one, and marry and have bairns." She sniffed.

"And that makes you weep?"

"I'll . . . I'll miss our . . . our friendship, is all. Is that so daft?" she demanded damply.

For a moment he listened to her sniffling. This concept of him marrying had evidently come from her conversation with Sir Hamish, and she'd said it had cut her. And if something in all that had hurt her . . . He smiled in the darkness. "Would you say I'm a straightforward man, Fiona?" he asked.

"Aye. That ye are."

"Then when I say I can't even imagine selecting some dainty finishing-school heiress, you would believe me?"

Silence. "What ye cannae imagine now and what might happen in six months are two very different things, Gabriel."

Well, he was very much the living example

of that. He could announce that he already had a bride in mind, but that was more likely to begin another argument about how he had no idea what it meant to be a duke. She preferred deeds to words, anyway. He meant to provide her with deeds aplenty. And when she looked at him and saw results rather than her very determined hope, he would say the words. All of them.

But he couldn't leave her to dwell on Hamish Paulk's words, either. Those ugly things could defeat both of them before they had a chance to begin. "I promise that I don't give a damn how your uncle thinks my life should proceed. And I promise that you will never be alone as long as my heart is beating." Again he had to hold himself back; this didn't seem the time for words he'd only been repeating to himself for the past day or so. "Does that suffice for today?"

"Gabriel, ye dunnae —"

"Does that suffice, Fiona?" he repeated, more forcefully.

Another surprised breath. "But ye cannae, because —"

"Do you believe me?" he insisted, taking a careful step in the direction of her voice.

Her sigh didn't sound particularly happy. "Aye."

"I'm sorry. Was that 'I' or 'aye'?" he asked,

trying to put in the inflection she used with the latter word. He took another step, banged his shin, and corrected course.

"That's nae amusing," she retorted.

"How do you think I feel?" he countered. "I just promised you support and friendship, and you —"

"I said 'aye.' Yes. It sounds grand."

That stopped him. "Am I saying the wrong thing?" he asked slowly. "I did warn you that I've had very little experience with personal entanglements."

"Ye're going to have experience with me punching ye in the head if ye dunnae stop trying to reassure me, ye lummox."

His seeking fingers touched cloth, and he closed his hand over her hip. "Then I'll stop reassuring you. I'm here. I'm not going anywhere. There is no woman in my thoughts but you, Fiona."

He could feel her shaking. If she had truly been speaking of nothing but friendship, if he was just the instrument through which she could save her beloved MacKittrick, he'd likely just doomed them all. Love, he was swiftly discovering, was not the wisest of emotions. It was, however, the one most difficult to ignore. And quite possibly the most difficult to prove to a stubborn Highlands lass.

A finger poked him in the eye. "Damnation!"

"Oh! Oh, I'm so sorry," Fiona exclaimed. "I wanted to touch yer face."

He blinked tears away. "You did, in a manner of speaking. You were going to slap me, I suppose?"

She reached out again, more carefully, touching his ear and then cupping his cheek. "I wasnae going to slap ye," she whispered, and her lips brushed his. "And I'll nae abandon ye."

Gabriel closed his eyes, wrapping his hands around her waist and pulling her against him. He wasn't alone, either; he didn't have to do this alone.

"Ye spin my world aboot, Gabriel," she murmured against his mouth. "But heaven help me, I believe ye."

Less than a fortnight ago he'd arrived at Lattimer, and in so doing had upended her entire life. Almost from the beginning he'd known what he wanted of her. Luckily logic and facts had formed the bridge, because his heart had already leaped across the river. All *she* had to keep herself afloat was hope, and for some reason the belief that he would do as he promised. Before he proposed to Fiona, before he declared himself to her, he meant to give her more than a promise. He meant to give her proof.

The trio of coaches stopped well into the trees and out of sight of even the highest rooftops of Lattimer. The door of the lead coach opened, and the Duke of Dunncraigh stepped to the ground, Sir Hamish Paulk on his heels like a faithful dog.

Once they emerged, Ian Maxwell kicked his heels into his gelding's ribs and made his way down the hillside to the road. Then he dismounted, removed his wool tam, and bowed. "Yer Grace, Sir Hamish."

"Ye made it look like thievery," Dunncraigh snapped. "I wanted accidents."

"I'd already brought doon the cliff and moved half the flock before Lattimer arrived." He shrugged. "I didnae know he'd be so curious. And I'd nae idea he'd be a fighter."

"He's a damned devil, is what he is," Hamish grumbled.

Dunncraigh put up a hand. "Spitting and growling doesnae accomplish anything. Lattimer's the new savior here — fer the moment. The clan'll see him fer who he is once anything turns ill." He fixed his hard gaze on Ian. "We tried draining resources, but now we're against a man willing to lose blunt to keep his hold on this place."

"Aye," Ian agreed. "He does seem a stubborn, proud sort."

"It isnae aboot ruining finances any longer. It's aboot the curse. Ye drive it doon their throats, lad. I want Lattimer to beg me to purchase this land so he can be rid of it. It's time fer the Sassenach to go. This is Maxwell land. Ye ken, lad?"

Ian put his hat back on his head. "I ken." He hesitated. If he didn't press now, though, he'd likely never get another chance. And he'd definitely never get a better one. "And Fiona Blackstock?"

Sir Hamish spat over his shoulder. "Do with her as ye want. She's as useless as her brother was. Neither of them owns an ounce of loyalty to their own clan. I'm done with her."

Swinging back up on the gelding, Ian nodded. "Consider it done, Laird Dunncraigh."

"If ye dunnae see to it, I'll burn Lattimer to the ground."

"My lads and I willnae fail ye. Ye've given me all the incentive I need, Yer Grace."

Gratitude from the chief of clan Maxwell, money, and now Fiona. As the coaches departed and he trotted back up the hill, Ian grinned. The mighty Duke of Lattimer wouldn't know what hit him.

"Read it to me," Gabriel said, stroking the straight razor along his right cheek. "Your voice makes everything sound more palatable."

Fiona watched the sure-handed, soapy glide for a moment, unexpectedly mesmerized. It had been so long since the castle had seen anything resembling traditional domesticity, and Gabriel Forrester's bedchamber would have been the last place she expected to find it. If she kept staring, though, he would accuse her of being softheaded. And if there was one thing she was not, it was softheaded.

Smoothing the missive against her knee, she lowered her gaze to the neat, precise writing. The solicitor probably used a ruler to measure the height of each letter. " 'Yer Grace,' " she read aloud, " 'We can of course accommodate yer request to pay from yer accounts the goods ye've ordered to be delivered to Lattimer, as well as freeing more funds fer yer use in Scotland.' "

"Well, that wasn't as bad as I expected," he commented, moving on to his left cheek. He took more care there, moving the razor parallel to his scar rather than over it.

"Does shaving there hurt ye?" she asked, leaning closer.

"No. I'm just trying to avoid gouging myself." His light-eyed reflection gazed at her from the dressing mirror. "You're not helping."

"Fine, ye ungrateful lout." Resolutely she returned her attention to the letter. " 'As we have been charged, by ye, with overseeing yer investments, however,' " she went on, " 'I feel we have a duty to inform ye that yer stated plans to restore the Lattimer property are disproportional with regard to the income therefrom derived.' "

"Hm."

"That means ye'll be putting in more than ye'll be getting oot," she translated.

He made a sound that might have been a chuckle. "I prefer your way with words, my lass. Go on."

She grinned as much at the way he'd addressed her as his good humor. As he'd said, whatever else happened in their lives, they stood together. As for the fast patter of her heart, she would keep that to herself. Aye, she'd fallen head over heels for him, but Gabriel didn't need to know that. He had other, far more important, things on his mind. " 'In addition,' " she continued, " 'ye havenae provided us with instruction as to the budgetary requirements of yer Cornwall and Devonshire properties, which could result in their maintenance and repair needs nae being met in the upcoming fiscal year.' " Fiona scowled. "Ye cannae neglect Hawthorne or Langley Park, Gabriel."

"I won't. I'll send letters this evening to my stewards there and ask for their — what was it? — budgetary requirements. Is there more?"

"Mostly some reminders aboot how long these soliciting lads have represented the Lattimer interests and how they look forward to continuing to do so." She skimmed through the rest of the letter. "And one more important bit. 'Please understand that if ye continue to put this amount of money toward yer least profitable property over an extended period, ye will be in the position of overseeing nae a shrinking income, but a negative one, which situation cannae, of course, be sustained withoot putting ye in danger of losing assets.' And then it's signed and cosigned by a half-dozen men with letters after their names."

Gabriel wiped the remaining soap off his face with a cloth. "That makes sense," he said, turning in the chair to face her.

"And ye dunnae find it alarming?" she asked, lifting an eyebrow. "Because I do."

Even if it meant he shouldn't devote so much time and money to Lattimer so quickly. They'd been failing for a hundred years. He didn't need to try to restore it in a month.

He reached over to take her free hand and pull her off her perch on his camp trunk and onto his lap. "If the paper men were truly alarmed, they would have used less flowery language," he quipped, leaning in to kiss her. "They think I'm a half-wit." Another kiss, openmouthed to meet her eager lips.

"That isnae answering my question," she insisted, trying to stay on topic even with her voice muffled against his mouth.

"Hard-hearted lass." With a sigh he touched his forehead to hers. "I think the estate owner in question can devote some unallocated funds to the Highlands property, given the previous decades of neglect it was therein accorded."

That made her chuckle. "They were correct; ye are a half-wit."

"Thank you. But if I have to sell off some investments, then so be it." He kissed her again. "I'm accustomed to not being a wealthy man, Fiona."

"But ye're nae a man alone, any longer."

"Then I need to figure out the minimum

numbers necessary to sustain my other two estates, the house in London, and the one in Inverness, and keep that amount available. The rest I can damned well spend as I please. And I please to spend it here."

He was likely the first duke in history who didn't care about increasing his wealth and influence, and Fiona truly didn't want to point that out to him. In fact, the idea of using every available penny to improve Lattimer appealed to her greatly. But was it fair? Not necessarily to the other estates, but to him?

She put her hands on his shoulders and shoved. Gabriel kissed her again, likely to point out that he didn't have to cooperate if he didn't choose to do so, before he backed away a breath. "What is it?" he asked.

"I'm worried ye're doing all of this fer me. That if things dunnae work oot here as they should, ye'll resent me fer pointing ye toward failure. And ye'll blame me fer the fact that ye're neglecting yer other properties when ye shouldnae." Fiona plucked at the buttons of his coat. "I couldnae bear that, ye ken."

"Of course I'm doing this for you," he stated.

Oh, dear. "But ye cannae, G—"

"And I'm doing it for me," he continued,

400

over her protest. "The idea of helping people improve their lives appeals to me. A great deal." He grimaced. "I'll make some idiotic mistakes with it. I'm accustomed to dealing in absolutes. I have no idea how to be wealthy. Or how to manage the fact that people apparently listen to me because of some title I didn't earn."

Fiona gazed at him for a long moment before she realized she was still tugging on his lapels. "Ye're a very interesting man, Gabriel Forrester."

He grinned. "I'll take that as a compliment." Glancing over at the small, unadorned clock that sat on the hugely ornate mantel over the equally ostentatious limestone and marble fireplace, he returned his attention to her and ran a finger slowly down her throat to the lace-lined neck of her gown. "When are we supposed to be at the church?"

Attempting to ignore the silly flutter those words caused, she shrugged. This wasn't about her daydreams. It was only that she still wasn't accustomed to being part of a "we," and today people would see it. They would know she'd fallen for a Sassenach. And a duke. Even if all he'd promised her was friendship, at least presently the definition of that involved kissing and sex, thank goodness. "Ye set one o'clock fer the picnic. Ian brought by some rabbits earlier, and he said people are already gathering in the churchyard. And the wagons have gone oot to begin bringing in the cotters by the river."

"The food's going down at noon; we'll do the same. No reason for people to wait about looking at perfectly good sandwiches."

She nodded, agreeing. "And I'm nae to tell ye, but the cotters working at the factories think there are enough of them settling along the river now that they can call it a village."

"Why aren't you supposed to tell me that?"

"I think they want to see how ye react. So be surprised, and pleased, and approve of whatever name they've decided to give it. Because there was some brawling and profanity involved before they sorted it oot, from what I hear."

He sighed. "It's all a test, isn't it?"

"Aye. Every step ye take. And if ye falter, they'll all be cursing ye fer nae selling to Dunncraigh."

"I could have done without hearing that today."

Even with the amount of weight that had landed on his shoulders over the past few days, she'd yet to see him give any indication that he found it overwhelming. He seemed to understand that this would not be a quick battle and a long victory celebration. Because it would be just the opposite — a long struggle, a brief celebration, and then another siege. Perhaps a soldier was the perfect match for Lattimer, after all. Providence was an odd creature.

"Noon, hm?" he drawled. "Whatever shall we do until then?"

Fiona grinned. "I'd say ye need to go meet with Oscar Ritchie aboot the stable's grain requirements fer autumn and over the winter, but from the state of yer trousers that could be a wee bit awkward."

"It is not a 'wee' anything, madam," he countered, backing her toward his bed.

"I'll nae argue with ye aboot that," she said, chuckling, delighted shivers running up her arms.

He'd replaced the old monstrosity of a bed with a much simpler oak frame and a much firmer mattress. Likewise the room itself had been stripped of most of its ornamentation. The heavy wood paneling was gone, replaced with fresh, light green paint. The animal heads gave way to paintings of the Highlands, and most of the dusty books and knickknacks were now almanacs and planting guides and studies about soil erosion, and several vases of fresh wildflowers. It suited him even without all the last touches finished — straightforward, charming, and practical.

"I used to hate walking into this room," she said, stopping her backward steps as her calves touched the bed frame. "It always felt stale and ostentatious and haunted."

"And now?" he asked, pausing to take in the room again.

"It has its attractions," she returned, grinning.

"Does it now?"

Gabriel wanted to bend her over, lift her skirt, and take her. That, however, was both ungentlemanly, and far too quick. For the picnic she'd donned a pretty white muslin gown with deep red flowers and green leaves embroidered throughout. Her clan colors, more or less. She looked delicious, and he spun her around to view the dozen tiny buttons running down her spine to her waist, trying to figure out how he was going to open the damned things without pulling them off.

When he began tugging at the first one, though, she whipped back around and slapped his hands away. "I'll nae have ye ruining my dress or my hair," she stated.

"Today is too important."

He scowled. Several minutes ago he'd stopped thinking about the picnic and speeches and having to smile far too much. At this moment he'd stopped thinking about anything but burying himself between Fiona's thighs and hearing her cry out his name in ecstasy. "Then you take it off," he said, turning her away from him again so he could slide his hands around her hips and then up her front to cup her breasts over the thin muslin.

When she started wriggling her bottom against his front, he clenched his jaw. She was doing it on purpose, making her rules and then pushing to see whether he would go along with her wishes or not. As long as he ended where he wanted to be, he would play along — to a point.

"Your clothes are still on," he pointed out, slipping one hand inside her gown to pinch a nipple.

She gasped, arching against him. "Ye make me a bit giddy, Sassenach," she managed, her voice a purr of desire.

"Then you should lie down," he returned, licking the curve of her ear.

"Nae. I think *ye* should lie doon."

"I see. I think I could manage that." Still playing with her, he unbuttoned his trousers with his free hand and kicked out of them, thankful he hadn't yet donned his boots. God, she was so close, and it was so tempting.

He had to close his eyes to steady himself before he released her to sit on the edge of his new bed and scoot backward. With his proper shirt and cravat, waistcoat and dark jacket above, and nothing below, he must have looked quite a sight, but he didn't give a damn.

"Come here," he growled, reaching out and catching hold of her skirt.

With a breathy laugh she complied, hiking up her skirt and clambering onto the bed beside him. He took her hand so she could steady herself as she straddled his hips and then far too slowly sank down around him.

Finally. Sliding his palms up her thighs, he thrust upward, meeting her as she bounced up and down on him. Hot, tight, and his. For a man who'd never expected to fall in love, much less see a future the two of them could share, the desire, the possessiveness he felt both aroused him and shook him to his core.

But with her hands planted on his chest and her head thrown back as she made mewling sounds in time with his thrusts, she *was* his. All he needed to do was prove to her that he was the man she and Lattimer needed. And inside her, feeling the exquisite ecstasy of her climaxing around him, he felt like he could do anything.

For a veteran soldier it was an unexpected and heady sensation. He didn't quite trust it, but he damned well enjoyed it. As the tension inside him stretched to breaking, he sat up to take her mouth. "Do I stay or go?" he groaned, finesse drowned out by need.

She wrapped her arms around his shoulders, sinking onto him almost frantically. "Stay," she moaned thickly, shuddering again.

He couldn't hold back any longer. Spilling into her, he lifted his hips convulsively. *Mine, mine, mine,* thudded through him as he came hard and fast.

For a long time he held her, feeling her heart pounding over his. Gabriel tried to catch his breath, sinking back onto the mattress again. Fiona fell forward to sprawl across his chest. He wanted to tangle his fingers through her hair, but settled for curling a straying strand behind one ear.

Whoever the tenants here claimed allegiance to, for the past four years Fiona had looked after all of them. And still she'd managed to find room in her heart for one more lost soul. With her in his arms, he could see a future. And it had been a very long time since he'd even thought in terms of years rather than days, or even hours.

"You are a very bonny lass," he murmured, stroking her cheek.

"Ye're nae so bad yerself, Gabriel. And thank ye fer nae mussing my hair."

He chuckled. "You're welcome. Tonight, though, no clothes."

Fiona lifted her head to kiss him. "I find those terms acceptable."

His door handle rattled, accompanied by a thud and a wumph. "Damnation," Kelgrove's voice muttered. "Your Grace?"

"I really need to find him a position he wants to take," Gabriel murmured, wrapping his arms loosely around Fiona. "What?" he called.

"Oscar sent a stable boy up to the castle to request that we borrow all available farm wagons. It seems half the county is gathering at the river and means to come to the picnic to 'set their oon eyes on His Grace.' That is a quote."

Fiona nodded against his chest. "That would be grand, to include them."

"See to it, Sergeant. Make certain you ask, not order."

"Yes, sir."

"Have the kitchen bake more bread,"

Fiona whispered. "And pull another barrel of whisky from the larder."

"Adam," Gabriel called, "you should also ask Mrs. Ritchie to bake as much bread as she can manage. We can always send back up to the house for additional supplies, if that proves necessary."

"I'll see to it, Your Grace."

"And pull another barrel of whisky out of the larder."

"Yes, Your Grace." Kelgrove paused. "Is there anything else?"

"Is there anything else?" Gabriel whispered to Fiona.

"Nae, I cannae conjure anything at the moment," she returned softly, her voice amused.

"That will be all, Sergeant!"

"Thank you, sir!"

The footsteps retreated down the hallway. "I'm glad you locked the door," Gabriel said, running his fingers idly down the length of buttons he wasn't permitted to open.

"Kelgrove's doing my tasks," she returned, sitting upright, away from him. "I should be helping. Who knows how many questions will come up, last minute."

"He's aiding," Gabriel returned. "It's what he does. But since I've discovered his hidden passion for facts and figures, I'll find something useful for him. I do have three estates and people telling me where I should spend my money."

"Ye do mean to set yer own eyes on Hawthorne and Langley Park, I assume?" she asked, black eyes gazing down at him.

"I will," he agreed. "Once things have calmed down here."

"Good. Ye need to know what ye own. Ye might even decide ye prefer one or the other of them to here."

He'd never heard anything more unlikely. She lived here, and so he preferred to be here, as well. If this was supposed to be a test of his connection to her, he could think of better, more tactile ways to demonstrate how much she meant to him. Gabriel eyed her. If he meant to be a competent landowner, he also needed to learn some finesse with words. He put his hands over hers. "Would you like to tour them with me? I'd value your opinion. And your company. And if *you* find somewhere you prefer to Lattimer, then we'll talk."

Her brow furrowed. "I'll nae find anywhere I prefer to here, Sassenach."

"And I haven't had a home since I was seventeen. This one suits me quite well." Tightening his grip on her hands, he pulled her down again. "I like the view," he murmured, lifting his head for a kiss.

Every time she moved his cock throbbed, and as her tongue danced with his the fellow seemed to decide he was ready for another go. He could tell that she felt it, and she groaned as she moved over him. "Yer lad's very spry today," she noted, grinning.

"We both had a good breakfast."

Forty minutes later he finished refastening his trousers, pulled on his boots, and did his best to straighten his cravat. He knew he looked English, and saw no reason to pretend to be anything else. His tenants knew him to be English, even the ones who hadn't yet seen him. The sooner they could become accustomed to him, and the sooner he could become accustomed to this version of himself, the better.

It would be a fraction easier without the uniform, and he'd packed those away in his trunk. Eventually, when the idea of parting from them didn't open a hole in his gut, he would send them up to the attic. At the least, he knew he wouldn't be wearing them any longer. This battle required a different uniform, a different strategy, and promised a very different, and a very precious, reward.

Chapter Fifteen

"Fleming, are you joining us at Strouth?" Gabriel asked, as the old duke's newly polished barouche stopped on the front drive.

"I . . . hadn't considered it, Yer Grace," the butler replied.

"I know you have duties here," Gabriel said, handing Fiona into the open vehicle and feeling her squeeze his hand in approval, "but I also know the cotters see you as the household's representative. I leave it to you to decide."

The butler's cheeks darkened. "In that case, I would be honored, Yer Grace," he stated, bouncing on his toes.

Gabriel motioned him toward the barouche as Kelgrove took the seat facing Fiona. "Allow me to give you a ride, then."

Fleming practically beamed. "I . . . thank ye, Yer Grace. That would save my old legs the walk. Very kind of ye." The stout Highlander stepped up and sat beside the sergeant.

Still no "laird" within earshot, but Fleming's willingness to join them signaled some progress. Fiona had pointed out to him several times, generally while angry, that his staff and his tenants were not an army. As the barouche topped the rise twenty minutes later and crossed from the trees into the large meadow where Strouth lay, however, he wondered if she was wrong about that.

They'd planned a picnic in the shady churchyard opposite the graveyard. With an hour still before the al fresco luncheon was even set to begin, however, he could see that the well-manicured lawn wouldn't be sufficient. All across the meadow people stood talking, children running between the clusters and shrieking in delight at the holiday.

If he took the village and quadrupled the number of inhabitants, he still wouldn't come close to the number presently filling the clearing. "These are all my tenants?" he muttered at Fiona, who sat beside him with a smile pasted on her face.

"Aye," she returned. "But I didnae expect this many. They've come from all the way across the loch and up into the mountains, even. I doubt there's anyone left oot there at all but fer the shepherds and the extra men ye sent to guard the flocks."

"Can we feed them all?"

Fleming cleared his throat. "With all due respect, Yer Grace, I heard a rumor or two aboot how far word had spread, and I advised Mrs. Ritchie to begin baking two days ago."

"Ye might have said someaught, George," Fiona exclaimed. "I thought we'd have maybe two hundred."

"I apologize, Miss Fiona," the butler said. "It was only a rumor. If I'd been wrong, we'd have been donating biscuits to the church fer the next fortnight."

"Thank you, Fleming," Gabriel put in, before Fiona could do more fussing. "You may well have prevented this from becoming a disaster."

"I'm pleased I could be of assistance, m'laird."

Gabriel nodded. He was counting every "laird" as if it were a precious diamond. Whether Fleming had simply forgotten or he'd meant the word intentionally, it doubled his total.

The barouche had to slow to a walk amid the crush of people. When it began to look like someone might be injured if they continued to press forward, Gabriel instructed Kevin to stop. "We'll walk from here," he said, reaching over the door to open it.

Fiona stepped down first, closely followed by the butler. "If they turn on you," Kelgrove murmured, standing, "there won't be a damned thing either of us can do about it."

"I know. You can return to the house if you wish."

The sergeant frowned. "Whether you're still my commanding officer or not, Your Grace, I don't think there's any call for you to insult me."

Gabriel grinned, clapping Adam on the shoulder. "That's what I wanted to hear. If anything does go awry, stay close to Fiona," he said, turning to watch as she threw her arms around a young lady who looked enough like her to be a cousin.

"You expect me to hide behind a woman's skirts?" the sergeant returned, his posture indignant.

"No. I expect you to protect her."

"I . . . Very well, sir."

That seen to, Gabriel offered his arm to Fiona. They could all say he was just being polite if they wanted to; as long as she was beside him, he didn't care what anyone else thought. The crowd immediately surrounded them. The majority of his tenants appeared mostly curious and a little shy at meeting their landlord for the first time in twenty years. For his part, smiling and being friendly and appearing . . . harmless wasn't anything to which he was accustomed, but he did his damnedest. It went with the civilian clothes and riding in barouches and the stunning woman by his side.

Not everyone, though, seemed happy to see him. Those men, the ones on the fringes and the others who kept themselves shadowed behind their fellows, they caught and kept his attention. Had Dunncraigh sent him some troublemakers? Or were these men simply more wary and more suspicious of his motives than the rest of them? If it was the latter, they could still be reasoned with, convinced if not by his words then hopefully by his deeds. If they were the former, he might well find himself with a fight on his hands, after all. He refused to be comforted by that thought.

"Don't glare," Fiona said through her clenched smile as they made their way toward where the main tables had been placed. A hundred blankets covered the meadow grass around them — at least the villagers had come prepared to sit on the ground.

"I'm assessing," he countered, but smoothed his expression anyway.

"They like ye, I think," she continued after a moment. "I ken they've heard aboot the sheep, by now, and how ye helped Ailios. They'll listen, at least, which was more than I expected."

He lifted an eyebrow. "Just what *did* you expect?"

Fiona shrugged, her eyes dancing. "A few cabbages thrown at ye, at least."

If she was teasing, the day must be going well. "I'll remember you said that."

Rather than climbing on a chair again, this time he opted for the top of the church's steps. Father Jamie joined them, and though Gabriel had been somewhat suspicious of the parson after Sir Hamish had spent so much time supposedly reassuring him about the Englishman who'd arrived at Lattimer, today the man looked ready to weep with joy at the sight of all his flock gathered together.

"This is grand," he breathed, clasping his hands together. "Och, this is grand."

Gabriel waved a hand as the horde crowded before the church. If he had his say, this would only be the first time they saw Fiona and him arm in arm here. That, though, was a promise for another day.

"Good afternoon," he called. "Thank you all for coming. Most of you have likely heard by now that the Duke of Dunncraigh offered to purchase this property from me, and that I refused his offer."

"We heard he's banished us all from clan Maxwell!" an angry male voice called out — one of the men hiding himself from clear view.

"That isnae so," Fiona took up. "We're as important to the Maxwell as we ever were — which isnae much at all. When's the last time any of ye set eyes on him?"

"Yesterday!" another one yelled.

"Aye, yesterday, because Lattimer being here finally made him notice us. Did ye see him when Brocair burned to the ground four years past? Or when the irrigation dam broke and flooded all the fields east of the loch? I saw his men every year, coming to collect his tithe, and I saw him when my uncle Hamish took me to Dunncraigh, but he's nae come to visit on his own fer at least a decade."

"My Harold died of fever three years back," an older woman stated. "Miss Fiona came to see me and sat with me and brought me a nice meal, and saw that my roof was patched. I nae heard a word from Laird Dunncraigh, and Harold served his da' fer all those years."

"Laird Lattimer saved my life," a more familiar voice said thinly. Gabriel looked over to see Ailios Eylar sitting on a chair, a blanket across her knees. "And he went oot of his way to do it."

"I'm pleased to see you out of doors, Mrs. Eylar," Gabriel returned, inclining his head. "But I have to argue with you on one point: I didn't go out of my way. I've lived most of my life as a soldier. I looked after my men, I fought beside them, and I went where I was ordered to go. This — Lattimer, MacKittrick, whatever you choose to call it" — and he gestured at the expanse around them — "is the first time I've felt like I've had a home since I was seventeen years old."

It felt odd to say it all aloud, but he didn't see any point in creating some elaborate, heroic fiction about destiny. He would tell them the truth, because that was who he was. They could take that truth and either believe he could and would help them, or not. As he looked out over the sea of faces, he hoped he'd chosen the right tack.

"I'm a simple man," he went on. "I had no idea I was related to a duke, much less that I had become his sole heir. Before this happened I thought I would be a soldier until I died or grew too old to hold a rifle."

He smiled ruefully. "I reckoned it would be the former. I didn't expect this life. I certainly didn't expect to find a home, or a place where I could be useful. I know you don't trust me. You have no reason to do so. My great-uncle neglected this place to a shocking degree. But I'm not him. And it is my goal, my duty, to do better than he did."

"That sounds like a load of shite to me!"

Fiona jabbed her finger at the light-haired man who'd yelled. "I see ye there, Cuthbert Dinwoddie. And I saw ye sleeping when a dozen head of sheep went missing. *Our* sheep. Ye've nae right to insult His Grace if ye cannae tell the difference between watching sheep awake and counting them in yer dreams."

Cuthbert went red-faced as the villagers laughed. "And why are ye defending a Sassenach, Fiona?" he countered. "Is it because ye've had him beneath yer skirt, ye whore?"

Gabriel stepped forward before he'd even realized he'd done so. "You," he said, indicating the shepherd. "Cuthbert. Come here."

"Gabriel," Fiona hissed behind him.

He kept moving forward, the crowd parting to let him through, until Cuthbert Dinwoddie had to choose between running away and facing him straight on. The man lifted his chin, his fists curled. "I'm ready fer ye, English," he growled.

"Good. Then listen," Gabriel snapped back, the clarity of his anger surprising him. "Say whatever you like about me. Respect is earned, and I haven't earned it yet. But if you insult that woman again after all she's done here for you and your family and your neighbors and your fellow clansmen, I will drop you where you stand."

Cuthbert's gaze darted here and there as he no doubt searched for an ally — or an escape. "Aye, ye're a big man, ye are, making threats in front of all these people."

"Look at me," Gabriel instructed.

The shepherd hemmed and hawed for another bit, then finally met his gaze. "What?"

"Do you think I'm jesting?" He paused. With no answer forthcoming, he advanced another step. "Do you think I would hesitate for a damned second?" Another pause, silence meeting him again. "Remember that." Gabriel took a breath. "When I arrived here, I did so with the idea of leaving again as soon as I could hire a proper steward. It took less than a day for me to realize what a mistake that would be. Fiona Blackstock literally devotes every waking minute to you and to this land. And as compelling and . . . inspiring as she is, I can do no less."

Fiona had watched Gabriel stride down the steps and make directly for Cuthbert Dinwoddie, and for a long space of heartbeats she thought he actually meant to hit the shepherd. Instead, and with a few succinct words, he won over everyone in the meadow — with the possible exception of Cuthbert.

As much as she wanted to sit beside Gabriel, they'd already decided that splitting up would benefit them more. And so she sat between Ailios and William MacDorry, while the duke's table had filled with what looked like every unmarried lass in the county.

"He seems to have a head on his shoulders, at least," Tormod the blacksmith commented. "And Cuthbert's a bloody idiot, which we all knew, but now it's fer certain."

"Ye ken ye'll have fights, if the duke decides to repair one lad's fence before another man's," William noted.

"Aye. What do ye think of a drawing, of sorts?" Fiona asked. "We'll have to see to the major repairs first, like the irrigation gates, but then we'll put all the houses with roofs that need patching on papers and draw them from a hat. They'll all be done, but nae one person will decide the order."

"I reckon I could live with that," one of the fishermen farther down the table said, nodding. "It'd be fair, at least."

"What aboot the curse, though?" came from one of the picnic blankets to her right. "It's all grand plans, but we've seen it before. Mr. Kieran managed to get the mill working again, and then Brocair burned three nights later. And a week after that, Mr. Kieran rode into the bogs and only his horse came back."

Fiona wanted to pretend not to hear that, because she had no idea how to answer it. Facts and plans were well and good, but folk had blamed every bad bit of luck on that curse for the past hundred years.

"They say only an Englishman turned Highlander can break the curse," another voice took up. "We have an Englishman now, at least."

"Nae Sassenach can ever be a Highlander, and ye know it," a third villager contributed. "It's a curse that cannae be broken. If we fight against it, then we'll only be putting ourselves in harm's way. 'His allies shall perish.' That's what MacKittrick said."

"What, are ye a witch now, Letitia Garretson?" someone else countered. "Does that mean ye'll nae ask to have yer window replaced or yer pig fence mended when the time comes fer it?"

She'd expected the pessimism and doubt, but the number of hopeful voices pleased Fiona greatly. They had a chance, she and Gabriel. They truly had a chance to make things right here. And the villagers were past ready for that, as well, or there would have been a great many more of them fretting about Dunncraigh threatening to turn his back on them. They'd realized — or some of them had, anyway — that he'd already done so.

A high-pitched scream pierced through the cacophony of conversation. Fiona looked up, alarmed. "Where did that come from?" she asked, and Ailios put a hand over her heart.

The sound repeated, a young girl's scream, and a trio of young ones ran into view from the middle of the village. "The well!" the youngest of the Dinwoddie boys yelled. "She's in the well!"

Dear God. Fiona shot to her feet, ice slicing through her. Gabriel had already launched himself across the top of his table, charging for the well with dozens of men and women on his heels. *Not this,* she prayed silently, hiking her skirt to her knees and sprinting to catch up. *Not this, please.*

■ ■ ■ ■

Gabriel ran, barking orders for someone to fetch rope, ladders, anything they could use to reach the bottom of the well. He couldn't remember even setting eyes on the damned thing, and now —

Christ. The thought of a child drowning while he dined on sandwiches both sickened and horrified him. He'd seen dead children, and they still haunted his dreams. This, though, was one of his. His responsibility, his care, his duty. He could be sick later, horrified when lives didn't depend on his actions. If nothing else, being a soldier had taught him that. Act first, feel later — if at all.

A half-dozen more children stood leaning over the three-foot stone circle to look down the dark hole in the middle. "Get back," he snapped, jumping up onto the foot-wide lip and squatting to look down. He was ready to jump, but he wasn't going to risk landing on a struggling child's head. He needed to see, first.

The well looked like a gaping, bottomless black maw. Even worse than the dark, though, was the silence. He sank down onto his stomach, shading his eyes from the sunlight. Behind him adults chattered in a panic, trying to figure out which child was missing.

His eyes began to adjust, and slowly a thin white shape came into view, protruding from the still black surface of the well water. He felt like ice inside. An arm? A leg? Abruptly the shape registered, and air flooded back into his lungs.

"It's a cow," he said, looking up to meet Fiona's horrified gaze, to see relief return blood to her face. "It's Brian Maxwell's cow."

Fiona's hands went to her mouth, her eyes bright with tears. "A cow?" she repeated, visibly shaking. "Are ye certain?"

He nodded, wanting to hold her. "I can see an upturned horn and part of the muzzle."

"Oh, thank God," she breathed. "Thank God."

"How the devil did a cow end up in the well?" Niall Garretson demanded, the miller's voice unsteady.

They'd all been shaken. Around Gabriel, relieved, half-hysterical laughter filled the air, coupled with speculation about how any cow had ended up at the bottom of a well. He sat as the big blacksmith pounded up, ropes coiled over his shoulder. "Any idea how to pull a cow out of here?" Gabriel asked him, gesturing.

"A cow? Thank Saint Andrew." Tormod leaned over the lip beside him. "Horses and rope, I reckon. Someone'll have to go doon there to get a line around her."

Abruptly Brian Maxwell was there, peering over the side. "My red?" he asked, tears running down his freshly shaved face. "Oh no, lass. Ye ken she likes to wander, Yer Grace, but she's a clever one, she is. She'd nae just jump into a well."

Gabriel refrained from pointing out that the first time he'd encountered the red-furred cow, she'd been trapped up to her chest in a mudhole. That didn't seem especially clever of her. "However she got in there, Brian," he said, gripping the farmer's shoulder, "we need to get her out. This is the village's main water supply."

The farmer nodded. "Aye. Aye, I ken. My Brady, he'll do it. He's a good lad." A young man of about fifteen stepped forward, his expression grim.

It had been on the tip of Gabriel's tongue to countermand that suggestion, and to announce that of course he would go down there himself. Strouth was his land, these, his tenants. The risk should be his. Before he could say it aloud, though, he caught sight of the villagers around him nodding their approval at the farmer's words.

His pride didn't like it, but his common sense understood. Brian had been negligent — again — and allowed his cow to escape her pasture. Brian therefore needed to make this right. He held out a hand to the boy. "Come up here, Brady," he said. "We'll tie a rope around you and lower you down. You'll need to secure the second rope around both horns, and you'll have to do it mainly by feel."

The lad nodded. "I ken. Let's get her oot before she spoils the water."

Gabriel and Tormod tied the rope under the boy's armpits while several others unhitched three pairs of horses from the waiting wagons and harnessed them together. When everything was ready, Brady sent his father a nod and then scooted off the well's stone lip.

While Brian hung over the edge and motioned them to let out rope, Gabriel, Tormod, and two other villagers slowly lowered Brady Maxwell into the darkness. They played out nearly twenty-five feet of rope before the farmer announced that his boy was in the water.

More men lowered a second rope, and then what seemed like an hour later but must have been only a few minutes, Brady yelled that he'd finished. They hauled the boy up.

"There's blood in the water," Brady said breathlessly, as they freed him from the wet rope and Fiona threw a picnic blanket over his shaking shoulders. "I couldnae make oot how much, or where it came from."

"Let's get her up, and we'll find out."

With six horses, even the waterlogged weight of the dead cow moving straight up the inside of the stone wall of the well didn't present much of a problem. A moment later and the bloated carcass with its twisted horns bumped heavily over the lip of the well and thudded to the ground.

"She's well gone," Tormod noted, wrinkling his nose at the smell. "She must've wandered into the village last night, tried to climb up fer some reason, and fallen in."

"Aye," Brian said mournfully. "Dogs always spooked her. She might've been affrighted."

To Gabriel that didn't seem particularly plausible. The red beast had been accustomed to wandering and likely to all the dogs in the village, as well. But if it hadn't been an accident, then someone had dragged a dead cow into the middle of Strouth, dumped it deliberately into the well, and escaped — all without being noticed.

"It were the curse," the farmer said, toeing the cow. "We all knew someaught would happen. If the bairns hadnae seen that twisted horn of hers, we'd nae have noted anything was amiss until folk started getting sick."

Gabriel exchanged a glance with Fiona. Did she have the same questions? Was she wondering who might gain from poisoning the well water? "Let's get this away from the village and burn it," he said. "If some illness caused her to do this, I don't want anyone eating the beef."

"A good milking cow lost and nae a thing gained," Brian muttered. " 'Tis the curse, poor lass."

"We'd all best leave the well be fer a few days," Fiona said, putting her hand on Gabriel's arm for balance so she could lean over and look into the depths. "The water flows doon there, but we dunnae ken how slowly." She straightened. "There's food still to eat, and enough's been wasted today."

Gabriel placed her hand around his arm again as they and most of the villagers wandered back to the picnic. Several of them crossed their fingers and spat over their shoulders as they passed the well. "We were lucky," he murmured, low enough that only Fiona could hear him. "Twice over."

"I nearly choked on my own heart," she returned, "thinking it was a bairn who'd fallen in. But if they hadnae all gathered aboot to play here today, all we'd know fer a time is that Brian Maxwell's cow went missing again."

"Do you think it was an accident?" he asked, lowering his voice still further. "Because I don't."

"I hope it was. I truly do. But I wouldnae wager any coin on it." She glanced over her shoulder. "And I'm thinking ye should keep those extra men watching the sheep."

He nodded, a smile tugging at his mouth. "You are a sensible lass."

"And ye're a fine man, stubborn though ye are. I dunnae think I was the only one to notice how ye stepped right into the middle of the lads to help. And ye let Brian save face. It almost makes me want to kiss ye."

" 'Almost'?"

"Aye," she said, grinning at the ground. "Almost. I've nae wish to turn this from a picnic into a hanging. Though I'm beginning to believe ye'd get by with a good flogging, after this."

"That's encouraging. Thank you."

She bumped against his side. "I think ye

should thank me later."

Oh, that he would do. Several times.

CHAPTER SIXTEEN

Fiona wakened from a dead sleep, a sound she couldn't quite identify pulling at her. Warmth surrounded her, and she shifted just a little to feel Gabriel's solid form against her back. He had one arm stretched beneath her head, and the other draped over her ribs, and she wanted to stay that way forever. She loved the stubborn Sassenach and the way he was so willing to take on the impossible without even a second's hesitation. When they were like this, she could see them together in a future with fields full of butterflies and crops growing tall and green.

In the dark she could also acknowledge that her being in love with him wouldn't prevent him from marrying someone else, that he'd never mentioned words like "marriage" or "love" or "forever" in her presence. She took a breath. He was a soldier, accustomed to fighting in order to survive from one day to the next. Perhaps "forever" never occurred to him. And really, if all his day-to-days ended in her company, she had nothing about which to complain.

A low-pitched cry echoed dimly into the room, sounding like it had come from very far away. She couldn't make out the words, but that had to be what had awakened her before. The hair on the back of her neck pricked.

"Did you hear that?" Gabriel asked, his voice alert.

"I did. I couldnae make it oot, though."

He stretched, then sat up. "I'll go find out. Stay here and keep the bed warm."

Fiona scooted to the edge of the bed. "Ye can get a wee coal pan fer that, ye sluggard."

The voice came again, from closer, and this time she could make it out. "Fire!"

Gabriel drew in a sharp breath. "The cow wasn't an accident," he muttered, grabbing for his trousers.

She had nothing but her night rail with her. Cursing, she slipped it on over her head. "I'm getting dressed," she said, running for the door.

"Fiona, if you smell smoke, don't stop for a gown," he ordered, already stomping into his boots.

"If I smell smoke, I'm coming back fer ye," she shot back, and pulled open his door. The hallway was empty, but she could hear voices coming from the direction of the stairs. The air didn't smell of anything but an evening's chill, either, and so after a quick mental debate over whether she should dress or go find out where the fire was, she hurried to her bedchamber.

Muttering curses to herself, she yanked open her wardrobe. In the dark she couldn't tell which gown she touched first, but that didn't matter. She left on the night rail and pulled the gown on over it. It wasn't much, but it would provide her at least a little additional warmth. She also dug out her heavy work boots, which would likely serve her better than any of her prettier, less practical shoes.

A heavy man's coat went on over everything, and she headed back for the door, pausing only to grab a ribbon so she could tie back her loose hair. She still didn't smell any smoke, but it was a big house. And Gabriel would be ahead of her, diving directly into wherever the most danger lay.

On the second-floor landing she finally spied someone running below her. "Lochie!" she called, leaning down to see the second footman as he headed toward the front of the house. "What's going on?"

"The mill, Miss Fiona. It's blazing, Oscar

435

said. We're all heading up with buckets. The lads in the stable are getting wagons."

Her relief that Lattimer wasn't in flames vanished just as quickly as it came. "Go!" she said, motioning at him. "I'll catch up."

The footman continued on his way. Someone had thought to light lamps on the bottom floor, at least, so she could see where she was going. Fleming stood in the foyer, which would have been a normal sight except for the fact that he wore only his nightshirt with his coat pulled on over it. "Is the rest of the house awake?" she asked, moving sideways as another handful of servants ran outside past her.

"Aye, miss. The laird ordered me to stay, though, with some of the footmen. He said to watch for anyone who shouldnae be here."

She nodded. "First the cow and now this. Someone's doing this, George. It's nae some curse that sets a fire."

"Then watch yerself, Fiona, lass. And watch oot fer the laird. He took his horse; I heard someone say he rode oot bareback."

Of course he had. "I will. I'll send ye back word as soon as I know anything."

One of the wagons rolled past as she reached the stable, and she grabbed for the tail. Two of the grooms pulled her aboard, and she sat down between them. The road wasn't meant to be traveled this quickly at night, but the fire wouldn't wait for them. "Stop at the loch and fill the buckets," she ordered, as Loch Sibhreach came into view on her left. "Tilly, ye and Diarmid stay right here and make certain the wagons behind us do the same."

The footman and the maid jumped to the ground. "Aye, Miss Fiona. We'll see to it."

The moment they crested the low hill she could see the glow in the center of the valley. The villagers in Strouth must have heard the alarm being raised as well, because she could see the line of lanterns heading along the road that intersected with the path to the mill. Good. Strouth was a bit closer than Lattimer was, and every second would count.

"It smells like burned bread," one of the others said, as they rumbled and jolted toward the orange and yellow blaze.

"That's the sacks of flour and grain burning," Hugh replied grimly, nothing but a dressing robe and a pair of breeches between the footman and the chilly night.

They needed to move faster. Gabriel's comment that they were being attacked, that this and Brian Maxwell's cow hadn't been accidents, made sense. And added in with

Lattimer's other misfortunes over the past years, it infuriated her.

Someone had stolen sheep, yes, but she'd put that to poachers, to the desperate act of a few desperate individuals. The irrigation gates that failed one by one, the mill's grindstone that seemed to crack at least once a year, seed grain that got wet and rotted — everyone else had put those and dozens of other incidents to the MacKittrick curse. She'd decided it was general bad luck, brought on by the property's slowly diminishing finances that kept her constantly behind on repairs.

But if someone had done this . . . Fiona clenched her cold fingers into fists. She needed to talk with Gabriel. Previously her familiarity and friendship and kinship with everyone had given her an advantage over him, made her necessary — or so she'd thought. Now, though, all this pointed to someone she knew, and she hadn't a clue who it might be. Nor could she go about threatening and accusing people. As much as she would hate to see him do it, Gabriel could be more forceful than she. And he was certainly more cynical and suspicious to begin with.

The trees gave way to meadow, and she gasped. The grain mill wasn't merely burning. It *was* fire. She couldn't make out anything but orange and yellow flames roaring halfway to heaven, obscured only by black smoke and broken here and there by black sticks that had once been beams but that now looked crazily like some giant's burning bones.

A line of people stretched from the stream to the fire, the buckets they passed along heavy and reflecting wet in the light from the fire. The wagon lurched to a halt, and Hugh helped her to the ground, grabbed up a bucket, and ran toward the fire. Fiona turned a quick circle, looking for Gabriel.

Her first concern should have been for Niall and Letitia Garretson and their young daughters Jenny and Rose, but she couldn't help herself. She needed to know he was safe. It was so odd to realize that nothing and no one mattered as much as he did, even weighted against people she'd known all her life. Even when she'd devoted the past four years to looking after all of them — every single life here in the meadow.

She frowned. Wherever Gabriel was, he would be helping. Grabbing an empty bucket and then a second one, she strode over to where the bank of the millstream flattened out into a manageable slope. Adding them to the pile being filled and handed off, she turned to go looking for more.

A wall collapsed, sending a shower of fire and sparks into the air. One fell on her skirt, smoldering, and she beat it out with her hands. Before she'd even arrived the mill had been completely engulfed; it was horribly clear that there was nothing left to save. The best they could hope for now was that they could keep the blaze from spreading to the wheat fields around the mill.

She retrieved bucket after bucket as they were emptied into the flames and cast aside. As the fire finally began to run out of fuel, the flames dipped lower over the glowing pile of timber and blackened stone. The black smoke became white steam, and she finally caught sight of Gabriel, beating out a long tendril of flame with a shovel before it could spread in the long grass.

Thank goodness. Tired as she was, the tension running through her shoulders eased a little. He was safe. Or as safe as any of them were, anyway. As she watched, he finished beating the spot fire out and went back to shoveling dirt and mud over the smoking wreckage.

When the parade of buckets began to slow and light began to glimmer on the eastern horizon, she handed the duty off to someone else and went to find the Garretsons where they stood in their nightclothes by the stream. She put a hand on Niall's slumped shoulders and then wordlessly hugged Letitia and the two lasses.

"I banked the fire in the cottage," Niall said. "Before we went to bed. Just as I always do. And I would nae leave a lantern in the mill. I wouldnae do such a thing. My lasses . . . I might have lost my lasses. We were asleep, Miss Fiona. If we hadnae . . . Someone fired a shot, and that woke me."

"Thank goodness it did," she said aloud, though the gunshot troubled her as much as anything else. "Did the shot come from close by, then? Do ye ken who did it? Did they help ye flee the cottage?"

The miller blinked, clearly only hearing half of what she was saying. "I didnae see anyone till old Reggie Eylar came running up the road, yelling fer us to get oot of the hoose because it was afire. We were oot by then already, but he helped me with the pigs and sent his boy doon to alert the castle." A sob broke from his chest. "My da' and his da' and his da' before him worked that mill. What will we do now? Where will we live?"

A hand touched Fiona's shoulder, warm and firm. "Firstly, Mr. Garretson," Gabriel said, "you and your family will stay at Lattimer as long as you need to. Secondly, once this fire is well out, you and I and some of your neighbors will pull the wreckage apart and see if anything can be salvaged. Thirdly, I will expect your assistance and advice when I arrange for a new cottage and mill to be built here."

Letitia burst into tears, hugging her daughters to her. "Oh, my laird, thank ye so —"

Gabriel held up his hand, and she immediately subsided. "You just spent half the night watching your home burn, Mrs. Garretson," he said. "You don't owe me anything." He tightened his grip on Fiona's shoulder. "Will you see them to Lattimer, Fiona?"

"Aye," she returned, holding out her arms to herd the family to the nearest wagon. "We'll find ye someaught to wear, and Mrs. Ritchie'll have a nice, hot breakfast fer ye."

"I'll stay," Niall stated, looking again at the smoking ruins.

"No," Gabriel countered. "Eat, and get some sleep. There's nothing to do now but make certain the fire doesn't flare up again, and there are plenty of men here to see to that."

The miller nodded. "Aye, m'laird. I will thank ye, too, and I reckon ye cannae stop me."

With a brief smile, Gabriel inclined his head, then turned away. "Give me a moment," Fiona told the Garretsons, and walked after him. "Gabriel."

He immediately turned around again. "They could have been killed," he said, his voice low and hard, fury in the stiff line of his spine. "Those two little girls. This is far beyond stealing some damned sheep."

"It makes me wonder," she said, not certain she should say anything that could potentially make him even angrier. "Has anything that's ever gone wrong here been an accident?"

"That's a very good question, Fiona. I have several others, myself." Gabriel looked around the clearing, at the dozens of people, mostly men now, who stood surveying what little remained of the mill and attached cottage. "I want to take a quick look here, before anything can be moved. Or removed."

"If it makes a difference, Niall said the sound of a shot woke them up in time for them to escape the hoose."

"It makes a difference if our arsonist wanted mayhem but balked at murder." He tilted his head, his expression easing as he gazed at her. "Do you have any idea how much I want to kiss you right now?" he

443

murmured.

"I ken I do," she returned, doing her best not to smile in the midst of the destruction, "because I'm near to tackling ye to the ground and having my way with ye. Ye look very fine with yer shirt untucked and soot smudged on yer face."

His brief, precise smile made her forget how tired, cold, and dirty she was. When he reached out and hooked her forefinger with his, she didn't even care if anyone else saw them.

"I love you, Fiona Blackstock," he said quietly, then released her hand to return to the smoking pile of timber and stone.

For a long moment she simply stood there, seeing her own breath as she exhaled in the dawn light. Whoever had said words had less impact than sticks or rocks had no idea. This morning she could fly. All she needed to do was jump, and her feet would never touch the ground again. *He loved her.* It didn't matter whether that altered anything or not, because in her heart it changed everything.

"Are ye ready to head back, Miss Fiona?" Oscar Ritchie asked, as he walked up to her. "I reckon Niall's bairns could use some breakfast."

She shook herself. Contemplating everything those three words meant to her could wait for a more opportune moment. Four of her kinsmen had just lost both their home and their means of earning a living. "Aye. I could use some of the duke's American coffee, myself. I reckon he could part with two cups, if ye'll join me."

The head groom grinned, then dropped the expression as they reached the wagon where the Garretsons waited. "Aye, miss," he returned, handing her up and then clambering onto the seat beside her. "Ye've persuaded me, if ye think the laird willnae mind."

Oh, she didn't think he would mind at all. And as for him being convinced that no one would ever see him as the laird of MacKittrick, he wouldn't mind being wrong about that, either. It made for an unexpectedly fine morning despite the troubles of the night, at least as far as she was concerned.

Gabriel stomped into the house, trying to get the last of the soot and mud off his shoes so he wouldn't track it through Lattimer. Fleming had found time to dress in his proper livery, though the dark circles under the butler's eyes told their own tale of a sleepless night.

"We found two adjoining bedchambers fer Niall and Mrs. Garretson and the wee lasses," the butler said, taking Gabriel's filthy coat with two careful fingers. The rest of him likely reeked of smoke, as well. Apparently he could be as hard on civilian clothes as he could his uniform. "Those girls said they'd nae seen such a grand bed in all their lives."

"Make certain they have whatever they need," Gabriel returned. "No one unexpected came calling while we were away?"

"Nae, m'laird."

"Good." As much as he wanted a hint or two about who might be sabotaging Lattimer, they'd had enough damned excitement for one day. "Where's Miss Blackstock?"

"In her office. She asked to see ye after ye had a chance to eat and clean yerself up."

"Thank you, Fleming."

Eating and changing his clothes could wait. Trudging up the stairs, he pushed the half-closed office door open. She sat at the desk with an open ledger beside her as she scribbled madly on another sheet of paper. She'd bathed and changed into clean clothes, but had left her hair down but for a loose ribbon holding the mass back from her face. It was quite possibly the most enchanting sight he'd ever seen. That in itself proved either that he'd gone mad, or that he was in love. And he'd told her so. Seeing her at the mill with her singed dess and the wreckage all around them, not telling her how he felt would have been absurd.

The scent of coffee touched him, and he narrowed one eye. "That smells suspiciously like my coffee," he said aloud, indicating the cup at her elbow.

Fiona looked up. "However can ye tell, over the smoke smell ye've got aboot ye?"

"A man can tell." Wearily he sank down onto one of the straight-backed chairs opposite her. Sitting seemed like something he hadn't done in a year.

"Then I confess. It *is* coffee," she returned, setting down the pencil. "And I offered Oscar a cup, as well. He blessed ye fer it."

"Well, I can always use a blessing."

She eyed him for a moment, then picked up the pencil again and began doodling. "Did ye find anything?"

"Kelgrove and I poked through the mill's ruins as best we could, with it still smoking. I could smell a trace of kerosene, but there was no sign of a lamp, broken or otherwise."

Her lips pressed together tightly enough to turn them white. "Niall's been running that mill fer fifteen years," she returned. "I've nae known him to be careless aboot it."

"At this point I would be happy to hear that it *was* an accident," he returned, dragging a hand through his hair.

"But ye dunnae think it was one."

"No, I do not." He sat forward. As much as he wanted to know what she thought of his declaration, they had several more pressing worries. "Nor do I think Brian's cow was an accident. And for both of them to have happened within a day? I don't know what those odds are, but I wouldn't take them."

"Nor would I."

"I have to blame the Duke of Dunncraigh, Fiona. This began after I refused to sell Lattimer to him."

She shook her head, her expression grim. "Nae. It didnae begin then." Fiona turned around the paper on which she'd been working, pushing it in front of him. "The sheep, the irrigation system, the flooded fields, the rotted seed — Lattimer's bad luck has been going on fer years."

He looked down at the list. Beside each incident she'd noted the approximate loss of income and the repair cost. With the mill added at the bottom, the amounts were staggering. "No wonder Lattimer hasn't been making a profit."

"Aye. Part of that's my fault, fer hiring so many staff here. If ye hadnae come, and after what happened last night, I would have had to let some of them go."

And he was very glad, for more than one reason, that he'd arrived here when he had. But his current ability to replenish Lattimer's coffers couldn't continue indefinitely. And if the number with which she'd provided him equated to only four years' worth of misfortune, they were even closer to the edge than he'd realized.

"These circumstances," he said slowly, not wanting to see more pain in her lovely black eyes, "aren't sustainable. Which, I imagine, is the idea. If it is Dunncraigh, and I have no reason to think otherwise, he's making this place as undesirable as possible. Just looking at the figures without knowing the tales behind them, no one in his right mind would want to own it."

"Gabriel."

Holding her gaze, he smiled. "I'm not in my right mind. I haven't been since I set eyes on you."

That at least earned him a smile in return. "Ye dunnae need to use flattery to win me over. Ye've already had me."

He took her fingers in his. "I'd jest with you if I wasn't so tired, my lass, but at the moment I'm being perfectly sincere."

"The first time ye set eyes on me, ye grabbed me aboot the chest and nearly drowned me."

"You're the first woman I've ever met who didn't want or need to be rescued."

Her eyes filled with tears, and he cursed to himself. Making her cry had not been part of the equation. Why was it easier to charge into battle than to tell a woman how much she'd come to mean to him?

"That was supposed to be a compliment," he offered.

Fiona stood up and leaned across the table to kiss him. "I think I did need to be rescued, Gabriel," she said. "If ye hadnae come up here, I'd slowly have drowned beneath the weight of all this, and I'd have thought it was all my fault."

"It is definitely not your fault," he returned emphatically, lifting her over the desk to sit across his thighs. "It is Dunncraigh's fault. He might have thought he was doing nothing more than turning Lattimer into a money sinkhole, but he forgot that this place is more than just land."

Resting her forehead against his, she slid her arms around his shoulders. "And here ye are, a man accustomed to fighting over land and territory and politics, and ye've nae forgotten fer a moment aboot the people here." She kissed him again, long and slow. "Ye told me someaught this morning, Gabriel Forrester. I'd like to say it back to ye. I dunnae ken what'll come of it, but I love ye."

She loved him. He'd felt it in his bones, but hearing her say it aloud meant . . . more. It gave him a connection to this place, to this life, that he couldn't otherwise have hoped to find. And he would do anything to keep it from slipping through his fingers. "Considering how we did meet," he murmured, stroking his hand through the long, loose tail of her dark hair, "I mean to have revenge on whoever killed Brian Maxwell's cow."

"Do ye think Dunncraigh intends to bankrupt ye, then? Ye refused his offer, so he'll cost ye so much money to keep Lattimer that ye end up having to sell it to him, after all?"

"That's entirely possible. He said that he petitioned the Crown for the property after my uncle died. The old duke wouldn't sell to him, so that was his next option. And now I won't sell it, so he's decided to be less subtle."

"It's still subtle enough," she muttered, her muscles tightening. "We cannae prove anything. And even if we could, ye ken half of clan Maxwell will think we're lying. Neglecting the people here is one thing. Doing someaught to hurt them, that's something else entirely."

All he needed was another round of "blame the Sassenach" to begin if he did find proof of Dunncraigh's misdeeds and decided to bring charges. On the other hand . . . "I can't do nothing, Fiona. That's not in my nature. And I *will* eventually run out of the blunt to keep this place."

She held his gaze for a long moment, then nodded. "Then we'd best make certain he cannae wriggle oot from under the blame." Closing her eyes, she leaned against his shoulder. "I'd be inclined to accuse my uncle fer yesterday and last night, but Hamish couldnae walk into Strouth unnoticed with a great cow slung over his shoulder, even in the middle of the night. And he's nae inclined to dirty his hands, anyway."

That made sense. Hamish Paulk was a spiteful sycophant, but as Fiona had noted, hauling dead cows about didn't suit him. And if he had set the fire at the mill, Gabriel doubted he would have bothered with trying to wake anyone to warn them. "Most of the things on your list happened at night, didn't they?" he asked, freeing a hand to lean over and pick the paper up again.

"Aye. Which means it could be nearly anyone." Fiona grimaced. "I dunnae like having to suspect my own."

"No one does. But *I* have no difficulty with suspecting *your* own."

"At this point, Gabriel, I'm grateful fer that."

It would be so easy to sit here in the quiet office, Fiona in his arms, and Gabriel swore an oath to himself that one day he would be able to do so. For now, though, the need to resolve Lattimer's substantial troubles outweighed his yearning for a moment or two of peace. "Let's look at this logically," he said slowly, gathering his thoughts back together.

"There's nae anything logical aboot anyone willing to harm his own people."

"You'd be surprised what little it takes sometimes," he returned. "But let's begin with facts rather than motives. How many men would it take to maneuver a large, healthy heifer into a well?"

"I reckon she had to be dead first, or everyone would've heard the commotion. Poison, likely, since the only wounds on her were from hitting the walls on the way doon."

Gabriel nodded. "The dead weight of a cow, heaved over three feet of well wall. Eight full-grown men? Nine?"

"I'd agree with that."

"And knocking down the cliff face, making off with half the flock of sheep, and getting them away before the shepherds could get over the landslide to find them?"

"Aboot the same, I'd say. Between eight and ten." She shifted a little, twining her fingers with his, a simple intimacy he found fascinating. "The irrigation gates would've taken fewer than that," she went on, "since it didnae all happen at once. And one man could've set fire to the mill."

"Not considering any matters of suspicion, who could go about at night in numbers eight or ten strong without being noticed?"

Fiona scowled, clearly not happy with the line of thought. He didn't expect her to be, though. It wasn't pleasant, especially for her, but it was necessary. And after last night, figuring out who was doing Dunncraigh's dirty work had become more urgent than ever.

"We've had extra men oot watching fer thievery at night since the sheep began going missing. They're nae noticed, but the thievery came before we sent them aboot."

"Who else might be out of doors at night?"

"The shepherds, though they generally have the dogs watching at night, with only one or two men up and aboot. Ian and his gamekeepers go oot at night when we have vermin aboot. Some of the drovers, when they're bringing cattle through the property on the way to market." She paused. "The drovers come from all over the Highlands, from a dozen or more different clans."

That sounded interesting. "Are there always drovers in the area?"

"Nae. They come when someone has a herd or a flock to drive to market. Ye can find them anytime except fer deep winter, but unless ye send fer them fer yer own animals, ye can only guess when and where they'll make an appearance. It could be some of them, Gabriel. They've nae loyalty to clan Maxwell. It'd be a small matter fer the duke or my uncle to pay them to create some mayhem here."

Hm. It made sense that Fiona would want to blame the nomadic and ever-changing group of drovers. If she knew any of them personally it wasn't well, and they weren't people with whom she shared a past or kinsmen to whom she'd devoted so much time and effort. "Did any of the estate's misfortunes happen over the winter?"

"A few. Some of them might have been accidental, after all." She stood, leaving his front feeling cold. "I can fetch Ian Maxwell. If there's a herd and drovers nearby, he would know it."

From the pattern of disaster beginning to take shape, it made more sense for the culprits to be local, but Gabriel didn't feel ready to dismiss her idea simply because it was convenient for her. "That sounds like a good beginning." Slowly he pushed to his feet, his muscles protesting at being asked to do more work already. "I feel the need for a hot bath and a change of clothes. You're welcome to join me for the former."

A smile curved her mouth. "Ye say such romantic things. But I need to send fer Ian and look in on the Garretsons and see to —"

"Stop," he protested, chuckling. "I'll join you after I've cleaned up. I know I still smell like smoke." Taking one of her hands, he pulled her in for a kiss. "And you smell like heather."

"Smoky heather now, ye heathen," she returned, kissing him back before she walked to the door. "I may join ye yet, if the water's still warm when I finish."

"I'll still be warm," he noted, as she

headed down the hallway. "And naked."

Staying with her would mean a lifetime of joint baths missed because she had people after whom she needed to look. And it would also mean a lifetime of nights where he went to sleep with his arms around the same lass, and mornings where her smile was the first thing he saw. For a man who'd meant to spend his life as a soldier, just the idea was both foreign and intoxicating. To have actually found the woman who made him want to have a life beyond daily fights to the death . . . He couldn't even put it into words.

Hoping at least some of the buckets had made it back to the house, he requested a bath be brought up to his chambers and then went upstairs to find some clean clothes. After that, he had traitors to discover, a mill to rebuild, and a lass who needed proposing to and marrying. And knowing Fiona, it would be in that order.

Chapter Seventeen

Rolling her tired shoulders, wishing she'd had more to offer the Garretsons than some encouraging words and biscuits, Fiona paused outside Gabriel's closed bedchamber door. Yes, she'd cleaned the soot off herself with a bowl of scented water and a cloth, but whatever he'd said, she doubted she smelled like heather. The idea of a hot bath sounded heavenly. A hot bath with Gabriel Forrester sounded even better than that.

She put her hand on the master bedchamber's door handle. At that same moment Tilly emerged from a neighboring room, linens in her arms, and Fiona quickly turned and made for her own bedchamber. "Blast it," she muttered under her breath. People were suspicious of her and Gabriel, she knew, but she didn't feel quite ready to confirm anything yet. Not until she knew what it all meant.

Shutting her door behind her, she turned around — and stopped in her tracks. "Ian? What the devil are ye doing in here? Oot with ye."

The gamekeeper turned from looking out one of the narrow windows that faced the loch. "I rode by the mill this morning. The family got oot?"

"Aye. Nae a one was hurt."

"Thank God. Did Niall kick over a lamp or someaught?"

She grimaced. Poor Niall. However careful the miller had always been, there would be doubts from now on. Or at least until they found someone else to blame. "He says he didnae. But we can converse doonstairs. I have someaught to ask ye anyway. Meet me in my office. I'll be doon in just a minute."

The gamekeeper nodded, walking toward her. "What did ye want to ask me, lass?" he murmured, stroking a finger down her cheek. "I told ye I'd help ye get rid of the Sassenach. Is that it?"

A fortnight ago she'd actually contemplated such a thing. That almost seemed a different lifetime ago. "Nae. I need to know if ye've seen or heard of any drovers aboot. We reckon they could be the ones making trouble here."

"Trouble? The sheep, ye mean?" He leaned in, his gaze lowering to her mouth.

At the last second she shoved him back, stepping sideways to avoid the kiss. "That's enough, Ian. Go doonstairs."

"Ye didnae used to mind it when I kissed ye, lass." He grinned that charming, seductive smile of his. "And more. The Sassenach willnae miss ye fer a bit, I reckon," he said, putting an arm around her. "Ye can go back to managing his estate fer him later."

With that he tried to pull her in again for a kiss, but she elbowed him in the ribs. Yes, they'd spent the occasional night together before, but his smugness about his own irresistibility had grown tiresome. And that had been before she'd met Gabriel, anyway.

"I'm nae jumping into yer arms, Ian," she said more forcefully. "I told ye that before. I'm happy to be yer friend, but I'll nae share a pillow with ye again."

His level gaze unsettled her a little, and he didn't back away. "Is it true what I've heard, then? Ye and the English soldier?"

"Ian, I'll nae tell ye nicely again — go wait fer me in the office." And she would make certain she had Gabriel with her when she next spoke to the gamekeeper, as well. Just to avoid any more complications. "As fer the rest, who I do or dunnae kiss has naught to do with ye. Oot."

He didn't move. "Ye've gone mad, Fiona. Ye turn yer back on yer own clan chief, on yer own uncle, fer an outsider? Ye let him inside ye but now ye cannae bear to be in the same room with me? Because of him?"

A shiver of uneasiness settled into the pit of her stomach. With what had happened last night, half of the house's excessive staff was below stairs, resting. And Gabriel was four doors down, likely asleep in his bath. She should have been in there with him. What did it matter now if Tilly — or anyone else — knew she loved a Sassenach? "I'm nae having this conversation," she stated, and turned on her heel. Four doors. She could make it that far.

Ian grabbed her shoulder and pulled her backward, forcefully. "Ye need to have this conversation," he retorted. "And ye need to listen to what I tell ye."

In the middle of the room she couldn't reach anything to use as a weapon. Several possibilities stood by the hearth, but she wasn't anywhere near them now. She needed time, and a bit of luck. "Say yer piece, then, and get oot. Ye ken I dunnae like a bully, Ian, and that's precisely what ye are."

"And ye sided with that damned Sassenach against yer own. Do ye nae realize? Ye've nae clan, Fiona. And only me to protect ye from the wrath of the Maxwell when Dunncraigh purchases MacKittrick back."

"Gabriel isnae selling MacKittrick, so none of what ye just said signifies."

"He *will* sell. It's aboot pride now, I ken, but when it's aboot money and keeping away the debt collectors, he'll sell. He can pay to have one mill rebuilt, but what if someaught happens to the blacksmith's next? Or the church? Or Ailios Eylar's cottage with her pretty new windows? What if someaught happens to poison the cattle? If he doesnae do what's right, someone *will* get hurt. And it might be him, Fiona. Ye ken how deadly the MacKittrick curse can be."

That did not sound like idle speculation. Rather, it sounded almost like someone's plan, laid out step by step. Fiona kept her expression level, but inside she felt like she was running full tilt toward a cliff. What was she supposed to do, agree with him? Argue with him? Which one would see her out of the room so she could go fetch Gabriel and tell him she'd found their traitor?

"I didnae see ye at the picnic yesterday," she said aloud, trying to purchase herself a moment to think.

"I was oot watching over the flocks," he said. "Ye shouldnae have been at the village yesterday, either. Lattimer thinks he can win the loyalty of clan Maxwell with pretty sandwiches and a dram of whisky." Ian snorted. "He couldnae even protect a single cow."

Fiona took a quick breath. "I have to say, Lattimer nearly pissed himself when he saw that heifer in the well. Nearly thought himself cross-eyed, too, trying to figure oot how she jumped up and then fell in tail first."

The gamekeeper stopped smiling. "So that's how it's to be, then?" he said, closing on her again. "I'm supposed to tell ye all my secrets because ye pretend fer five seconds that we're friends again after ye call me a bully? Yer own uncle's washed his hands of ye, Fiona. If it wasnae fer me stepping forward to claim ye, it might have been ye going into the well instead of the cow. I'm yer only protection, lass."

"No, you aren't."

She and Ian both turned toward the voice by the fireplace, and Fiona hissed in a breath when she saw Gabriel standing in front of the tapestry there. Whatever he'd had in mind when he'd slipped through the

463

secret passage, he wore only his trousers and boots. His hair was damp and disheveled, but as attractive as he looked physically, and as keenly relieved as she was to see him, the expression in his eyes turned her insides to ice. This was the face, she realized, his enemies saw before they died.

"Ye heard her, aye?" Ian asked, moving a half step away from Fiona. "Laughing at ye after she had her lads throw that cow into the well? She's turned traitor on ye. She answers to Dunncraigh himself, I reckon."

The swiftness with which he threw her beneath the proverbial carriage wheels stunned her. And for heaven's sake, was that what Gabriel had arrived to hear? "Ye black-hearted, lying sn—"

"I heard you threaten Fiona," Gabriel interrupted in a flat voice. "Not the words I would choose to take me to the grave, but not the only poor choice you've made."

"And those are bold words fer an unarmed man," the gamekeeper returned. "I've nae reason to want to see *ye* kept safe." He pulled a pistol from beneath his coat and aimed it at Gabriel.

"Nae!" Fiona grabbed his arm, wrenching it down. He cuffed her across the face, sending her reeling. Stumbling, she fell against the side of the bed. "Nae!"

Before Ian could straighten again, Gabriel tackled him. The two men crashed into her dressing table, shattering the mirror. Sharp glass showered onto the wood floor. Her chair went over in the tangle of limbs and nearly cracked her across the skull. For God's sake, they were going to kill each other.

Fiona staggered to her feet, her ears still ringing from Ian's blow. "Stop it!" she shrieked.

The pistol flashed into view, caught between the two of them. She wanted to jump in, to do *something,* but if she struck at the wrong moment and the gun went off, it would be her fault. And if it hurt Gabriel — or worse — she couldn't . . . It would be too much.

Gabriel twisted, ramming his shoulder up into Ian's chin. The gamekeeper stumbled, and a hooked leg sent him to the floor on his arse. The Duke of Lattimer rolled to his feet to press the pistol against Ian's temple.

"Gabriel, ye cannae!" she called out, putting both hands over her heart.

"I most definitely can," he snapped back, his gaze fixed on Ian's face. "For twelve years I did it almost daily. And for less cause."

"Get on with it then, English," Ian spat,

blood running from his nose and dripping onto the wooden floor.

Hardly daring to breathe, Fiona stepped up to Gabriel's left side, away from the weapon in case he might think she meant to take it from him. Instead, she put a hand carefully on his free arm. His muscles twitched even beneath her light touch. "He fired a shot to wake Niall and his family," she said, keeping her voice low and quiet even if she couldn't stop it shaking.

"After he set fire to their home." Finally he sent her the briefest of glances, his expression cold and distant. "Why are you defending him?"

"If ye kill him, Dunncraigh will have everyone saying ye murdered one of yer own servants so ye'd have someone to blame fer yer misfortunes," she went on. "Ye've won over most of the people here. Dunnae throw that away."

Abruptly Gabriel lowered the pistol and took a step backward. "You heard the lady," he growled. "At this moment your life is more useful to me than your death. I suggest you keep it that way."

Ian climbed to his feet, wiping blood from his face. Fiona had known him for her entire life. She'd shared his bed on occasion. And he'd used her friendship and her trust to undermine everything she did. Moving around Gabriel, Fiona took a long step forward and slapped Ian hard across the face.

"I reckon ye have one path ahead of ye," she stated. "It leads ye with us to Inverness, where ye'll write oot everything ye've done to this place, and ye'll write doon the name of the man who put ye up to it and why."

"He'll murder me, ye stup—"

She slapped him again. "And when ye've done that, the Duke of Lattimer will decline to press charges against ye." At that Gabriel stirred, but he kept his mouth shut. "He will also give ye a thousand pounds, at which point ye'll purchase passage on the first ship headed fer America."

"Well, ye've thought this all oot," Ian retorted. "But it relies on me cooperating with ye. What if I choose nae to be the traitor ye are?"

"You stopped being a part of clan Maxwell the moment you did the first thing to harm this place." Gabriel gripped the pistol so hard his knuckles showed white, but he kept the weapon pointed at the ground. "If you think I'm speaking out of turn, then please don't do as Fiona suggests. I'll put you in a room with Niall Garreston and Brian Maxwell and every villager in Strouth whose well water you tried to spoil. We'll see if they think you're a bonny Maxwell lad or not."

"With ye here, none of us are Maxwells any longer," the gamekeeper returned, but his shoulder lowered and he seemed to get . . . smaller. "I'll do as ye say. After this I'll nae have a place in the Highlands any longer, anyway. I dunnae want one." He glanced up at her. "Whatever I swear to on paper, ye'll nae get the law to move against Dunncraigh, ye ken."

"Aye," she returned. "But everyone will know that he went against his own. And if someaught ill befalls MacKittrick after this, the blame and the fault and the shame of the deed goes to him."

"That, my lass," Gabriel said, his hard-eyed expression easing just a little, "is a very good idea."

The ride back into the valley reminded Gabriel strongly of his first trip to Lattimer Castle six weeks earlier. Seasoned and cynical as he was supposed to be, he couldn't resist repeated looks out the window even if it made him feel like a farm boy on his first visit to London.

Snow blanketed the ground, thick enough to keep its crisp white coloring, but thin enough to be broken by vast purple patches of late-blooming heather and thistle. The color of Loch Sìbhreach deepened from blue to onyx, with thin black ice rimming the near shore. In the still air and gray sky it looked like the landscape of a madman's dream, exotic and enticing. His dream. But not only his.

"Is this usual?" he asked, returning his attention to the only vision more enchanting than an early snowfall in the Highlands.

"Nae," Fiona said, not bothering to hide her amusement from him. "It's barely September. The snow's a month early, at least. It'll nae last, but it does make a bonny sight."

"Aye, it does," he returned, taking her hand and tucking her closer against him. "Very bonny." He kissed her, need and desire spinning against the odd sense of contentment that had drawn around him like a warm blanket. *Him, content.*

"Are ye truly pleased to be back here?" she asked, stroking her palm along the side of his face. "Inverness was very grand, compared to Lattimer. And much more civilized."

With a grin pulling at him, he kissed her again. A hundred thousand kisses still wouldn't be enough to satisfy him, but they would be a damned fine beginning. "Do I strike you as being a civilized man?" he returned, releasing her fingers to open the buttons of her heavy crimson pelisse and then slipping a hand inside to cup one warm, soft breast.

"Nae," she whispered back, kissing him more urgently. "Ye strike me as an insatiable man."

Gabriel chuckled as he teased at her nipple with his thumb. "Three weeks in a house with less than a dozen servants was very like being alone with you," he murmured, jumping as she stroked a hand over the growing bulge in his trousers.

"Aye. Everyone else thinks so too, I reckon." Slowly she opened the quartet of buttons closing the flap of his buckskins. "And that's nae even considering the two of us traveling alone in a coach. I'm scandalized, ye ken." She freed him, then sent a single fingernail trailing lightly across his balls and then down the length of his cock.

Groaning, he shoved her hand aside, yanked her gown up around her waist, and lifted her over his throbbing member. "If I hadn't lost the ability to speak just now," he returned, half closing his eyes as she lowered herself tightly around him and then started bouncing, "I'd say you . . . ah . . . were more wanton than scandalized."

"Fer a man withoot speech," she returned breathlessly, nibbling at his ear, "ye talk too much."

He thrust up into her, meeting her downward strokes with a grunt. Again and again, deep and fast, until she gasped his name and collapsed, spasming, around him. Gabriel splayed his hands around her bared hips and hammered against her twice more, then spilled himself hard inside her. "Fiona," he breathed, shuddering.

The coach's cushions would have to be restuffed after the two-day drive back from Inverness, given the abuse the poor things had taken. He rested his head back against the seat, closing his eyes as his breathing and heartbeat slowed, and very aware of the warm, vibrant woman panting against his shoulder and still straddling his hips.

"How do you say 'I love you' in Gaelic?" he asked, lowering his face into her dark, sweet-scented hair.

"I think ye just said it in every language, *leannan,*" she returned, laughter in her rich brogue.

"Very amusing, Fiona. Tell me."

She sighed deliciously. *"Tha gaol agam ort,"* she said.

He repeated it to her. *"Tha gaol agam ort.* Aye?"

"Aye." Stretching, she put her hands against the seat back on either side of his head and kissed him again. "Ye're a quick study. Aboot a great many things. Niall Garretson's likely to begin weeping when ye show him the plans ye drew up fer the mill."

"Weeping with approval, I hope. It's a mill that'll never fall in a siege, at least." As he took another glance out the window, he straightened. "Christ," he cursed, and lifted her off his lap.

"What?" she demanded, twisting hurriedly to follow his gaze and shoving her dress back down around her legs. "Lattimer hasn't collapsed, has . . ." She trailed off. "Oh. Oh, my goodness."

People lined the road ahead. A great many people, in both livery and farm attire. With another curse he refastened his trousers before the coach drew close enough for any of them to see in through the open windows. "Am I about to be burned at the stake?" he asked, knocking on the coach's roof.

"I've nae idea," she returned, busy stuffing her breasts back inside her gown and fastening her pelisse over the lovelies.

The coach rolled to a halt a few feet short of where the young footman, Hugh, stood on one side of the snow-covered road, Ailios Eylar's daughter Eppie opposite him. Ga-

472

briel opened the door and hopped to the ground, then turned around to take Fiona around the waist and lift her down, as well.

"Hugh? What's wrong?" he asked, buttoning his caped greatcoat against the chill before he took Fiona's hand to help steady her as they walked to the beginning of the parallel lines of tenants and staff that continued all the way up the drive to Lattimer's front doors. At least the old place still stood, dark and impressive beneath the overcast sky.

The footman bowed at the waist, then straightened again. "There's nae a thing wrong, Yer Grace," he said, his voice wavering just a little. Nervous? What was the lad nervous about? They'd just spent three weeks making statements and exposing Dunncraigh's misdeeds, resolving what he'd hoped was the last of Lattimer's troubles. And now before he'd even stepped through the door something else seemed to be rearing its head.

"Hugh, I ken I dunnae need to tell ye," Fiona took up, "but everyone's ootside. And it's snowing. What's amiss?"

"They put me here on purpose," Hugh said, "and told me what to tell ye. We didnae know what was afoot when Yer Grace and Miss Fiona and Ian rode off to Inverness. But Fleming's been reading us the newspapers and yer letters, and now we know. He told us what the Maxwell did, and how he turned Ian and the others against their own." He squared his shoulders. "So we're here to tell ye that we're nae clan Maxwell, any longer. Some of us are named Maxwell, but Dunncraigh's nae our chief."

"Ye dunnae have to do that," Fiona burst out, her expression shocked. "I'm the one who's made him angry. There's nae need fer ye —"

"There is," Eppie said, unexpectedly from behind them, the first time Gabriel had ever heard her speak. "We all talked aboot it. Some of us wanted to send a letter to Dunncraigh and tell him what we thought. Some others, though, said he wouldnae care, and that we'd be asking fer trouble where he'd be happier just to keep ignoring us. But we all decided; withoot Miss Fiona we'd all have been in fer it a long time ago. And Miss Fiona chose ye, Yer Grace."

"I'm supposed to tell it, Eppie," Hugh broke in. "Miss Fiona chose ye, Yer Grace, so we reckoned that's good enough fer us."

Gabriel frowned, not quite certain what was going on. "Thank you, but what —"

"Ye're the Duke of Lattimer," Hugh interrupted, clearly warming to the topic. "But only the Sassenachs call this place Lattimer. So in London ye can be the Duke of Lattimer. But here, if ye dunnae object, Yer Grace, ye're Laird MacKittrick."

It wasn't even a title. It hadn't been since the Crown had taken away the land from the last, curse-prone, Scottish lord who'd resided here. Beside him Fiona had tears in her eyes, and she nodded at him emphatically. She'd chosen him, they said. Without her, he would have been back on the Continent by now, and he likely would have sold Lattimer to Dunncraigh without a second thought. It had been a burden. Now, though, and so swiftly it still stunned him, this place, this woman, had become his life.

"I would be honored," he said, raising his voice so they could hear him down the line. "It doesn't seem right, though, for me to take credit when we all know who truly deserves this. As you said, without Fiona, all of us — including myself — would be in much worse shape."

Turning around to face her, he sank onto one knee, taking both her hands in his. The collective gasp of the gathered onlookers clouded the air with fog. It likely wasn't fair, for him to do this with all these witnesses, but in this circumstance he was much more interested in getting what he wanted than in being fair.

"Get up, Gabriel," she hissed, her cheeks growing pale.

"I can't be Laird MacKittrick without a Lady MacKittrick," he said, looking up at her. And this, this moment, worried him more than any fight on any battlefield. This moment didn't rely on his own skill. It relied on someone else's heart. Every minute since he'd arrived in the Highlands, though, had been about facing his own worries and doing things he would previously have thought impossible. "And a duke needs a duchess. You are the heart of this land, Fiona, and I can't ask for any more for your kin and for me. I love you with every ounce of my soldier's heart, and everything else you've enabled me to become. *Tha gaol agam ort,*" he went on, hoping he hadn't mangled it. "Will you marry me?"

For a handful of hard beats of his heart she stood there, staring down at him while tears ran down her face. Then she launched herself against his chest, pushing him backward into the snow and kissing him as cold wet went down his neck. Laughing, he threw his arms around her, holding her close.

"You didn't give me an answer," he said when he could breathe again, as their newly formed clan gathered around them making their own sounds of congratulations and delight.

"Aye!" she yelled, and her kin cheered. "Aye," she repeated more quietly, touching her forehead to his. "I love ye something fierce, Gabriel Forrester. Ye're nae what I expected, and I cannae imagine tomorrow withoot ye beside me."

He smiled, lifting his head to kiss her again. "You don't have to. The MacKittrick curse doesn't stand a chance against us, my lass."

"Nae," she returned, grinning down at his face. "It doesnae."

The employees of Thorndike Press hope you have enjoyed this Large Print book. All our Thorndike, Wheeler, and Kennebec Large Print titles are designed for easy reading, and all our books are made to last. Other Thorndike Press Large Print books are available at your library, through selected bookstores, or directly from us.

For information about titles, please call:
  (800) 223-1244

or visit our Web site at:
  http://gale.cengage.com/thorndike

To share your comments, please write:
  Publisher
  Thorndike Press
  10 Water St., Suite 310
  Waterville, ME 04901